STRIKE
OF THE
COBRA

ALSO BY TIMOTHY RIZZI

Nightstalker

STRIKE
OF THE
COBRA

A NOVEL BY

TIMOTHY RIZZI

DONALD I. FINE, INC.

NEW YORK

Library of Congress Cataloging-in-Publication Data
Rizzi, Timothy.
Strike of the cobra / by Timothy Rizzi.
p.   cm.
ISBN 1-55611-359-5
I. Title.
PS3568.I835S75   1993
813'.54—dc20   92-54980
CIP

Manufactured in the United States of America

10   9   8   7   6   5   4   3   2   1

Designed by Irving Perkins Associates

This novel is a work of fiction. Names, characters, places, and incidents are either the product of the author's imagination or are used fictitiously. Any resemblance to actual events, locales, organizations or persons, living or dead, is entirely coincidental and beyond the intent of either the author or publisher.

For My Parents,
Leo and Dolly

ACKNOWLEDGMENTS

Special thanks to Major General Joe H. Engle USAF (Ret.) for spending the time to answer my endless questions about shuttle operations, space systems and aerodynamics.

To the 336th Fighter Squadron based at Seymour Johnson AFB, North Carolina. Especially Major Miles Crowell USAF, for the tactical briefing on the new composite air wing and answering my questions on air-to-air and air-to-ground tactics. The time spent in the F-15E simulator was extremely educational and ended way too soon. We should all be thankful the 'E' is on our side.

Captain Michael Villalva USMC for his help in verifying sniper and scout tactics.

Paul Fling, Unit Chief of Design for McDonnell Douglas, for solid counsel and clear thinking. Yes, I too miss the sunshine.

Dr. Robert Arnio for the insight into the paranoid mind.

To NASA's Public Affairs Office for allowing a tour of the Houston shuttle training facilities and Mission Control.

I would especially like to thank Don Fine and my editor Andy Zack along with the entire team at DIF. Without their support this would not be possible.

Most of all to Diana, for your understanding, strength and patience throughout the process.

GLOSSARY

ACO —   Aircraft Control Officer

ASAT —   Antisatellite Weapons. Launched during a crisis or staged
            in orbit, these weapons are used to destroy an enemy's
            communication and reconnaissance satellites.

CDC —   Combat Direction Center

CINCs —   Commanders in Chief of the ten unified & specified U.S.
            commands.

CSOC —   The Air Force's Consolidated Space and Operations Cen-
            ter (pronounced See-Sock).

DCI —   Director Central Intelligence

ELINT —   Electronic Intelligence

EORSAT —   Electronic Ocean Reconnaissance Satellite

FLIR —   Forward Looking Infrared

INS —   Internal Navigational System

IRST —   Infrared Search and Track

MFD —   Multifunction Display

NORAD —   North American Aerospace Defense Command

NPIC —   National Photographic Interpretation Center is located in
            Federal Building 213, eight blocks from the Capitol on
            New Jersey Avenue. Using a massive array of computers
            the NPIC is responsible for analyzing billions of bits of
            satellite information into usable intelligence.

NSA —   National Security Agency. Located at Fort Meade in Mary-
            land is responsible for intercepting and decoding foreign
            electronic communications.

PVO —   *Protivovozdushnoy Voidka Oboroni,* the Troops of the Air
                Defense Forces for the former Soviet Union.

RORSAT —   Radar Ocean Reconnaissance Satellite

SA-6 —   NATO code name 'Gainful', this mobile low-altitude sur-
                face-to-air missile system can attack targets out to 34.5
                miles with a ceiling of 59,000 feet. The twenty-foot-four-
                inch radar-controlled missile carries a 176-pound high-
                explosive warhead and can accelerate to Mach 2.8.

SA-8 —   NATO code name 'Gecko', this surface-to-air system is a
                highly mobile all-weather tactical missile. The tracking ra-
                dar is a pulse type, and the missile has a range of 18
                miles. The ten-foot-six-inch missile has a maximum speed
                of Mach 2 with a ceiling of 24,000 feet.

SAM —   Surface-to-Air Missile

SARSAT —   A NOAA-9 Search and Rescue Satellite

SEODSS —   Sea-Base Electro-Optical Deep Space Surveillance System

Spetsnaz —   Special purpose units of the former Soviet Union. These
                troops consisted of highly skilled men able to perform
                unique and difficult missions.

STA —   Shuttle Training Aircraft

ZSU-23-4 —   Commonly referred to as a Shilka, or simply a ZSU-23,
                this four-barreled twenty-three-millimeter antiaircraft gun
                can fire up to 1,000 rounds a minute at low flying aircraft.
                The gun is mounted on a SA-6 Gainful chassis and is
                guided by a self-contained microwave target-acquisition
                and fire-control radar.

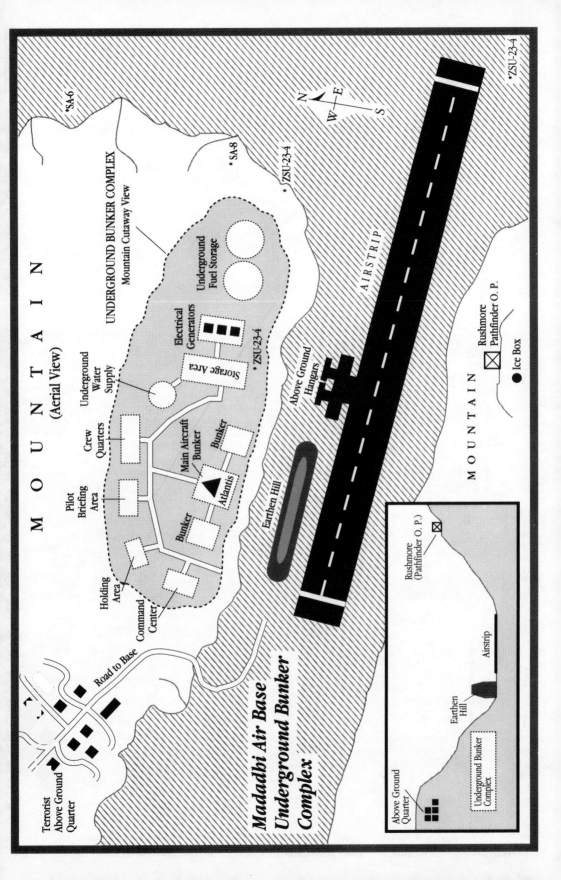

Madadbi Air Base
Underground Bunker
Complex

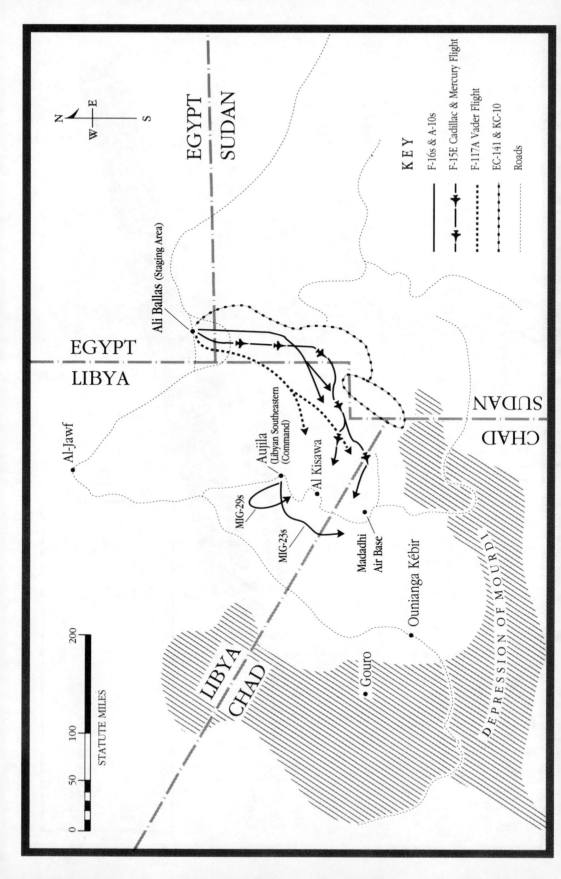

STRIKE

OF THE

COBRA

DAY
1

FRIDAY, SEPTEMBER 17

1

The day had come for Adib Hamen to die. He did not want to die, but he did not fear death either. When it came he would embrace it as a welcome friend.

Adib Hamen had been long committed to his fate. He had trained for seven months at a Libyan air base, south of Timassah, flying his silver gray MiG-23 interceptor at least once a day, often more, including sorties at night. Now he had come back to the place he called home, a secret base located west of the Depression du Mourdi, in Chad's northern desert. A place of few comforts, but a place he had grown to respect. He had many friends here, men like him, men of vision, men filled with anger and hatred.

The desert training camp fell under the command of Abu Ajami, the commander of the Fatah Revolutionary Brigades. Hamen and Ajami had planned this mission together. It would fulfill the last promise Abid had ever made to his wife.

At the age of twenty-five, Adib Hamen married a young Palestinian girl and dreamed of having many children. One month to the day after his wedding, while on a trip to visit her family in Amman, Jordan, his bride was killed by an Israeli bomb intended for a PLO terrorist. As he buried the pieces of a body that was once his lovely bride, Hamen had sworn he would someday avenge her death. Four years had since passed. Now he felt a sense of pride to be the first to pilot the sleek, Soviet-made, single-engine fighter. It was a new weapon in his people's fight for a homeland.

Sitting on the edge of his cot, Hamen finished zipping his blue flight suit and bent over to tie the laces of his black leather boots. A short man, Hamen stood five feet three inches tall and weighed just 140 pounds. He kept himself in shape by exercising each morning and eating a steady

3

diet of rice and boiled chicken. His face was thin with sunken cheeks and a broad flat nose. His only facial hair was a small neat mustache, and he kept his black hair short so that the undersized flight helmet would fit properly on his head. His dark eyes were stone black and cold.

Hamen stood, surveying his quarters one last time. The barren rock walls of his room were dark and the air frigid. *I will not miss this place,* he thought.

He moved closer to the burning candle on a wooden dresser next to his cot. The light from the candle filled the room with an amber glow. Hamen glanced at his flight plan one last time. He would take off to the east and cross the southern tip of Libya before entering into Egypt. He would then turn north, drop to 1,000 feet above the western desert, to avoid radar detection, until he reached the town of Siwah. He was then to bank northeast, flying over the coastal city of Ad Dab'ah and out over the Mediterranean. Radio contact would be established with a Libyan military freighter shadowing a cruise ship loaded with American tourists. His final duty would be to point his fighter at the ship for a direct collision and join his wife with Allah. It would be a blow to the very people who supported the Israelis.

"Your fighter is ready." Yusuf Kamal, the camp's security officer, stood at the door. He moved into the light where Hamen could see his face. A large muscular man in his late forties, Kamal stood nearly six feet tall. Barrel-chested, with a bushy black and gray beard, the bald-headed Kamal was the second in command at the base. Only Abu Ajami had more authority.

"Are you ready?" Kamal asked.

"I am ready," Hamen responded firmly. He picked up his helmet as he blew out the candle, turned and exited his quarters.

E-2C HAWKEYE, BULLDOG 602

Lieutenant Commander Ben Rificoff sucked in a long breath of stale recycled air and rubbed his eyes with his fingertips, trying to relieve some of the stress. He straightened his back and flexed his leg muscles, hoping to get the blood flowing again through his five-foot-ten-inch frame. Just on the downhill side of a six-hour mission the soft hum of the Grumman E-2C Hawkeye's twin turboprop engines were lulling him to sleep. He tried to shrug off the lethargic feeling pulling at him.

With his back perfectly straight and his fingers hovering above the computer keyboard, Rificoff focused on watching for any changes in the sea or sky. He had qualified for the position of aircraft control officer eighteen months earlier and to his surprise still liked what he was doing. He had gotten married right after qualifying and would be a proud father in just two more months. If things worked out he would return home several days before his wife was due. He had not seen her in half a year. Before joining the navy he had never stayed at a job longer than three months. His father had been right: the military was what he had needed to help him grow up and become responsible.

Rificoff's job was to operate the APA-171 air surveillance radar and advanced radar processing system. The system's twenty-four-foot radome, located on top of the aircraft, rotated once every ten seconds, covering a circular surveillance envelope of three million cubic miles. The system could analyze more than 600 individual aircraft while still tracking ships or ground targets. At the same time Rificoff and the other members of the crew could direct forty intercept operations simultaneously.

He and the other members of the five-man crew had launched off their carrier, the USS *John F. Kennedy,* patrolling the southern Mediterranean, at 0200 hours. The black sky had been clear and the sea calm. Rificoff hoped they would both remain that way until the crew touched down on the carrier again sometime after the sun was up.

The *Kennedy*'s battle group was operating off the northern coast of Egypt fifty miles west of Alexandria. They had spent the last six weeks cruising just outside Libyan territorial waters, monitoring the movements of the Libyan navy and air force. So far everything had gone off without a hitch. It seemed the Libyans were in no mood to challenge the *Kennedy.* The carrier was now in Egyptian waters and in three days would be heading north to Italy, for a little R&R.

Rificoff, the senior ACO, was looking forward to a hot shower and breakfast. His red hair was oily and his clothes felt moist and sticky as he sat in the dark, trying to concentrate on the ever-changing seven-color Loral display unit. The deep blue eleven-by-eleven-inch monitor showed the air and sea traffic around him. Sitting next to him were the combat information center officer and the flight technician. Rificoff shifted his attention to the center of the display, focusing in on the flashing computer-generated image of his carrier. It was making a wide turn back to the northwest, into the wind.

Rificoff keyed his mike. "Diamond Back Lead Three Zero Niner, this is Bulldog . . . turn left to a new heading of zero eight eight, maintain altitude at seven thousand. New traffic to the north at zero one one. Looks like a civilian heavy . . . heading west and climbing." He watched two blips representing a pair of F-18s as they started their turn northeast. The F-18s were flying BAR CAP (barrier combat air patrol), making sure no unidentified aircraft came close to the battle group.

"Roger that Bulldog . . . turning," came the response from the lead F-18.

The two-tone white and gray E-2C Airborne Early Warning aircraft was orbiting at 28,000 feet above the Mediterranean. Rificoff felt the aircraft come out of a slow banking turn and sensed the craft's changing posture as the pilot throttled back and adjusted his flaps to a ten-degree down setting for optimal radar performance. The plane then continued on its racetrack flight path around the carrier.

Rificoff scratched his day-old beard as he watched an electronically generated yellow triangle, representing a new surface radar contact, turn to blue and then back to yellow as the tracking computer tried to get a positive fix on it. This indicated the computer wasn't receiving a strong enough return to track the contact, a ship. The new blip was to the east of the battle group moving to the northwest, barely readable at the outer edge of the radar's 245-mile range. Rificoff was somewhat amazed that the radar was even tracking it. Because of the distance it would take a few seconds before the computer could sort out all the data he would need to make a preliminary report. He waited as the data started to appear next to the blue triangle representing the contact.

SPEED—18 KNOTS, HEADING—237, LARGE SURFACE VESSEL.

"I see you." Rificoff whispered. He hit the send button on his console, dumping the data to the *Kennedy's* combat control computers. A second later he lost contact with the target. He would have to wait until it sailed closer, he figured another five or ten minutes.

USS *John F. Kennedy*

The Combat Direction Center of the USS *John F. Kennedy* was bathed in shadowy turquoise-colored light. The room was relatively small, only twenty by thirty feet, with low ceilings and a grooved metal floor. Only six men monitored the equipment in the completely computerized combat nerve center of the ship.

The low light allowed four combat tactical action officers to study the immense amount of information available to them from an assortment of wall-sized screens. The four men, schooled in the art of threat analysis and operation, relied heavily on the eight-color Navy Tactical Data System, the main screen on the wall ahead of them. The flickering yellow, red, blue, and green authority lights of the NTDS immediately identified threats in the air and on the surface with the *Kennedy's* own radar and increased coverage from the Hawkeye circling above. A large electronic screen on the left wall contained a map showing the location of each ship in the fleet and an outline of the northern coast of Egypt. To the right, a status board of which pilots and aircraft were in the air was updated continuously. In addition to the main NTDS screen, each officer had access to a standard computer directly in front of him.

Commander Lawrence Doherty, a pudgy-faced man with a big smile and thick glasses, leaned against the doorway nursing his fourth cup of strong black coffee, wondering if he was going to be able to sleep when his watch ended. He surveyed the room. Doherty may not have looked the part, but he was considered one of the best ops officers in the navy. A seasoned officer, he never got excited—about anything—and that was his strength. He always thought things through even if there were only minutes to make a tough decision. His twenty years of experience spanning five tours in the Middle East, including the Iraq war, reassured everyone in the CDC that things were in capable hands.

Doherty took a seat next to Chief Emerson. Nathan Emerson operated the computer and communications equipment that tied the carrier into the Hawkeye orbiting above them. As the Hawkeye surveyed the area, it relayed all of its information directly to the ship. Commander Doherty liked Emerson, even if he was jumpy. Emerson was bright, he just needed to calm down. Doherty knew a lot of this had to do with the fact that Emerson lacked experience and only time would build his confidence.

"Anything happening out there?" Doherty asked.

"Just received a new surface contact bearing one one eight, sir. It's still 240 miles east and heading northwest." Emerson didn't bother to lift his head from the scope.

"Hmmm . . . is it military?" Doherty watched the dancing red and green lights of the control console reflect in the chief's glasses.

"Checking now, sir," Emerson said, quickly referencing his electronic computer log, which updated him on what ship traffic should be in the area. "Whatever it is I don't show a record of it."

Doherty took another drink of his coffee. "Keep an eye on it."

Stars shone bright in the desert sky as Adib Hamen approached his fighter. A single white spotlight marked the location of the MiG-23MF parked next to one of the base's hardened underground aircraft bunkers. Hamen stopped for an instant, studying the MiG. The single-engine swing-wing fighter was still very capable after twenty years of service with the Libyan government. Forty-five feet in length, the aircraft had been designed in the early sixties as a multirole attack fighter and trainer. The MiG had a round, pointed nose, swept-back tail, and variable geometry wings mounted high on its fuselage. Its original brown and gray desert camouflage paint scheme had been replaced with a simple silver gray without any markings to identify its country of origin. Purchased from the Soviet Union, the MiG had been used by the Libyan air force as an air-to-air intercepter before being given to Abu Ajami and his band of terrorists.

"My brother . . . this is a glorious day." Abu Ajami stood next to the nose gear of the jet, the desert breeze blowing his long black hair across his face.

Hamen walked up to him. In the crisp night air Ajami wore only a solid white dress shirt and black wool pants. Strapped to the waist of his six-foot frame was a nine-millimeter automatic pistol.

Hamen searched his leader's eyes for the conviction and strength he knew he would find there. He felt in his heart that this man would someday be remembered as the greatest Arab that had ever lived. If he had one regret it was that he would not be alive to see that day.

"I am ready, Ajami," Hamen said, his voice firm with certainty.

Ajami extended his arms, grabbing the smaller man by the shoulders. "You are a great warrior. Today you shall join with the brothers who have gone before you . . . in paradise." Ajami wrapped his arms around Hamen, embracing him. "Go now, Adib. Strike a blow against the Great Satan."

"I will miss seeing our victory," Hamen said.

"Allah is waiting for you."

Kamal approached the two men. "It is time."

Hamen climbed up the five metal stairs leading to the cockpit. The engine was already running, its high-pitched whine tingling his ears. He stepped onto the dirty gray ejection seat, then placed his legs on either side of the control stick before sliding down. The seat was cold and hard, but he barely noticed.

Kamal had followed him up the ladder and was now helping strap him in. When the harness was in place and snapped together, Hamen put on his helmet, plugging in his oxygen mask and radio.

"Allah be with you!" Kamal shouted. He climbed down and helped the ground crew pull the wheel blocks away.

Hamen hit the switch, closing the canopy. It came down with a blunt thud, quieting the interior of the jet. He switched on a light and began his preflight checks. After a few minutes he was ready to taxi into position at the end of the narrow 10,000-foot runway. A solitary row of lights blinked down its center, and he could see a half dozen men standing near one of the parked trucks.

Hamen scanned the instruments one last time. Everything checked out. He wrapped his gloved left hand around the throttle and advanced it slowly, letting the thrust build. He then eased off the brakes, feeling the 38,000-pound swing-wing jet leap forward as he jammed the throttle to the stop, forcing the engine into afterburner. An instant later the fighter sprang into the air. As Hamen passed over the end of the runway, he retracted the gear and cleaned up the flaps. He swept the wings from twenty-six degrees back to forty-five degrees, banked to the north, and watched his airspeed climb on the HUD to 380 knots. The heads up display allowed him to fly the fighter without having to constantly refocus his eyes from the cockpit instrumentation to the sky around him. The HUD provided visual indication of his airspeed, altitude, and heading, which were projected on a clear piece of Plexiglas and focused out to infinity. Everything he needed to fly the fighter was right in front of him.

When Hamen hit 1,000 feet, he disengaged the afterburner. His jet faded into the night sky.

Ibn Ghallan

Libyan Naval Captain Malek Bani unbuttoned the top of his thick black wool coat as he paced back and forth on the bridge of the thirty-year-old Polnochny Class LSM, a 780-ton landing ship. His steps were short and his pulse quick as the tension built within him. He could feel sweat building under his heavy garment and was becoming uncomfortable. In the distance he could see the first hints of a red glow signaling the coming dawn, now only thirty minutes away.

A small, thin-faced man, Bani had a stringy brown mustache and yellow teeth from a three-pack-a-day cigarette habit. He considered smoking his only real vice and one that he very much enjoyed. He took one of the brown paper cigarettes out of its pack and moistened the end of it with his lips and tongue. He knew he had to clear his mind and concentrate on the situation around him. This could be the beginning of a victory or a disaster.

By all outward appearances the *Ibn Ghallan* seemed insignificant. Rust stained, with large sections of her gray paint peeling away, it was slow, barely able to make twenty knots under full power. Yet the *Ibn Ghallan* carried an impressive mix of weapons, including sixteen Soviet-made SA-N-3 surface-to-air missiles and four CPMIEC C-801 ship-launched medium-range antiship missiles.

This massive amount of firepower did little to relieve Bani's anxiety as he watched the lights of an Egyptian tanker slowly cut across his bow two miles away. It was heading toward the southeast, angling away from him. This would slow him down. For the last twenty-four hours he had been shadowing the *Song of Flower,* a medium-sized cruise liner. The nervous captain had been careful not to get too close and yet make sure the ship was always in sight. He now had to change course and reduce his top speed because of the Egyptian ship. Bani couldn't do this for long and still be able to follow the cruise liner. His ship didn't have the speed he needed to catch up.

Bani had intended to follow the *Song of Flower* as it moved up the Egyptian coast on its way to Taormina, Sicily. He had hoped he would be able to slip in closer under the cover of darkness so he could guide the MiG to its target. He checked his watch. If everything went as planned, and it rarely did, the MiG would be in radio range in just over forty-five minutes.

"Damn," Bani cursed under his breath. He turned to his second in command. "Go down below. Tell the engine room I want every ounce of power on my command."

"Yes, Captain," the younger officer responded as he swiveled on the heels of his boots and left the bridge.

"Take a new heading of two three two," Bani barked. "Reduce speed to ten knots and wait for that fool to sail clear. Bring up the surface to air radar and activate our IFF receiver. I don't want any surprises."

Rificoff keyed the Hawkeye's internal mike, which allowed him to talk directly with the pilot of the E-2C. "How long before it's light enough to get a visual? I'm showing some new surface traffic."

"Fifteen . . . twenty minutes," came the reply.

"Roger." Rificoff watched as his unidentified target continued to move west. Only now there was another ship trailing the first one six miles behind it.

Rificoff was having a hard time getting a clear picture of the two ships on his radar screen. Obviously the radar signal was bouncing off something solid, yet he still wasn't getting the data he wanted. There was the possibility some of his radar energy was glancing off a thick fog bank that was interfering with the return signal. He couldn't be sure. What he was certain of was his computer still needed more time to sort things out and every second both of those ships were getting closer.

"Let's try this," he said to himself as he tapped a new set of commands into the radar computer, instructing the beam to narrow its width of electronic energy and increase power to ninety-five percent.

Instantly the information on his scope changed. The triangles representing the first and second contacts turned blue. The computer had gotten a solid fix on them.

Rificoff smiled.

The radar return now looked like many of the ships he had seen in the waters off Libya. Nothing more than a pair of medium-sized, steel-hulled boats moving at moderate rates of speed.

He adjusted the beam width again, this time widening it. He would now try to clarify the images of each ship. At the same time he punched the computer keyboard, telling the system to call up the data he would need for the carrier's CDC. In a flash he had his answers. The closest target was now 229.6 miles to the east and heading directly toward them at a steady eighteen knots. The second target was moving a little slower than he had first thought, sixteen knots.

"Strike, this is Bulldog, I'm showing two unidentified targets two hundred twenty-nine point three miles, bearing dead ahead. Speed . . . eighteen knots," Rificoff radioed the *Kennedy*'s CDC.

The instruments were now showing a strong K-band surface-to-surface and surface-to-air radar sweeping from one of the unidentified ships. The emissions coming from the ship were on the low side of the K-band frequency at 13,500 MHz. His basic ESM/ECM (electronic support measures/electronic counter measures) equipment provided identification, warning, and bearing of the surface radar. The ESM/ECM would also give confirmation when an enemy activated its fire control radar and warn him if a radar-guided antiship or antiaircraft missile had been launched. Rificoff's computer program had been recently updated with visual displays that were simple and easy to read. It gave his E-2C a full 360 degrees of instantaneous frequency measuring coverage over the entire radar spectrum. The system was so good that on a clear day Rificoff could tell if a commercial airliner was using its weather radar as it flew 300 miles out.

It only took a few seconds for the ECM computer to identify the type and make of the radar. It was an older Soviet-made system, code-named Spin Through, used for surface-search, air-search, and navigation. It was a common medium-range radar used on most of the Eastern Bloc ships that were exported to other countries during the eighties. Rificoff was concerned but not worried. The Spin Through wasn't used to launch weapons, and he had encountered it on a few civilian-operated vessels licensed by Libya, Iran, and Oman. As long as the frequency stayed the same, there wasn't much danger.

2

MiG-23 Flogger

Adib Hamen watched the flickering lights of the Egyptian town of Siwah grow closer. Even though it was still night, flying at 1,000 feet he could make out much of the details of the ground below. Buildings, parking lots, and roads were easy to see under their bright street lamps. Hamen streaked over the only highway leading out of the town to the north. He watched several cars traveling down the single road, their headlights leading the way. Enough sight-seeing, he told himself. His attention returned to the cockpit and his HUD.

Hamen was right on schedule. His mission clock showed 0554 hours and he was maintaining a speed of 380 knots. Everything was going as planned. He had half of his fuel remaining and the jet was operating flawlessly.

Hamen nudged the stick to the right, taking a new heading of zero four nine, northeast. He watched the top of the HUD as the greenish compass swung around and his airspeed fell slightly, then sluggishly crept back up as he came level out of the banking turn.

The hardest part of the mission was before him. The western Egyptian desert had been devoid of search radars. He knew that would not be the case as he approached the more populated area around the northern coast of Egypt. He had to stay alert and concentrate. It would be light shortly and he would lose another of his advantages, the night.

Suddenly a warning tone sounded in his headset. It was faint at first, but as he flew farther to the north the signal grew stronger, more even. Hamen's insides rolled over, even though he had been expecting this. It was the long-range early warning radar based at West Cairo airfield, an American radar system used to defend against an enemy air attack. Hamen had been trained to respect the quality of American military

12

equipment, and he had hoped he could avoid a confrontation with Egyptian fighters.

Without a second thought he dropped the nose of the MiG, picking up airspeed as he flew toward the ground. At 700 feet he forced the stick back and felt the Gs climb to 2.5 before he came level again and added power. At 425 knots he eased off on the throttle and readjusted his grip on the stick. A drop of sweat ran down his forehead stopping at his brow.

The night sky was growing lighter and Hamen could see the small hills and rock formations lying ahead of him. In twenty minutes he would pass over the coast. He flicked on his IFF transponder signal. His destiny awaited him.

F/A-18C DIAMOND BACK

Lieutenant Commander Kirby ("Blade") MacLear scanned the clear sapphire blue sky above his F/A-18C looking for air traffic. MacLear, flying Diamond Back 309, was the lead Hornet of a two-fighter formation, heading northeast at 7,000 feet away from his carrier. The sea below was covered with a thick layer of white fog. The fog generally burned off once the sun came out, revealing the sparkling water of the Mediterranean.

MacLear looked back at the HUD, then at the center MFD, which showed current radar information. He double-checked, making sure the radar was set on the velocity search mode and positioned for maximum range. This mode allowed him to pick up bogeys at extreme range, sacrificing detail for distance and providing him with a target's azimuth and velocity data only. The Hornet's AN/APG-65 radar was his extra pair of eyes and ears, and he relied on it heavily. The system used a Doppler beam coherent transmitter, which worked equally as well in day, night, or adverse weather. It was on mornings like this that he was glad he had the system. A film of haze was starting to build above the ocean below. It was just thick enough to cut his visibility.

MacLear watched the round orange sun slowly move above the horizon. He was glad it was up. It wasn't that landing on a carrier at night bothered him, he just preferred to do it in daylight.

Kirby MacLear had gotten his call sign Blade in flight school because of his Romeo appearance and a fixation on sunshine, cold beer, and his surfboard. MacLear wasn't conceited, but he knew he was good-looking. He had dark skin, green eyes, and black curly hair and weighed in at 190 pounds of muscle. Because of this many people just assumed he was a womanizer. Yet MacLear was just the opposite. A strong Catholic, he had only slept with one woman his entire life, that being his wife.

Now at twenty-nine he was a veteran of thirty-one missions over Iraq. He had downed one Iraqi helicopter while on an air-to-ground mission during the second day of Desert Storm and had assisted in bringing down an Iraqi F-1A. Other than that he had spent most of his time flying combat air patrol for A-6 Intruders and A-6B Prowlers during their ground attack missions.

"Diamond Back Three Zero Niner . . . this is Bulldog. Request a visual on two unidentified surface ships bearing one six four to your south, range . . . two hundred sixteen miles."

"Ah, roger that, Bulldog," MacLear could tell by the voice it was Rificoff giving him the orders. "Diamond Back Lead on the way. You with me DB two?"

"Roger, Lead. I'm with you," came the response from his wingman.

The two dirty gray F/A-18Cs instantly banked to the south, long lines of white condensation streaking from their wingtips.

The *Ibn Ghallan* was back on course and at full power. The Libyan ship vibrated as her twin diesel engines struggled to push her toward nineteen knots. With calm seas Captain Bani hoped to gain on the cruise liner. He put his binoculars to his eyes. Through the morning mist he could just barely make out the *Song of Flower* churning up the water in the distance.

"Captain Bani, radar room reports two small unidentified aircraft closing from the north at high speed. Range seventy-four miles," the second officer reported.

"Are you certain?" He lowered the heavy glasses, catching the eyes of his second in command.

"Yes, sir. Radar has been tracking them for thirty seconds. They are flying in a loose military formation."

"Probably an American fighter patrol," Bani muttered. His last report from Libyan Naval Headquarters had confirmed the *John F. Kennedy* had sailed away from the Libyan coast heading north. It was obvious she had turned east and was probably out in front of his ship somewhere. Bani wasn't surprised; he had seen this same tactic many times. He checked his watch. The MiG would be showing up in thirteen minutes.

"Bring our surface-to-air missiles on line but don't activate the radar until I give the order," Bani commanded.

Hamen's MiG-23 crossed over the coast five miles west of the Egyptian city of Ad Dab'ah. He was sure someone on the ground would see him. The sound accompanying a low-flying fighter was hard to ignore.

Hamen just hoped he was moving so fast no one would realize it was an unmarked MiG-23.

He checked the mission clock below his HUD. He was now three and a half minutes behind schedule, but well within the fifteen-minute window outlined in the mission planning. So far, so good. As far as he knew, Egyptian radar hadn't detected him, and no other military aircraft were in the area. Hamen was twenty minutes away from his target. Even if the Egyptian air force did come after him now, it would be too late by the time they figured out what he was up to.

Hamen surveyed the horizon. His altitude was such that a wispy mist hanging over the blue water limited his visibility to less than seven miles. He hoped the sky would clear as he flew farther out into the Mediterranean. His eyes returned to the instruments; he saw no problems. He nudged the stick straight back and added power. He watched his altitude and airspeed climb at the same time. With his left hand he turned the MiG's IFF transponder to full power and aligned his radio to the designated UHF channel. Shortly, he should be picking up a radio message from the *Ibn Ghallan*.

Hamen readjusted himself in the seat, feeling the lap belt tug at his stomach. His finger brushed the trigger of the twenty-three-millimeter cannon. It was the only weapon the fighter carried. The weapon racks had been stripped off the wing roots to reduce drag and save fuel. He wouldn't need anything else. The explosive impact of his aircraft with the ship would cause more than enough damage.

At 2,000 feet he leveled the fighter, trimming it up for level flight. He should be high enough for the Libyan ship to register the signal from his IFF transponder.

E-2C HAWKEYE, BULLDOG 602

"Thirty-one miles and closing. The ships should be off your starboard on the edge of the fog bank. Maintain current heading and descend to three thousand," Rificoff directed. He watched the surface targets on his radar scope and the two F-18s approaching.

"Roger that, Bulldog. Visibility limited to six miles . . . descending to target," MacLear radioed.

Captain Bani was now in the radar room of the *Ibn Ghallan,* several decks below the main bridge, a darkened room with no bright lights or windows. He stood looking at the black console, watching the amber-colored scope.

"Radar contact, Captain, bearing one seven one. I have IFF confirmation . . . it's the MiG." The radar operator aboard the *Ibn Ghallan* had just caught sight of a new target approaching from the south. Directly under the radar blip was AZN-16, its IFF signal confirming it was the aircraft they were waiting for.

"How far out?" asked Captain Bani.

"Eighty-six miles, altitude 2,000 feet."

"And the targets overtaking us from the north?"

"Twenty-five miles, sir, and heading straight for us."

Bani swallowed hard, contemplating his options. "Contact the MiG."

The radar operator keyed his mike. "Flight one one zero . . . this is control base. Do you copy?" They waited; no response. "Flight one one zero . . . this is control base. Do you copy?"

"Copy . . . con . . . base." Hamen's static-filled answer broke up.

"Praise Allah's holy name, you have arrived," Bani whispered. "Keep him on a course for our ship."

"Flight one one zero. Turn left to three four seven and maintain heading." The radar operator released the button on his mike and looked at Bani.

"Now . . . where are those other targets?" Bani asked.

"Eighteen miles out at 3,000 feet. Speed constant at 400 knots . . . they'll be approaching off our starboard."

Bani didn't like what was happening. His orders from his commander were direct and simple: Control the MiG to the cruise ship but don't provoke the Americans. Libyan leader Colonel Muammar Qaddafi had learned his lesson in 1986 when the Forty-eighth Tactical Fighter Wing flying F-111s bombed Tripoli, nearly killing him. The goal of today's mission was to covertly assist Abu Ajami in returning the Palestinians to their homeland, but not get bombed by the Americans again.

Bani knew he needed to divert the American fighters from the MiG. *If they come within ten miles, I will bring up the fire control radar. That will keep the bastards busy and away from my brother,* he thought.

"Stand by to bring up the fire control radar," Bani ordered.

MacLear could clearly see the two surface ships on his F-18's powerful radar. The first target was six miles out and slightly east of his flight path. His eyes went from the radar screen to the airspace out in front of him. A broken layer of fog hugged the ocean below him, making it difficult to see what was on the surface.

As far as MacLear was concerned, this was shaping up to be a standard surface ship interception. He and his wingman had participated in a dozen interceptions just like this in the Gulf of Sidra during their six-week patrol. The Mediterranean was full of surface ship traffic, and sometimes he wondered if the crew in the Hawkeye were just a bit paranoid. The F-18s would both break formation flying on each side of the ships at 1,000 feet. After appraising the situation, they would make their report, hook back up, and head for home.

"You see anything, Mad Dog?" MacLear radioed his wingman flying 500 yards off his left side.

"Negative, Lead," Lieutenant Hugh Calderone answered. He was four years younger than MacLear and still green, with only 300 hours behind the stick of one of the U.S. Navy's hottest fighters. Calderone didn't fit the standard tough-guy image of a fighter jock. He was only five foot five and weighed in at 142 pounds soaking wet in his flight boots. His hairline was receding and the other pilots gave him a hard time, saying he had more hair on his chest than on his head. When he was inside his fighter, he made up for his wimpy size. Calderone gave flying everything he had and when in a battle he fought like a mad dog, not knowing when to quit.

"When we reach the lead ship, you break left. I'll go right and cross its beam. Let's get a quick visual and then move on. Probably the same ol' nickel-and-dime shit." MacLear still couldn't see anything below him.

"Roger, Lead."

MacLear's aircraft rocketed away from his wingman, banked left, and came level a little below 2,000 feet.

"One pass and we're out of here." In the distance MacLear could vaguely see the outline of the first surface ship. He maneuvered his fighter into a shallow dive. A glance told him Diamond Back Two was in sight and following his lead toward the ocean.

He rolled his F/A-18C left to get a better view of a pearl white cruise liner cutting through the water.

"Looks like a love boat, Lead," Calderone radioed. Then he began a poorly sung version of the TV series' theme song.

"Roger that Two . . . and you sing like you fly . . . like a Mad Dog." MacLear grimaced as one of his wingman's badly hit notes pummeled his eardrum.

"Activate the radar now," Captain Bani called out from the *Ibn Ghallan's* radar room. His plan was simple. *Their attention will have to be on me now. I am the threat.* He could see the two aircraft on the radar scope ten miles from his ship. "I'm going topside." He made his way to the doorway leading to the bridge.

The *Ibn Ghallan* came alive. The eight-foot open-mesh parabolic dish located on the top of the bridge started to turn counterclockwise, sending out a steady G/H-band radar beam. Below it a smaller dish turned in the opposite direction; it would control the missiles once they launched. The dual-rail launchers, located on the bow of the ship, rotated forty-five degrees to the west and stopped. One white and black 1,200-pound air-to-air missile hung below each rail.

Rificoff heard the warning tone in his headset first as the Hawkeye banked in a slow turn. It was a high-pitched buzzing sound like an electric razor. His eyes burned in on the ESM/ECM equipment to the right of his radar scope.

"Holy shit!" He blurted. His tactical display was flashing a yellow warning. The ESM antenna was picking up a change in the second target's radar emissions from a constant stream of K-band emissions, a navigational radar, to a short, pulsing frequency in the G/H-band range. A fire control radar was now painting the area around the F-18s with strong bursts of radar waves. The computer automatically accessed the radar threat library of over 2,000 known hostile radar transmissions. It then cycled through its 80K memory in 4.7 seconds giving him an answer. A single Head Lights B fire control radar system. The system was used to control SA-N-3 naval air-defense missiles.

"Radar has locked onto target . . . permission to fire," the second officer reported from his position next to the ship's internal intercom system.

Bani spun around and gaped at the nervous and confused man, not believing his ears. *What did he say? Did he really think I was going to challenge an American carrier battle group?*

"Fire? Is that . . ."

"Fire . . . fire," the second officer responded.

"NO . . . NO!" Bani shouted. *"Don't fire, you idiot!"*

It was too late. Bani felt the floor rumble as the first and then the second SA-N-3 left its launcher, both heavy missiles struggling to gain altitude. A few seconds later he lost sight of the missiles as they entered the sky above his ship. The smoky trails from their exhaust blended into the fog perfectly.

As Rificoff's thumb went for the communication button, the warning light flashed from yellow to red. The surface ship had just launched on the F-18s.

"Threat . . . threat!" Rificoff's heart pounded every beat. "Diamond Back, I show a launch of two . . . I repeat two . . . radar-guided missiles heading in your direction . . . active and tracking, ETA thirty seconds."

* * *

"Watch your six, Mad Dog . . . break." MacLear caught sight of two bright streams of fire rising out of the clouds to the east. He jammed his throttles forward, bringing the nose of his fighter up ten degrees while keeping his eyes on the accelerating missiles. He needed airspeed and altitude.

In the distance the dual-thrust solid fuel rocket motor of the first SAM had already pushed it past Mach point five as the missile broke through 750 feet and started to arc toward its target, Diamond Back Two. The missile's internal guidance system had locked on to the reflecting radar emissions of the American fighter. The SA-N-3 was an older type SAM, which only allowed the system to attack a single target at one time using two missiles. The SAM was not designed to engage low-flying, high-G targets such as fighter aircraft. Each missile was steered by four stubby rear fins, making it only moderately maneuverable. The fins were tipped with either a rearward- or forward-pointing antenna linking it with the G/H-band fire control and engagement radar aboard the *Ibn Ghallan*.

MacLear stiffened, watching the two missiles gain speed and streak toward his wingman.

"Hold tight, Mad Dog, hold tight," the more experienced pilot urged. He was afraid Diamond Back Two would break too soon, allowing one of the SAMs to stay locked on to the fighter.

"I got'em, I got'em." Mad Dog's tone was calm and even.

MacLear followed the missiles as they continued to accelerate. He watched the F/A-18C bank slowly back to the northeast, slicing across the nose of the lead SAM and gaining altitude. Mad Dog was doing exactly what he was supposed to do, put the SAMs at a right angle to his aircraft.

"That's right . . . that's right," MacLear whispered under his oxygen mask. "Now wait . . . wait."

The first missile was rocketing directly at the steel bird. It made a slight course correction, following its target. A thousand yards behind, the second SAM was at a slightly lower altitude.

"Break left . . . left!" MacLear bellowed.

MacLear watched as Mad Dog put his fighter into a maximum G left turn, dropping his nose toward the water and gaining airspeed. The first SAM couldn't follow. It raced past in a blur. The internal radar seeker head had lost lock on the target.

The remaining SAM made a slight trajectory adjustment to the east as it pushed over into a curving dive. Its guidance system continued to hold steady lock on the fighter a few seconds longer, then flashed by only fifty yards away, close enough to activate one of the four proximity

fuse strips along the nose of the SA-N-3. In a white puffy explosion, the
SAM sent hot steel into the F/A-18C's rear section.

"Fuck!" Mad Dog's angry shout reverberated in MacLear's ears. *"I'm
hit and losing hydraulic pressure, Blade."*

"Roger, Mad Dog, let's get the hell out of here." MacLear slammed his
throttles forward, driving them to the stop, into afterburner. He snapped
his fighter into a hard left turn, feeling the sharp cutting pain of 6 Gs
rolling over his body. As his wings came level, he placed the center of
his HUD right on Mad Dog's tail and started to accelerate toward him. A
quick scan of his cockpit instruments and the silence of his RHAW
equipment ensured him the threat was over for the moment. His concern now was to get the injured fighter back to the *Kennedy* in one
piece.

"Arrest this man!" Bani screamed at the top of his lungs. "Put him in the
brig . . . I will deal with him later." Two armed men dragged the ship's
second officer off the bridge. Bani lit a cigarette, his hands trembling,
hoping the nicotine would calm his nerves. He looked through the dirty,
pitted window of the bridge at the gray ocean. The morning fog was
beginning to break up, and he could see patches of blue sky above his
ship. His career as a Libyan naval officer was over. The Americans
weren't going to sit back and not take action against his ship or his
country. Bani's body weakened. *I will be shot when I return. I am a
dead man,* he thought, resigned to the fact.

He sucked in a deep breath of cigarette smoke. *Unless the mission
. . . Of course! Unless the mission is successful,* Bani thought. Bani
pushed the button on the intercom. "Shut down the fire control radar.
Where are the American aircraft?"

"The American fighters are retreating, Captain."

"ETA for the MiG?" Bani felt himself becoming sick. By shutting down
the radar he hoped he had just bought the few minutes needed to vector
the MiG to its target.

"Ten minutes, sir."

"Heading?"

"Five degrees off course for our present location."

"Contact the MiG. Have the pilot adjust his heading."

"Yes, Captain."

The *Song of Flower* was still sailing away from them. He hoped they
had not seen the SAMs launch.

USS *John F. Kennedy*

Commander Doherty let out a deep sigh of relief, watching the two blips leaving the hot area. There was a controlled chaos in the CDC, as was to be expected with any surprise attack. Washington had been alerted and was standing by for further developments, already planning what retaliatory actions would be taken, if any. Doherty left for the ready room and instructed Emerson to keep him updated.

Aboard Bulldog 602, Rificoff wiped the sweat from his face with the back of his shirt sleeve. "Diamond Back, this is Bulldog. Damage report and current status."

"Bulldog, this is Lead. I got out in A-1 shape, but Two took one of those SAMs up his butt. He's losing hydro, but I think we can make it to deck. Visual on first target appeared to be a tourist cruise ship. What the hell's going on?" MacLear's tone sounded his frustration for having been caught with his fly open.

"Data shows the missiles came from the second target. We're still piecing things together. I have backup on the way; you guys hang tough out there."

"Roger, Bulldog, I copy."

"I can't believe those bastards launched on us," Rificoff swore under his breath. His eyes went back to the two blips on his scope representing the F-18s. They were now thirty-five miles away from the enemy ship on a direct course back to the *Kennedy*. Rificoff had vectored two other F-18s into the area; however, it would be another eight minutes before they could be of any help.

MacLear slid in under Mad Dog's Hornet to survey the damage. It was more extensive than he had hoped. There were several grapefruit-sized holes cut through the right tail fin and horizontal stabilizer. He could see a thin stream of black smoke coming out of the number two engine and long streaks of reddish brown hydraulic fluid from several small punctures. MacLear flew his 18 up and around so he was flying off Mad Dog's left wing. He was close enough to see his wingman's face.

"How's she doing, Mad Dog?" MacLear referred to the handling qualities of the damaged aircraft.

"A little rough, but I can hold her together," Mad Dog radioed back. *"I don't want to ditch her."*

"There's smoke coming out of your number two engine. Keep an eye on it."

"It's running hot now. I'm shutting it down. Shit . . . I waited too long to make my break, Blade."

"Bullshit, you did good. Now let's just get you down. How's your hydraulic pressure?" MacLear asked, making sure his wingman didn't overlook anything.

"Falling . . . but slowly."

"It'll be all right. I'm on your wing, ol' buddy."

3

Rificoff's eyes watered as he maintained vigil on the scope. He felt responsible for not getting ample warning to his fighters and was determined not even a flea would get past him this time. Searching the bottom of his scope, he saw a new blip. This one was smaller and wasn't a ship. An aircraft moving at low level with a moderate rate of speed toward the two original targets. He quickly scanned over the entire scope for other bogeys.

"Damn it." Rificoff's adrenalin raced. "Diamond Back, this is Bulldog. New target approaching hot area. It's definitely an aircraft; we need identification."

"Negative, Bulldog. Request to stay escort."

"Negative on escort, Diamond Back One, you're the only aircraft in the area and this one could be military. ETA for other 18s is five minutes." Rificoff hated making this demand, knowing MacLear just wanted to bring his wingman within safe distance of the *JFK. This job can make you feel like a real shithead,* he thought. He released his mike and listened in on the two Hornet pilots' conversation.

"Blade, I can make it," Rificoff heard Diamond Back Two radio.

"All right, see you back on deck, Mad Dog. Bulldog . . . Diamond Back One breaking to engage."

Ibn Ghallan

"Captain . . . an aircraft is turning from the north. One of the American fighters. It's returning," the radar operator reported.

Captain Bani finished lighting another cigarette. "They must have picked up the MiG. Ignore it. We have done our part. Contact the MiG

23

pilot, vector him to the target. Then I want complete radio silence. I want flank speed . . . get back into our waters. Is that understood?"

"Yes, Captain."

MiG-23 Flogger

Hamen let his silvery fighter drift up to 3,000 feet as he eased the steering symbol on his HUD back to a heading of 347 degrees. He was seven miles out at 380 knots. As he cut through the morning fog, he could see the gray water of the Mediterranean flash below him. The *Ibn Ghallan* and cruise ship should be out in front of him, somewhere.

"Flight one one zero . . . turn right to three four zero. Target should be visible," the hollow voice of the *Ibn Ghallan*'s radar controller cut into his headset. *"Final transmission."*

Hamen pushed the stick down, forcing the MiG into a shallow dive, and banked a few degrees to the west. He switched off the radio and throttled back, reducing his airspeed.

F/A-18C Diamond Back

MacLear tracked the new air target. The APG-65 radar fed him constant updates as the target changed position, speed, and altitude. He didn't like what he saw. The aircraft had reduced its airspeed and changed course to the west. It was pointed directly for the cruise ship at an altitude below 1,000 feet. Possibly it was having some sort of engine trouble, but MacLear doubted it.

The F/A-18C pushed over at 5,000 feet and headed for the water, gaining airspeed. At ten miles out the visibility was limited.

"Damn fog!" he cursed into his empty cockpit.

At 2,000 feet he hauled back on the stick, coming out of the dive pulling a steady 3 Gs. If the target stayed on course, he could intercept before it reached the cruise liner.

Between broken pockets of fog Hamen saw a fuzzy outline of the cruise liner. It was five miles out off the left side of his MiG's nose. Churning water trailed behind the ship. Hamen was only a few degrees off course, but it didn't matter. His attention centered on the target of his mission.

MacLear squinted, trying to catch sight of any unusual glitter or flash of light. His radar told him the aircraft was out there in front of him. He lowered his helmet visor, eliminating the glare from the rising sun. The bow of the cruise liner came within sight 3,000 feet below. The sound of his twin jet engines would be quite a wake-up call for most of the passengers. At the same time his thumb moved the weapons select switch from long-range AIM-7M Sparrows to short-range AIM-9L Sidewinders, air-to-air missiles. MacLear knew his target was close. The faint pulsing tones of the super-cooled heat seekers, trying to acquire a heat source, filled his headset.

He strained his eyes, following a silvery silhouette moving fast to the north a thousand yards away. The color was unlike any other aircraft he had seen. Nevertheless, the profile indicated it was a MiG-23. MacLear held the powerful fighter steady, hoping not to give off any glimmers of light himself.

When the MiG passed before him, he banked sharply to the east, coming in behind and beneath the aircraft, taking a position 300 yards off its six o'clock. He watched the swing-wing MiG for a moment. The aircraft was bare, not carrying any missiles or bombs. It also didn't have markings to identify its country of origin. He checked his threat panel; no electronic emissions were radiating from the MiG. Its air-to-air and terrain-following radar must be turned off.

"What game are you playing, buddy?" MacLear questioned aloud. He figured the pilot had not seen him and watched the MiG pitch up and down as much as 100 feet as it maintained the current course straight for the cruise ship. *Either this guy has very little, if any, training or he isn't competent,* MacLear thought as he shook his head.

"I have a visual, Bulldog. Your target is a MiG-23 . . . no markings," he radioed. "Better try radio contact."

"Roger, Diamond Back."

The *Song of Flower* was much larger than Hamen had pictured. The exterior was a soft ivory with neat rows of windows running parallel to the water along its sides. He could see the turquoise swimming pool on the upper deck lined with lounge chairs. He smirked under his oxygen mask. This was nothing more than a floating luxury hotel full of lazy, fat westerners. Hamen banked a few degrees west, careful not to fly his MiG too close to the *Song of Flower.* As he came even with the stern, he angled away from the ship, putting the fighter into a gradual climb due north. He would swing around 180 degrees and strike the north side of the ship. Sleeping passengers would never know what hit them. The memory of his wife surfaced as he began praying.

* * *

MacLear rolled his fighter forty-five degrees, keeping his eyes locked onto the MiG.

"Negative response from radio contact, Diamond Back One," Rificoff reported.

"Roger, Bulldog, what about the second ship?"

"She did a turnabout and is quiet."

"You want me to spook him?" MacLear was hoping he'd have a chance to let off steam.

"Strike orders you to maintain visual contact. You have permission to fire if the target shows any hostile intentions."

MacLear watched the MiG glide through the sky in front of him. It was at 4,000 feet and two miles out. "Okay, turkey, make a move," MacLear challenged. As if on cue, the nose dropped and the mysterious fighter hit 380 knots.

"What the hell?" MacLear exclaimed, watching it head directly at the cruise liner. Instinctively, he followed. In one fluid motion he kicked the Hornet into afterburner, slicing through the air next to the older MiG in just seconds.

"Bulldog, this is Diamond Back . . . we have a possible kamikaze situation here. Stand by." MacLear then slid in under the right side of the unmarked plane and let his F/A-18C drift up so his cockpit was even with the MiG's. He lifted his visor, wanting to make eye contact with the pilot.

Hamen jumped involuntarily as out of the corner of his eye he spotted another aircraft. His head snapped around to the sight of a fully armed American F-18 Hornet less than thirty yards away. He lost his breath momentarily as his mind swirled with emotion. How long had the American been following him? Why hadn't his leaders told him Americans would be in the area?

He turned his head back to his HUD. In the distance he could see the *Song of Flower*. He was at 2,500 feet, a mile and a half out. Hamen turned and looked at the American one last time. *I cannot fail,* he thought. He mashed the throttle forward, putting his fighter into afterburner. The added kick in acceleration pushed him back into his seat as his airspeed built.

"No way, man, no way," MacLear declared into his empty cockpit, watching the MiG try to pull away. He could see its tail exhaust glowing dark orange. Banking his Hornet seven degrees left, he whirled in behind the MiG. His left hand pressed the two throttles forward just short of maximum power. A constant, even tone sounded in his helmet; the Sidewinders had locked up.

"Bulldog . . . Diamond Back. Enemy fighter is descending toward cruise ship. Permission to fire."

"Weapon's free . . . weapon's free," Rificoff replied.

MacLear was in perfect firing position. If he was going to kill a man, he wanted to be certain there was no room for doubt that his intentions were a definite threat. He stroked the release button with his thumb as the MiG streaked onward.

Hamen used both hands to move the stick back and forth, jinking his fighter slightly left to right. At 1,200 feet, he centered the stick. His fighter stabilized and he put the cannon aim point, in the center of his HUD, on the middle of the ship. Hamen squeezed the trigger, bringing his twenty-three-millimeter cannon to life. The MiG shuttered as a steady stream of cannon fire exploded from beneath the fighter. Hamen sucked in what he thought would be his last breath and whispered his wife's name. The water erupted in front of him as the first rounds fell short of their mark.

There was no question now what the MiG was about to do. MacLear could wait no longer.

"Fox two!" He gave warning and punched the weapons release trigger, sending a single olive drab Sidewinder to its target. He nosed his F/A-18C up, keeping his eyes on the fiery smoke trail.

MacLear watched as the tail section of the MiG burst into a red sphere of fire. A series of twisted aluminum chunks could be seen cartwheeling through the sky. With its tail gone, the aircraft began a slow roll left, its nose pitching down.

Hamen heard a loud thud and his aircraft shook violently. The stick went dead as his MiG rotated completely over.

"No!" he shouted with anger and disbelief. "I must not fail." Using all his strength, he tried to level his stricken aircraft. He looked up to see gray ocean fast approaching. His last conscious thought was the hope that Allah would let him be with his wife, even if he had not succeeded with his mission. The rear fuel tank of his MiG exploded.

* * *

"Splash one MiG," MacLear radioed as the ocean shot up with the impact of the downed fighter. "The stupid bastard must have thought he still had a chance."

He made a wide banking turn over the cruise liner, cutting his airspeed as he circled the wreckage. The MiG-23 had missed the ship by only 200 yards to the rear. The waves behind the big ship were filled with floating debris and a light slick of fuel.

MacLear unhinged his oxygen mask, letting it dangle from his helmet. He smiled at the sight of a pair of F-18s. His backup had arrived.

"Diamond Back One to Bulldog . . . I'm homeward bound."

4

Nikolai Leonov could clearly see the details of the city below; they were gradually descending. The morning sky looked frosty and he wished for another cup of hot coffee. The former Soviet army general had been up for six hours and had spent four and a half of them in the air. He was on his way to a Russian military space control and tracking center at Yevpatoriya in north central Russia. A military satellite was spinning out of control, and he had been told to make sure it was dealt with in the appropriate manner. Whatever that meant, he wasn't sure. As the new deputy minister of defense, there were going to be many assignments he would have to figure out as he went along.

Leonov closed his eyes and rested his head on the back of the soft leather chair, feeling his collar pinch his neck. He didn't fit the image of the stereotypical Russian officer. A medium-sized man, he had a clean-shaven face, a double chin, and bushy black eyebrows. He combed his graying hair, what was left of it, straight back and wore round glasses when he had to read something. Slightly overweight, he was having a hard time getting used to wearing European-style suits, button-down collars, and silk ties. He now carried a businessman's briefcase and worried about the way he used his words, not wanting to offend any-one. The changes in his country's government was one thing, but having to totally restructure the way he dressed, talked, and presented himself was quite another. After all, he had spent the last twenty-seven years of his life in the uniform of the once glorious and mighty Soviet military. He had worn the uniform with pride, and from time to time he would remove it from his closet and look at it. He remembered the first day he slipped the heavy brown wool coat over his shoulders and left his home behind to protect his country.

Leonov had worked hard to achieve the rank of lieutenant general of

29

the Spetsnaz, the Soviet special forces. He was not like many of the
other officers in the Soviet army, who were promoted easily because
they had followed in their father's and grandfather's footsteps. Leonov
had come from humble beginnings. Born into a family of six, he was the
youngest of three sons and two daughters. His family lived and worked
in the small farming town of Frolovo. His father had worked in several
of the large warehouses that distributed food to the other communities.
Leonov recalled his father coming home at night so tired he could barely
walk or eat. But never did his father complain about the hard work. His
mother had labored in one of the nearby factories, manufacturing shirts
and pants. Memories of his childhood were of being happy and care-
free. He never went hungry, and his parents had done their best to make
sure his brothers, sisters, and he always had had good clothes and
shoes.

After graduating from high school with honors, Leonov was the only
member of his class to be selected to attend airborne school in Ryazan.
It was an honor that had given his family much pride. It was there that
he had first met the men assigned to the special troops of the Spetsnaz.
They possessed inner strength, and Leonov had been impressed by a
quiet quality he could not see in others in the military. He knew he must
become a part of this elite group. He continued his studies and two
years later was asked to join the Spetsnaz special forces.

It was 1964 and the Soviet Union was at the height of the cold war
with the United States. War always provides opportunities for quick ad-
vancement, and Leonov proved himself to be a good and loyal soldier.
He moved up the ranks easily with many acts of valor.

"Mr. Leonov, we're fifty kilometers out and descending. We should be
on the ground in twenty minutes." The sound of the pilot's voice crackling over the intercom startled him from his thoughts.

Leonov opened his eyes and his breath fogged the window as he
stared out at the dawning day. He felt the jet bank to the left and come
level, as the pilot throttled back and slowed the twin-engine aircraft.

In many ways Leonov longed for the old days, the days when he
knew right where he stood. His mind wandered through the past to
deep inside a heavily forested hill, a bunker with no air shafts and
only one entrance, a fortified *Raketniye Voiska Strategicheskovo
Naznacheniya*—Strategic Missile Forces—command and control center.
On the lowest level of the bunker was an impregnable room. In this
bunker he had been introduced to the nine senior members of what was
called the inner circle. They were the up-and-coming members of the
Soviet command structure. They were in charge of secret military plans
and reported to only one man, Yuri Andropov, leader of the KGB and
general secretary of the Communist party after Brezhnev's death.

Leonov soon became the new junior ranking officer. They promoted him to lieutenant colonel, and he was given command of a Spetsnaz regiment with 650 men. Many careers and fates were planned or guided during the inner circle's intimate meetings. A man was given only a single chance to join this clandestine segment of the Soviet military. Surprisingly, he had had the choice to refuse without consequences to him or his family, as long as he never spoke of the group's existence.

Each member of the inner circle controlled a key element of the military's structure. This was all done in the name of state security and, of course, made it easier to direct the future. There was only one man who had the real power to wipe out the enemy's national command authority centers with a single lethal blow. This man was General Major Dimitri Popivich, commander of the Soviet Union's military space operations at Yevpatoriya. In 1981, Andropov and the inner circle had feared a nuclear war with the West was imminent. They secretly built a satellite armed with independently targeted nuclear warheads. This first-strike weapon would be used against NATO and American nerve centers in the first minutes of nuclear conflict.

However, in the fall of 1984 everything changed. A new Soviet computer radar shield had been built to protect the country from an attack. In a secret mission the United States boldly attacked the new computer center, destroying it. Leonov had later learned that a single prototype B-2 Stealth bomber had penetrated the Soviet Union's best air defenses and demolished the last hope his country had of keeping up with the West. So began the disassembling and reform of the Soviet Union's military strength and nuclear firepower.

Leonov forced himself to think about the present. General Popivich's acceptance of the ongoing reforms greatly concerned him. When the Soviet Union collapsed, it severely weakened the military's command and control structure. Not surprisingly, Popivich had survived when the empire crumbled. Following the orders of Andropov, Popivich had been instrumental in constructing and controlling the Soviet Union's secret military space weapons program. Because of his knowledge, he still maintained his post at the space operations center and was stubborn enough to hold on to what power he had left. The old man was one of Leonov's former comrades in the inner circle, and Leonov hoped that relationship would be of service and not prove to be a detriment. Yet Leonov wasn't too optimistic. General Popivich had deep roots going back generations in his native Ukraine. He had grown up in the small village of Sokal near the Polish border, where most of his family still lived, and he came from a long line of military leaders. What troubled Leonov the most was Popivich's vocal opposition to Russia's military restructuring and his unyielding desire to hold onto the old ways. His loyalty wasn't with Russia, it was with the missile forces. *One thing is for certain,* Leonov thought. *When I'm finished with this assignment,*

Popivich will be relieved of command. The man has outlived his usefulness.

Leonov tugged his lap belt snugly around his waist and rubbed his face as the landing gear came down. He was glad they were finally landing.

SHIMANOVSK STATION, RUSSIA

Eight hundred and nineteen kilometers northwest of Vladivostok, near the banks of the Amur River, the Russian tracking station of Shimanovsk was cold and silent. It had been five years since the last technicians were stationed there. They had been replaced with more reliable computers. Now only an occasional engineering team visited to make sure all the telemetry, tracking, and communications equipment was operating properly.

The enormous tracking antennae had been built twenty-five years earlier to assist the monitoring of a Soviet fractional orbiting bombardment system, or FOBS. The system had been developed to deliver strategic nuclear weapons, utilizing an Antarctic trajectory, against U.S. naval targets operating in the South Pacific. It had been created when the Americans had little early warning capability if an attack came from over the South Pole. At that time, American strategy relied heavily on north-looking ground-based radars as their major defense. This made the prospects of an Antarctic attack strategically attractive, even if the distances were extremely long.

Since that time, U.S. early warning satellites in geosynchronous orbit and phased-array warning radars sweeping to the south had largely negated the FOBS threat. The station at Shimanovsk was now used to track various Russian military satellites.

The eight radar dish antennae rotated three degrees left and five degrees north. The overlapping white aluminum dishes sent a steady stream of C-band radio waves into the air. In a matter of seconds it would once again lock on to a large Russian satellite in low earth orbit and relay its position to the control center at Yevpatoriya.

Leonov pulled out a cigarette and hesitated before lighting it. His personal physician had told him that cigarette smoke was one of the worst offenses to an ulcer, but he couldn't break the habit. *It's bad enough all I can eat is bland food and drink only one small glass of vodka a day,* he thought. *My God, how many sacrifices do I have to make for this job and the new government?* It just wasn't worth it. When this project was over,

Leonov planned to take some time off. The last thing he needed was a bleeding hole in his stomach.

He drew in a full breath of smoke, holding it a moment before exhaling. The sun, burning through the overcast, allowed him to see the layout of the base at Yevpatoriya. There were a dozen large structures containing the computers and communication equipment. Surrounding the primary buildings were smaller ones, along with the white radar domes and microwave antennae.

The driver turned north, away from the main part of the compound, and accelerated down another dirt road. A high barbed wire fence bordered the road on both sides. In the distance were a couple of single-story buildings. As they drew closer, Leonov saw a man standing alone.

It's about time, Leonov thought. He crushed out his cigarette and waited for the car to come to a stop before reaching for his briefcase.

A young man, wearing a neatly pressed air force uniform, spoke as he swung the car door open, "Good morning, Mr. Leonov. Welcome to Yevpatoriya. I trust your trip was uneventful." He was nice looking, with straight teeth and black hair. His name badge read First Lieutenant Alexei Teshev.

Leonov exited the car and shook the man's hand. A blast of cold wind took his breath away. "Thank you . . . my flight was fine, no problems."

"I apologize. The weather could have been a bit warmer for your visit."

Leonov just shrugged. The weather was the least of his concerns. Besides, he would be leaving again in a few hours to return to Moscow.

"Have I arrived in time?" Leonov asked.

"Yes, the satellite will be in range shortly. General Popivich has been expecting you. We are just minutes away from giving the command. Come, let me show you the way." Teshev turned up the collar on his jacket and started toward the nearest building. "This is not the normal command center that is used. Because of the nature of this assignment, General Popivich decided to use the emergency command bunker." Teshev was speaking loudly, over his shoulder.

The two men entered the building, closing the door quickly behind them. Seated at a desk was an elderly security guard. He motioned for Teshev to proceed with a nod of his head. Leonov followed the lieutenant along a dimly lit corridor to a set of concrete steps leading down to a bunker. Leonov held the cold metal handrail, being careful not to miss any of the steps.

"When we reach the command center, I would prefer to observe the operation unnoticed," Leonov said.

"I will return to my post then," Teshev replied.

The two men reached the bottom of the stairs. Leonov estimated they

were at least sixty meters underground. They turned right and entered
the command center. Leonov unbuttoned his coat and stood in the shadows near the back of the room. He could see Popivich standing in the
middle of the room.

The beginning of a new day was the furthest thing from General Major
Dimitri Popivich's mind as the first bits of telemetry started to fill the
large color radar screen before him. He stood with his arms folded in the
darkened military space control center. A tall, trim man, Popivich stood
right at six feet, his shoulders square and back straight. His face, however, showed his age. In his late sixties, deep wrinkles surrounded his
eyes and cut into his forehead and cheeks. Virtually bald, what hair he
did have was a yellowish gray. Popivich stood motionless, seemingly
mesmerized by the dancing green and yellow lights of the underground
command post.

The center was a small room in the shape of a horseshoe. Ten technicians sat in two neat rows in the middle of the room, manning the
center's computer terminals. They could track everything from perimeter
security to the weather. On the wall before them were three viewing
screens. The largest screen displayed an outline of the eastern half of the
former Soviet Union in red. In the upper section, a bright blue line out of
the north traced the trajectory of a satellite in a north-south orbit.

General Popivich was a veteran controller of over 400 military space
launches. The facility at Yevpatoriya was currently responsible for tracking and operating sixteen Russian satellites: four Kosmos photographic
reconnaissance, eight Kosmos 1603-type ELINT (Electronic Intelligence),
and three ocean reconnaissance satellites. The final satellite was simply
known as Kosmos 3-1660, and it was on this satellite that the entire
station now focused its attention.

Popivich watched the data appear on the screen before him. The
tracking ship *Akademic Sergei Korolov* had lost contact with the satellite
six minutes ago as it started its orbital swing above the Arctic Ocean.
Soon it would pass directly over the tracking station at Shimanovsk. At
this point, Kosmos 3-1660 would be closer to the earth than at any other
point in its orbit.

"Everything is ready," the general grunted, as he scanned the room
with his eyes. He wasn't so much stating it as he was verifying.

Leonov remained in the shadows, standing behind Popivich, watching his actions. "I trust this plan of yours will work . . . General," he
said softly. Leonov took a long drag from one of his Turkish-made cigarettes, exhaling the pale blue smoke through his nose.

The sound of the voice told Popivich who it was, but he didn't turn to
acknowledge his former colleague. In his eyes, Leonov was just a

mouthpiece for the new leaders of Russia, a betrayer of the Soviet Union, a traitor to the country he had been trained to defend. And now Popivich would have to submit to *his* scrutiny.

Finally, Popivich turned around. "The deputy defense minister knows nothing of what I am trying to do here?" Popivich looked Leonov directly in the face, leaving him to wonder if the general had already been aware of his presence.

Leonov only stared back in reply. Popivich had aged, but his eyes were still bright and full of fire.

The general turned away and took a step forward as the down-link telemetry continued to appear on the main viewing screen.

"Apogee two seven four kilometers. Perigee . . . two hundred twenty three kilometers." First Lieutenant Teshev relayed the data at the same time the computer plotted the course of the Kosmos. He was now monitoring a computer display showing a thin blue line, the path of Kosmos, moving twenty-five times the speed of sound to the southeast.

The room fell silent as the other nine technicians sat stone faced. The only sound that could be heard was the tapping of the computer keyboard and Lieutenant Teshev's voice.

"Three minutes to SUBK ground," he stated. The SUBK system operated the satellite's two basic modes with either radio control from the ground or automatic functions programmed in its memory.

"Transfer control from automatic to radio ground control on my mark," General Popivich ordered. Kosmos 3-1660 inched closer to the Shimanovsk tracking station on the large screen before him. "Pressurize the maneuvering thrusters."

"ODU up-link operating at full power, General. Operating frequency 399.97 MHz," the technician to the general's right informed him. The ODU controlled the satellite's low- and high-thrust maneuvering engines.

The technician paused to make sure his readings were correct. He then keyed a new set of instructions into the computer. "Ready on your signal, General."

Popivich leaned over in an unconscious effort to get closer to the larger screen. His pale face hardened in concentration. The general knew this would be his last chance to boost the satellite into a higher orbit. For the past nine months, 3-1660's orbit had been steadily deteriorating, and at its current rate of descent it was predicted that the Kosmos would fall out of orbit within the next few weeks. If everything went as planned today, they would send it up to a storage orbit, keeping it in space for another five years. If not, Kosmos 3-1660 would come down and bring with it a political disaster, not only from the deaths that might occur, but because the Russian government had failed to abide by the Outer Space Treaty prohibiting nuclear weapons in space.

"Thirty seconds to optimum range." Lieutenant Teshev's hand hovered above the thrust control button on his keyboard.

"Standby, Lieutenant. On my command only." The General sensed the young officer's intensity.

"Five . . . four . . . three . . . two . . . one. Now, General."

Popivich waited a few moments until the satellite was directly over the tracking station. The blue line depicting its path across eastern Siberia intersected the red dot representing the tracking station.

"*NOW*. Fire the thrusters," the general demanded.

Leonov's body tensed and he straightened to get a better view.

Two hundred seventy-four kilometers above the cold brown earth Kosmos 3-1660 shuddered to life. The 7,000-kilogram satellite resembled a gray boxcar with gold and silver solar panels. The northern end was a large round sphere containing computers and navigational equipment. Protruding from the sphere were a number of short radio antennae and sensors.

The Kosmos wobbled slightly as the four thrusters, two on each side, glowed white from the blast of the small hydrazine and nitric acid rockets straining to push it higher.

"Fuel at thirteen percent," Lieutenant Teshev announced. "I show some oscillation. It is starting to roll and pitch."

"Damn it," the general grunted. That was the last thing he wanted. If the Kosmos started to roll, it could tumble. That would add further atmospheric drag, causing it to come out of orbit more quickly. If he ordered the thrusters to be shut down completely, his plan would certainly fail. He had to make a decision and make it quickly.

"Continue," Popivich said stiffly.

"General—" Leonov began to protest.

General Popivich held up his hand. "Full power, Lieutenant. Take the fuel down to five percent."

"I'm showing minimal altitude gain. Twenty-five, thirty . . . fifty kilometers." A red warning light started to flash on the left-hand side of the control screen. "Premature shutdown on number one and three thrusters. It is starting to—"

"Initiate emergency cutoff, Lieutenant!" The general's eyes were locked onto the screen. He clinched his fist, jamming it into the palm of his other hand.

Lieutenant Teshev hit the emergency shutoff button twice, sending a signal to the Kosmos telling its computer to cut off the fuel supply to the maneuvering thrusters.

"Damage report," Popivich demanded.

"Waiting for computations, General. Telemetry is down-loading into the computer now," replied Teshev.

Popivich didn't have to wait. He could read the data appearing on the screen just as well as anyone. The dark blue vein running down the center of his forehead pulsed as he said, "We're going to lose it."

Kosmos 3-1660 was now tumbling out of control. When the number one and three thrusters had shut down, the other two had pushed the satellite into an end-over-end spin. The 3-1660 was slowly spinning, like a giant football heading through the goal posts, high above the earth.

"Calculate time to reentry," Popivich barked.

Teshev turned in his chair, this time looking at his commanding officer's eyes. "Because of the tumbling, atmospheric drag has been increased by thirty-eight percent. At this point, I can only speculate."

With this, Leonov stepped out of the darkness. "Then speculate. I need to know, Lieutenant. A day, a week, a month. How long?" Leonov spoke to Teshev; however, his eyes bore in on Popivich.

"We will know more after the first few orbits . . ." The lieutenant stopped, knowing he must give some sort of answer. "I would say it is now weeks . . . possibly two or three. Or even sooner."

Leonov crushed his cigarette on the concrete floor with the heel of his black shoe. He slowly turned to watch the blue line as it continued to plot the Kosmos' southerly course.

"May I have a few words with you, General?" he asked abruptly after a moment.

Popivich's jaw visibly tightened before answering. He stood there as if he could will the satellite back into a higher orbit.

"This way," Popivich answered gravely. He knew what was coming. Both men turned and the general lead the way to his office in the rear of the complex.

Popivich waited for Leonov to be seated before he closed the heavy metal office door. Because this was an emergency command and control bunker, the well-lit office was compact, neat, and almost humble for a man in Popivich's position, unlike the elaborately decorated and furnished rooms his colleagues occupied in Moscow. A simple wooden desk stood against the far wall below a set of two shelves. The desk was uncluttered with the exception of three phones and a few papers. On the wall to the left hung a picture of Cosmonaut Yuri Gagarin. General Popivich took his time as he made his way to the worn black leather chair.

Leonov waited patiently. He watched the man make his way around the desk and wondered if he would be in as good of shape when he reached his late sixties. General Popivich had an impressive record, no one could deny that. Rumor had it he had been selected to be the first Soviet to be launched into space. But two weeks before the flight he sprained his ankle while practicing a parachute drop. Yuri Gagarin was the number two man and got the spot. But that didn't change things now. *Popivich should have retired when he still had dignity,* Leonov thought. Kosmos 3-1660 was the last residue of Popivich's and Andropov's grand plan to control the world. The general may have been a great man at one time, but now that part of their country's history was over. Leonov was a realist, knowing Russia had to join the rest of the world.

Leonov lit his last Turkish cigarette. He sighed, angry at his lack of foresight. The thought of smoking Russian or American cigarettes held little appeal for him.

"I am more than disappointed you didn't succeed. The minister of defense is meeting with key members of the government tomorrow. He will not be pleased." Leonov spoke in an even monotone, as if Popivich were a foreign delegate.

Popivich studied the man before him. He had known Leonov for over twenty-five years and still didn't trust him. *How can this man be lecturing me on what is good for the government,* he thought. *Saving face for his precious new Russia. It is men like this . . . corrupt bureaucrats with selfish greed . . . that destroyed the Soviet Union and made the black market strong, not the military.*

Popivich drew a deep breath before he spoke. "Let me remind you once again, Mr. Leonov, I can solve this problem by pushing one little black button. Kosmos 3-1660 will disappear in a cloud of vapor and no one will know the difference. In the old days we would not have hesitated to take care of this problem ourselves. This is not the first time we have had such mechanical malfunctions."

"Stop it, Dimitri, listen to yourself. This is not one of your standard Kosmos surveillance satellites . . . is it?"

"Yes, you are right, of course. It is the most advanced satellite we have ever put in orbit."

"It's just too bad your engineers were not capable of building a satellite that could stay in orbit for more than ten years," Leonov said, looking away. He felt his stomach rumble with pain and bile bubble up his throat as his anger built. This was the last thing his ulcer needed, an argument with a pigheaded man still living in the past.

"Listen to what I say. I can *solve* this problem," Popivich demanded quietly. "I can blow it up over the southern Pacific Ocean. No one will know what was on board."

"I cannot take that risk. There is too much at stake now. This could be disastrous for Russia. The West will never trust us again. Everything we have tried to build could be lost." Leonov loosened his tie, but found no relief with the gesture. "Article four of the Outer Space Treaty clearly states that neither side would place offensive weapons of mass destruction into orbit. I have not forgotten there are ten nuclear warheads as well as a plutonium reactor carried aboard that satellite. You yourself said the chances of the reactor core and the warheads surviving the reentry is extremely high. Does it not concern you that our country will suffer embarrassment and thousands of people may die if just one of those bombs explodes? We do not need that kind of publicity."

Popivich snorted, shaking his head in disagreement. He understood precisely what Leonov was saying. This was a problem for the new Russian government, not the Russia Popivich had worked and sacrificed his life to protect.

"Dimitri," Leonov continued, almost pleading with the old general, "that satellite is still classified as most secret. Only a handful of military people know what is really aboard 3-1660. After the coup attempt everything changed so rapidly . . . loyalties switched overnight. If our new leaders find out I have deceived them by not disclosing the existence of the warheads, I will spend my last days rotting in prison."

"You should have told them. It is not my problem." Popivich's mouth curled into a smile.

"Damn you, Popivich. If I go to prison, you will be there with me. I will see to that!" Leonov shouted. *"I do not want that. Do you?"*

"Of course not." Popivich averted his gaze, feigning acquiescence.

"We know the Americans have mistakenly classified Kosmos as what they call a RORSAT satellite. They believe we used it for ocean reconnaissance. If this situation is not handled correctly, there is no doubt we will be held accountable." Leonov paused, aware of his own guilt, but unable to control his irritation. "Think about it . . . Our economy is slowly coming around. We are now tied to the West. We need their trade, money, and technology to avoid more hunger. If the Americans find out that we have not been totally honest with them, I can only imagine the damage that will be done. I am afraid our options are limited." Leonov winced as he sucked in another smoke-filled breath.

"Your decision must consider the consequences to the military as well . . . our strength as a nation," Popivich chided. "What if things change again . . ."

"It is too late. You had your chance today. I will recommend to the minister of defense that we ask the Americans for assistance. They have a space shuttle scheduled to go into orbit within the week. It is our only hope." His eyes pleaded with Popivich. "You must agree, the options are limited."

"I cannot agree to such a possibility. We have years of technical research and some of our most vital secrets built into that satellite. Target imaging, solid rocket fuel mixtures, laser guidance, and communication codes. You can't blindly trust the Americans!" Popivich slammed his open hand onto his desk. He had no comprehension of how this former comrade could behave so impetuously. "Do you understand how important the Kosmos is?"

Leonov thought for a second; this was going further than he had anticipated. He needed Popivich on his side if his rescue plan was going to work. He took a breath, making sure his next words would be calm and clear. "I will make sure that when the satellite is recovered and sitting on the ground in the United States a team of Russian engineers will be on hand to secure it. I promise you the Americans will not be allowed to walk away with our—*your*—technologies. This is the best I can offer, Dimitri."

"And the satellite?"

"It will be returned here to you. You and your team can dismantle it. No one will ever know what was on it," Leonov said with confidence.

The general nodded, knowing this argument was over. *There must be other alternatives, you fool,* Popivich thought. Even the cost of a few hundred lives was a more acceptable prospect.

"Tomorrow we will ask the Americans for their help. I will need one of your false technical manuals, the one you prepared for the party when the Kosmos was first constructed." Leonov rose from his chair, fixing his tie, his ulcer protesting the movement. "I will be leaving for Moscow within the hour to meet with the minister of defense. I will inform him that you and I recommend this course of action." He paused before leaving the room. "This is for the best, General; you will see."

5

Mark Collins felt homesick. He told himself it was the change of food and tried to downplay the fact that he missed his wife, Christine, and their newborn daughter. Thinking of them only made it worse. Of course, the general turmoil of the Mideast didn't help his attitude either. After a decade of lying low, Libya was stirring the fires of political unrest again, and the CIA feared that Qaddafi could be preparing to heighten his terrorist activities. At a recent meeting of Arab leaders, Colonel Qaddafi had boasted publicly it was again time to put the West back in its place for failing to resolve the plight of the Palestinian people. It was a threat the CIA took very seriously.

Collins had just about gotten used to being a "spook." He had become a full-time employee of the CIA just three years earlier. Before that, he had worked with the agency off and on as a liaison for the army. When the cutbacks came, he retired with the rank of major at the age of thirty-three. The CIA then asked him to take a full-time position with the Directorate of Intelligence. For several years, Collins's main responsibility had been piecing together information on the acquisition of advanced weapons from European arms manufacturers by the nations of the Middle East. About eighty-five percent of the data Collins analyzed came from open sources, CNN, overseas broadcasts, the markets, trade publications such as *Aviation Week,* and computer bulletins. The other fifteen percent came from covert sources, human spies, satellites, and communication intercepts. The information then was refined and used to draw up national intelligence estimates. These estimates, actually lengthy memos, were designed to give the policy makers in Washington a fundamental understanding of a nation's military threat to the United States.

Eighteen months ago, Collins transferred to the Directorate of Operations. Involving roughly 5,000 of the CIA's 21,800 full-time personnel, the DO is the most secret branch of the CIA. Collins's military background and understanding of how the analytical side of the CIA worked made him a perfect candidate for a position in Operations. After completing his training program, he was assigned to the counterterrorism division. He found it a hell of a lot more exciting than examining international freight transfer documents.

Collins liked to think of himself as the average American with a better-than-average job. If he stood in a crowd, he wouldn't stick out. That was probably one of the main reasons he had gotten the job at the DO. Ordinary looking, with short light brown hair that was graying on the sides, and standing not quite five feet nine inches tall. Collins kept himself in fair shape with regular workouts. But he wasn't a fanatic about his appearance. Probably his most distinctive features were his intense gray eyes.

Collins slipped on his sunglasses and looked out at the vastness of the desert as he made his way from the officers' cafeteria toward the main part of the air base. He had been in Egypt two weeks and could already tell it was going to be another blistering day. The young CIA counterterrorism officer was wearing his standard dark blue sports jacket, neatly pressed khaki pants, and white shirt, no tie. In the next thirty minutes the base would be crawling with pilots and technicians. In the distance he watched a C-130 cargo plane taxi into position, ready for takeoff. Its brown desert camouflage made it easy to spot against the dark background of the runway.

Collins still hadn't adjusted to the time difference and had awakened earlier than usual. Before he had married, it had been routine for him to be the first one to work, but he'd gotten out of the habit. His early start each day was actually working out fairly well; it helped him to get a lot of work done. *Maybe I can go home sooner,* he thought.

Collins was assisting the Egyptian army and air force on developing better ways of securing their military bases from weapons theft and terrorist attacks. The Egyptians welcomed the American's help and in return Collins was learning about the Arab culture, which would contribute to his understanding of the terrorist mind. If that was possible. In addition to his official duties, he met with senior Egyptian intelligence officers and was briefed about their extensive antiterrorist network.

Collins's assignment to the CIA's antiterrorist department and specialization in the Middle East provided him with a direct pipeline to the CIA's deputy director for operations, Tom Staffer. With the World Trade Center and Sears Tower bombings still painful memories, his department had high priority. Before moving into Operations, Collins had been working side by side with the Naval Investigative Service's Antiterrorism Alert Center, headquartered in Suitland, Maryland. Both jobs were challenging, and Collins had heard rumors he was being groomed for bigger things. Being conservative, he ignored the rumor mill.

"Good morning, Mr. Collins." A young Egyptian air force officer had jogged up alongside him.

"Good morning, Lieutenant."

"I have a message for you. Please come this way."

A few minutes later, they entered the air base's communications room located below the control tower.

The Egyptian officer didn't waste any time getting to the point. "Sir, earlier this morning an unmarked MiG-23 attempted a suicide mission against an American cruise liner. The MiG was shot down by one of your F-18s just before it impacted the ship." He handed Collins a fax.

"Let me guess . . . since I'm in the area, why not fly out and pick me up to help put the pieces together, right?" Collins breathed heavily at having to delay his present work. *Why'd this jerk have to pick an American cruise liner?*

"Yes, sir. An F-14 from the carrier *John F. Kennedy* is on its way here to pick you up. Approximately thirty minutes from now." The lieutenant smiled sympathetically.

"Thank you. I'll be ready."

MOSCOW, RUSSIA

Petr Czerlinsky, Russia's newly appointed minister of defense, looked older than his years. His wavy gray hair had an oily sheen to it, and the crow's-feet around his eyes were deep and long. Years ago he had stopped worrying about his weight. Now fifty pounds heavier than his doctor recommended, Czerlinsky kept himself alive with daily doses of blood pressure medicine. At sixty-two he was not a logical choice for the defense minister's job. There was opposition to having one of the former military establishment hold the position. However, that was the very reason he had been hired to help the military's transition to the new form of government. Ironically, though, his military background didn't make his job any easier. Czerlinsky still battled with his generals and admirals.

Czerlinsky had been working in his office for eleven hours and was growing tired, his mind wandering as he finished the last of the day's business.

"Minister Czerlinsky, Deputy Leonov is here to see you," his assistant's deep voice came over the intercom, bringing him back to the matters at hand.

"Ah, yes. Send him in," he said with a yawn.

Leonov entered the large plush office and walked the fifteen meters to the rear of the room. The rich-colored walnut paneling, vermilion carpet, and soft lighting relaxed him a bit after his fast-paced trip.

"Good evening, Nikolai. I take it the chill I feel is our winter returning again," Czerlinsky stated pleasantly. "Ah, September in Russia . . . summer ends and winter begins. There is nothing in between."

Leonov grinned wearily. How true that was. "Yes, Minister Czerlinsky, I agree, there is no in-between." He removed his gloves, stuffing them into the pockets of his black wool overcoat. He then removed his scarf and coat, placing them over the back of the chair.

"How was your visit with General Popivich?" Czerlinsky didn't wait for an answer as he studied Leonov's lethargic movements. "You look tired . . . is it your ulcer again?"

Leonov just nodded. He was more concerned with collecting his thoughts and how to present the dreadful news to the minister.

"I trust you have a favorable report for me?" Czerlinsky grew impatient for the man to tell him what had happened.

Leonov sighed before answering. "No, Comrade. I am afraid not. Kosmos 3-1660 is still in trouble."

Czerlinsky sank back into his massive chair, looking at the ceiling. He then turned his attention to his deputy.

"I see." He leaned forward, his arms on the glass-topped desk. A bronze statue of a wild horse sat on the right corner. A picture of his second wife, twenty years younger than he, was on the other side.

"I'm afraid the satellite is in more danger now than it was before we attempted to boost it to a higher orbit." Leonov finally sat in the chair, crossing his legs.

The minister leaned back, again frowning. He was having enough difficulty trying to keep his critics silenced. This would not help him remain in his position.

"Explain." Czerlinsky's voice was barely audible.

Leonov touched on the events that led up to the malfunction of the two thruster rockets earlier in the day and how the satellite was now tumbling out of control.

Czerlinsky listened intently, only nodding once or twice.

After a few minutes Leonov concluded, "I contacted General Popivich after I returned to Moscow. They are more closely able to calculate the satellite's decaying orbit. It will be entering the atmosphere within the next ten days, they believe."

"Have our options changed?"

"No, Petr, I'm afraid they haven't."

"So," Czerlinsky pressed, "General Popivich was in agreement with asking the West for assistance?"

"Yes. He knows there is no other solution." Leonov shifted his weight in the chair. "I have thought this through . . . completely. Asking the

Americans for help is the only way we can save face as a country and dispose of the satellite at the same time."

Czerlinsky sighed again and rubbed the bridge of his nose. He was not convinced himself of the idea's merit. But realistically, they were running out of time. "What am I to say to assure our president that going to the Americans is the best recourse?"

"I share your concern. However, I have been following Kosmos 3-1660 for the last ten months, and I have made you aware of the consequences that must be considered. I believe that should be enough explanation in itself." Leonov paused. He opened his briefcase and removed his notes. He put them on his lap and flipped through until he found the page he was looking for. "Kosmos 954 came out of orbit in 1978 over northern Canada. That satellite was one-fourth the size of 3-1660 and its reactor reentered intact, scattering radioactive debris over 500 square kilometers." Leonov put the report on Czerlinsky's desk.

"Yes, I have read the reports." Czerlinsky groaned. "But I am not a diplomat."

"Simply say we have a satellite in a decaying orbit. It is powered by a plutonium-fueled nuclear reactor similar to the one that was on Kosmos 954. However, it is bigger and potentially more dangerous. Unlike the previous satellite, the radioactive core could fall onto a populated area." Leonov pressed on: "Play on the Americans' sympathies and then ask for their help. Of course, their silence should also be requested for the sake of our fragile new government. After this is agreed upon, we can then work out the details of a joint effort in rescuing it. When it is safely out of orbit, we can make a public statement, telling the world about the successful mission. I would also suggest that one of our cargo ships be used to pick up the satellite after the Americans bring it back to earth."

Defense Minister Czerlinsky sat silent and pensive.

"We have a man in Washington based at our embassy; his name is Georgi Soloyov. He has been stationed in the United States as part of our technical exchange program. I have worked with him on several projects. He is loyal and can be trusted. I suggest he become our liaison. It would be wise to insist that Russian technicians be at the landing site and allowed to take immediate control of the satellite when it returns to earth. For safety, only our engineers must be permitted to shut down the Kosmos' systems. Once the satellite is turned over to us and secured, we can transfer it to the cargo ship," Leonov finished, clearing his throat. He placed his notes in front of the minister and went to the bar for a glass of water.

Czerlinsky had become overwhelmed with the numerous details of this plan. Possibly it would be best just to let the satellite reenter on its own and pay the price.

"This never should have happened. We should have been ready for an emergency such as this." Czerlinsky's thoughts shifted. "You are well prepared, my friend. Perhaps I should step aside and let you handle the matter."

"I am only doing my job. And you will do your job just as well. If we all keep our wits about us, this can be accomplished without any repercussions." Leonov took a package of Zantac from his coat pocket. He removed one of the prescribed pills and swallowed it with a gulp of cool water.

Czerlinsky swiveled around in his chair and looked out the window behind his desk into the growing darkness. "I'm meeting the president tomorrow morning for breakfast. I will tell him your recommended course of action and persuade him that involving the Americans is in the best interest of our country."

"Good." Leonov rose from his chair, preparing to leave. He was feeling weak and nauseous as his ulcer continued to burn inside him.

"Can you control Popivich? I know he has agreed, but I am not sure he should be trusted or left unobserved," Czerlinsky said.

Leonov finished putting on his coat before he answered the question. He had the same worries and was surprised Czerlinsky hadn't asked sooner.

"Leave Popivich to me. I will be watching over his shoulder every second of this operation." Leonov slipped his scarf over his neck and picked up the briefcase.

"I will speak with you tomorrow. Go home. Get well, Nikolai, we have a big project ahead of us."

"Good night," Leonov said as he headed for the door. His thoughts turned to a hot bowl of soup and a warm bed.

USS *John F. Kennedy*

Collins wished he had dressed warmer. A cool wind blew across the steel deck of the *Kennedy,* sending a chill down his spine.

"There she is," Commander Earl Chadwick, the carrier's intelligence officer, shouted.

Collins looked into the bright sky, not seeing a thing.

Twenty minutes earlier Commander Chadwick had received a radio transmission that the crew of a Sea King helicopter, on station over the MiG-23's wreckage, had spotted and retrieved a body. They were now on deck waiting for the chopper to return.

"Just off the starboard bow," Chadwick pointed. "That's our bird." The distinct sound of a helicopter cutting through the thick afternoon air grew louder.

Collins shielded his eyes from the sunlight as the SH-3H helicopter hovered above the flight deck for a few seconds. After the pilot got his bearings, he inched the mouse-gray aircraft toward the deck, gently touching down. A half dozen men ran toward the big chopper, securing it.

"They'll be bringing the body to sick bay. This way, Mr. Collins." Chadwick gestured.

Collins buried his hands deeper into his pockets, trying to stay warm. He followed the shorter and rounder commander down several flights of metal stairs and passageways until they reached a part of the ship that smelled of disinfectant. The two men entered a crowded room containing a long medical examining table.

"I'm not sure what shape the body will be in. The F-18 pilot reported the aircraft blew up just before impacting the water. I've seen the bodies of other pilots from downed aircraft. Sometimes you can learn something, sometimes you can't." Chadwick shrugged. "Want some coffee?"

"No thanks, Commander." Collins watched the middle-aged intel officer disappear and return with a white Styrofoam cup filled with steamy black liquid. The naval officer leaned against the wall, sipping his coffee.

The sound of men entering the outer room caught their attention. A navy doctor, assisted by two armed guards, wheeled a stretcher into the room. Resting on it was the covered body of the terrorist pilot.

"Commander . . . ," the doctor shook hands warmly with Chadwick.

"Doctor Shayler, this is Mark Collins. He's with the CIA . . . I guess you can figure out why he's here." Steve Shayler, the chief flight surgeon, offered his hand to acknowledge the introduction.

"Nice to meet you, Mr. Collins. Hope I can give you the information you need."

"Hello, Doctor." Mark wasn't even sure if there would be anything of significance that could come from this. But as a rule you check out everything for the slightest possible leads when it comes to terrorism.

"Well, gentlemen, let's begin." The doctor flipped back the white sheet, uncovering the dead man's face and upper body. The corpse was still wearing a blue flight suit. It was ripped and singed black in several places. Both of the man's eyes were open, staring blankly at the ceiling.

"As you can see, there's very little damage done to the pilot's face or upper chest area. He must have been wearing a helmet, preventing burns or flailing to his face." Shayler touched and maneuvered the body with his latex gloved hands. "Although, his neck, back, and forearms are charred."

Chadwick and Collins looked on as the doctor began feeling along the limbs.

"Both legs are broken, possibly a couple of cracked ribs." He continued, putting his right arm under the small of the pilot's back and lifting him up. With his left hand he opened the corpse's mouth, tilting the head back. Shayler lifted him a few inches higher, trying to see if any water ran out of his lungs. None did. After a moment he let the body fall back on the examining table.

Shayler stopped to look over the chart his assistant was making notations on. "I would say he died before he hit the water."

"How can you tell?" Collins quizzed.

"No water in his lungs. On the report it says he was found drifting face down, tangled in his parachute." Shayler hadn't bothered to look up and was busily marking skin samples.

"His ejection seat could have been triggered by the explosion or even from the impact of the water." The commander spoke thoughtfully. Collins moved around to the front of the stretcher to get a better view of the lifeless body. The man's face was vaguely familiar, even though it was enlarged, ashen, and dirty.

The doctor continued, "The exterior tissue is swollen and pale due to exposure to the salt water. I would guess he was in his mid-thirties and whoever he is—"

"Adib Hamen," Collins interrupted.

"What?" Chadwick and Shayler asked at the same time, looking at the CIA man.

Collins moved in closer, staring at the dead man's face. *The bastard was flying a MiG-23. Where the hell would they get a MiG-23?* "I said this man is Adib Hamen. He is a terrorist. I can't believe we've got him. Well, we didn't quite get him, but at least we can identify him."

"What makes you think it's him? Perhaps the ocean has distorted his features. I wouldn't get too excited until we can get something more positive." Shayler was skeptical.

Collins paused, thinking of the last time he had reviewed the classified data. The file contained a two-year-old color picture of Hamen and his leader, Abu Ajami. They were eating dinner in a small out-of-the-way restaurant in the southern part of Tripoli when a fast-thinking Mossad officer snapped the picture. The officer tried to follow them but lost both men two days later. Shortly after that, the Israelis learned that Hamen had entered a hospital.

"He should have an appendicitis scar on his abdomen," Collins threw out as his memory raced.

Shayler unzipped the man's flight suit down to his navel. On the left side was a three-inch scar. "Well, there's definitely a scar." The doctor leaned over to the assistant, again making more notations.

"Israeli agents almost caught up with him. It was . . . in Tunis. That's right. They had missed him by less than an hour. He checked out of the hospital and disappeared," Collins went on, his mind still racing.

The doctor cut away the wet flight suit for a more thorough exam, prior to an autopsy. Collins's mood darkened. His thoughts went back to the picture of the restaurant and the two men seated at the table. Ajami with his smooth, pale skin and black hair was not smiling. The CIA had a nickname for the handsome killer, the Black Prince.

"Ajami . . ." *Was Abu Ajami alive?* He had been out of action for more than a year. There had been talk he had retired, given up his vision of a homeland for the Palestinians, or that the devil had finally reclaimed his lost son. Could Ajami be operating again? And, more immediately, where had he moved his base of operations?

Collins spoke to Shayler and Chadwick: "Before the autopsy, I would like this man's picture and fingerprints sent to Langley for verification, along with the radar telemetry from the E-2. I want to know where this MiG originated from."

"No problem, Mr. Collins," Chadwick replied. "I'll put my best man right on it. I'll be on the bridge if you need me."

"Doctor, if you wouldn't mind, I'd like to know when everything's been completed: the autopsy, identity verification, and any test results that you conduct. This may be something very important and time is vital."

"I understand," Shayler nodded, noticing Collins's heightened tension.

Five minutes later, Collins closed the steel door to the cramped compartment, turned on the light, and opened his briefcase. Removing an Acros 486/50 notebook computer, he opened it and turned on the machine. The hard drive contained an electronic file holding every shred of information the CIA had on terrorists and their operations, including Abu Ajami. Collins entered his security code, disabling the self-destruct mechanism, and typed in ABU AJAMI followed by three asterisks. A small green light, located on top of the computer, flashed, telling him the hard drive was working, looking for the data.

"There you are," Collins said. The color screen showed a replica of the CIA's latest photo. Under the picture was ABU AJAMI—LEADER OF FATAH REVOLUTIONARY BRIGADES.

Collins studied the picture. Ajami was a good-looking man with strong facial features, a long, structured nose, and convincing eyes. He moved on to the text portion of the report. It contained the standard mix of data: where he was born, parent's background, estimated age. That wasn't what Collins was looking for. He scrolled the screen until he reached Ajami's psychological profile. Psychofiles, as the operations side of the CIA referred to them, were extremely important. The CIA went to great lengths to make sure each profile was as accurate as possible. With some people, particularly fanatics, this was nearly impossible. However, over the years the CIA had been able to put together quite a bit of

information on Ajami. On the second page, third paragraph, Collins
found what he wanted.

. . . IT HAS BEEN REPORTED THAT AJAMI IS A PARANOID SCHIZOPHRENIC AND SUFFERS
FROM ONE OR SEVERAL FORMS OF PARALOGICAL THINKING. AT TIMES HIS REASONING IS
SOUND AND WELL THOUGHT OUT. AT OTHER TIMES HE IS IRRATIONAL. PARANOIA SEEMS TO
OCCUR WHEN AJAMI IS UNDER STRESS FOR LONG PERIODS OF TIME. HIS THINKING BECOMES
DISTORTED ALONG WITH HIS PERCEPTION OF REALITY. MEMBERS OF HIS LEBANESE OPERA-
TION HAVE REPORTED THAT AJAMI ROUTINELY CLAIMS TO HAVE CONVERSATIONS WITH
ALLAH. ALLAH APPEARS TO HIM IN DREAMS AND VISIONS, HELPING TO GUIDE AJAMI IN HIS
TERRORIST ACTIVITIES. HE WILL CONFORM HIS PERSONAL AND DELUSIONAL DESIRES INTO
ILLOGICAL THINKING THAT FUELS HIS PARANOID BEHAVIOR FURTHER. SEVERAL MOSSAD
REPORTS HAVE NOTED THAT AJAMI IS PRONE TO FITS OF EXTREME HOSTILITY AND VIOLENCE
FOLLOWED BY HYPERSENSITIVITY, SUSPICION, AND ISOLATION.

Collins read on, letting his mind soak in the data. He turned the
computer off and lay down on his bed, studying the rust-blotched ceiling. His mind rehashed what he had just read. U.S. and Israeli intelligence had learned that Ajami wasn't operating in Lebanon, Syria, or
Jordan, and the CIA was confident he could have been tracked down if
he was operating out of Libya. Collins knew when a terrorist lives on the
edge, constantly hiding and attacking, he had a tendency to become
paranoid, making him a prisoner of his own fear. Yet Abu Ajami was
different from other terrorists Collins had studied. He not only was smart
and skilled in the art of deception, but he had a true passion for his
cause. This made him inordinately dangerous. As far as Collins was
concerned, he was one of the most dangerous terrorists alive. The file
said the Mossad had captured and interrogated several of Ajami's men
during a covert raid three years ago in southern Lebanon. The Mossad
then shared the intelligence with the CIA—for a price, Collins was sure.
The captured terrorists talked of moments of compassion, then crazy
tantrums. There were times when Ajami appeared to be possessed by
Satan and others when he was calm, insightful, and manipulative.

Collins rolled over, resting his head on his arm. Ajami had been traced
to the bombing deaths of several American businessmen in Turkey three
years ago. Evidence also pointed to his involvement in at least three
other bombings in Paris, London, and Rome, killing and wounding a
total of ninety men, women, and children. In over four years there was a
single common thread connecting Ajami with each bombing. The terrorist and his men used a powerful, specially designed plastic explosive
known as Semtex 801. During the cold war, Semtex, manufactured in
Czechoslovakia, was sold to just about every terrorist organization in the
world. However, Semtex 801 was heavier and denser, leaving large
traces of hydrocarbons and ammonia after it exploded. When East-West

tensions had ended, Collins had been able to track down to whom all the 801 formula had been sold . . . to Ajami and his followers.

Collins smiled. *I'm going to get this asshole. A dead pilot and some wreckage isn't much to go on, but it may be all I need.* After all, Ajami wouldn't know that Hamen was dead. Word hadn't even gotten out yet of the attack. The only information the press had to report was that two Libyan SAMs had been fired at an American aircraft. And Ajami wouldn't know it had been just a coincidence that F-18s were in the area to intercept the MiG.

Collins rubbed his chin, trying to think this through. He could create a rumor that Adib Hamen was still alive. Maybe fabricate a story he had been tortured . . . did some talking . . . then maybe he could rattle Ajami and his men into making some kind of a mistake and exposing their camp. Or better yet, Collins could leak false information into the Arab community, saying an American agent was operating inside Ajami's camp and that was how the fighter patrol knew where and when to intercept the MiG.

Collins smirked; that was it. The CIA operated a Syrian double agent out of the Directorate of Operations. Mark could create a story, phony up some pictures, and make sure Syrian intel got their hands on it. And with a little luck word would filter down to Ajami. It was a long shot, but it was better than sitting like a lump on a log, as Grandpa would say.

In the morning, I'll leave for Langley, Collins told himself, as he rolled over, hoping to fall asleep quickly. His mind drifted to images of his wife and little girl.

6

They knew him only as Ajami. He was their strength, their teacher, and their leader. They were his chosen ones, the *Muminin*—the followers. They were his sons, his brothers, his *Pasdars*—guards.

Ajami considered himself a new breed of terrorist. His background was dissimilar from most of the men he led. He had grown up knowing wealth and pleasure in the small town of Yaamouni, Lebanon, twenty-five miles north of Baalbek. He was the only child of a Palestinian businessman, a hashish trader. His mother was a beautiful woman with dark hair and a fair complexion. Her features helped her blend in with the people of the village. She was an excessively religious American Muslim who had turned her back on her country and family for a new life in Lebanon. She spent many hours each day preaching to Ajami the word of Allah and the evils of the Western world. His father had become rich young, trading and selling the immense hashish crop that was grown in the hills and valleys near Yaamouni.

Ajami attended college in Lebanon, studying marketing, politics, and engineering. But most importantly, he learned how critical it was for him to continue his peoples' struggle for what was theirs: a God-given right to a homeland.

As he grew older, Ajami began to realize that other Palestinians were not as fortunate. They lived in poverty and were a people without a country. He began to loathe the lavish lifestyle and material goods his father cherished and his mother enjoyed. Ajami remembered his father as a man of greed and his mother as a weak hypocrite.

In his mid-twenties Abu Ajami met other people who shared his hatred for the West and its culture. Like most young Palestinian men his age, he began a quest to learn a new way of life with his newly found brothers. They isolated themselves from the impurities of the outside world. He made several trips to the freedom and education camps his religious brothers frequently visited. The training camps completed the final preparation for Ajami's life.

He acquired the skill to master and control his hatred, storing it and calling upon it at will, like a craftsman's tool. Hate was an energy, giving him a power he had never felt before. It kept him alive and inspired through the days and nights of training and studying in central Iran and later North Korea. The different camps instructed Ajami in various methods of terrorism. Attending as many as he could, he became knowledgeable in areas of weaponry, leadership, and strategy, including manipulation and intimidation tactics.

Physically Ajami was a tall man with a lean build and deep blue eyes accentuated by dark, thick lashes. His stare was unnerving and to most women exciting. He had learned at a youthful age to use it to win the favors he desired, if only for the night. He intentionally kept his thick black hair at shoulder length and his face clean shaven. This gave him a fresh, virile look. His nature was reserved and quiet, adding to his mysterious personality.

Ajami's promise to himself and to the people who now followed him was uncomplicated. He would continue the fight until the wrongs of the past were corrected or until his death. His past had proven him a fearless and ruthless fighter for the cause. At eighteen, he volunteered with two other members of the Palestinian Fatah's Revolutionary Council, headed by Abu Nidal, to attack one of their most hated enemies.

On a moonless May night, off the southern coast of Lebanon, they slipped into a rubber dinghy and motored their way into the darkness. The salty sea stung his eyes and left an unpleasant taste in his mouth as the polluted water splashed around them. Ten miles out they cut the engine and silently drifted toward the Israeli coast, using oars to push them through the black ocean, past the patrols.

Their target, a newly built hotel in the Israeli port of Haifa, was alive with life that night as they approached from the west. The air was filled with the sounds of music, dancing, and laughter. Ajami remembered the warm spring breeze helping to push them ashore and the feel of the sand beneath his feet. He pulled their small boat onto the darkest part of the beach, securing it with a spike in the sand. Dressed as western tourists, they concealed their AK-47s, the wooden stocks having been removed, under their clothes as he and his fellow terrorists reached the hotel pool. The strong aroma of food swirled around them as they took up their predetermined positions. No one noticed them. Even when their weapons came out, the people just stared, not believing what was about to happen.

After seventeen years the memories were still sharp and crisp. The rifle pulsing in his hands as he emptied the magazine into the crowd of people. An elderly woman screaming as the bullets ripped through her vibrating body. Her face and dress bloodied, she fell to the ground with a groan.

An Israeli security guard pulled his pistol, but it was too late. Within moments it was over, their mission completed. Strangers lay dead and dying on the red splattered cement before them. The music had stopped and the air was now filled with sobs and cries of disbelief.

As they reached the beach fifty meters away, Ajami's own excitement turned to horror as his heart beat wildly in his chest. He faced true fear for the first time. He would never forget the sound of the bullets striking the wet sand around him nor the last gasps of his companions as they were struck down. Climbing into the rubber dinghy, he motored away as bullets ripped the air over his head and hit the water next to him. Ajami made it halfway back to Lebanon before Israeli helicopters arrived overhead, slicing the night with powerful searchlights. He slipped out of the dinghy into the icy cold water and swam the remaining distance to shore, knowing it was only by Allah's will he was allowed to live.

That night he would be the only one to escape with his life, the only one to tell the stories of glory, triumph, and losses. Abu Ajami had been the victor.

He reached down now and picked up a handful of warm desert sand, rubbing it gently between his smooth fingers. The fine powdery grains felt good. A person becomes immune to the revulsion of death when witnessing it day after day, but they never forget the first time. *So long ago,* he thought.

The next morning a flight of four American-built F-4 Phantoms, with Israeli markings, cut across the sky into southern Lebanon. Without warning, they dropped their bombs and streaked out of sight, leaving behind columns of thick black smoke, fire, and death. Ten minutes later, another flight hit the Fatah's camp again. The F-4s were swift as the pilots twisted their huge aircraft into and around the triple A positions, dropping the bombs on several two-story houses.

When it was all over, twenty-two Palestinians were dead. Four of them were young children, found among the burning debris. Their life-less bodies were displayed on the sidewalk next to the burned out buildings to fuel anger. Seeing your own people murdered has a greater impact than any speech for justice could accomplish.

The celebration of the night before had turned to a day of retaliation. The Israeli pilots knew precisely where to drop their bombs, and in-stantly brother turned against brother. Every member of the camp was suspected of aiding the enemy. Ajami felt the people's mistrust. He was one of the newest members of the terrorist camp and was almost one of "them"—he was half American. Each member of the Fatah knew that without the American jets, bombs, and rifles, and especially their money, the Israelis would not be as strong.

To prove his loyalty, Ajami spoke through actions rather than words. Soon the leaders of the PLO became aware of Ajami's vision and passion, quickly growing to trust and even admire him. He was finally assigned to lead Force 17, the Fatah's protection and security force. His job was to protect Yashir Arafat. He frequently traveled under diplomatic cover and was given the job of inspecting the security at each PLO embassy around the world.

Ajami watched as events changed the world around him. Egypt made peace with the evil. Fatah's bases in Lebanon were raided and ripped away. His leaders ran to Tunisia to fight among themselves. The training camps in the Soviet Union were no more, and Iraq had been defeated in a great battle against the world's greatest satanic force. Some of his previous freedom fighters talked of coexisting with the enemy and sharing the land. To Ajami and the men he now led, this was the talk of weakness and lost hope. The idea of compromise sickened him.

Through all this his vision never wavered. However, Ajami came to realize that the Fatah Revolutionary Council was no longer driven. The years of failed battles had softened their hearts.

Ajami had broken away from the Fatah, taking the most radical and hard-line members of the Revolutionary Council with him. He did not take all who had wanted to come, only the ones he knew would fight and die if he commanded it. Ajami knew loyalty and devotion created a worthy opponent. His disciples must remain committed to their cause. He would not, could not, tolerate mediocrity.

He had established his camp and training grounds in an extremely remote section of northeastern Chad, twenty-five miles south of the Libyan border on the edge of the Aozou Strip, a narrow section of land running the length of the Libyan-Chadian border. This strip of land had been claimed by both countries. However, a UN cease fire prohibited each country from flying into or massing troops in an attempt to retake the forsaken strip of desert. In a sense it was a no man's land. The Aozou Strip acted as a buffer between two hostile countries.

Ajami knelt down, leaning his back against the hard rocky entrance that led into one of the natural caves he now called home. He looked to the west, where the sun hung low, casting slashes of red and yellow into the coming night sky.

The nearest paved road was seven miles to the north. The only people his men had contact with were the Magarba and Zuwaya desert traders. These tribesmen, who had roamed this dry and desolate land for hundreds of years, occasionally traveled south of the base on their way to and from southeastern Egypt. An agreement had been made between their leader and Ajami. Stashes of food and medicine given to the nomads would buy their silence and allow the terrorists to move about freely.

The jagged rock ledges of the ancient riverbed offered them safety, a place where they could train and hide, planning the future. Supplies were easily trucked from the town of Ounianga Kebir, forty-two miles southwest, or flown into their remote airstrip under the cover of darkness. The airstrip had been built by the Libyans while occupying the land in northern Chad. The runway ran east and west with two large hangars on the northern side. Buried into the barren mountainside were three hardened aircraft shelters and a network of command bunkers. They were of West German design and reinforced with layers of nickel carbon, steel and concrete. The massive concrete doors, facing outside each shelter, were painted in brown desert camouflage. Each of the bunkers was connected by a series of underground tunnels leading to the central command and control bunker buried 100 meters deep. Two of the shelters were big enough to house Soviet-made T-16 Badger bombers, which are about the size of a Boeing 767 airliner.

The entire base was the size of two dozen football fields. A narrow 10,000-foot runway stretched across the flat valley floor between two 2,500-foot brush-covered ridges and was big enough to handle anything up to heavy transports. Only a few hundred meters away, a fortified storage bunker contained fuel, small arms, aircraft spare parts, food, and water. There was also room for 250 air force personnel should Libya decide to return to the base. The runway and aircraft shelters took twelve months to build during the late eighties and had been abandoned when Libya withdrew from Chad.

Behind a series of high rippled cliffs, raising straight up for 50 feet, was a chain of sharp rock fingers and boulders rising 2,000 feet higher. There, in elaborate seclusion, was the camp. A winding row of steps led up to the quarters above the main part of the camp. Stone houses, built from rocks scattered about the mountainside and reinforced with steel, gently sloped so they blended into the countryside. They were hard to distinguish in the long shadows of the setting sun. Simple doors bolted into the rock face of the cliff were the entrances to each small cave overlooking the airstrip. These fortified stone shelters were what the freedom fighters called home. The interiors were humble, consisting of only straw beds, a stove, table, and chairs. Walls were smudge stained from camp fires of the past. The men had chosen to live above ground rather than in the bunkers themselves. Ajami wasn't a fool. Fresh air and sunlight were good for keeping his soldiers' spirit alive as they trained for the future.

It was supper time on this cool fall evening and wisps of gray smoke curled up from the chimneys. Ajami watched a man dressed in brown desert camouflage slowly climb the stairs below him. It was Yusuf

Kamal, his most trusted friend. He waited for him to reach the top and their eyes to meet.

"The supply trucks are coming, Ajami," the big man's deep, throaty voice broke the silence. His shirt was unbuttoned to the middle of his sweaty chest, and Ajami could see the brown dust of the desert in his beard.

"How many?" Ajami asked.

"I count three, maybe four, trucks. This must be the shipment we have been waiting for to complete our defenses," Kamal grinned. "It is finally happening, Ajami. All the work and planning is paying off. Soon no one will threaten us."

Ajami rose from his kneeled position and nodded. He hoped what Kamal was saying proved to be true. The Libyans had promised to supply them with a number of SA-7 hand-held surface-to-air missiles. It was worth the three-month wait so they would no longer have to worry about an attack on their camp from the air.

"Good. Gather the men. Standard procedure. I want a roadblock set up. Do not let any of them enter the camp. Have your men blindfold the drivers and whoever is on board those trucks. Take them to your security area and feed them, but make sure they see nothing." Ajami wanted to ensure their operation would not be compromised by the talk of idle men.

"And the trucks, what about the supplies? Should we unload them at once?"

"I want the trucks driven to the storage bunker and parked. Wait until the sun goes down and the temperature falls before you have the men unload them. We can get the trucks out of here early tomorrow morning. The sooner they leave, the better."

"Yes, my leader," Kamal replied, not taking his eyes away from Ajami.

"You wish to say something else; what is it?" Ajami asked.

"It is time for your medication. You will be feeling . . . uneasy soon if you do not . . ."

"I know how I will be feeling, Kamal." Ajami's tone was empty and hollow. He used an antipsychotic drug to help keep his paranoia in check. Ajami considered his disorder a great weakness, and Kamal was the only one in the camp that knew of it. Each month a single injection abetted his sensations of anxiety and mistrust for approximately thirty days. The only thing he hated more than taking the drug was being reminded when to do it. "I will tell *you* when it is time."

"Yes, my leader," Kamal said, walking away.

Ajami followed the man with his eyes. Kamal had been Ajami's friend and trusted adviser for more than twelve years. They had studied together in Iran and fought side by side when the Israelis moved into southern Lebanon. He was the only one Ajami trusted as his second in command and chief of the camp's security.

Gazing into the distance, Ajami found faint spots of dust slowly moving through the vast desert. The Libyan trucks carrying their goods were still a good distance away. He walked down the steep steps to the center of the camp. It was time for him to join his men and start the celebration.

7

Major General Richard ("Duke") James's intense hazel eyes watched the altimeter slowly climb as the instructor pilot nosed the shuttle training aircraft over at 35,000 feet. He felt the Gs let off as the specially engineered Grumman Gulfstream II executive jet came level above the early morning haze hugging the ground below. Duke barely made out the contour of the land and buildings beneath him. To his left he could see the murky waters of Galveston Bay and farther out the darker blue of the Gulf of Mexico.

The cockpit of the STA was split into two parts, one half orbiter trainer and the other half executive jet. The forty-three-year-old general prepared to bring the jet in for a dead-stick landing. In his mind he was at the controls of the shuttle *Atlantis* on final approach. An orbiter-style control stick replaced the standard yoke control and the flight instruments resembled that of the shuttle. The instructor pilot sat next to him in the right seat behind the standard controls of the Gulfstream. In just seconds Duke would be flying a giant glider that responded just like an orbiter.

"All right, Duke . . . she's all yours," Joseph Carney, the instructor pilot, said as he took his hands off the control yoke. "This is your last check ride before the real McCoy."

"Thanks, Joe." Duke wiped the sweat from the outer edge of his helmet, which covered his salt-and-pepper hair. He straightened his six-foot frame before wrapping his right hand around the black rubber control stick, scanning the instrumentation one final time. The aircraft was his as he started the process. His square jaw tightened and his eyes narrowed in concentration, making a deep scar above his right eye more prominent.

Duke had been married to the same woman for fourteen years. He

59

and Katherine, or Katie, as Duke called her, had three children. Matt, the oldest, was ten, Pamela five, and Sean two and a half. Duke had started his air force career after graduating with a bachelor's degree in science from Colorado State University. His first assignment was flying F-111s. In 1979, he transferred to B-52s, eventually making his way to the B-1B program at Ellsworth Air Force Base in Rapid City, South Dakota.

His career had changed in the fall of 1984 when, as a lieutenant colonel, he climbed into the cockpit of a prototype B-2 Stealth bomber code-named Nightstalker for a mission into the Soviet Union. Duke completed the top-secret mission, destroying a Soviet computer command center that threatened the balance of power. A month later, he was awarded the Distinguished Flying Cross, along with a Purple Heart, and was promoted to general, taking a position in Washington on the staff of the National Security Council. After a while, flying a desk just didn't cut it. He jumped at the chance to start his astronaut training in Houston six years ago.

"Ground, this is *Atlantis*. Do you copy?" he radioed.

"*Atlantis, this is Ground, we copy. Looking good. Initiate landing sequence when ready.*"

"Roger, all systems go, out." Duke's voice was even and steady.

The jet trainer vibrated as the automatic flight computers converted the red, white, and blue business jet from powered flight to a mini space shuttle ready to glide back to earth.

A red light flashed, showing that the computer had switched on the in-flight thrust reversers. The autopilot and computer-controlled simulation system were now electronically talking to each other in order to maintain the correct speed and rate of descent. Duke punched in the proper instructions, telling the computer he would be landing the shuttle manually.

"Hold on, Willie, here we go," Duke radioed to the T-38 chase plane, which could be seen out his right window doing a slow turn. He nudged the stick of the STA trainer to the right and pitched the nose down three degrees. His eyes stayed on the altitude direction indicator, which showed his pitch and yaw.

"*Don't screw this one up,*" Willie Quandt radioed back from the T-38.

"Not on your life," Duke announced into his oxygen mask. "You just stay awake out there and keep an eye on me. Maybe you'll learn something."

Willie Quandt banked his white jet right to get on Duke's wing. He watched as the trainer started to nose down and pick up airspeed. Willie would be flying in the pilot's position next to Duke on the upcoming mission into space. At thirty-five, he was eight years younger than Duke and had been into space once before. A naval commander, he had been an F-14 test pilot before entering the astronaut program five years ago. Quandt was unmarried and had only one other passion in life than flying: he loved to hunt big-game animals. His Houston home had a trophy room that would rival many museums. His pride accomplishment was a grand slam consisting of a bighorn, desert, stone, and Dall sheep. He was one of the few hunters in the world that had achieved such a feat.

Willie's first spaceflight had been an eight-day DoD mission to deploy two new-generation military communication satellites. At least, that was the story leaked to the press. It was partially true; they had deployed one new satellite, but their main mission had been to recover a Chinese reconnaissance satellite that was tumbling out of control in a low earth orbit. The Chinese had written the satellite off and had expected it to reenter the atmosphere in a few weeks. Willie was the pilot on that mission also, and the thought of getting back into space once again made his stomach turn with excitement.

"Glidescope twenty . . . twenty-one . . . steady at twenty-two degrees. Rate of descent 12,000 feet a minute." Duke started to flare the air brakes as he radioed the data for the benefit of Willie and the ground controllers looking at him on radar. The STA was falling more like a rock than an airplane.

"Looks good," Willie's voice crackled.

Duke didn't reply. A dead-stick landing was one of the toughest parts of being a shuttle pilot, and it took all of his concentration.

"Atlantis . . . Ground Control. You should now be in contact with autoland." The ground controller watched the STA on his two-color radar scope approaching from the east of Ellington Field.

"Roger that, Ground. Thirteen thousand, glidescope twenty-two percent," Duke said, as the trainer broke through the light morning overcast. He could now see the ground clearly below him.

The instruments on the STA automatically started receiving landing data from the microwave landing system on the ground. In addition, the tactical air navigation locating system and radar altimeter supplied Duke with a constant update of his position and altitude.

"Fifteen seconds to preflare," Willie radioed.

"Roger that." Duke scanned the instruments. The horizontal situation indicator told him his approach was a little high and two degrees off center. "Come on, baby, get back on course." Duke coaxed the trainer back in line with the instruments and the runway.

Duke had been at the controls for less than five minutes. Things were beginning to happen fast now, and he didn't have any margin for mistakes. He was three miles from touchdown at 2,300 feet, air speed 384 knots. The black and gray runway, stretching out before him, was growing larger by the second.

"Okay, baby . . . nice and easy." With steady back pressure, Duke pulled the stick toward him. The nose of the STA pitched up as his airspeed started to bleed off. He watched his altitude continue to fall, but not as rapidly. The STA was now thirty seconds from landing, altitude 1,900 feet.

Willie throttled back and lowered the landing gear of his T-38 in an effort to stay even with the larger trainer.

"Ground, *Atlantis*. Preflare initiated, glidescope on landing profile," Duke radioed.

"*Roger,* Atlantis."

Duke glanced to the right side of the control panel where the landing gear switch was.

"Six hundred, five hundred . . . three fifty," he counted off.

"Atlantis . . . *Ground Control. Eighteen seconds to touchdown.*"

"Roger, Ground, preflare complete at one point five degrees. She feels good."

Duke lifted the cover of the black metal switch and armed the landing gear. He lined the nose of the trainer up with the white center line of the runway as his eyes went back to the altimeter.

"*One hundred and ten . . . one hundred,*" Willie called out. He was now just fifty feet off Duke's right wing, hugging the ground.

"Atlantis, *Ground. Main gear down . . . nose gear down.*"

Duke keyed his mike and flared the air brakes to 100 percent at the same time. "Roger . . . gear down and locked." The STA was now over the runway, only seconds from touchdown.

Willie leveled his jet as he slid in a little closer to the trainer. "Atlantis, *main gear at ten feet . . . five feet . . . three . . . two . . . one . . . contact.*" A puff of blue smoke exploded from under the tires of the STA as they hit the runway.

"*Nose wheel at five, four, two . . . touchdown.*"

Duke applied pressure to the brake pedals, and the trainer started to slow.

"*Picture perfect, Duke. Do that at Edwards and you'll get a standing ovation,*" Willie Quandt radioed.

"Roger that, Chase. See you in a few minutes." Duke looked over at the IP, wanting his approval.

"Couldn't have done it better myself," Joe smiled with a nod as he took control of the trainer.

Willie's T-38 rocketed out of sight ahead of them. He would circle around once and join Duke back at the hangar after landing.

Duke unhinged his oxygen mask, letting it dangle from the left side of his helmet. An uneasy feeling came over him as the STA swung around and slowly taxied to the hangar area. It was as if things were happening too fast. He had been training for this mission for over two years, but it was still hard to believe. In four days he would be sitting in the cockpit of the shuttle *Atlantis,* ready to blast into space. The name itself conjured up images of unknown mysteries of the past. His wife Katie had hoped he would fly the *Atlantis* the day they learned about his new assignment. She thought it would be romantic to fly a shuttle named after a lost city, as long as he didn't get lost coming home.

Duke grinned. Katie was a hopeless worrier. She really hadn't wanted him to get this position; but knowing how much it meant to him, she tried to stay involved in the excitement.

The STA came to a stop a few hundred feet from the entrance of the large white hangar. The ground crew would refuel her before the next shuttle pilot would take Duke's seat and the process would start over again.

It was almost too good to be true. What had started as a distant dream was now a reality. And a scary one at that. It seemed like only yesterday he had moved Katie and the kids from Rapid City to Georgetown, D.C., and now to Houston. The physical geography was a shock in itself. The metropolitan areas of Georgetown and Houston had many times more people than the entire state of South Dakota. Duke still wasn't used to the traffic and honestly felt he never would be. Thank God, Katie had had the insight to find a house in Sea Brook, which was only a few minutes away from NASA. The townhouse they bought was in a complex on the shores of Clear Lake, just off Mariner Drive. The exterior of the buildings reminded Duke of an old western ghost town. They were a combination of stained brown wood with a green and gray hue. The salt air kept the local maintenance men busy as they tried to keep a fresh coat of stain on the outside of each home.

Duke never thought he would like living by the sea, but he soon found it to be pleasant and enjoyable. The community they lived in surrounded a large artificial lagoon where his neighbors kept their boats, everything from single-engine motorboats, which were used only on the weekends, to forty-foot sailboats. Many nights he and Katie opened a window, falling asleep to a cool breeze and the sound of the clanging of the rigging hitting the aluminum masts.

Duke unbuckled himself and prepared to leave the aircraft. As he climbed his way to the exit door, he saw two flight technicians approaching the STA.

A blast of humid morning air hit his face as he helped prop open the door of the jet. He climbed down the ladder and looked over his left shoulder to see Willie parking his T-38 a hundred yards away. Duke walked closer to the jet.

Willie clambered out of the cockpit and made his way to Duke, who was now standing between the two aircraft. He carried his helmet under his left arm and Duke could see his big grin under his short-cropped mustache as he approached.

"Ninety-six hours and counting, General. Are you ready?" Willie asked.

"Ready as I'll ever be," Duke said, walking toward the main hangar, his thoughts drifting to the mission.

8

The fragrance of boiled mutton filled the air. Abu Ajami and several other men sat in a circle surrounding a glowing orange fire, eating their evening meal. The crackling sound from the burning wood and smoke curled unevenly as it crept into the still night air. The heat of the camp-fire warmed them as they talked of their past and future. The atmosphere was one of joy and anticipation.

Ajami looked around to each man seated with him. They were smiling. Some in the group had trained with him in the camps of North Korea. They were now using that training to teach the other members of Ajami's army how to fight. Every man was an expert in one or more areas: communications, defensive and offensive tactics, bombs and booby traps. They were all qualified to operate the camp's antiaircraft artillery and antitank weapons, as well as everything from heavy machine guns to hand guns. They all could hit a silhouette of a man at 500 meters with an AK-47.

The best weapons and training were given to his men, and, in return, he expected their best. However, Ajami knew a leader could have the finest weapons and men in the world but without their conviction he was doomed to failure. It was something to be earned over time. Ajami had learned his lessons well in southern Lebanon. He vowed he would never be driven away again without inflicting heavy damage on the enemy. But if he should need to flee, a series of tunnels connecting the rock houses to the air base's underground bunkers awaited his escape. There was enough food and water stored to remain holed up for at least two months. Ajami was proud of the complex he had assembled.

Tonight, Ajami didn't share in his men's laughter and conversation, for his mind was filled with other matters. The glow from the embers cast

65

dancing shadows, distorting the features of their faces as they talked and drank.

Ajami watched their actions and expressions. Much could be learned by the way a man carried himself in the presence of his companions.

Out of the darkness a man slipped into the gathering. It was Kamal. He stood for a moment, waiting until Ajami acknowledged him.

"We must talk," Kamal said.

They walked away from the others so as not to be overheard.

"The Libyan truck drivers are secured in their quarters. I have posted guards outside their doors," Kamal stated. "I have instructed Yari to take meals to the men." Kamal watched Ajami's face in the firelight.

"Very well, and what of the weapons?"

"I have inspected the guns being unloaded from the trucks. There is much more than we had hoped for in this shipment. Captain Jibril was not lying when he said he now had access to many weapons." Jibril was the Libyan army officer who coordinated terrorist activities with Ajami. He was also Ajami's only contact with the Libyan government.

"Explain." This information caught Ajami's attention.

"Along with the six SA-7s he promised, we also received SA-16 missiles—"

"Sixteens! How many?" SA-16 air defense missiles were a more advanced version of the SA-7, faster, with a more sensitive seeker head.

"I count two. There may be more. We also received a half a million rounds of ammunition and the RPGs you requested. We still have one more truck to unload. I am sure that one contains our food and medicine." Kamal could not contain his exuberance and let a smile cross his face.

"I am pleased!" Ajami exclaimed, joining in the good cheer. "I am pleased. Allah's will be done."

"Allah's will be done," Kamal repeated.

"Go monitor the radio and see if you can pick up any Israeli or Egyptian news channels. I want to tell the men of our camp's victory today." Ajami's confidence was evident. There was no question in his mind Hamen had succeeded in attacking the *Song of Flower,* and the news of their triumph would be broadcast around the world.

"Yes, Ajami," Kamal disappeared back into the darkness, walking up the hill around the back and to the west of the main bunker complex. After climbing several hundred rock steps, he entered the main passageway that led through the center of the camp. The passageway was narrow, barely wide enough for a jeep to navigate. The terrorists had built a string of one-room stone huts from the natural surroundings consisting mostly of rocks. Many of the rooms were occupied, and Kamal could see the yellow lines of candlelight seeping through cracks in the walls.

Kamal traversed left, down a narrow stone path, to a rock and mud hut. It was in an unused section, fairly secluded, and because of this fact he liked to have his Libyan visitors stay there. The less they knew, the better.

As he neared the door, Kamal was aware that something was not quite right. The guard was not at his post, and the door to the hut was not completely closed and locked as it should be. He searched the surrounding area quickly and spotted the metal panel lock on the ground.

He drew his gun and moved closer to the door, stopping just outside. He heard a faint whimpering from inside. He gently pushed the door open, looking left to right, assessing the situation. The room was gloomily lit by a kerosene lantern burning on the far table next to a tray of uneaten food. He scanned the rest of the hut in the soft flickering light.

The whimpering was a woman's weeping. Kamal's eyes adjusted to the shadows, and he could see two figures wrestling in the corner.

Kamal tried to utter a sound, but his fury choked him. It was Yari, one of the young Zuwaya girls from a local nomadic tribe, that helped out in the camp. A Libyan was on top of her, his pants pulled to his knees. He held one hand firmly over her mouth, pressing her upper body down with his forearm.

"Stop this . . . *STOP!*" Kamal shouted. He reached down and grabbed the man by the hair, pulling him off the girl. The man fell back, stumbling across the dirt floor.

Kamal was enraged even more by the wild fear in the young woman's doelike eyes. Yari was trembling, and tears streamed down her dusty cheeks. She rose shakily from the mattress, bringing her torn abbayah up to cover her bare breasts.

"It is all right, my child. It is all right." He took off his jacket and placed it around her shoulders. "Go. Wait for me outside. Go quickly, Yari."

She ran from the room with her face in her hands, sobbing.

Kamal was standing over the Libyan. "Get up. I said, get up." He kicked the man in the side, hoping to break his ribs.

"Leave me alone, you maggot," the man mumbled. He rolled over on his back and pulled up his pants. He then stood and smirked, showing his brown placque-covered teeth.

"Damn you, little man." Kamal spoke low, his voice controlled. "You have just taken her family's dignity. You stripped it away like a pig."

Kamal removed a stainless steel knife from its sheath. In one move he wrapped his left arm across the man's throat, swinging his leg out, closing the door. He could smell the man's strong body odor in his nostrils as he jammed the point of the knife into the base of his skull. The Libyan jerked, but it was already too late. Kamal rotated the knife in a short circle, cutting the muscle and soft bone. Within a heartbeat, the Libyan's brain stem was severed and he was dead.

Kamal dropped the man's body to the ground. He watched it twitch for a few seconds before it was still.

"You are scum." He kicked sand in the dead man's face and spit.

Kamal came out of the hut and found Yari huddled on the ground. She was no longer weeping, and her body was eerily relaxed. Kamal picked her up, carrying her down the steep incline. He entered his quarters and placed her on the mattress.

"You will be safe here," Kamal said softly, leaving the room.

Several minutes later, Kamal was alone in the camp's only radio room. The chamber was dark, the sole light coming from the backlit dials of the equipment. It was barely enough for him to see. He listened to the hum of static fade in and out in his headset as he adjusted the radio, trying to clarify the weak AM radio signal. He continued to move the knob, sweeping the indicator back and forth across the number 90.

Radio Al-Quds—The Holy—the Arabic name for the city of Jerusalem, should be on the air for its nightly news broadcast. Kamal hoped it would carry news of his religious brother's successful raid against the American cruise liner.

He bent forward and closed his eyes, straining to listen. The radio station broadcasting was in the Libyan town of Ma'tan Bisharah, 250 miles north of the camp. Kamal knew they were on the edge of its broadcasting range and if there was any interference in the area there was a chance he would not be able to pick up the drifting signal of the station.

". . . at dawn this morning American fighter aircraft provoked an attack by a Libyan missile cruiser fifty-nine kilometers north of the port town of Alexandria. According to informed Libyan government officials, who witnessed the act of air piracy on ground control radar, the American aircraft were flying on a parallel course with the Libyan cruiser Ibn Ghallan when the Americans opened fire on the ship. The cruiser defended itself by returning fire on the hostile aircraft with surface-to-air missiles, downing one of them. The Libyan government has filed a formal protest with the United Nations against the United States and is asking all Arab countries to join them in their call for justice.

"In other news . . ."

Kamal turned off the radio, rubbing his face. Nothing. There is nothing about the attack. It must have failed. Adib Hamen must have failed. How could this be? A surge of panic shot through his body. Ajami would not be pleased. He would be furious.

DAY 2

SATURDAY, SEPTEMBER 18

9

General Dimitri Popivich sat slouched in a tattered plaid green chair, alone in his one-bedroom apartment. The only noise to be heard was the static of his fifteen-inch black-and-white TV. It filled the room with a pale gray radiance from the picture that was only short wavy lines on the screen. The station had gone off the air for the night long ago. Next to the general was half a bottle of Russian vodka. It had been full only four hours before.

Life has not always been this way, he reminded himself. There had been a time when the men in the military were respected and beyond reproach. It had been military leaders, not civilians, who first had the vision to send a man into space. The world had looked upon the Soviet Union as a great and powerful country, one to be admired and feared. The men before him had died for that honor.

The early days of Soviet spaceflight were dangerous and glorious. As a young captain, Popivich was one of the first test pilots to be chosen for the secret missions. His skill in flying experimental aircraft and his ability to remain calm in moments of extreme stress were remarkable. On more than one occasion Popivich had managed to fly and land some of the PVO's unstable experimental aircraft safely when the laws of physics ruled against it. He understood the one basic law of aerodynamics: What goes up must come down. Truly, though, he instinctively knew which planes would be winners and which would prove to be lemons before he even got into the cockpit. Maybe that was why he still craved spaceflight after all these years; it was the ultimate challenge, pushing the limits of man and machine further than ever before.

Popivich's first assignment as a cosmonaut was to work with the ground recovery team of a precursor Vostok capsule, which had carried two dogs into space. Popivich was scheduled to launch next. However,

71

the dogs never returned to earth. They burned up on reentry. Popivich didn't sleep for several nights, the horrifying howls of the dying dogs filling his mind. Yet his resolve to be the first man in space never wavered.

Two weeks before the mission, during a routine parachute jump, Popivich's left foot hit the ground wrong. The navicular bone was fractured and the doctors recommended he be grounded. Ten days later, Yuri Gagarin became the first man in orbit, three weeks before Alan Shepard became America's first astronaut. They had beaten the Americans once again.

Popivich's turn would come sixteen months later. He and two other crew members climbed into a newly redesigned Voskhod spacecraft in October of 1964. Their quarters were so cramped that, due to weight and space restrictions, they were not allowed to wear pressure suits. The mission was simple: prove the design features of the new spacecraft and use its success for political propaganda gains. They stayed in orbit for three days, following a structured schedule of experiments. The mission was picture perfect until the time of reentry. The new spacecraft used a supplemental rocket system, which was to slow the capsule's rate of descent before it impacted the earth. The rockets were to be fired four miles above the landing site, allowing the crew, with the assistance of a parachute, to land gently. Only one of the three rockets fired properly. The other two exploded, filling the capsule with fire and smoke. When they landed, two of the three crew members were dead. The only survivor was Popivich. His skin and lungs had been badly burned. He spent the next six months in the hospital recovering. He would never fly again. That was the last time cosmonauts were sent into orbit without life-saving pressure suits.

Popivich gently rubbed the twisted burn scars on the side of his neck, feeling the tissue beneath his fingers. The scars were a constant reminder of the sacrifices he had made for the motherland.

Popivich stared blankly at the television. Its hypnotic effect comforted him as his mind wandered. He raised the glass to his lips and sucked in another mouthful of the colorless liquid, numbing his mind and body. *Everything I have worked for is falling apart. The principles I stand for are nothing now. The honor I risked my life for . . . meaningless.*

The general dwelled on early times of jubilation. He had been named to that rank, placed in command of the antisatellite weapons research at the Northern Cosmodrome, at what would be considered an inexperienced age, his diligence and labors having won him this trophy position. While working with this team, they successfully tracked and killed a satellite in low earth orbit. It was a triumph his country and the Communist party could be proud of, and Popivich was honored. The West was far behind them in ASAT technology, and Popivich was determined that the Missile Forces would maintain that lead.

He lifted the glass under his chin, looking into it. Yuri Andropov, his comrade, the leader of a strong nation, was dead.

"Yes," Popivich spoke out loud, slurring his words, "that was the beginning of our dissolution." After Andropov's death the country had turned down a different path. They called it glasnost and perestroika. The military leaders became docile children, no longer worthy opponents. He lowered his head and closed his eyes. *Now they ask the* Americans *for help with one of* my *satellites.* Popivich's entire life had been devoted to challenging and defeating the Americans.

They tell me I am part of the old thinking, the old ways. They think I am an old fool. But I will be remembered. And I will be in the history books . . . as the one who preserved our country's honor. Leonov will regret his cowardice.

He got up from his chair, turning off the TV, then shuffling the distance to his bedroom. He undressed in the darkness. He cursed himself for his night of weakness, realizing there was much to be done. It would be morning soon and he was not looking forward to the pain he would awaken to. Yet he knew the pain would help drive him to complete what he must now do.

ALEXANDRIA, VIRGINIA

"Have my car waiting for me in ten minutes. Oh, and, Nancy, see if you can get a hold of Congressman Dansforth. Tell him I'll have to cancel. Thanks." Tom Staffer set the telephone down and picked up a coffee cup. He raised the warm liquid to his lips, at the same time pulling down the middle section of the white blinds just far enough to see a crystal blue sky with the sun coming up over the horizon. His two-bedroom apartment overlooked a row of nearby spruce trees. He studied them for a moment. They didn't move; not a breath of wind blew. It was going to be a beautiful autumn day and now he was going to miss it. *Well, not all of it, if I have anything to say about it,* he thought. His mind shifted gears as he changed clothes. The thought of going to his CIA office in a polo shirt and cotton pants was depressing. All it would do was remind him of what he was missing.

Taken as a whole, Tom Staffer enjoyed being the deputy director of Operations for the CIA. He didn't have a lot of people to report to, and his twenty-six years of experience gave him a well-rounded background for the position. To be totally honest, Staffer had worked hard to get where he was in the organization. An East Coast Ivy Leaguer, he had been prodded into joining the CIA by his best friend after the two had graduated from Princeton with law degrees. Staffer soon learned that if he was ever to get to the upper ranks of the CIA, he would have to learn the ins and outs of the four directorates: Operations, Science and Technology, Intelligence, and Administration. It had taken him twenty years, but Staffer knew the organization inside and out. The downside was that, in doing so, he was a logical choice to pull double duty. He had just gotten off the phone with DCI Anthony Brady. A Russian Kosmos satellite was tumbling out of control, and they were asking the U.S. for help in recovering it. The president and Joint Chiefs needed to know what data the CIA had on the Kosmos, and the director didn't want anyone below a deputy to be in charge of the project. Vance Edleman, the deputy director of Intelligence, was out of the country attending a conference on Asian affairs, so it was only natural that Staffer be called in to cover for him.

It doesn't matter, Staffer told himself. After all, he lived alone. His children grown and divorced from his wife, he could work the long hours the job required without restrictions. Although being bothered on Saturday morning just before stepping out the door for his favorite golf course irritated him. It wasn't that Staffer had a thing about working on Saturday, but he had been planning this particular date for a month. It wasn't easy to get three congressional members of the House Armed Services Committee on the green at the same time. Not to mention they were all Democrats. Staffer knew if he was ever to get the funding he needed for the final production model of the new KH-16X satellite reconnaissance system, he would have to have their support. This was part of what he called his "politics improvement strategy."

Staffer tossed his pants onto the bed, knowing his maid would hang them when she came in today. He reached into the closet, pulling out a dark gray wool suit.

He stood in front of the mirror for a few minutes, straightening his paisley silk tie before slipping on the jacket. His graying hair was thinning, but his mustache was still thick and black. He had lost a few pounds after his last checkup. The doctor had seen signs of possible trouble in the tests and chided him. He figured he'd quit smoking, too. He laughed inwardly, knowing he had been trying to do that for five years, without any success. A knock on the door told him his driver had arrived.

Twenty minutes later, the black Cadillac limousine came to a stop at the back entrance of the CIA. Staffer quickly exited the car and made his way up to the seventh floor. After passing through three security checkpoints, he walked through the waiting room and into his office.

"Good morning, sir. Everything is on your desk," Bob Russell, Staffer's administrative assistant, said.

"Thanks." Staffer closed the door, removed his jacket, and sat down.

Unlike in the movies, Staffer's office was average and plain. He had a window behind him, although he kept the drapes closed for security reasons, and bookshelves lined the walls in front of him. The wall to the right contained a map of the world, and on his left side was a round table with four green chairs. The table was used for impromptu meetings the director liked to hold in Staffer's office. His desk was organized and neat, the carpet was grey, and the outer edges of the ceiling were yellow and water stained.

Sitting in the middle of his desk was a plain brown folder. He opened it, removed the documents, and glanced over the pages. Staffer looked over the formal request twice, making certain he was reading it correctly. It was written on Russian stationery and signed by their minister of defense. It looked real all right, although it was only a copy.

The Russians were reporting that they had lost most of their technical data on Kosmos satellite 3-1660 when the Soviet Union crumbled. The satellite was in a decaying orbit, and they had no means to stop it or recover it. The only information available was the fundamental development materials, which told them the satellite could be dangerous if it came out of orbit because of its large plutonium reactor. The Joint Chiefs wanted to know, within twenty-four hours, of course, everything the CIA had on this particular Kosmos-class satellite, its mission, original orbit course . . . the standard stuff.

Why couldn't this wait till Monday, Staffer thought, turning in his chair to the computer terminal on the left side of the desk. He flipped through the plastic holder next to the keyboard and pulled out a 3.5-inch disk. Staffer smiled to himself. There wasn't anyone else in the room with him, yet he felt uncomfortable having to refer to the computer without his secretary. *I guess I can fumble through it by myself.*

A second later the screen flashed, showing a breakdown of departments. Staffer paused, reading the computer monitor. *Let's see, do we have a category for crippled Russian satellites with plutonium core reactors?* He tapped the cursor a couple of times before finding the computer file for the Space Defense Operation Center at Cheyenne Mountain. He studied it a few more seconds. The file showed a Vice Admiral Francis Petersen. He was the man Staffer needed to contact.

JOHNSON SPACE CENTER, HOUSTON

"You tell those idiots at the Cape I want full OMS engine pressurization in one hour or I'm recommending to the launch director we put everything on hold. I know the safety manual says we can launch with ninety percent pressurization, but the damn safety manual doesn't run the show once *Atlantis* is in orbit, I do. My crew's lives depend on those engines, and I want them 100 percent operational. Is that clear?" General Terrance W. Novak, the flight director, rolled an unlit cigar between his thumb and forefinger. Novak had a square, flat face and huge hands. He wore his hair in a crew cut and looked more like a worn-out linebacker than a man with 10,000 hours in high-performance jet aircraft.

"Sir, it's going to take at least forty-five minutes to—"

"I don't give a rat's ass about your excuses. Those tanks need to be run up to 3,700 PSI, and not one pound less. That's what's needed for a normal burn. It should have been done right the first time. You have one hour. Now, stop wasting time." He hung up the phone.

That was all it would take for an OMS engine failure, some engineer trying to do his job the easy way. Safety manual or no safety manual, Novak had his own ideas of how things should be done.

Terrance Novak hadn't risen to the top of the ranks by doing things the easy way. A lieutenant general, he was responsible for all joint military-civilian spaceflights. He had two more years before retirement and then planned to start a new career with NASA.

The phone rang again. He picked it up abruptly, saying, "Novak here."

"This is the chairman of the Joint Chiefs of Staff's office. Please hold for General Jack Dawson."

Novak sighed, remembering when Dawson was a first lieutenant puking his guts out after his first check ride in an F-86. Now he was too good to dial his own phone.

"Novak, this is Dawson."

"Hello, Jack."

"I need you in Washington ASAP. I'm having a jet dispatched to Ellington Field at once. You're to leave within the hour."

"What's this about? Can't it wait? For heaven's sake, I'm in the middle of a countdown!"

"I know that," Dawson replied. "This phone isn't secure, Terry. You'll have to trust me that it's absolutely necessary you come immediately. I'll see you this evening and we'll have dinner together. I've got to go. See you then." The line went dead with a click.

"Well, of all the crap—" Novak bit off the end of a fresh cigar and spit it directly in the wastebasket.

USS *Templeton*

The frigate slowly turned southwest at five knots, her bow stealing into the gloomy night. Her single screw beat the water behind her into a white foam as the *Templeton* sliced through the rolling two-foot waves. Operating fifty-two miles north of Guam in preparation for the next shuttle flight, the thirteen-year-old Oliver Hazard Perry–class warship was one of the ships used by NASA and the Pentagon as part of the Space Detection and Tracking System. The ship and its specialized crew were responsible for helping to keep track of over thirty thousand satellite observations a day. All of its data was transmitted to the Space Surveillance Center in Guam. The data was then retransmitted to the Space Defense Operations Center, or SPADOC, computer banks in Cheyenne Mountain. There the *Templeton*'s transmissions were analyzed and referenced to the standard characteristics of satellites currently in orbit. Between five and six thousand objects, ranging from Chinese and Soviet weather, reconnaissance, and early warning satellites to discarded rocket boosters and nonfunctioning equipment, were tracked with extreme accuracy by SPADAT's worldwide sensor network.

At 0300 hours, the control center of the ship was quiet, dim, and shadowy. The only lights were those of the instruments flickering on the walls and ceiling, casting a Christmas tree–like array onto the faces of their operators. Only necessary personnel were at their posts. All nonessential crew members were in their bunks asleep.

Captain Scott Reader watched, over the shoulder of an operator, the ship's color radar spinning clockwise. The only clouds on the screen were thirty miles to the east, heading away from them. Ten hours ago a high-pressure system had moved into the area, clearing the skies and calming the seas. The moonless night was close to perfect for their latest set of orders.

"Bring her around to two eight seven. Slow speed to two knots," Reader ordered.

"Aye, Skipper . . . two eight seven . . . speed two knots," came the response from the com.

Chief Harold J. Cook studied the light blue and black radar scope before him. For fifteen minutes nothing had moved across it. The sky above the *Templeton* was empty of aircraft and not a single satellite was orbiting overhead. The chief was starting to feel drowsy. According to his calculations, they should have had radar contact three minutes ago. His eyes shifted to the lower left corner of the screen. A slight grin came across his face.

"We have radar contact, sir. Kosmos 3-1660 should be in sight in thirteen minutes."

"Good." Reader's attention went to the other side of Cook's control panel.

"I am positioning the mirrors now, Captain. We'll be ready." Cook caught Reader's eyes.

"Nice work," Reader nodded with satisfaction. "There's enough time for us to get a stable look at her on two passes before it turns light." He straightened up. "Twelve minutes till show time, gentlemen. Let's get it right the first time."

In the center of the ship's upper deck sat a TRW-built Sea-Base Electro-Optical Deep Space Surveillance System. The crew referred to it as the SEODSS. The surveillance system was basically a sixty-inch reflective mirror telescope linked to a Masthead Imaging III Digital computer. It rested on a movable compensation platform that consisted of a series of six sensor-controlled hydraulic arms. The arms were attached to large silicon-filled bladders on which the telescope sat, dampening any vibrations and motion. This simple system enabled the telescope's aperture to remain rock solid and spot movement of extremely faint objects, while compensating for the movement of the earth and sea. The light gathered by the telescope was then fed into a computer linked to a charge-coupled device for real-time transmission. The CCD was nothing more than a large advanced home video camera containing 687,000 pixels. The images produced by this electro-optical observation system were so clear and well defined that intelligence officers at NORAD could actually count the number of screws the Russian and Chinese engineers used to close the access panels on their satellites.

"She's coming into view, sir." Cook watched as the red triangle representing the Kosmos moved across the upper part of the screen. "We should be seeing something."

Reader finished filling his coffee cup before walking back over to the monitor.

"Can you magnify?" he asked.

"Magnifying to one half." Cook moved the black joy stick with his left hand, commanding the telescope's mirrors.

A second later the faint image in the center of his screen began to clear. The wavy round outline of the satellite became a grayish white oblong shape slowly tumbling end over end. Its two gold solar panels were waving and flashing the reflected starlight against the blackness of space.

"Computer lock in fifteen seconds," Cook sounded off. The ship's long-range acquisition radar dish was pointed at a seventy-degree angle to the horizon.

"What's happening?" Reader asked.

"Focusing now, Captain." Cook didn't bother to look up.

Faded red letters of the CCCP could be seen on the side of the satellite. The lower section of the satellite was bleached and peeling, while the upper section's bare metal remained unscathed. The intense heat and long-term effects of the ultraviolet light had peeled most of the protective coating away.

"Give us a closeup and start recording," Reader ordered, checking his watch. He had been up for twenty-two hours, and his body and mind were letting him know they required rest. *I'm getting too old for this,* he thought.

"If you have any problems, I'll be in my quarters." Reader disappeared through the heavy canvas curtain covering the doorway of the command center.

DAY
3

SUNDAY, SEPTEMBER 19

10

Vice Admiral Francis Petersen yawned while stepping out of the C-21 transport plane. His puffy and droopy eyelids were the tell-tale signs of his flight from Colorado Springs to Andrews Air Force Base. Sleeping on planes was a lot like sleeping on a ship: either the sound lulled you to sleep or it kept you awake. All his years in the navy and he couldn't remember sleeping through an entire night. He would doze off a few minutes at a time but would never really get to a deep sleep. His wife joked it was because he was like a small child, afraid he'd miss something.

Petersen stepped off the aluminum staircase onto the tarmac. The early dawn air was a bit colder and thicker than in Colorado. It was a wet cold, not the dry cold he had gotten used to in the Rocky Mountains. A shiver went down his spine; it would be at least another month before it got this cold in Colorado Springs.

Fifty feet away was a DoD limo. A neatly dressed marine major approached.

"Admiral Petersen." The marine saluted.

Petersen nodded, returning the salute.

"This way, sir." He moved to the right, opening the door and letting Petersen into the car. He then climbed in next to Petersen, closing the door behind him.

The warm interior enveloped Petersen as he slid over to the far side of the backseat.

"Would you like some hot coffee, sir?"

"Yes, thank you. Black's fine." Petersen watched him carefully pour a half cup as the limo rounded a corner.

"That's good." Petersen took the cup and sipped down a quick mouthful, burning the roof of his mouth.

"It should only take us a few minutes, Admiral."

Petersen moved his briefcase from his lap to the seat between himself and the marine. He turned and looked out the window. The sun wasn't up yet, but the brightening eastern sky showed slashes of clouds cutting across it. He wondered if his wife was all right and reminded himself to call her in a couple of hours. *What I should be doing instead of daydreaming is concentrating on what I'm going to tell the CIA and the chairman of the Joint Chiefs,* he told himself. He continued staring out the window. How long had it been since he was last in Washington? Two, three years maybe. Petersen hadn't been back since he left his job as a space weapons analyst for the DIA.

"How was your flight?" the marine asked.

"No problems . . . just an airplane ride." He turned his head and looked out the window again, hoping the major would get the hint. Within a few minutes the limo pulled to a stop.

Petersen exited the car and entered the guarded River Entrance of the Pentagon. This was the entrance used by the Joint Chiefs of Staff. He showed his ID and made his way into the building.

Turning right into the E-ring, he walked down a darkened corridor. Petersen expected to see more people about but quickly remembered why it was so quiet. It was Sunday morning; everyone was at home. *Didn't the Japanese attack on a Sunday?* he wondered, knowing the answer.

Passing through a junction of two hallways he turned left, walking by the portraits of Sheridan, Halsey, and Stilwell. Petersen moved quickly, finally reaching conference room 173.

The room was plain and simple, just like he remembered. Two rows of fluorescent lights ran across the ceiling, making the room bright. A large round table in the center was surrounded by chairs, many occupied. Along the far wall were several TV monitors and a large laminated plastic map of the world. One of the monitors, a Sony high-resolution big screen, was on a metal cart directly behind the table. A VCR was beneath it with its clock flashing 12:00 in green.

"Frank, good to see you," Tom Staffer said as he rose from his chair.

"It's good to see you, Tom. How have you been?" Petersen held out his hand and they shook with a firm clasp. Staffer looked good, Petersen noticed. He had known Staffer for ten years and had worked with him daily during the Iraqi war. In Petersen's opinion, Staffer was one of the most intelligent and insightful men he had ever worked with. During the war, Petersen had been in charge of the NORAD team that had supplied the Pentagon and CIA with launch warnings and probable launch sites for SCUD missiles in western and southern Iraq. Staffer had coordinated the data and earned a great deal of respect, not only from the U.S. Air

Force, but also from the Israelis. Staffer's fast analyses allowed the United States to attack mobile SCUDs minutes after they were launched.

"I'm doing well. We've been waiting for you." Staffer motioned to an empty seat.

Still seated at the table were Air Force General Jack Dawson, the chairman of the Joint Chiefs, and the DoD's director of shuttle operations, General Terrance W. Novak. They rose at the same time to greet Petersen and nodded their heads in mutual acknowledgment.

Petersen's eyes met Novak's. "Know the name. Nice to finally meet you," he said, walking to the end of the table to shake hands. He removed his long navy blue coat and draped it over one of the chairs.

"We don't have a lot of time, so let's get started," Staffer announced.

Petersen felt the mood in the room change as he seated himself hurriedly, aware they had only been awaiting his arrival for Staffer to begin the meeting.

"As you all know, the Russians are asking us to help them out of a politically embarrassing and dangerous situation. Secretary of State Weber and the president have agreed in principle to assist them. The reason for this meeting is for you to voice any concerns and to start outlining the details for a smooth and successful mission." Staffer paused briefly, taking a sip of water from the glass in front of him. "The first thing we need to know is what we're dealing with. Admiral, were you able to obtain that information?"

Petersen was already one step ahead. On the table in front of him was an open file. He glanced over his notes before he spoke. "We were able to get some very good footage of the satellite in question, Kosmos 3-1660. This was transmitted to us less than six hours ago from one of our surveillance ships in the South Pacific as the satellite orbited over her. The SEODSS was able to take pictures of her on two orbits, and we spliced this together." He pulled a video cassette out of his briefcase, rose from his chair, and placed the cartridge into the machine.

"Tom, could you get the lights, please?" Petersen asked Staffer, as the screen brightened and he adjusted the volume. "The Soviets launched Kosmos 3-1660 on December 19, 1984. The launch site was Tyuratam. After an A-12 booster launch, it achieved a north-south orbit of 415 miles apogee with a perigee of 360 miles."

Staffer's expression asked his question.

Petersen held up his right hand and clinched it into a fist. "If my fist was the earth, Tom, the orbit would be something like this, the apogee being the farthest point from earth and the perigee being the nearest point." Petersen's finger went around, showing the orbit.

Staffer nodded, indicating he understood the explanation.

Petersen pivoted back to the screen, which was showing a faint picture of the Kosmos satellite. "The 3-1660 is sort of a strange duck. It really doesn't fit into any particular category."

"What do you mean by that?" General Dawson asked, folding his arms and slumping forward in his chair. The broad-shouldered chairman of the Joint Chiefs wasn't sure he liked the idea of pulling an old Soviet satellite out of orbit unless it had something directly to do with the national security of the United States.

Petersen hit the pause button of the video machine and went on. "Around seventy percent of the satellites the Soviets used to launch into orbit were military. We've been tracking Kosmos birds since 1962. We generally know if they're military by their orbits, launch sites, and communication signals . . . that sort of thing. From there we break the satellite's mission into several categories: ELINT, ASAT, navigational, communications, and a couple of other minor military operations. When 3-1660 was launched, we had a hard time classifying her. Oddly, she's the biggest Kosmos ever launched into orbit by the Soviets, and even today we don't have a clear picture of what its mission is or, I should say, was. It's been quite frustrating."

"Well, what do you do know, then?" Dawson asked.

Petersen sighed before continuing. "We've classified the 3-1660 as a one-of-a-kind RORSAT-EORSAT hybrid. We determined this by the shape, orbit, and electronic emissions, which are consistent with other Soviet platforms used for ocean reconnaissance. We believe, because of its size and the antennae it uses, that it has a dual capability: radar and electronic emissions detection." Petersen pushed the play button on the VCR. "As you can see, the 3-1660 is shaped like a Verera-series platform. It is square, with very few rounded corners. This is not the standard Soviet RORSAT shape."

Petersen waited a few moments until the satellite could be clearly seen slowly tumbling on the big screen. He pointed to the screen and explained the various features. "Ion engines, main maneuvering thrusters. Just forward of the main engine is the electronics and attitude control instrumentation and right behind that is the up-down link dish. Currently they are using a 16 MHz short-burst radio frequency to try and control it. And it's not working."

Dawson rubbed his chin. "Interesting. What kind of detailed data can —would—this type of thing supply them?"

"Well, it could possibly track a carrier battle group without any problems. Either by radar or by sensing the group's electronic emissions. From there they could target it with land-based ballistic missiles. That is, of course, if we have it classified correctly. Presently most, if not all, its systems are shut down."

Petersen continued. "The two main antennae protruding out of the top of the forward main body . . . here and here," he pointed to the screen, "receive and transmit radar and radio transmissions. We believe the power plant to be located in this section. From the data the Russians have supplied we know this Kosmos is powered by an advanced Topaz phase-three plutonium-fueled thermionic reactor. Only two of these reactors were made, a test model and the one that went into this satellite. We know the reactor was designed at the Kurchatov Institute of Atomic Energy in Moscow and is quite advanced, even for today. It's big, weighing 6,500 pounds, and can generate fifty to seventy kilowatts . . . over a twenty-year life," Petersen added. "Obviously, this is what the Russians are most concerned with." He froze the picture on the screen.

"How dangerous is this reactor core?" Novak interjected. He didn't want the *Atlantis* and its crew glowing in the dark after returning to earth with a rogue satellite.

"That's a good question. Unfortunately, it's one we'll have to let the Russians answer for us. We know that the RORSATs built in the mid-eighties were engineered to jettison their reactor core before the satellite reentered. In theory, this allows for the reactor to burn in the atmosphere, so it never hits the earth. But we also know they've had some problems with this system, and it doesn't always work like it's supposed to. I don't believe this satellite has that particular system or the Russians wouldn't need our assistance." Petersen looked around the table for any other questions.

Dawson spoke up. "Well, now that you've told us what you think this thing is, what other info do we need?"

Petersen finished swallowing the last of his water before answering. "I have a list of technical questions I would like to ask the Russian's space representative when we meet. But nothing that is critical at this point. My main concern right now would be if the nuclear reactor is leaking or not."

Staffer turned to Novak. "Terrance, what about it? You have anything to add? What do you think?"

"Frankly, we haven't been given a lot of time to figure this thing out. I would just like someone's reassurance that my shuttle and crew will be in minimal danger."

"How complicated will it be to bring it out of orbit?" Dawson was jotting down notes for his formal report.

Petersen moved out of the way as Novak stood and walked over to the TV set. He studied the picture for several minutes before answering. "From the looks of things, we should be able to handle it without any problems. I know the Russians use the same satellite-recovering system we do. It's hard to tell, but these . . . ," he pointed to a bright area under the Kosmos's antennae, "look like payload grapples. We just need to get our hands on their tech manual and make sure the damn thing can withstand twenty Gs of forward pressure. When my crew lands, I don't want that thing ending up in their laps."

"Frank, level with me," Staffer said. "What's your gut feeling?" Staffer knew that half a decision was made from facts and the other half from instinct.

"I really don't know. There is just something . . ."

"If you have a concern, Petersen, I want to hear about it, too," Dawson stated bluntly.

"It's not so much a concern, General." Petersen paused. "I know you're a man that likes to stick with the facts, but . . . take a look at this." He gave a weak smile to Staffer, deciding to take a chance and voice his uneasiness. "These pictures aren't as clear as I would like them, but let me show you something." He waited a few more seconds until the tumbling satellite rolled around and was facing them. He then froze the screen and pointed to the shadowy underside of the satellite. "This is the bottom of 3-1660. I can tell you with pretty good certainty what's in each section. However, I can't figure out what's in this section." His finger traced over the back half of the satellite. "If you look very carefully, you can see two rows of five round circles. I'd say they were some sort of access panels, or hatches, but it doesn't add up. Why would they be there?"

"Well, you must have some idea," Novak quizzed.

"Yes, in theory they could possibly be ejection ports for film canisters; however, they're awfully big for that. I don't know, maybe it's nothing to worry about."

Staffer studied the picture. To him, nothing looked out of the ordinary, but that didn't mean anything. "Give it some more research, Frank. I'd feel better if you knew everything checked out about this Kosmos. That's why I called you in."

"I understand. I'll keep digging."

Staffer got back on track. Returning to his notes, he asked Novak, "If we go with this, how will it affect our original mission?"

Atlantis was scheduled to carry a small proof-of-concept CIA prototype, Keyhole KH-16X. The satellite would be deployed and left in space only if all of its systems were functioning properly. Novak knew it was Staffer's pet project. "Hell, I don't see a problem with your part of the mission. We'll still deploy your satellite. The civilian end might have to be trimmed a bit, but I don't want to eliminate it completely."

Staffer didn't like Novak's answer. "Let me make something perfectly clear, General. That satellite needs to be launched on time and without any glitches. The systems we are currently relying on are ten years old. The agency needs that bird in orbit. If something interferes with that, we'll be up shit creek and it will be my ass on the line."

Novak pull a cigar out of his pocket. He rolled the tip of it on his tongue before he answered. "All right . . . let's do this. I'll cancel the civilian part of the mission altogether. The crew will deploy your agency's satellite before it maneuvers into position to pick up the Kosmos . . . as long as it's safe."

Staffer looked Novak in the eye. "I'm glad we could come to an understanding."

The room fell silent. *Well, one thing sure hasn't changed,* Petersen thought, as he turned off the VCR and ejected the tape. *When Staffer wants something, he can still get his point across.*

"When are you meeting with the flight crew?" Dawson asked Novak, breaking some of the tension.

"This afternoon. I've already put the flight on hold. If I get the go ahead, *and* I decide it's safe, we'll plan the mission and be ready to lift off in two days." Novak folded his arms and looked around the room, waiting to see if his timetable would be challenged.

"Jack, is the meeting set up with the Russian space attaché?" Staffer asked Dawson.

"Yes, it's set for ten o'clock this morning at the State Department." Dawson put the cap on his pen and closed his notepad.

Staffer took a breath, trying to loosen the knot Novak had created in his neck. It was 7:50 A.M. and it felt like he had put in a full day.

"Okay," he said, "the White House wants our recommendation on this thing by eight tomorrow. We still have a lot of finalizations to do. Let's plan on meeting again back here tonight at seven."

Dawson caught Novak's eye as he stood. "General, since you're going to the Cape, I'd appreciate your faxing me your recommendations no later than 1800 hours. I'll need some time to add your advice to our report." His attention shifted to Staffer. "Tom, I'll see you here at seven."

Dawson and Novak gathered their things and left the room, lost in their own thoughts. Petersen was purposely lingering and when the two men were out of the room asked, "What's Novak's background?"

Staffer thought for a moment, recalling what he knew. "Well, let's see, he's currently a lieutenant general with Air Force Space Command. He's flown a standard array of aircraft: fighters, bombers, that sort of thing. Other than that, he's been involved with the military space program for about ten years. He's also been involved in several CIA space projects in the past. From what I hear, he's very qualified and makes things happen. NASA will probably ask him to stay on as a civilian flight director after he retires in a couple of years." Staffer slipped on his overcoat. "Why do you ask?"

Petersen snapped the latches closed on his briefcase. "Well, to be honest with you, I just want to be sure he's the type that will be ready for anything. This Kosmos has always been a mystery to me. I'd like to have all the facts at my fingertips before I make a conclusive decision.

All I can tell you right now is I'm bugged by those rows of circles on the bottom side of the satellite." Both men made their way to the door.

"So, what do you want, Frank? On any mission do we ever have all the answers?" Staffer asked.

"Exactly. Yes, I think on most we know what we're getting into. This is like landing in the fog without instruments. We know we're flying the plane, but we don't see everything on the ground. Is there any way I can meet with this Russian attaché?"

Staffer hesitated. "Not at today's meeting. It's already been discussed. Secretary Weber doesn't want any military people there. I guess he thinks it will make the Russians nervous. I don't agree with him, but it's his call."

"Would it be all right if I submit some questions in writing, then?"

Staffer paused. "I'll tell you what. I'll see if I can set up a meeting with the Russian after lunch today without Weber knowing. Somehow, I have a sneaky suspicion that, with their necks on the line, he'll be very willing to cooperate with us."

"Thanks for humoring me on this hunch, Tom. I hope it's nothing, but I'd like to be sure."

"I'll get my office on it right away. If this turns out to be more than they say it is, and your hunch is right, there won't be anything humorous about it."

Petersen chuckled as he reminded himself that things in Washington were never the way they seemed. And if the State Department was involved in this, chances were the decision had already been made.

11

Duke James heard the buzz of the alarm clock but didn't move. It took him a few seconds to remember he wasn't at home. He lay there hoping the dull buzzing sound would just stop. It didn't. He hadn't thought the one-hour difference in the time zone would have much effect; however, his body was out to prove him wrong. Duke peeked up to the window, where he saw a hint of sunlight breaking through the clouds. He sat up, reached over, and turned off the alarm. His flight to Kennedy Space Center from Houston the previous evening had been uneventful. The day had been filled with the usual preflight briefings on weather, flight plans, and the customary final details. Last night the rest of the crew, their families, and the launch staff had had the traditional beach party for the flight team. James stayed an hour or so, making a point to see everyone and say hello. He didn't like socializing without his wife and also wanted to leave before the party got too rowdy.

He and the rest of the crew were on the third floor of the quarters, quarantined until the launch. It was Sunday morning, and Duke found himself wishing he could attend Mass with his family before the flight. He normally complained about going, but Katie kept on him, saying he should go for the kids. Now that Duke thought about it, that was why he missed it now. They would have been all together.

Duke ran his fingers through his hair as he made his way to the bathroom. A hot shower would feel good and get his blood flowing again.

As he stepped out of the shower, he heard the phone ringing. He quickly dried himself between the rings and answered it. "James here."

"Duke . . . where have you been? You're supposed to be quarantined. The whole staff has been looking for you." Willie's voice was about an octave higher than normal.

91

"Slow down. I was in the shower. What the hell's going on?"

"I've been trying to reach you for the last ten minutes. Did you hear about our mission?"

Duke sat down on the bed, wrapping the towel around his neck. "Hear what? Willie, you're talking too fast."

"Novak's postponed the mission and everything that was scheduled for today has been canceled. Security has put a lid on this thing, and I can't get a straight answer out of anybody."

"What does Novak say?" Duke grabbed an end of the towel, rubbing his head.

"I don't know. He's not even in Houston."

"Where is he?" Duke questioned, not expecting Willie to know.

"Flying in from Washington. We have a meeting set up at 1100 hours," Willie answered.

"Are there problems with the orbiter?" The thought of a hydrogen leak and a two-month delay flashed through his mind.

"I don't know. That's just it. Everyone is acting strange about this and no one will tell me anything."

Duke checked his watch: 0832 hours. "Are you in your room?"

"Yeah."

"Why don't you give Andrea a call and I'll meet you both there in about half an hour." Duke finished drying his legs.

"Okay, I'll talk with you then."

WASHINGTON, D.C.

Georgi Soloyov had been in the United States too long. His mind wasn't as sharp as it used to be. There were too many temptations, too many choices. Life was too easy. In an ironic way, he missed the toughness of his life back in his home country. Life in Russia made him appreciate things more: a warm bed, hot food, and the simpleness of his apartment. Here, in Washington, whatever he needed was at his fingertips. And if it wasn't, it didn't take long for him to get it. Today he wanted to be back at the embassy. But instead, he found himself on his way to the White House.

The driver changed lanes, unbalancing Soloyov as he crossed his legs in the back of the freshly washed limo. This wasn't a meeting he was looking forward to.

Officially, he was a civilian assigned to share his vast knowledge of the former Soviet and current Russian space program with the Americans. He had testified before Congress about joint Russian-American space missions and how the two countries could peacefully pursue space travel. The American Congress seemed to like his talk about peace and working together on new and adventurous projects. They liked him so much he found himself on Washington's dinner party A list.

Currently he spent his time split between Washington and Cape Kennedy. The Americans were eager to share their technology with him; it was beneficial for both countries. He had even sold the Americans a few nuclear reactors for use in space and some specialized life-support equipment his country had invented.

The driver came to a stop at the east entrance of the White House, and Soloyov showed the guard his identification. He was immediately waved through the gate, and the car halted less than a hundred feet inside the fence. A few minutes later, he was seated on an olive-patterned love seat across from the secretary of state, Irving B. Weber. Between them was a tray of coffee, tea, and sweet rolls.

"Georgi, I am glad you came to us with this problem," Secretary Weber said in his usual measured tone.

Soloyov sipped his tea before answering. "I certainly hope your government can help us. This is very embarrassing for my country and we wish no harm to anyone. I am sure you understand the seriousness of radiation poisoning from our satellite. My country does not wish for this to happen."

"Yes, I understand. I can assure you my country doesn't want it to happen, either," Weber agreed, offering a sweet roll from the plate he held in front of Soloyov. The secretary had met the Russian on two other occasions, and they were both social. He wished he had spent more time sizing him up under different circumstances.

"I spoke with your foreign minister, Mr. Dolezalek, late last night, and I assured him we were willing to assist you. I also assured him the mission would be classified, as per your request. Only our governments will know."

"That is why I am here, Mr. Secretary. My background is as such I can assist you in every aspect of the mission. My country is also setting up a committee, as we speak, at our space port in Tyuratam. With some software changes, we can link up with your flight center in Houston and help your NASA officials guide the shuttle to Kosmos." Soloyov took another sip of his tea. His mouth was getting dry. "I am prepared to hand over all the technical data we have. Of course, you are aware that some of the information was lost when the Soviet Union was dissolved. I hope what we do have will be enough for the recovery of the satellite." He opened his black briefcase, handing the secretary an inch-thick file. "This will answer many questions."

"Thank you; I will pass this on to General Novak. He is in charge of our team at NASA."

"Yes. I know him. We have worked together on several projects. I am pleased he will be working with me on this as well." Soloyov's genuine delight at this news was evident by his tone and expression.

Weber thumbed through the technical manual. It contained black-and-white scientific drawings of the satellite and descriptions of its internal and external systems. He finally said, "NASA's biggest concern, of course, is safety."

"Oh yes, I agree, Mr. Secretary. That is why my country is also proposing for you to allow us to assist you in the ground recovery operation, once your shuttle has landed. This would greatly increase the chances for success." His smile was wide.

This took Weber by surprise. No one had mentioned this to him before. After the thought sunk in a little, though, he kind of liked the idea.

"Interesting. But as you know, Georgi, this is going to be a military mission. I am not sure if that is possible." Weber's nature caused him to be cautious, thinking the Russian's real concern could not be so much for safety as it was for the security of their satellite. "We will consider it, though," he finally answered, not wanting to shut the door completely.

Soloyov nodded and took a long sip from his cup of tea. "How else may I be of help to you?" He had seen the glimmer of excitement in the secretary's eye at the proposal and hoped his disappointment wasn't showing.

Weber smiled. "I appreciate all you have done thus far, but now it is up to our president. If he says yes, I am sure we will have a few more questions and tasks for you then." The secretary stood, extending his hand. "Thank you again for coming, Mr. Soloyov. You will have our decision no later than 10 A.M. tomorrow."

WASHINGTON NATIONAL AIRPORT

Mark Collins was the third person off the United DC-10. He scratched his unshaven face and wondered if he looked as bad as he was beginning to smell. He had caught a military flight, a T-43A, out of West Cairo, which had taken him as far as Bonn, Germany. From there he climbed on a British Airways 310 Airbus to London, and then on to Washington via United. Sometimes the fastest way home wasn't the easiest, he reminded himself. *At least I'm back in the good old U.S.A.* There was nothing like being back home.

"Christine." Collins smiled, entering the main terminal. He put his arms around his wife, kissing her on the cheek. He took a step back, looking at her soft blonde hair, clear skin, and brown eyes.

"God . . . I'd almost forgotten how great looking you are," Collins grinned.

Christine smiled back. "Well, I guess this new dress did the trick."

"How's my other girl?" Collins looked down at his six-month-old daughter. He couldn't help thinking she was just as beautiful as her mother. Dressed in white, she had a round little head with dark hair. Her eyes were closed as she tried to sleep through the noise of 250 people all trying to exit the airplane at the same time.

"Well, she's doing a lot better now that Daddy's home."

"I can't wait to get home." Collins put his arm around his wife, and they walked toward the baggage claim.

RUSSIAN EMBASSY, WASHINGTON, D.C.

Petersen sat unhappily. It was now after lunch and in his mind he knew he should be back in Colorado Springs digging up every bit of data he could on Kosmos 3-1660. To make things worse, Staffer had been unable to pull off a meeting with Soloyov, the Russian space attaché, without Weber knowing, but at least he got one set up.

"Admiral Petersen, Mr. Soloyov will see you now." A pleasant-looking woman waited to show him the direction. "Right this way, please."

Petersen entered a large office. The carpet was a red floral pattern, and there was still a hint of the newly installed smell in the air. The room was well lit, with deep brown mahogany-paneled walls covered with pictures of famous Soviet scholars and diplomats. In the back of the room was a large desk with two brass lamps on each corner. A well-dressed man in his late forties stood and acknowledged him.

"Please come in," Georgi Soloyov said, as he made his way to the front of the desk. "I apologize for the delay. I am being—how do you say—pulled in many directions." He held out his hand.

"Nice to meet you, Mr. Soloyov."

"Yes, Admiral Petersen. Please sit down." Soloyov motioned to the chair in front of his desk.

The two men took their seats.

"Admiral, I see from the fax I received from the State Department you are in charge of satellite identification and tracking at NORAD. Is that correct?" Soloyov was holding the fax in his hand, looking intently.

"Yes, that's correct," Petersen replied. He was sure that Weber had also reassured Soloyov in the fax that the military wasn't going to get in the way of the mission.

"I certainly hope you found the information I presented to Secretary Weber helpful."

"Yes, it was. Unfortunately, it didn't answer all my questions. I hope you can help me," Petersen said. He looked the Russian directly in the eye, trying to get a feel for the man.

"I will do my best. However, I am sure I'm not as technically knowl-edgeable as you, Admiral Petersen," Soloyov stated with a straight face.

Petersen opened his briefcase, pulling out the file containing several photos of Kosmos 3-1660. He had had the photo lab wash out most of the color, clarity, and details so the Russian wouldn't know just how good the pictures had been or where they had come from. There was just enough detail to show what he was interested in.

"From what I've been told, this is the satellite in question." Petersen placed the picture on the desk. "Kosmos three one six six zero. I'm sure the information that we've classified it as a RORSAT ocean reconnais-sance platform has been shared with you," he said assuredly.

"That is correct," Soloyov said, grinning. "We used it to help keep track of our fishing fleet . . . but, of course, we don't do that sort of fishing anymore." He let out a short laugh, only to be cut off by Peter-sen.

"The question I have is this." Petersen pointed to the area of the two puzzling rows of circles. "Could you please tell me what these are? Your country's other satellites don't have anything similar to them."

Soloyov appeared to be genuinely studying the picture for a few mo-ments before commenting. "I am impressed. May I ask you how you got these remarkable pictures?"

"It was taken by one of our satellites that watches over *our* fishing fleet," came Petersen's snide response.

Soloyov grinned again. "We have nothing to hide. It is all in my re-port. But let me tell you personally: what you are looking at are several things. First, these two in the rear are nothing more than pressure vents. If anything goes wrong with our reactor, they blow off, releasing pres-sure. Second, these two are additional reservoirs for liquid nitrogen, which helps cool the reactor core in an emergency." He looked at Peter-sen and shrugged. "The last six are simply empty. When we designed this Kosmos, our engineers thought they would need the extra space for technical equipment. But, as you know, technology marches on and we were able to develop other designs to do the job. Kosmos 3-1660 is one of a kind. We didn't continue to deploy the system. It was just too big and bulky—how do you say—a clumsy design?"

Petersen watched the man's eyes carefully, looking for the slightest change in his expression. The Russian was either telling the truth or was the best liar he had ever met.

Soloyov went on. "I am glad you brought this picture with you, Admi-ral. It confirms what our engineers already know. From this picture I can tell the reactor is still sealed and not leaking. We shouldn't have any problems with our joint rescue." His attention went back to the photo. "If there were any problems, these doors would be open or completely blown off. This is good news. You can tell General Novak to tell his astronauts the satellite is certain to be safe." He paused with a broad smile. "No, I have a better idea. I will tell him myself."

"Yes. I was told you'll be going to Houston," Petersen said.

"Yes. I will be in Mission Control during the recovery and then the Cape to help direct ground operations when the shuttle has landed." Soloyov folded his hands. "Now, is there anything else I can help you with?"

Petersen cleared his throat, "No, sir, not at the moment."

"Good, then." Soloyov stood to show him to the door. He put a well-manicured hand on Petersen's back. "If you have any more questions, my door is always open. Otherwise, I hope we can talk again of something less—how do you say—less significant."

Two minutes later, Petersen was in his DoD limo heading back to the Pentagon. That uneasy feeling hadn't left him. Soloyov seemed honest enough, Petersen tried to reassure himself. Yet somehow his answers just didn't fit. Petersen had studied too many Soviet satellites, and they never designed anything if it didn't fill a need. Hell, they were notorious for taking a ten-year-old satellite and bolting everything from antennae to solar arrays to it just to get around the cost of constructing a new one. Why would they build a huge Kosmos and then leave half of it empty? It just didn't add up.

He felt the car stop. "Thanks," he told the driver as he exited the car. "I need to get back to Colorado," Petersen thought out loud.

The remnants of lunch were on the center table of the modest white-walled NASA Kennedy Space Center briefing room. The vanilla-colored cafeteria trays were stacked on one end of the table, with crumbled paper napkins and plastic forks scattered on top. The room was filled with the mingling smells of pizza and fried chicken. General Terrance Novak walked back over and took his seat, holding a full glass of iced tea. His stomach was still rumbling its objections to the several slices of pepperoni pizza he had just consumed.

Spread out in front of him were numerous charts, safety manuals, and five copies of the Russian technical report outlining the details of Kosmos 3-1660.

"Okay, let's get down to business. As you know, since 0700 hours today, this mission has been put in the black and is now classified. I don't want any of you talking to the press or anyone else who is not directly involved with this mission. That includes your wives and family. If the president approves, and I go along," he added, "we'll launch on Tuesday. This should give the control team enough time to get the computers reprogrammed and the data link set up between Tyuratam and Houston." He stirred in the glob of sweetener from four packages and looked around the table. "As you're aware, for speed and safety I've cut the crew down to just the three of you. And I've totally restructured the mission profile." He looked at each astronaut as he spoke. "Duke, you'll still be in command; Willie, you're piloting; and Andrea, you're going to be the only mission specialist."

Andrea Tilken lifted her head, catching Novak's eyes.

"Do you have a problem with that?" he asked.

"No, sir. I can handle it."

Novak nodded. He had no doubt she could handle any job given, as part of a team or alone.

"Good. All the experiments you were scheduled to perform are canceled. Your job now is to deploy the KH-16X and retrieve a Russian Kosmos. It's in a decaying orbit and could be an immediate danger if not rescued."

All three crew members looked around silently at each other.

"Willie, I'm counting on you to be a big help." Novak was banking on Willie Quandt's experience since he had been on the team that had taken the Chinese military satellite out of orbit. He gulped a fourth of his tea and continued. "There are five grapple hooks on the Kosmos. You'll need to secure one to haul the thing in. I've got Engineering making the modifications to *Atlantis*'s cargo bay and payload harness. Once the satellite is inside, you shouldn't have any problems securing it. Without any obstacles you'll land back at the Cape on Thursday."

"The Cape?" Duke looked up from the paper he was scribbling on. "I thought we were scheduled to land at Edwards."

"That's been changed also. The Russians have asked to take immediate control of the satellite once you're on the ground. They have technicians flying in as we speak to help unload and truck the Kosmos out of here. If we were to bring you back to Edwards, we'd have to truck the damned thing to the West Coast."

"What are the additional risks involved?" Duke asked.

Novak tapped a pencil on the table, eyeing Duke. "It shouldn't be much different than catching one of our own birds and bringing it back. I guess the biggest danger is leaving it up there." He pressed on, turning his attention to Andrea. "Your biggest challenge is going to be getting it into the cargo bay and securing it. That's why we'll be working so closely with the Russian technicians. We'll have another full briefing tomorrow for any other questions you may have."

Willie raised his eyebrows at Duke, knowing that meant the general wasn't going to say any more about it right now.

"The rest of today I want spent discussing the mission among yourselves and letting me know what further information you may need. Don't forget to anticipate and start planning for any miscalculations. I'll be working out of the launch director's office if you need me." Novak stared hard at the three crew members one more time. "I want everything worked out before I leave for Houston tomorrow evening. Is that clear? I don't want any screwups." He shuffled his papers into his briefcase and left the room.

"Oh shit. Is Novak in rare form, or what? Damn, I feel like I'm back in flight school," Willie joked.

"Novak's just nervous. And frankly, I can't blame him." Duke sat back in his chair and folded his arms.

Andrea reached over and picked up the photographs in the center of the table. The satellite looked awkward, square, and bulky compared to the ones she had practiced pulling into the cargo bay back in the water tank at Houston. Its dirty gray metal contrasted with the deep black of the sky around it. Much of the communications and tracking gear looked like it had been an afterthought.

Andrea's trade was designing satellites for Lockheed. She was their top engineer, with a Ph.D. in electronics and physics. Although technically she was an air force employee, she split her time between working on Lockheed's SDI research and helping the CIA develop its next-generation spy satellites. When it was decided an engineer should be on board all military missions, she joined the astronaut corps. The thought of losing an $800 million satellite with budgets as tight as they were didn't appeal to the CIA or the Pentagon. Her job on this mission was to deploy the KH-16X, which Andrea had helped design, and make certain it was working perfectly before leaving orbit. She thumbed through the pictures one by one, trying to get a mental picture of how she was going to wrestle the Kosmos into the shuttle's cargo bay.

"I can't believe how *big* this thing is. I'm only going to have about two feet of clearance on each side of the cargo bay." Andrea sounded worried, but deep inside she was excited about being able to get such a close look at an old Soviet recon bird. She wished she'd have time to examine it thoroughly.

"No sweat," Duke said. "Just rope it and drag it."

"At least now I can bet we're home in time to see the Raiders get their butts kicked by the Broncos." Willie jumped from his chair, running to the end of the room and pretending to catch the ball for a touchdown.

"I'll take you up on that bet," Andrea said, without looking up from the picture.

"Which bet?" Duke asked. "That they'll get their butts kicked or that we'll be home in time?"

Andrea and Willie looked at Duke silently. They had meant the game. The other thought had never occurred to them.

DAY 4

MONDAY, SEPTEMBER 20

12

THE WHITE HOUSE

Tom Staffer knew why it didn't feel like Monday. He was dead tired. Normally the week began after two days of leisure and at least one good game on the golf course. He had had neither. This morning he found himself standing in the Oval Office waiting for the president and secretary of state to show up for their meeting. The weariness he felt persisted as he took a sip of hot black coffee. *Sometimes there's no substitute for sleep,* he thought. He decided to stretch his legs and walked over to Jack Dawson, the chairman of the Joint Chiefs of Staff. To the general's left was Bill Bishop, the national security adviser, and standing next to him was Tony Brady, the DCI. The secretary of defense, John Turner, wasn't present, and Staffer remembered he was probably on an airplane on his way back from a fly-fishing trip in West Yellowstone, Montana.

"They've been able to react very rapidly," Dawson was saying to Bishop. "I talked with General Novak this morning, and he has everything falling into place nicely. The crew of the *Atlantis* is fully briefed and the countdown has begun."

"Novak's being kind of presumptuous, don't you think, Jack? The president hasn't even okayed this thing yet," Bishop commented, taking a sip from his white china cup.

"I think so. But Novak would call it being prepared," Dawson said. "They're going to launch *Atlantis* either way. Add to that how Secretary of State Weber feels about the Russians. And in case you've forgotten, Weber's got the old man's ear. I'm sure he wants to bail the Ruskies out and help them save face all in the name of democracy and the new world order." As chairman of the Joint Chiefs, Dawson didn't pull many punches.

Bill Bishop, the NSA, turned to Staffer. "What about you, Tom? Has your opinion changed since last night?" Staffer didn't answer right away.

103

As usual, Bishop was doing his prebriefing survey, trying to get a feel for how each person was going to advise the president. Staffer glanced at his boss, Brady, before answering.

"No, I haven't changed my mind. But I'm inclined to agree with Jack. I think Weber has probably already persuaded the president to proceed with the mission to rescue the satellite. And right now I can't come up with any reasons why we shouldn't help them. But CIA doesn't make policy. We just advise."

"Yeah, I know," Bishop said.

Staffer heard the door open and the president entered the room, followed closely by Secretary of State Weber and his chief of staff, Allen Manning. Each man in the room turned to greet their commander in chief.

Staffer watched the president survey the room. He knew the president preferred these somewhat informal ways of conducting a briefing to the heavy-handed ones that were sometimes necessary in the Situation Room. The president's experience in private business and Congress had taught him that he generally got more honest answers if the people advising him were relaxed and didn't feel like their backs were against the wall. Staffer couldn't disagree. The hardest thing in Washington was getting people to be honest.

"Good morning, gentlemen." The president checked his watch as he spoke. "I hope everyone had a restful weekend."

Staffer smiled politely. He wondered at times about the president's sense of humor. It was either very dry or nil.

With everyone seated and settled, the chief of staff started the meeting. "As you know, Mr. President, we were contacted by the Russians three days ago. They informed us they have a hazardous satellite in a decaying orbit and need our assistance in recovering it. We have been working steadily on this matter since then. We now have enough data that a decision can be made as to whether we should aid them or not. NASA is presently standing by. And as you are aware, sir, timing could become crucial."

With an open hand, Manning motioned to Dawson. "Jack, what do the Joint Chiefs say?"

"My basic instincts tell me to be vigilant when dealing with the Russians on military matters. I don't want *our* shuttle or satellite compromised because—"

Secretary of State Weber jumped in. "I don't believe we have time to fret over possibilities right now. This satellite is just too dangerous."

"This is a military mission, Mr. Weber. It is *my* job to scrutinize it from every angle, including the past." Dawson's burly body came forward to the table in Weber's direction.

It's going to be one of those meetings, Staffer thought.

"What does Novak say?" The president asked, interrupting the two.

Weber answered the question before Dawson. "He's cautious, sir, but thinks it can be done without any complications."

"Okay." The president shook his head in thought.

Manning filled the silence. "What's CIA's opinion?" All eyes turned to Tony Brady, the DCI.

"I'm going to let Tom answer that. He's the one on top of this." Brady looked at Staffer.

"Mr. President, I've been following the reports from our intelligence team at NORAD. They're supplying my office with hourly updates on the satellite's position. Its orbit is decaying very rapidly. We've checked the data the Russians have given us, and from everything we can see they're telling us the truth. If we don't take it out of orbit, it will come down on its own in a couple of weeks at most . . . or possibly only a few days." Staffer looked the president directly in the eye.

"What is the probability of it coming down inside the United States?" This time it was Bishop asking the question.

"Less than ten percent," Staffer answered unemotionally.

"I see," the president said. "And what, if any, are your concerns, Mr. Staffer?"

"My biggest fear has to do with the plutonium in the reactor. If the satellite is already leaking radiation, it will contaminate the *Atlantis,* and if there is enough, it could possibly kill the crew." Staffer handed the president a file containing the photos of the satellite. "From these pictures the satellite doesn't appear to be leaking, but we'll want to make sure it's clean before we load it into the cargo bay."

The president looked at the pictures for a few moments. "Is there anything more?" he asked, setting the photos aside.

"Only that my recommendation is we do it on the condition it's safe."

Weber finished up by adding, "The safety aspect of it goes without saying. As far as the political implications, Mr. President, the only down-side is the inconceivable disaster if we don't help them. I told you last night this is what the rest of the world would expect us to do. We have the power to assist them; therefore, it's only logical we should."

"I know," the president answered, looking hard at Weber.

The secretary, in turn, looked around the room. "I think we have a unanimous vote, gentlemen."

The president rose from his chair and walked over to his desk. The meeting had lasted a mere five minutes. "I spoke with the Russian president last night. He asked if we would keep a lid on this whole affair. Understandably, it would be a very big embarrassment for his country, and they don't need more trouble. I told him the mission would be kept under tight military security and we would do our best. I know a lot of people are going to be involved in this, but I want you all to make this a priority . . . keep it airtight." He turned to Dawson. "Jack, I want you and the Defense Department to head this thing up. I expect the Joint Chiefs' full cooperation also. Tony, you and Tom keep me updated from your end at the CIA. I'll call the Russian president myself and tell him we're on board. By Friday, I hope this will all be wrapped up."

Weber and Bishop were the first to stand, followed by Manning. They walked over and shook hands with the president. Staffer, Dawson, and Brady prepared to leave.

Staffer looked over at Weber, who was joking with the president. To him it was more than obvious the State Department had pushed this thing through. Now it was time for everyone else to make sure it happened.

KENNEDY SPACE CENTER, FLORIDA

Duke James watched a whisper of white vapor dance into the air above the burnt orange external tank of *Atlantis*. The liquid hydrogen condensed as soon as it hit the humid Florida air. The white wisps of steam lolled a few seconds before vanishing. The Florida sky was deep blue, highlighting the features of the black and white spaceship.

The orbiter was a mile away, with the late afternoon sun reflecting off its bright white paint. A steady warm breeze pinned Duke's shirt to his back as he walked a few feet closer. He could feel the magic of *Atlantis's* presence. Her size and stature alone were overwhelming.

So it all comes down to this, he thought. A career in the military, a family, and a dream. *Hell, getting here was half the fun,* he joked to himself.

Duke kept his distance, wishing he could reach out to touch *Atlantis.* This was his time alone with her. He had been waiting and training for this moment his whole life. A trip into space. He would proudly be at the controls of the most complex manned spacecraft ever built. She had crawled in under his skin and held his impassioned yearning in check with her awesome magnificence.

He turned and started his walk back to the security van. The dry sand crunched under his tennis shoes. The next time Duke would see her at 0400, he and the crew would be boarding for lift-off. The memory of *Atlantis* sitting on the launch pad was burned into his mind. It would be something that would always be a part of him.

NORTH AMERICAN AEROSPACE DEFENSE COMMAND, COLORADO SPRINGS

Admiral Petersen stepped inside the dark blue U.S. Air Force shuttle bus. The seats and gray rubber floor mats gave hint to the age of the vehicle, but it was clean and well maintained. The black vinyl seats were patched, worn from the constant exchange of passengers to and from the mountain complex.

Petersen took his usual seat on the right side next to the window. He patiently watched as a couple of air force officers finished parking their cars and climbed on board. Soon after the doors were closed, they were on their way. As the bus left the parking lot and turned onto the main road, the electric heater, in the rear of the bus, chattered to life and started to warm the interior. It would be a few minutes before the warm air would reach the front of the bus where Petersen sat. It was a price he was willing to pay in order to be the first person off.

The morning was frosty, giving the mountain air a crisp, fresh chill. The bus made its way up the winding road to the half moon entrance leading to NORAD. The night before, a quick-moving storm had passed through the Colorado Springs valley, leaving behind traces of white, fluffy snow. The direct rays of the sun would soon melt the evidence of the powdery glitter on the ground. In the coming months Cheyenne Mountain would soon be covered with a thick blanket of snow.

The mountain itself wasn't easy to miss. Located outside Colorado Springs, it stood proudly to the west. A passerby in the day, driving down I-25, would first spot Pikes Peak rising up behind it to the north. Its summit, over 14,000 feet, was snow-free only two months out of the year and was a much bigger tourist attraction. At night, however, the Will Rogers Shrine and the well-lit ski slopes led one's attention to the south, where telltale circular lights loomed out of the darkness. Many curious tourists made it a point to ask the purpose of the unusual glow from the dark mountainside.

During the early sixties, hard-rock miners had blasted over 700,000 tons of granite out of the heart of the small mountain to construct NORAD. They carved out a series of elaborate tunnels and caverns, making the interior a miniature city. Once the network of tunnels was complete, engineers went to work drilling over 115,000 ten-foot holes into the walls and ceiling of the complex. They inserted expandable rock bolts to create a layer of super-hard compressed granite. The rock was pressed together so hard it was almost impossible to dislodge anything larger than a pebble. The engineers then installed a layer of heavy steel wire mesh.

There were fifteen three-story buildings located inside the mountain's hollow interior. The buildings were all built on a series of 1,000-pound steel springs along with a computerized hydraulic system. Each building was designed to be completely freestanding, and they were not in contact with the walls and ceiling of the caverns. This design was developed to help the interior structures survive the wild oscillations and tremors caused by a nuclear attack.

Petersen put his hand on the seat, steadying himself as the bus chugged jerkily, entering the mile-and-a-half-long domed tunnel. The words CHEYENNE MOUNTAIN COMPLEX were painted in white letters above the entrance. The roar of the diesel engine drowned out the conversation of the two air force colonels seated behind him. The interior of the bus was enveloped with an eerie radiance from the yellow gas lights that hung from the rock ceiling. Petersen removed his sunglasses, putting them in his briefcase.

Two hundred yards from the end of the tunnel the bus came to a stop. Petersen watched as two guards approached. They were wearing calf-high black polished boots, green army fatigues, and heavy olive-colored winter coats. They each wore blue berets placed smartly on the side of their heads. Strapped to their waists were loaded, stainless steel Smith and Wessen .357 Magnum revolvers, with the hammers pulled back and cocked. The leather strap of the holster came across the top of the frame, which prevented the gun from firing unless it was removed. One of the guards snapped Petersen a sharp salute as he exited the shuttle bus.

"May I see your ID, sir?" the guard asked sternly. The frigid air inside the tunnel suspended the guard's breath.

Petersen's hand went up to the left side of his chest as he looked down. He had forgotten to clip on his security badge. Fumbling through his pockets, he muttered an apology and produced the small laminated ID. It was the size of a credit card, with his picture in the upper left-hand corner. Along the sides were a series of code numbers and symbols. The back of the card contained three electronically activated magnetic circles, which allowed him access to sensitive parts of the complex. He handed it to the guard as the two air force colonels walked by smiling. They had their ID badges pinned to their jackets.

"Thank you, sir." The guard handed the badge back to him, stepped aside, and saluted again. Petersen carefully clipped the badge onto his breast pocket and proceeded.

He walked past the second set of three-foot-thick steel doors and into one of the hallways leading to the operations center. The passage was narrow but well lit. A row of glass-covered light bulbs lined the hall, leading the way. Petersen passed several offices and doors before he turned sharply to the right. He waited for three air force technicians, wearing sweaters, to pass by before he climbed a set of metal stairs. At the top of the staircase, above a set of double-locked gray security doors, the words WARNING: AUTHORIZED PERSONNEL ONLY; USE OF DEADLY FORCE IS AUTHORIZED were painted in fluorescent orange letters. Petersen inserted his ID, magnetic side down, into the sensor and punched in the proper code numbers. With a snap and a pop the locks opened the doors and Petersen stepped inside.

"Hello, Admiral," one of the civilian tech representatives glanced up to greet him.

Petersen acknowledged the man with a nod and kept walking. The last thing he needed was to get corralled by someone who wanted to chitchat. Officially, Petersen wasn't supposed to be back from Washington and at his post until tomorrow morning. He lowered his head and continued on his way across the room, weaving through a half dozen other technicians and computer analysts.

"Admiral Petersen, Admiral Petersen," a soft voice called from the center of the room.

"Shit! I should have known better," he grumbled to himself, then turned smiling. "Yes, Lieutenant."

A young, round-faced first lieutenant approached him. Brenda Holloway had been assigned to Petersen's satellite tracking and identification team five years ago and was now in charge of programming computer models of orbiting satellites.

"I didn't think you were returning until tomorrow, sir."

"I wasn't." Petersen glanced at his watch. "And if I'm not out of here in thirty minutes, I'm going to miss a dinner date with Mrs. Petersen, and she may make sure I never return at all."

"I understand, sir. I'll make it brief. I've been doing some additional computer-tracking analysis on that Kosmos satellite you asked about before you left for Washington."

This brought Petersen's annoyed state to one of interest. "The Kosmos 3-1660?"

"Yes, sir, that's right. Well, at first I thought it was nothing. Then, the more I delved into it, I began discovering some things that are out of the ordinary. I think it could be important. May I show you?"

"Lead the way." Petersen gestured, following her.

"I compared my results to what was in the mainframe storage banks," Holloway said over her shoulder. She reached the computer station and sat down.

Petersen looked at the monitor. A close-up, four-color, computer-generated image of the Kosmos appeared on the screen. The computer displayed its course as it slowly tumbled out of control over the western Pacific.

Holloway continued to manipulate the keyboard while she talked. "This is the most current data I have to work with. What you're looking at are three orbits that were recorded starting early this morning. As you can see, the satellite is tumbling at a rate of one revolution every three minutes. That's about normal for a satellite of this size in low-earth orbit."

Petersen looked at the Kosmos twisting end over end in the center of the super VGA computer screen.

"This image is in real time. Now let me show you what happens when I speed it up." She fed some new commands into the machine. "This is two times its spin rate . . . three . . . six times." Brenda looked at the admiral. "You should be able to see what I'm talking about at ten times its normal spin rate."

Petersen watched. Sure enough, when the satellite was spinning at ten times its normal rate, he saw it. The Kosmos was tumbling in an uneven spin. The difference was subtle, but he could see it. Each time one particular end of the satellite came over the top, it picked up speed as it fell toward earth. Not much, but enough to be peculiar. Petersen knew in the weightlessness of space the satellite should be spinning consistently.

"What do you make of it, Lieutenant? Is it atmospheric drag, or is it heat expansion from the sun?" he finally asked.

"I don't know, sir. The only data in the mainframe that relates to this is when Skylab was out of control, and that data is over twenty years old. It tumbled like this also, but I had to speed up the simulation fifty times before I got the same kind of results."

"Interesting. Freeze the frame and magnify." Petersen was now bending over the monitor, getting a closer look.

The lieutenant did as she was told. The image of the Kosmos suddenly filled the entire screen.

"Now print that. I want to compare it to some other photos I have. And, Lieutenant, I want you to write up a comparison chart of Skylab and the Kosmos satellite. I don't care how insignificant you may think it is, I want to know every detail."

"How soon do you need it, sir?" she asked, checking her own watch now.

"ASAP. The sooner the better, okay?" Petersen pivoted on his heel and strode away. If that end matched up with the rows of circles still nagging at him, he would know for sure something was amiss. He was anxious, though, that it might be too late. *Atlantis* was scheduled to launch, and it would take a definite and drastic miscalculation to stop the mission.

As he entered the command and control center three stories above the operations room, he saw General Van Sheeden standing near the large glass windows overlooking the amphitheater below. The general looked a lot like his old calculus teacher back at Annapolis, with a protruding round nose and large hands. One major difference, however, was that he took his job a whole lot more seriously than his former teacher. The general was in great shape and as commander in chief of NORAD left no doubt as to who was in control.

"Frank, you're back. How was Washington?" Sheeden asked, looking over his left shoulder. In his right hand he was holding a steaming mug.

"Wet and cold," came Petersen's reply, as he placed his hat on a rack along with his coat. He walked over next to the general and surveyed the room below them.

The large twelve-by-sixteen-foot screen was currently exhibiting an outline of the western half of China. The screen to the right, and on top, marked the air traffic above the United States and Canada with a light green line. Directly below, on the same side, a screen showed the locations of American submarines and surface vessels.

"What's with the China map?" Petersen inquired. "I haven't seen that one up for a while."

"ICBM . . . SS 18 launch test. It was one of the ones they bought from the Ukraine six months back. It launched about two minutes ago. We thought it would take the Chinese at least a year before any were ready to test."

"Were you able to copy their down-link transmissions?" Petersen asked curiously.

"Not all of them. The RC-135 that should have been on station is down with mechanical problems. What we did get came off our satellites." Sheeden placed his hand over his right shoulder, rubbing the tense muscles. "We could have used that data off the RC." He sucked in a breath and released it.

"How was the accuracy? Any evidence the missile was guided by a laser gyro system? I would hope the Ukrainians weren't stupid enough to sell that to them also," Petersen commented.

"It's hard to say. They coded the transmissions, of course. It will take a while for the signals to be broken down." Sheeden sipped from his cup. "As you can see, it's been a busy afternoon."

The room below was calmly active. Men and women were on their phones or sitting at their computer terminals, studying the changing data. Organized routines prevented any havoc.

"Have you been able to act on the fax I sent you yesterday?" Petersen asked, changing the subject.

Sheeden walked over to the control board and pushed a button.

"Captain Riley, call up the screen in sector forty-five. I also want the overlay and crossing pattern for Lacrosse and the Soviet satellite three one six six zero we've been tracking."

"Yes, sir," Petersen heard the response over the intercom.

The captain in the room below typed a set of commands into her computer terminal. The large screen flickered and then went blank. Ten seconds later, an outline of the North Atlantic appeared. Petersen could see the rugged coast of Greenland to the north and Iceland in the center of the big screen. Intersecting the eastern edge of Iceland were two dotted tracking lines representing the path of each satellite Petersen had inquired about. One was red and the other yellow.

"The red line is the current and projected path of the Kosmos. The yellow line is the path of the Lacrosse. They will cross in about six hours. Lacrosse will be fifty miles higher than the Soviet bird, but we should be able to get you some good radar images. I've already contacted Sunnyvale. They'll give you four thirty-second bursts at full power. After that, she'll be out of range."

Petersen nodded. "Good. That should do it. How's the tie-in with Tyuratam going? Are the Russians cooperating?"

"Yeah, they're cooperating, all right. If they had it their way, we'd be linked up right now. Hell, Houston already is. They've been talking back and forth all morning. I'm being a little more cautious here. I had Colonel Hill reprogram some of our communication channels so they wouldn't know the exact frequencies we normally use. The White House might be excited about this, but we have security measures here."

The admiral and general were in full agreement with that statement, as they both turned back to face the main screen.

YEVPATORIYA, RUSSIA

General Popivich stood rigidly. His body language alone communicated his unyielding attitude. He was not about to give in this time. Yevpatoriya had been under his command for eight years. Deputy Minister Leonov, standing directly in front of him, was equally determined that the general carry out the given orders.

"Let me repeat to you, General, you are living in the past and do not have a say in this matter. You had your chance days ago when you told me you could save the satellite. You did not. You failed. We had no other choice but to go to the Americans, and you agreed. Now, we must cooperate with their military. Tyuratam is currently transmitting to Houston. They need the tracking data from this station to guide the American shuttle to our satellite." Leonov's hand chopped up and down, emphasizing his words. His face displayed his anger as he continued, "You must get this facility on-line and ready to transmit to the American space center at NORAD, or I will find someone else to do it. Do you understand?" He finished off with an audible rumble from the gases building in his stomach.

"And what about our monitoring stations?" Popivich persisted.

"Are you so stupid to think the Americans don't already know where our monitoring stations are? And what if they don't, and find out; what then? *Nothing,* that's what." Nikolai Leonov looked at him without blinking. He had anticipated this big battle, coming prepared with a full bottle of antacid. If he could get past this hurdle, he could lie down to rest after taking the medication.

"The American shuttle launches in eighteen hours," Leonov concluded firmly.

General Popivich watched Leonov's eyes flash with anger. *I have pushed this matter far enough. Arguing with this man is futile. The bastard will just relieve me of my command.*

Lowering his head as if humbled, he spoke. "I understand. I will not fail in my duty to serve our country. Communications with NORAD will be on-line in less than an hour."

The deputy minister breathed a sigh of relief. He had finally won the battle. "Thank you, General. I will be in my quarters, resting."

Popivich turned. "Contact Tyuratam; transmit the proper frequency codes in order to communicate with this station. Have them tell the Americans we are open for a satellite linkup and will be transmitting tracking data as soon as they come on-line."

"Yes, General," the communications officer replied.

DAY
5

TUESDAY, SEPTEMBER 21

13

Atlantis towered in the cool Florida night. Powerful high-energy search-lights lit up the shuttle in all her glory.

The entire shuttle system weighed a total of 4.4 million pounds and stretched 184 feet into the air. The largest part of the shuttle was the dark orange external tank, or ET. The orange color came from a spray-on polyurethane foam that helped insulate the entire tank. The tank itself was made from a lightweight high-strength aluminum alloy. The upper section was holding 143,000 gallons of liquid oxygen. The lower, larger internal tank held 383,000 gallons of liquid hydrogen. On the bottom of the tank were two large-diameter feed lines. These lines fed the space shuttle's main engines, which were referred to as SSMEs. *Atlantis's* three engines were the most advanced liquid-fueled rocket engines ever built. Together the three engines burned the high-pressure mixture of liquid hydrogen and oxygen to create over 375,000 pounds of thrust per engine.

Bolted to each side of the ET were the workhorses of the shuttle, two solid rocket boosters. These 149-foot-tall monsters were straightforward and simple when compared to the ET. The SRBs' job was to give the orbiter an extra kick. For the first two minutes of the flight they provided most of the thrust needed to get *Atlantis* off the launch pad and into the air. Each SRB was made in four separate sections. The joints connecting the segments were shaped into a U with three rubber O-rings and an additional flange to prevent the leakage of hot gases from the inside of the booster. The propellant burned by the SRBs was a standard mixture of aluminum powder used as fuel, ammonium perchlorate as an oxidizer, and iron oxide powder as a catalyst. The remaining propellants were a blend of binders and curing agents that gave the fuel its solid state. Each SRB weighed over 1.3 million pounds and produced 2.65 million pounds of thrust at launch.

The third and final section of the shuttle system was the orbiter itself. Approximately the size of a DC-9 airliner, seventy-eight feet from wing-tip to wingtip, the shuttle was one of the most remarkable flying machines ever built. Designed to take crews into orbit 100 times, it was covered with over 32,000 heat-resistant tiles made from extremely pure (99.7 percent) sand. These protected it from temperatures ranging from 1,200 to over 2,300 degrees Fahrenheit. The nose and leading edge of the spacecraft, which were exposed to the most heat during reentry, were reinforced with carbon-carbon. This dark gray material was capable of withstanding temperatures of more than 3,000 degrees Fahrenheit.

Duke James was surprised at how quiet it was as he listened to the faint hum of static in his headset. Somehow he had pictured an actual launch as different from the training flights in the simulator. But he had been wrong. It wasn't.

He and his crew were resting on their backs as *Atlantis's* computers continued to run through the prelaunch checks. Duke could feel his palms getting wet as he looked out the left side window of the shuttle. He took a deep breath to help calm himself. No amount of preparation could cork the flow of adrenalin on a first-time spaceflight. The flight deck of *Atlantis,* filled with switches, buttons, and knobs, would be overwhelming to the average person. To the crew, every little gadget had its purpose.

Three CRTs, two above and one below, were in the center of the instrument panel. They supplied him with most of the data he and Willie would need during the countdown and the flight. Between his knees was the control stick, and directly in front of him was the attitude direction indicator, or, as the pilots called it, the eight ball. It showed his pitch-and-roll movements and was very much like the standard ADIs found in all aircraft. The compass-looking instrument below the ADI was the horizontal situation indicator. It showed the location to various navigational points during entry and final approach to the runway. The altitude/vertical velocity indicators were on the right of the HSI and ADI and the alpha/Mach meter was on the left. Surrounding him above and below were the hundred other switches to control everything from the cabin temperature to an alarm clock.

Duke and his crew had been aboard *Atlantis* two hours and fifteen minutes in preparation for their launch. He couldn't help but wonder if they were really going to get off the ground today. History told him the odds on the first try were against it.

His eyes went to the number two CRT located on the upper left side of the control panel. The dark green numbers lit up on the internal measurement unit, showing that the preflight alignment instrumentation was stabilized for launch.

Duke keyed his mike. "Control, *Atlantis*. We have IMU alignment. We show two eight degrees, three six minutes, three zero point three two seconds north, by eight zero degrees, three six minutes one four point eight eight second west." This position was the location of launch pad 39A at Kennedy Space Center.

"Ah . . . roger, Atlantis. That is correct."

Willie was turning the three water-boiler preactivation switches and then the three nitrogen supply switches, giving the thumbs up.

"Control, *Atlantis*. Nitrogen supply switch is on. Boiler control is on," Duke reported.

"We copy, Atlantis."

The backup flight system guidance navigation and control memory flashed the number 3.

"Atlantis, this is Control. The ground crew is away and secure. You're on your own."

"Roger." Duke looked at the clock. Thirty minutes to liftoff. His eyes met Willie's. "How we doing?"

"No problem. Everything looks good." Willie beamed through the open cover of his helmet.

"Andi, you doing okay?" Duke asked Andrea, sitting in the center chair directly behind the two pilots. The bulkiness of his suit and his position prevented him from turning around to see her face.

"You bet. I'm going to just sit back and enjoy the ride." Andrea laughed.

At twenty minutes from launch Duke keyed his mike for a voice check. "Control, *Atlantis* here. This is shuttle commander Duke James and his voice check, over."

Willie spoke out next. "This is your pilot speaking. This is a nonsmoking flight; please buckle up and hold on tight. At Mach 25 anyone falling out of their seat will be left behind. Voice check, out."

"Roger. We copy you, Willie. Out." The ground controller's voice cracked with a chuckle.

Duke watched the number one CRT as the computer loaded the flight program into the shuttle's navigational and guidance system. He then entered SPEC 99 PRO into the computer keyboard and pressed enter. A second later the number two CRT indicated their launch trajectory of a thirty-eight-degree compass heading up the eastern coast of the United States. This would take them into a north-south orbit. Once again he checked to be positive the shuttle's backup flight systems were up and running.

At T minus nine minutes the final ten-minute hold of the countdown began. This allowed the ground controllers and the crew to catch up on any last-minute details they were behind on. Duke and Willie sat motionless, monitoring the shuttle's controls. The three crew members could feel the electrifying tension increase as the countdown marched on. They listened intently to the ground control staff running through the final prelaunch checks. To everyone's amazement, there was not a single problem. They had a green light for a launch.

At T minus seven minutes the shuttle's access arm retracted. The countdown seemed to accelerate.

"Atlantis, *Control . . . six minutes and counting. Initiate APU prestart procedure.*"

"Roger, Control," Duke advised. He waited a minute for the auxiliary power units to start. "Prestart complete. APUs powering up."

"We copy, Atlantis."

"APUs all look good," Duke confirmed.

"Atlantis, we have you switching to internal power."

"Copy, Control . . . switching to internal power." Duke's earthy tone was steady and smooth as his eyes swept across the instruments.

Ten thousand feet over the launch site a single NASA G-2 Gulfstream weather plane made its final report to launch control. The high-altitude winds *Atlantis* would encounter after lift-off were constant, out of the southwest at eighteen knots. There wouldn't be a problem.

The bottom of the sun was just leaving the horizon, casting long fingers of light over the cape. The pilot turned the yoke of the sleek twin-engine jet to the west and added power, climbing out of the area for a landing back at the center.

Five miles to the north a black-and-white U.S. Air Force T-38 made another pass to verify the airspace was clear of any unauthorized civilian or commercial aircraft.

Duke took one more look out his left side window, spotting the grayish fleck of a sea gull high above the orbiter heading for the water in the distance.

"Atlantis, *this is Control. We show H-two tank pressurization at 100 percent. You are a go for launch.*"

Duke felt his body quiver. "Ah . . . roger, Control, we copy." He keyed his internal mike. "Adjust your restraints. I don't want to lose anybody. We're going." Duke felt a bead of sweat roll down behind his ear.

Willie and Andrea were silent, absorbed in their own thoughts.

The solid rocket boosters' APUs burst to life. *Atlantis's* on-board computers took charge of the countdown.

"Atlantis, *we show APUs start is go. On-board computer is go.*"

"We copy that, Control." Each astronaut's heart rate increased above 120 beats per minute.

With 6.9 seconds left, sparks could be seen swirling out around the base of the three main engines. The number one SSME thundered and roared, followed immediately by the deafening onset of the number two and three engines. *Atlantis* soared forward forty inches as the slack was taken out of the holding brackets. As *Atlantis* rumbled upward, Duke's eyes went to the Pc gauge. It read 100 percent. No problem.

Computer control of all the shuttle's functions was automatically transferred to Mission Control, in Houston. The capsule communicator, or capcom, Brody Johnston, watched the engine performance data on his screen. A split-second apart, each of the three main engines powered up, putting tremendous strain on the bolts holding the shuttle in place.

"*Five . . . four . . . we have main engine start.*"

Duke's muscles unconsciously flexed as he breathed heavily. "We have three at one hundred," he called out.

"*Three . . . two . . . one . . . zero. SRB ignition.*"

Atlantis's computers commanded the release of the five pyrotechnic bolts. In the midst of the boiling white smoke and gold flames, *Atlantis* ascended.

"Here we go!" Duke shouted excitedly. The exhilaration was incredible. The upward thrust kept his head firmly in place on the back of the seat.

"*Atlantis, you have cleared the tower. All engines looking good.*"

"Houston, *Atlantis* initiating roll program." Duke flipped a couple of switches and executed a 142-degree roll maneuver, placing the orbiter on its 38-degree compass heading.

"*Atlantis, roll maneuver complete.*"

"Go, sweetheart, go!" Willie howled. "Feels like we have a smooth ride . . . keep 'em burning." The shuttle was riding a tower of flames four times her length.

"Houston, *Atlantis* throttling down. Main engines at sixty-five percent," Duke called out.

"*Ah . . . roger,* Atlantis, *we copy,*" Brody Johnston replied from Mission Control in Houston.

"Thirty-nine thousand," Duke called off. "Max Q is over, Houston. We're go at throttle up."

YEVPATORIYA, RUSSIA

The down-link data from the American relay satellite was being received. General Popivich watched the big screen in front of him display the marked line of *Atlantis* making its way north from the eastern coast of the United States. Tracking computers had been programmed to plot only the courses of the American shuttle and the Kosmos 3-1660.

The general had ordered everyone he could out of the Russian tracking complex. Popivich did not wish to flaunt the betrayal of his country's national secrets to every officer under his command. For the next three days, the station would be operated by only four other junior officers and himself. He tried to ignore the fact that the deputy minister was shadowing his every move.

"It looks like a normal launch, General," Lieutenant Teshev reported.

"Very good. Call me when the Americans are near the Kosmos. I will be in my office." He dropped his hands from his waist and left the dark control room.

A bright flash reassured Duke James they had solid rocket booster separation. He keyed his mike, "Houston, *Atlantis* . . . we have SRB sep."

The shuttle was traveling at Mach 4.5 at an altitude of 147,000 feet. The burned-out rocket motor casings plummeted to the ocean below, where they would be picked up by a NASA recovery ship. The shuttle now consisted of only the orbiter and the orange external tank.

MISSION CONTROL, HOUSTON

A feeling of relief came over everyone. Georgi Soloyov was standing beside General Novak. Both men were directly behind the flight control officer, watching the launch on the various viewing screens on the wall before them. Soloyov coveted the modern American control facility, thinking, if his country had only half the technology he would not be standing where he was, relying on them for help. The enthusiasm was contagious, though, and he was thankful he had been allowed to witness another shuttle lift-off. He guessed by the computer screens and the tones of voices, accompanied by wide smiles, that everything was going well.

Brody Johnston was accustomed to the attention his station was receiving. He wasn't bothered by the two men standing behind him and was focused on his work. Normally, Novak would be pacing the entire room, but obviously this launch was different. This was Johnston's eighth shuttle launch. However, this was the first time he would guide the shuttle into a north-south orbit. He watched the computer generate the trajectory of *Atlantis* as it matched its predicted flight path. In three minutes, the shuttle would be traveling at Mach 15, eighty miles above the earth.

Johnston's eyes shifted to a secondary screen with the status of the ECAL (East Coast Abort Landing) sights. Each sight had a green light flashing next to its name. If one or two of the main engines failed after the negative return call was given, *Atlantis* could currently land at Cherry Point Marine Air Station in North Carolina. Or, depending on when the engine failure occurred, they could land at Otis National Guard Base in Massachusetts, farther north.

Satisfied that everything was normal, Johnston looked at his main viewer. *Atlantis* ascended at Mach 13, only forty miles east of Cape Hatteras, North Carolina. He keyed his mike. "Talk to me, Duke. How's the ride?"

"No problem, Houston. We are single engine to orbit."

"Roger, *Atlantis,* we read you. Watch your Gs."

Duke James didn't know it, but he had a smile on his face. The bumpiness of the last few minutes had leveled off into a smooth and easy glide. The roar of the main engines had graduated into a soft hum as they headed into the thin air of the upper atmosphere. Even Duke's heartbeat seemingly reduced its pounding.

"Atlantis, this is Houston. You're go for main engine throttle down."

"Roger, Houston, we copy. Throttle down. Acceleration is 2.2 Gs." Willie called out the procedure as Duke eased the throttle back to sixty-five percent of thrust. The cockpit windows were now filled with the blackness of space. Duke and Willie could clearly see thousands of stars dancing ahead of them. The upper bluish atmosphere faded into a deep purple. Neither astronaut had time to admire the beauty of it. That would have to come later.

"Atlantis . . . Houston. Go for MECO."

"Roger, Houston, we have main engine cutoff." Duke looked at the F7 console above his right knee. All three of the main engines' status indicators were red. The engines had stopped.

"Atlantis . . . ET sep in thirty seconds."

"We copy, Houston. ET sep is go." Duke James chuckled, shaking his head and letting out a jubilant yell. *Atlantis* and her crew were in space.

"They are safe in orbit. My countrymen will be very pleased," Georgi Soloyov said, blinking at the main screen in Mission Control. "Everything is going as planned, I trust?" he asked.

"Everything is normal," Novak responded, pulling a fat cigar out of his shirt pocket and sticking it in his mouth.

NORTH AMERICAN AEROSPACE DEFENSE COMMAND, COLORADO SPRINGS

First Lieutenant Brenda Holloway brushed her hair away from her left eye and tucked it neatly behind her ear. She wouldn't see the sun come up and didn't expect to see it set, either. The twinkling lights of Cheyenne Mountain's dark interior weren't a substitute for the warm glow of the sun. She would have to wait for the weekend.

NORAD's midnight cowboys, the men and women who monitored the nation's defenses during the off hours, were at their posts. Soon it would be 0700 hours and the day crew would be coming on. Brenda didn't mind the thirteen- to fourteen-hour days she worked at times. They were well worth the opportunity to live in Colorado, or God's Country, as the natives called it. And even though the work load and long hours occasionally cut into Brenda's social life, the upside was she got to play with the big boys. She believed she had more computer power at her fingertips than half the universities in the United States. If she ever chose to leave the air force, all the experience she was acquiring would look great on a résumé.

Brenda opened her top desk drawer to place her car keys neatly in the corner. She spotted a computer disk, containing the flight path of Kosmos 3-1660, lying out in the open.

"Good job, Holloway," she muttered. If the floor security supervisor had discovered that Brenda had mistakenly left the classified disk unsecured at her work station, she would have been history. She scolded herself for being so careless and vowed to be more alert. The disk contained the digital down-link from the three Lacrosse passes over the Soviet Kosmos satellite. She flipped the computer on and inserted the light gray diskette, punching in her security pass code. A small red light, on the side of the monitor, blinked on and off. The disk was cycling and the green light flashed, verifying that the code was valid.

"All right, let's see what Langley has for me." Brenda watched a fuzzy gray-and-white image take shape on her screen.

The information she was looking at had been down-loaded from the CIA-controlled Lacrosse C radar-imaging satellite. The Lacrosse was an advanced version of two smaller satellites built by the Imaging Radar Geology group at the Jet Propulsion Laboratory. The SIR-A and SIR-B prototypes had proven the concept that a powerful space-based radar could effectively see through darkness, clouds, and smoke, giving the CIA the capability to get real-time information anytime, anywhere. The synthetic aperture radar was so concentrated, it could not only define contours of the ground down to three meters wide, but it could also see through the surface of the earth. The radar's low-frequency pulse could penetrate snow, ice, and several feet of rock and sand. Generally, the CIA used the Lacrosse to track shallow-running submarines and to map the command and control bunkers of unfriendly nations. As far as Holloway knew, though, this was the first time it had been used to take a radar profile of another satellite.

Holloway tapped instructions, trying to clarify the picture. Nothing happened.

"Shoot . . . I've got the wrong program," she said softly, switching to a digital program rather than the analog.

Radar images transmitted from the Lacrosse C came in two different forms. Either one could be transformed into a photograph. However, with a digital program she could also manipulate the electronic signals and get a crisp picture of what she was looking at.

"There. Now I want a picture from directly overhead." She pushed the page down button, rolling the screen until a frame where the 3-1660 was perfectly centered on the screen appeared. From there she ordered the computer to digitally rotate the picture of the satellite so she could see it from all sides. Next she froze the scene and added color.

"It's too early in the morning for this," she moaned, rubbing her eyes.

A color picture of Kosmos 3-1660 now filled her computer screen. One end of the satellite had two rows of five black blotches. The other end had dark blue spots and lines, but they were in a random order.

"Let's see what you look like from the other end." She ordered the computer to give her the same type of color enhancement on the opposite side of the Soviet spacecraft.

Again, the same dark blue blotches. Only this time they were much darker.

Brenda leaned back, staring at the screen. The radar waves from the Lacrosse must have been powerful enough to penetrate the alloy skin of the satellite. The blue and black color told her that whatever was in the interior of the Kosmos was dense and heavy, one side being more dense than the other.

Of course! That's why it's tumbling unevenly, just like Skylab before it went down. Holloway pushed the print button and checked her watch. It had taken her nearly two days to complete her report for the admiral.

She pulled the Skylab file from her drawer and set it next to the computer. *If this leads to something important, maybe they'll give me a few extra days off,* she thought. She knew it was wishful thinking.

SPACE SHUTTLE *Atlantis*

"Come on, let's get this show on the road," Duke said, laughing as he floated out of his seat to the top of the crew cabin.

The shuttle had just come off a thirty-six-minute orbital maneuvering burn, raising their perigee to give it a 138.7-by-137.6-nautical mile orbit. This orbit was ideal for deploying the KH-16X, and Duke would have to maneuver only sixty miles to the west in order to intercept the Kosmos. A glimpse of the advancing dawn snuck through the front windows. The colors combined a unique glorious mixture of blue, red, and yellow.

Andrea Tilken and Willie Quandt took their posts directly behind the cockpit. Andrea's first task was to get the cargo bays open. Radiators were built into the inner surface of each door in order to rid the spacecraft of excess heat. If the doors weren't opened, *Atlantis* could remain in orbit for only a few hours. Andrea watched through a small window on the right side of the rear crew compartment as the bay doors slowly opened, exposing the KH-16X to the blackness and tranquility of space.

Willie stood next to Andrea and watched her work the controls. He would pilot the shuttle out of the way once the satellite had been deployed. Duke floated near the ceiling, watching the two prepare to deploy the experimental CIA spy satellite.

"Cargo bays open," Andrea announced. "Running communications check now." She manipulated buttons and switches, jotting info on the chart in front of her. "Life-support systems up and running. Oh two and nitrogen mix, cabin pressure, heat, and electrical power are A-OK. Everything checks out. Looks like we can stay up here for a while."

"CSOC and Houston, this is *Atlantis*. Do you copy?" Andrea spoke, adjusting her headset. CSOC (pronounced See-Sock), the air force's Consolidated Space and Operations Center, was located near Colorado Springs at Falcon Air Base. The main building contained a semicircular room similar in size to the one at Mission Control in Houston. Its primary mission was to control various military satellites, but the technicians and engineers working there also supervised Star Wars research equipment and several CIA satellites. Even though the air force officially operated CSOC, there wasn't any question in Andrea's mind several CIA personnel were controlling this part of the mission. After all, the KH-16X was their bird.

"We read you loud and clear," came the report from both stations.

"We should be ready up here in five minutes. What's the status on your end?" There was a short delay as the signal bounced off the western tracking and data relay satellite to the CSOC controller in Colorado Springs.

"We're ready when you are, Atlantis," the ground controller at CSOC responded.

"Okay, CSOC, you should be picking up a signal from the payload."

"We copy the down-link, Atlantis. *Give us a few minutes to make sure everything is on-line and operating properly."*

"Roger, CSOC."

As Andrea waited, she moved the power lever for the dual heavy lift payload assist, or PAM HL, to the on position and then ran a second diagnostic check. The results were satisfactory.

"Atlantis . . . *this is CSOC. Deploy payload at your discretion."*

"*Atlantis* requesting clearance from Houston for deployment," Andrea radioed.

"This is Houston. You have go for payload deployment."

"Roger, bird will be free in ten minutes."

Andrea gave the commands to mechanically separate the umbilical cable that had been supplying power to the satellite's upper stage. She then raised and tilted the payload table, which secured the satellite, to fifty-eight degrees. It was now pointed away from the shuttle and the sun. With that completed, she began venting the water/glycol mixture used to keep the liquid helium monochrome infrared sensors cool. After deployment, the satellite would use a simple thermoelectric generator to keep the sensors at maximum performance. If the IR sensors worked as advertised, the CIA would be able to detect troop and aircraft movements from 22,300 miles up in space, through several layers of clouds and ground fog. It was rumored that on a clear night the sensors could see a lone man strike a match to light a cigarette.

Three hours and twenty-two minutes into the flight, *Atlantis* was beginning its third orbit over the North Atlantic. Andrea hit the switches, firing the Super Zap explosive straps holding the payload in place. Seven springs tenderly pushed the 18.5-ton satellite out of the cargo bay at a speed of 0.05 feet per second.

"Payload is away," Andrea's thoughts came to words.

"Good job, Andi; couldn't have done it better myself," Duke joked from behind.

"We copy, Atlantis. *Everything looks good from here,"* Houston reported.

Andrea's eyes met Willie's. "Okay, hot shot, I like a man with a slow hand. Back us away nice and easy."

"That's me . . . Mr. Slow-and-Easy," Willie said, smiling as he wrapped his left hand around the black rubber orbiter hand control. He pushed it ahead slightly, firing the nose jets of the shuttle and pitching the orbiter away from the payload.

"Houston . . . we are pulling out. Give me one more diagnostic okay before we send this baby on her way."

"We read you loud and clear, Atlantis," Brody Johnston replied. *"Let it be written that this crew is batting one thousand."*

"We second that," the controller from CSOC chimed in.

"Yeah . . . well, we're only in the first inning," Andrea commented cynically. "I'll initiate boost phase in two minutes."

"Atlantis and Houston, you are go for satellite boost," CSOC replied.

Andrea sat patiently as Willie continued to put distance between *Atlantis* and the satellite. She watched the octagon-shaped satellite, its flat gold sides twinkling as it revolved in the sunlight. The top of the Keyhole contained a large radio dish that could be repositioned to transmit its data anywhere in the world. When the satellite reached its stationary orbit, two large solar panels would deploy to help supply it with electricity. This satellite was the test bed for a new generation of spy satellites that was so advanced the CIA would need only two of them to cover the entire world twenty-four hours a day.

"Ground . . . this is *Atlantis,* we are boosting now." Andrea swung around to Willie and Duke. "Close your eyes; this is going to be bright." She pushed the button activating the twin 1,171-pound thrust rocket motors.

In an instant of dazzling glare, the KH-16X disappeared into the heavens as the satellite began its final flight to an orbit 23,300 miles above the earth.

"*Atlantis . . . CSOC. Nice job, the payload is on track and looking good. If any of you make it to Colorado Springs, let us know. The Rocky Mountain brew's on us. CSOC signing off.*"

"Roger that, CSOC, we may just take you up on that." Willie grinned. He wasn't one to turn down a free beer.

Duke floated up between Willie and Andrea, placing a hand on each of their shoulders. "One down, one to go. We have a date with a Kosmos and we don't want to be late."

14

The desert sky was a pale hue of pink and orange from the setting sun. The brightest stars could be seen as night approached. Twenty miles to the southeast, intermittent lightning struck the ground from an approaching thunderstorm. The bursts of light illuminated the barren ground and rocky horizon.

Abu Ajami, distanced from the storm, instinctively knew his evening would be still, clear, and windless. He could feel the dry heat of the day transforming into the piercing cold of night. The temperature difference was comparable to seasonal changes taking place in just a few hours.

Kamal stood next to Ajami. Although the two men were nearly the same height, Kamal's bulky mass made him appear twice as large as Ajami. His muscular arms were folded across his broad chest as they waited in the dusk at the edge of the runway. The headlamps of their Soviet-built Ural 375 truck, parked behind them, cast long shadows onto the black pavement of the runway.

"He is twenty minutes late," Kamal commented. "The pilot will have a hard time seeing the runway."

"It is unlike Jibril," Ajami agreed, his voice uneasy. He checked his watch once and then a second time, all in the space of a few seconds. "Give them another ten minutes. Then we will return to the camp."

Kamal looked down, noticing Ajami's right leg twitching. It was evident to him that Ajami had still not taken his medication. He would have to make sure his reluctant leader received his shot soon.

The buzz of turboprop engines could be heard. Like many times before, the gray-and-brown-camouflaged Antonov twin-engine AN-32 light transport roared down the center of the runway, a couple of hundred feet off the ground, at high speed. After the pilot decided it was safe to land, he pitched the nose up and banked sharply to the north. Seconds later, he turned his landing lights on and glided toward the runway. The aircraft seemed to hover for a moment or two, wings fluttering back and forth, before its main gear touched down.

Ajami and Kamal stood on the west end of the runway, watching the airplane as the pilot steered straight toward them. The wind from the prop whipped their clothes as the aircraft made a semicircle and came to a stop only a few yards away. The engines powered down and the door opened. A short man with a small wiry build, Faisal Jibril was dressed in a neatly pressed khaki uniform. He had a thin, leathery face and pointed nose that looked as if it had been broken several times. He kept his angular mustache neatly trimmed, and atop his head sat a black beret. He walked down the ladder, followed closely by two other Libyan army officers.

"Captain Jibril," Ajami greeted him.

"Abu Ajami. It is good to see you, old friend," the captain shouted over the noise of the airplane. The two men clasped hands and hugged. They then stepped back, sizing each other up.

It had been more than three months since Jibril had been at the base. A lot could happen to one's loyalties in that time, Ajami told himself. The thought that Jibril was here because Qaddafi had changed his mind about supporting his cause crossed his mind.

Ajami, eight inches taller than Jibril, probably outweighed him by only ten pounds. Both men searched the other's eyes unsuccessfully for a hint of betrayal.

"Kamal, help my men secure the transport," Jibril ordered. "Store it in bunker number one and have it refueled."

Kamal, looking at Ajami, did not move.

Jibril sneered. "Very good. I see Kamal is still loyal only to you."

Ajami nodded his permission. Then the two men turned silently, walking toward the main part of the camp a quarter of a mile away.

Ajami was prudent in his trust for the Libyan, and it was no secret that Captain Jibril felt the same way. As head of the Libyan-controlled Palestinian terrorist training base, Jibril was the only man who didn't need Ajami's permission to enter the camp. Ajami didn't like it, but he knew he had to live with it. Jibril provided Ajami's men with arms, intelligence, money, and foreign passports. Consequently, he came and went as he pleased. If Ajami had a superior, Jibril was the closest person to it.

This trip was like all others. Ajami had received a simple radio message telling him Jibril was already in the air and would arrive shortly. Normally, this gave his men only an hour to prepare. There was no question in Ajami's mind that if the captain thought he could land at the airstrip and surprise them without getting shot down, he would.

Unlike many Palestinian-born Libyans, Jibril wasn't motivated by money or power. He had been born into a poor baker's family near

Jaffa, a small village just outside Tel Aviv. His family had been forced to flee to Tripoli, Libya, one week before the Israelis' declaration of independence, when he was fourteen years old. It would change his life forever and shape his feelings of great hatred against the Israelis, and their allies, the Americans and the British. At the age of twenty, he entered the military, where he was later drafted into the Libyan intelligence service. By his own accounts, Jibril still considered himself a Palestinian nationalist, which served him well in his current position.

"I understand your last mission did not go as planned." Jibril didn't lift his head while walking up the rocky hill in the darkness. The thought of a twisted ankle made him watch where he placed each step.

"No. It did not go as planned," Ajami stated flatly. Chances were Jibril had more details of what had actually happened. "Come, we can talk in my quarters."

It was pitch black when the two men reached the main trail curving through the base. Jibril was amazed and annoyed that Ajami still preferred to walk, rather than ride in a truck, to his quarters. Walking through the rocks and boulders might be shorter, but he was getting too old for walks in the desert at night.

As they entered the main part of the camp, located in the west hills above the runway, Jibril took notice of the several dozen crude stone houses the men of the camp lived in. He was impressed they had come this far in such a short time. Jibril also understood why the men preferred to live above ground rather than in the aircraft bunkers carved into the side of the mountain. He had been stationed at Madadhi during the war with Chad. Living underground for days on end was not good for morale.

Ajami continued to lead the way. At the end of the path was a steep hill. Fifty yards up the side of the mountain was Ajami's quarters. It overlooked the entire camp and gave him a feeling of being in control. The two finished the climb up the steep hill and passed the guards standing outside Ajami's hut. Ajami lit two kerosene lanterns, filling the room with yellow flickering light. As with just about everything in the camp, the room was simple and clean, containing only a wooden table, two chairs, and cot. On the table was a stack of western news magazines and in the corner were several AK-47s.

Jibril wasted no time beginning. "Two of our oil platforms were destroyed by American naval gunfire two days ago."

Ajami didn't say a word, his stare steady on Jibril's little eyes.

"It was in retaliation for the *Ibn Ghallan*'s attack on the American fighters," Jibril continued. "Colonel Qaddafi is not pleased."

"Was anyone killed?" Ajami asked.

"No one was killed. The Americans ordered the platforms abandoned before the attack."

"Then why are you here? Is it to tell me the mission failed? I know that," Ajami snarled, his temper showing. He wasn't in a mood for Jibril's condemnation.

"Contrary to any reports you may have heard, Adib is not dead. The Syrians have a source placed in one of the American intelligence agencies. When your MiG was shot down, he must have survived. The American Navy pulled him from the water and is holding him aboard one of their carriers."

Ajami stood up and walked away from the table, his mind trying to sort out what this meant. Syrian intelligence, known as the *Deuxieme Bureau,* was the best in the Arab world. It was entirely possible they had an American agent working for them. And Ajami also knew that Syria and Libya routinely shared intelligence when it benefited both their countries. *How could this be?* Ajami thought.

"How can you be sure? The Americans are full of trickery," Ajami tested.

"I have confirmed it. The Syrians have his picture. He is alive, I tell you."

"Adib Hamen . . ." Ajami whispered. "Oh, Allah, Adib is alive." There was a confusion of emotion within him at this unexpected news.

"He is alive, all right, and you can be sure the Americans are forcing him to talk." Jibril lowered his head in thought. "This could be a problem for all of us, Ajami. Why did you let him go? He was not a Palestinian."

"He was as much Palestinian as you or I. And what do you mean, *let* him? The mission was for volunteers only. He was one of the best men I had. And he knew the risks. They all did," Ajami answered, enraged at being challenged about his command decisions.

"Damn it, you stupid idiot! Why did you not think this through? This could endanger your operation; this will no longer—"

"The attack was well thought out." Ajami's voice was firm and forceful. The purpose of Jibril's trip was now apparent.

"If it was, like you say, then why did it fail? My leaders are furious at your stupidity. You gave the colonel your word the MiG would not be traced back to him. He now hides in the desert. Has it occurred to you that the Americans knew your plans all along? Someone in this camp is supplying the Americans or the Israelis with information," Jibril spoke slowly and through his gritted teeth.

Ajami's boiling rage brought him around. He lunged at Jibril, grabbing him by his collar. The older man's wrinkled face was distorted in the shadows. "Do not ever call me stupid again. Do you understand me, Jibril? And how could the CIA or Mossad know of this camp? How?"

Jibril didn't waver. He grasped Ajami's wrists at his throat. "The Americans are not as helpless as you may think. I am sure Adib has told them where your camp is located. They now know where you are, Ajami. Now, release me or—"

"Or what?"

"Let me go, Ajami," Jibril commanded sternly.

Ajami gave him a hard shove and Jibril fell backward, hitting the ground. He felt several sharp rocks cut through his uniform, digging into his skin.

"You are lying to me. Only myself and two other men knew the exact mission profile. I personally outlined every detail with Kamal and Adib —" Ajami stopped mid-sentence. "What is this, one of your loyalty tests?"

Ajami's hand unsnapped his holster, exposing the handle of his cocked nine-millimeter automatic. If Jibril persisted, the conversation would end with a bullet. "Where did you get your information? I want to know its source."

Jibril was not a fool. He knew Ajami would not have any qualms about putting a bullet in his head. The only way he could deal with a man of Ajami's excessive personality was not to show any weakness or fear. With his hands plainly in sight, he picked himself up, facing him. "I am not lying, Ajami. A traitor is here in your camp. And what purpose would it serve me to lie? Think about what has happened, and you will know I tell the truth." Jibril held Ajami's dark, ominous glare without flinching.

Ajami's mind raced as he replayed the events of the last few days and the failed mission. The only other man who knew the exact time the MiG was to attack was Kamal, Ajami reminded himself. It could not be his trusted friend. They had fought side by side, together for their cause. Not Kamal . . . He had always been loyal. The memory surfaced of Kamal sticking the barrel of his rifle in the mouths of eight captured Israeli foot soldiers, telling them to pray for Allah's forgiveness. One by one he blew the back of their heads off with a single bullet from his AK-47. When the men refused to open their mouths, Kamal broke the butt of his rifle through their teeth.

Ajami brushed his straight black hair out of his eyes. *If anyone could be trusted, Kamal could, couldn't he? After all these years I know Kamal* —Ajami stopped. *When you trust, you are weakened. Wasn't it Abu Nidal's confidant who betrayed him, bringing about his death? It had happened in history many times before. Maybe it* was *Kamal.* Ajami visibly shuddered, the conflict mounting.

Jibril knew he had to ask the next question cautiously. "Who is in charge of your security and who has access to your outside radio frequencies?"

"You know who it is. Only Kamal. He is in charge of all my—"

"Yes, he is in charge of all of your security. And now the Americans know that you are alive, as well as where your camp is located. All that you have built could be for nothing if this information is given to the Israelis and they attack." Jibril concluded his thoughts for him. "Kamal must be dealt with, Ajami. He is no longer a freedom fighter." Jibril had pushed his case against Kamal far enough.

Ajami snapped the black leather strap back over his pistol. "Is this what you came to tell me? That I have a traitor in my camp and it is Kamal?" Ajami's voice and manner regained their eerie composure. He walked over and pushed open the door. "Majeed. Come."

Jibril watched a muscular young man enter the room and stand rigidly before Ajami. Jibril guessed him to be in his late twenties. A week-old beard covered his face, with the exception of a wide scar across the lower part of his right jaw. The man was large, standing well above six feet, with broad shoulders like Kamal. He, however, was trim and fit. An Israeli-made Uzi nine-millimeter machine gun hung from his side, along with a few extra magazines of ammunition. The man was one of Ajami's personal bodyguards, one who had earned Ajami's trust, at least for the moment.

Ajami paced back and forth in front of the waiting guard. He felt the walls of his room closing in on him once again. His mind was drifting, unable to focus; it was as if he were afraid and fearless at the same time. In his building rage, the thought of his mental condition and the medication he needed to subdue it never came to mind. Ajami was losing control rapidly, and he didn't even know it.

Was Kamal a traitor? How could this have happened? Ajami was unsure of how to handle this, knowing every man in the camp would be watching him, looking for signs of weakness. *If I do not kill the traitor, I will lose their loyalty. I will lose everything I've worked to achieve.*

"Majeed, I have a . . . no . . . *we* have a problem, and you must trust what I say to you." Ajami held the soldier with both hands on his upper arms, staring into his face. "I want you to take several men, find Kamal, and bring him to me at once."

"Kamal?" Majeed questioned, his expression one of disbelief.

"You heard me . . . *Kamal.* Take his weapons from him and bring him to me. Now."

Majeed turned and left without saying another word. The pitch of his leader's voice spoke the implication.

Space Shuttle *Atlantis*

The mission so far, as the NASA public relations people like to put it, was picture perfect. The shuttle was running like a finely tuned sports car, handling every turn, bump, and rock in the road.

Duke James gazed out the window at the earth and stars. It was hard to believe that only four inches of glass and metal protected him from the killing elements of space.

Below, the earth was alive with green and brown shades of land. The rainbows of blue waters and mountain ridges with white translucent clouds circled overhead.

"General James, are you daydreaming, sir? That's not on our schedule today." Willie floated up next to him. His face looked round and puffy from the lack of gravity. And smiling gave his cheeks the chipmunk look.

Duke grinned, answering, "It's really something, isn't it?"

"I'll say," Willie agreed. "You can't explain it, even once you've been up here."

The two men watched the western coast of Africa pass by in slow motion.

"Come here. I have something to show you." Willie motioned, pushing off the wall and shooting over to the opposite window.

Duke followed.

"Look ten degrees off the wingtip. Do you see it?"

"See what?" Duke asked, pressing his face against the window.

"There, that flash . . . about every sixteen seconds." Willie checked his wristwatch. "Right about now."

A faint glimmer of light flickered in the distance right where Willie said it would. "See it?"

"Yeah, I see it. Let me guess; it's our friend, Kosmos?" Duke pulled away from the window disappointedly.

"Sure is, General. The rendezvous radar is locked on and we should be coming up next to her in eleven hours. Come on. Andi's wrapping things up with Houston. It's time to eat."

"Great. What's on the menu?"

"My personal favorite—spicy meatballs in barbecue sauce."

"I can't wait." Duke snickered, pulling himself through the hatch and into the lower section of the crew cabin.

Mission Control, Houston

"Sir, take a look at this," Brody Johnston said, pointing to his screen.

General Novak walked over and gazed at the computer terminal. An orange failure warning light was flashing next to the number two tracking and data relay satellite. The satellite, stationed 22,300 miles above the earth, allowed for communication and data relay between the ground and shuttle.

"It looks like an electrical failure. S- and K-band channels are down.

Solar arrays don't seem to be charging the batteries. We're going to have to shut it down," Johnston said.

Novak contemplated the situation while scratching the back of his head. His attention drifted back toward the main viewing screen. *Atlantis* was over the southern Pacific, heading toward Antarctica. Three TDRSs were needed to communicate with Duke and his team full time. With one down, a small zone of exclusion, or dead zone, would be created until the fourth or backup TDRS could be moved into place and brought on-line. "All right. Notify James and the Russians of the problem, then shut it down. And I want that backup on-line ASAP."

Johnston keyed his mike. *"Atlantis,* this is Houston. We have a problem."* His voice was calm.

MADADHI AIR BASE

Ajami probed Kamal's dark brown eyes. *Why has this man, my friend, betrayed me?* He knew the Syrians had a very trustworthy intelligence network, and he respected them. Kamal had turned and was now working for the enemy. And, undoubtedly, other members of the camp were also involved. Ajami unconsciously began jerking his head, searching the room, and seemed unable to stand in one place for long. *I will find the traitors and I will have them killed.* It was the only way he and his camp would be safe again. Ajami glanced at Jibril as the questioning continued.

"How did you contact the Americans?" Captain Jibril shouted into Kamal's face.

"I did not contact the Americans. I am being falsely accused." Kamal's eyes followed Ajami in his seemingly lost state.

"You are lying! How many other men are working for you?"

"It does not matter what I say. You will repeat these same questions another hundred times and I will answer the same each time. You have made up your mind I am guilty." Kamal's back was against a wall, and Majeed stood with his nine millimeter cradled in both hands, pointing it at his head.

"Yes, my mind is made up." Jibril indicated to Ajami it was left up to him.

"Adib is alive and in the hands of the Americans. Our entire operation is in jeopardy. How did they know when to attack the MiG, unless you supplied them the information?" Ajami asked desperately, not looking at Kamal's face.

"I do not know. I only know that I have always been loyal to you—"

"Stop!" Jibril cut off the reassuring speech of loyalty. "Who is in charge of your communications into and out of this camp? Who is autho-

rized to use the radio to make outside contacts? Only one man, Kamal. You. Are you working for the CIA and the Mossad? Why, Kamal? Why did you turn against Ajami and your brothers?"

Ajami paced back and forth, rubbing his thumb across the top of his pistol. His head was down and his ashen face seemed lifeless, his eyes distant. Everything was happening too fast. He could feel it. His camp was in danger, and the cause for which he fought had lost another battle. *This is happening because Kamal knows too much. Allah has warned me not to share my dreams with men.* But Ajami had told Kamal of his many dreams of leading the Palestinian people out of bondage. Now Kamal wanted to become as powerful as Ajami and replace him as the true leader of the Palestinian world. The vision of Allah warning him to be cautious because his men would conspire to steal his power suddenly flashed through his mind. *I cannot let this happen.*

Ajami removed his pistol from the holster. Walking up, he stuck the barrel to the side of Kamal's head. "Remember when you killed the Israeli soldiers in Lebanon? Now I tell you to pray to Allah. I have no other choice, Kamal."

"Then do what you must. I am your loyal servant, even in your misjudgment. I will be avenged in my life with Allah." Kamal breathed in, raising his frame proudly.

"Ajami, stop. If you kill Kamal, you will not find the others. No one operates alone," Jibril warned.

Ajami stared at the Libyan, his eyes coming back to life. "Yes . . . the others. I will need to find the others."

He turned to Majeed. "Bind his hands and legs. Take him to the holding area inside the bunker. See he gets no food or water. I will deal with him later." Ajami stuffed his weapon back into its holster and stormed from the room.

Majeed motioned for Kamal to turn around and face the wall.

YEVPATORIYA, RUSSIA

General Popivich brushed the sleep from his eyes as he looked over the control center. He had needed to rest and was glad to have slept. It was dark and sedate. The men sitting at their stations looked bored and lifeless, and the multicolored display screens on the front wall danced with ever-changing data.

"Status report," he barked, as he emerged from the back of the control center. The general's gruff voice immediately put everyone in the control center on alert.

"*Atlantis* is currently forty-seven kilometers behind the Kosmos. Approaching at six point eight kilometers per hour, General." Lieutenant

Teskev slipped back into his seat now that the general was up from his nap.

Popivich's eyes focused on the screen. The Kosmos and *Atlantis* seemed to be flying at the exact same speed only a few inches apart. He quickly calculated the time until they intercepted each other, in his head. "Seven hours," he thought aloud.

"The American shuttle should be in position to intercept our satellite in seven hours," Lieutenant Teskev confirmed.

"I know, I know, seven hours. I can read simple telemetry," Popivich snapped back, rubbing his neck. "What are the latest transmissions from Houston?"

"Nothing since word of their tracking satellite malfunction, General. All is quiet."

Popivich looked around the room. He did not see the watchdog from the Kremlin, Deputy Minister Leonov. He was astonished the pudgy-faced little rodent wasn't standing guard.

"Where is Leonov?"

"Resting, sir. He does not feel well."

His ulcer again. Maybe he will die, Popivich thought to himself. "And did he ask to be awakened?"

"Not until the Americans are ready to load Kosmos into their shuttle, General," Lieutenant Teskev answered.

Popivich nodded. "I see . . . Well, if he is truly sick, I suggest we do not disturb him."

The lieutenant's insides dropped at the general's suggestion. He cleared his throat, agitated. "General, I am under direct orders from the deputy minister to awaken him when it is time."

Popivich didn't answer the younger man. He folded his arms, not taking his eyes off the main screen. *When it is time,* I *will be giving the orders,* Popivich thought.

15

General Dimitri Popivich cracked the door open, peering into the room. He allowed just enough light to filter in so he could see. The room was nothing more than an unused office with two double bunk beds along the far wall. It was for his men to use when they were tired. In one corner was an overflowing ashtray on a grubby yellow table surrounded by four chairs. The sink and toilet were on the other side. The room's odor was evidence it had not been cleaned for some time.

Popivich's eyes swept the room until he came to a bundle of dark green blankets and wrinkled clothes. Lying on the bottom bunk, half covered, was Nikolai Leonov.

"Come in . . . I am awake," Leonov spoke, as he rolled over and sat up in the darkness. "What time is it?"

"Not to worry . . ." Popivich reached over, turning on the small lamp next to the bed. "How are you feeling?" he asked.

"Oh, it is you, Dimitri. I thought it was . . ." Leonov yawned, stretching, then stopped, surprised. "I am not doing well; it is my damned ulcer again." The deputy minister fumbled for his pack of cigarettes. His face was white, and Popivich could see his hand tremble as he pulled one out.

The man really is sick, Popivich thought. He had had his doubts. Now he knew he must take advantage of the situation. "You should eat something, Nikolai. You look tired and weak. Should I call you a doctor?"

"I am tired, but I am not weak, and I do not want a doctor unless it is my doctor from Moscow. Once this satellite project is over and done with, I will go and see him." Leonov filled his lungs with cigarette smoke, holding it. He paused. "Why did you come to wake me? You shouldn't have bothered yourself. I left instructions with Lieutenant Tes-

139

kev." As he became more alert, he thought it was strange for Popivich to be here, chatting like an old babushka. *What does he want?*

"I merely came to check on you, to be sure you were all right. As long as you are awake, you might as well know there is a delay. So you should go back to sleep; I will wake—"

"What! Is it serious?" Leonov, moving to stand, was held back gently by Popivich.

"No, sit down. It is nothing like that. The Americans are experiencing some kind of computer problem. That is all. It should be fixed in the next few hours. It is nothing for you to worry about. I will call you when it is cleared up and they are placing the satellite on board the shuttle." The general's face, filled with sincerity, was most unusual, and Leonov couldn't help but think under different circumstances he might laugh.

The deputy minister could not relax at Popivich's insistence. "If you would excuse me, General, I must use the toilet." He set his smoldering cigarette on the edge of the table, walking over to the lavatory.

Popivich inspected the room with his eyes. He had to react now. There had to be something he could use.

"I am so glad that we are finally coming to an understanding between us, General. It would have been very difficult to do this operation without you," Leonov spoke, standing over the toilet, urinating. "I mean, at first I had my doubts, but—"

The stinging crack of a blunt object striking his head took the breath out of him. An intense, dull pain began throbbing, throughout his head, neck, and upper body.

Leonov caught himself on the edge of the sink. He couldn't understand what was happening. He strained to pull himself upright. Dazed, he could taste blood in his mouth; he had bitten his tongue. Again, without warning, another striking blow fell upon his head. He tried to yell out but was unable to. His vision grew fuzzy. He crumpled to the floor, blacking out.

Popivich took the heavy glass ashtray to the sink, wiping away the blood. He then replaced the cigarette butts and ashes in the ashtray, returning it to the table. He lifted Leonov, smearing some of the man's blood and hair on the edge of the sink basin. Impulsively, Popivich slammed the deputy's head against the sink one more time, making sure the man was dead.

When Popivich was certain Leonov was no longer a problem, he wiped his own hands and brushed the wrinkles out of his clothes.

When he returned to the control center, no one had noticed his disappearance and he stood for a minute scratching the day-old stubble on his face. As he watched the S-band radar tracking transmissions from the shuttle come back on-line, he felt victorious. It is said when a person steps over the line of sanity that they become expertly cunning and invincible. General Popivich agreed with that statement. He felt as if no one could stop him now.

Popivich had spent much time deliberating over any holes in the American tracking and relay system. Impressively, there weren't any . . . until now. It was the dead zone created by the malfunctioning tracking and data relay satellite.

The Soviets had solved a similar tracking problem years ago by building a large tracking station on a remote island. It was located 152 kilometers to the south of Cape Horn on the Antarctic Peninsula. The Russians affectionately referred to it as Station Goldfish. The name derived from an old Russian folklore about an elderly man who, while fishing one day, caught a golden fish. The fish told the man if he let him go free a wish would be granted. The greedy man complained that one wish wasn't fair and made so many demands the fish finally grew tired, swallowing him angrily. Many men never returned from icy Goldfish Island. It is said that if a Russian soldier complains about being stationed on the island, the goldfish would swallow him.

"Houston reports *Atlantis* is ready to recover Kosmos. They are requesting solar panel separation," Lieutenant Teskev informed Popivich. "I must awaken Deputy Leonov now." He scooted his chair back to get up.

"Stay at your post! If he is still not feeling well, we should let him sleep. I will take full responsibility for your not waking him." Popivich glared at the young man, daring him to disobey his order.

"But the deputy has given me direct instructions. I must—"

"*Lieutenant* . . . I don't give a damn what he told you. I am in charge here, not the deputy. Now leave the man alone."

Teskev pulled himself resignedly back into position in front of his monitor. Popivich moved in closer behind the men sitting at their computer stations.

"Give me an update on *Atlantis's* distance to Kosmos." The dotted lines on the main viewing screen representing the two had now merged into one.

"One point two kilometers and closing, General."

"What is the satellite's electrical power level?" The technician monitoring Kosmos's internal power systems answered, curious about the strange question, "Ninety-two percent."

Popivich's expression didn't show his satisfaction. "Very well. Begin solar panel separation sequence when ready."

SPACE SHUTTLE *Atlantis*

"There they go," Andrea said. She and Duke were now standing at their stations in the aft part of the crew cabin, looking out the two large windows directly above them. "Right on schedule." The two large steel supports holding the gold and black foil solar array panels in place blasted away from the side of the Kosmos.

"See any problems?" Duke asked. His hands were on the thrust control stick, ready to maneuver *Atlantis* out of harm's way if need be.

"Clear on my end," Willie called, keeping watch out the front windows.

"Nope . . . looks good." Andrea keyed her mike. "Houston, tell the Russians whoever set up the computer sim on this one was right on."

Atlantis was now a quarter of a mile away above the tumbling Soviet satellite. The Ku-band rendezvous radar had steered them this close. Now it was up to General James to do the tricky part.

"Give me about a half a degree nose left and start to inch us down, General," Andrea commanded. She flipped the cargo bay floodlights on and hit the switch activating the two black-and-white video cameras located on the remote manipulator system. Next she triggered the TV down-link, allowing Mission Control to see what was happening.

"Okay . . . bringing her in closer. If I'm going too fast, say so." Duke, barely nudging the hand controller to the left, mobilized the forward reactive control system. A short blast of hydrazine and nitrogen tetroxide shot out from one tiny rocket motor, pushing the orbiter to the left.

"That's good . . . perfect." Andrea regulated the arm out of its storage area, directing it to the Kosmos. She hesitated, playing with the camera command switch until the picture was bright and clear.

"We're approximately a hundred meters out. I'm extending the arm and checking radiation readings." At the end of the arm, clutched in the grip of the payload snare, was a football-sized black box containing a radio transmitter and a remote control Geiger counter. With *Atlantis* in sufficient range of the satellite, Andrea turned to Duke. "Okay, I need to take control."

"You got it, Andi," Duke said, taking his hands off the controls. Andrea manipulated the arm with her right hand and commanded the orbiter rotational controller in her left. She pointed the appendage directly at the Soviet satellite, edging the shuttle in closer.

MISSION CONTROL, HOUSTON

The hushed control room watched the shuttle creep into position. The Kosmos was clearly seen hovering above the space plane's cargo bay on the two giant TV screen displays. Soloyov and Novak exchanged glances, hoping the same thing: that the radiation readings were correct and the satellite wasn't contaminated.

"Anything yet?" Novak demanded.

"No, sir. Radiation levels are normal." The answer came from a white-shirted technician who looked in the general's direction. Novak's expression prompted the man to further detail. "Sir, if there were any high or moderately dangerous levels, they are close enough to have picked them up by now." He referred back to his computer screen. "I'm not showing anything. I'd call it clean."

"Anything on your end, Houston?" Andrea radioed.

"There's nothing registering down here. You may proceed with phase two when you're ready."

"Roger that, Houston." Andrea looked over her shoulder at Duke back at his station, then at Willie floating up by the ceiling with his leg braced against the cabin wall. "I need to stabilize this thing and then search for the best grapple to clamp onto."

The payload snare probe, at the end of the arm, was designed to work with a standard grapple; it looked like a large nail with a heavy-duty triangular head. The grapple was fastened to current U.S. satellites, or free-flying payloads, for an easy retrieval out of orbit. Since Kosmos 3-1660 was also designed for shuttle operations, Soviet ones, it also had grapples. Andrea stretched the arm only a few inches at a time. All she wanted to accomplish now was to gently tap one end of the Kosmos and slow its spiraling. The tricky part was the timing; it had to be just right. She concentrated on the squared end of the Kosmos, containing the large down-link antenna as it somersaulted toward her.

"A little to the left . . . easy," Duke coached.

Andrea moved the snare in place, allowing the Kosmos to roll on to the end. She gently lowered the arm, giving with the momentum. The satellite bounced up slightly, coming back down and nearly stopping dead in front of Andrea and Duke.

"There, I see something." Willie pressed his face close to the glass. "I think . . . Yup, there's one protruding out the main body. About half-way down the left side. See it?" Willie spun around so he could point out the grapple to Duke and Andrea. "See the larger round antenna in the middle . . ."

"Yeah." Duke and Andrea were both elevated on their toes, struggling to see.

"Okay. Follow it down until you get to the main body. See where the metal has faded away? Now, look about three feet to the left. You can barely see it in the shadows."

"Okay, I got it." Duke spotted the grapple. "It looks just like one of ours." He pointed to the small piece of metal. "Andi, do you see it?"

"I sure do. Let's give Houston a peek and check with Tyuratam. Hopefully, they'll know if it can take the stress." She swung the probe out next to it, centering the picture on the TV screens. "Houston, this is *Atlantis*. How about it, guys?"

"Ah . . . roger, Atlantis. *We're having a conversation now. Stand by."*

"Ever rope a steer that big, Andi?" Duke asked, not taking his eyes off the Kosmos.

"No, and like I guessed, there's not going to be a lot of room left in the cargo bay." Andrea felt her palms growing sticky as she adjusted her grip on the hand controller. "Not much room for error anyway, is there, General?"

"Hey," Duke's eyes met Andrea's. "You didn't get this far by being perfect. You're here because everyone knows you'll do your best. It's your specialty. Hell, imagine if we had Willie the hot dog trying to wedge this thing in."

"Now, that's an ugly thought," Andrea replied, knowing Duke was trying to boost her confidence. She rolled her eyes and they both laughed, easing the tension.

"Hey, I heard that," Willie said from above them.

"Atlantis . . . Houston here."

"Go ahead, Houston."

"Tyuratam reports give it a try. That grapple should work. You've got a green light."

"Roger, Houston . . . here it goes."

Andrea twisted her wrist in a half circle and the arm responded by swinging in close to the satellite's body, a few feet away. Zooming back and forth, she acquired a static-free picture to monitor her movements. Easing the arm to the left and up a few inches, she rotated the snare in position, then slipped it over the short grapple.

"Contact," she said to herself. Squeezing the trigger on the hand control, she tightened the three internal wires inside the snare's head until they were solidly around the grapple. She immediately placed the payload arm-stick mode to the ORB LD position, preparing the computers to move the satellite.

"We show a positive connection, Atlantis. *Good work, Andrea, and you did it on the first try."*

"Thanks, Houston." She brushed her fingers through the loose, wispy bangs on her forehead.

"Well, now that you have it, what the hell are you going to do with it?" Willie joked from behind.

"Good question," she said.

"Houston is reporting that *Atlantis* has successfully secured the satellite, General Popivich. Should I give the command to shut down all remaining electrical systems?" asked Lieutenant Teskev.

Popivich didn't answer. His thoughts dwelled on the past. *Isn't this a parallel to the many times before when I put my life on the line for the glory of my country?* In his heart, Dimitri Popivich felt he was about to do the right thing.

"General, request permission to shut down the satellite's electrical systems?" Lieutenant Teskev asked again.

"No. Do not turn off anything."

"But, General, we must. The Americans can't be allowed to—"

"Lieutenant, must I remind you again that I am in charge here? If you cannot follow my orders, then you will be relieved of your duty!" Popivich's fury shook the young man. "We are under secret orders from the Ministry of Defense. It is not for you to worry. Men like myself know what is best and will make those decisions. Now, sit down and do as I tell you or leave the room."

"Yes . . . General." Lieutenant Teskev, realizing something wasn't quite right, sat down anyway. Popivich, as he had previously learned, was not a man to tangle with.

"Contact Tyuratam. Tell them all electrical systems on board the Kosmos have been shut down and we have ended all radio transmissions. It is safe for the Americans to load our satellite onto their shuttle."

"General, I request to have everyone in this room witness that you are responsible for this fraudulent message." Lieutenant Teskev was in a no-win situation. The tense silence was brief.

"Very well. I alone am responsible for the information Lieutenant Teskev is giving to the Americans. Now, *DO IT!*"

"Yes, General."

"Copy, Houston . . . the bird is dead." Andrea wrinkled her face, thinking that phrase wasn't very pleasant.

"Atlantis, we also have two engineers down here that want you to make sure the large antenna, at the base of the satellite, is kept away

from the port-side bulkheads. It could possibly tear the insulation when you close the bay doors. Place it on the starboard side. Do you copy that?" Brody Johnston asked.

"Copy, Houston," Andrea replied. She instructed the arm to swing the big satellite around. Lining it up parallel to the cargo bay, she very gently started pulling it toward *Atlantis.*

"Hot damn, Georgi! We did it." Novak was talking out the left side of his mouth. A large half-chewed cigar filling the other side moved unpredictably as he spoke. "I can proudly say that we are beginning a new era in space. And I'm proud to be part of it."

Soloyov only nodded. He wouldn't feel like celebrating until the satellite was safely back in Russia. He turned to General Novak. "My country is very grateful to the United States. This is a day we can all remember." The two men shook hands vigorously.

Soloyov looked back to the large display screen in front of the room. Live pictures from *Atlantis* were still being shown. One side of the dirty Kosmos could distinctly be seen as it rested inside the shuttle.

Lieutenant Teskev's anxiety increased with each hour. Disobeying the deputy defense minister was alarming enough to him, and now he was being forced to not only lie but to deliberately not shut down the Kosmos's electrical systems. He was truly torn. Independent thinking was still not looked upon in the Russian military as a strength, and the lieutenant had always been a good soldier.

As he looked at the display, he could see the U.S. shuttle starting its third orbit after securing the Kosmos. The shuttle was 200 kilometers off the western coast of South America, near Cape Horn, moving south. He could hear General Popivich pacing the floor behind him.

"When will *Atlantis* be in position to be tracked by our southern station?" Popivich barked.

The lieutenant checked his down-link telemetry. "It should be in range in approximately three minutes, General."

"Good. Very good." Popivich walked up behind Teskev and, speaking quite calmly, said, "You are relieved of your command."

The lieutenant's head snapped around. He wasn't sure if the general was talking to him.

Popivich only stared, then repeated, "Lieutenant Teskev, I said you are relieved of your post. You may leave."

Teskev glanced nervously at the other three technicians sitting to his left. Their eyes remained focused on their computer terminals, as if they had not heard. It was obvious they weren't going to get involved. He rose from his chair, stood at attention for an instant, and walked away.

Popivich slipped into the warm, empty chair. He studied the computer keyboard a few seconds, familiarizing himself with it. He knew it wouldn't take long for it to come back to him. Checking the main viewing screen, he saw a flashing red dot representing the American shuttle. It was now in a position where the Russian Antarctic tracking station could pick it up.

He turned, addressing the communications officer next to him. "I want to know when the *Atlantis* enters the dead zone. The precise second the communications stop between Houston and the shuttle, I want you to tell me."

"Yes, General. It should be entering the communications blackout in forty-five seconds."

Popivich sat erect in the seat, punching in COM SAT KOSMOS 3-1660 SUBK AUTO CANCEL RELAY. He waited for the computer to process the instructions and indicate that the Kosmos had switched from automatic to manual ground control. The computer beeped and data rolled down the screen. He was now controlling Kosmos 3-1660's internal functions. Keying in EXT MANUAL RELAY ODU UP-LNK MANUV, the Antarctic station instantly broadcasted a 399.97 MHz radio signal. It instructed the Kosmos's low- and high-thrust maneuvering engines to come on-line. Each of the satellite's eight fuel tanks received a fresh shot of helium gas, pressurizing them.

Popivich studied the new facts appearing on the screen. The PSI of each fuel tank was increasing. The low-thrust maneuvering engines contained 9.1 percent of their original fuel load. The high-thrust engines, however, contained only 4.8 percent of their fuel. *It will have to do,* he thought.

"On my mark, General." The officer's hand quivered as he stammered through the count. "10, 9, . . . 7, 6, 5, 4, . . . 2, 1 . . . they're in the dead zone."

Popivich tapped in instructions for the thrusters to rotate and point straight down. He estimated that would take about fifteen seconds. The shuttle would be out of radio contact with Houston for less than three minutes.

Lieutenant Teskev, comprehending the general's intentions, rushed from the room to awaken the deputy minister. In the darkness of the hallway, he broke into a run for the sleeping quarters located in the rear of the complex. His faint knock was muffled by his heart's hammering. Afraid he wouldn't hear any response, he cracked open the door.

"Deputy Leonov . . . I hate to bother you, sir, but I must speak to you . . ." He hesitated, straining to hear over the resonant noise in his head. "Deputy Leonov, I'm sorry to bother you. However, something—" He opened the door further and saw Leonov's body lying on the floor.

The gruesome scene combined with his agitation whirled the young man into delirium. He spoke aloud, all the while trying to pull the deputy's pants up. "You must get up, sir. Quickly. There isn't time. The general he's . . ."

Only five of the eight thrusters were pressurized to their capacity. The old general knew he could wait no longer. He typed in the final computer commands: COM SAT KOSMOS 3-1660 EXT FULL PWR THRUST MANV SUBK. Popivich stood tall, the chair toppling back as he did so, and pressed the fire control button, igniting the hydrazine and nitric acid mixture.

"Holy shit! What was that?" Willie exclaimed, as the orbiter rocked violently back and forth. All three astronauts were bounced around in the main crew cabin. Abruptly, it happened again. A high-pitched whine preceded muffled, thundering vibrations through the orbiter. The turbulence in *Atlantis* threw them against each other and everything that wasn't secured.

Andrea reached a window first. Her face ghostly pale, she shrieked, "*My God!* We're on fire!"

Duke twisted around and was confronted by an intense white light before he could shield his eyes with his hands. A bright yellowish glow of sparks and flames exploded out of the open cargo bay from the side of the Kosmos. Bits and pieces of molten metal shot past the windows.

Clinging to the rear window overlooking the cargo bay, Andrea tried to deduce what was happening, averting her eyes. The sides of the Kosmos appeared to be evaporating along with the sides of the *Atlantis*.

"I can't see. What the fuck's going on?" Duke blinked his eyes, trying to regain his sight.

"I don't know . . . it looks like we're melting!"

Duke hollered out, "Willie, get Houston and start preparing to deorbit." His vision cleared and he could see flames flickering in Andrea's eyes as he clamored up beside her. "Can't you jettison the fucking thing before we go up with it?"

Andrea was already standing at her station punching buttons and typing furiously on the keyboard. "I'm working on it, but nothing is responding." She tilted her head, avoiding the now blinding fire. "Shit! I can't move the arm. The components must have welded together from the heat."

"We're still in the dead zone. Houston isn't receiving our signal," Willie called back, holding one end of the headset to his ear.

"Great. Just keep trying, Willie, keep trying."

"Look, it's burning out." Andrea pulled at Duke's sleeve, getting his attention. All that could be seen now was glowing hot metal in the blackness.

"Hit the lights," Duke ordered. "Let's see what kind of damage we have back there."

Willie came back and joined the other two to assess the situation.

"Ah, shit! What a mess. We're in deep trouble, man; that does not look good."

"Shut up, Willie," Duke snapped, then softened. "We're prepared for emergencies. We'll just go one step at a time." He looked out over what he believed to be a living nightmare. The cargo bay was smoldering with ashen smoke and hot gases. The insulation along both sides of the fuselage was burned away, and long streaks of debris were floating out into space. The sides of the Kosmos were a warped and twisted clump of metal. Duke, astonished, wondered how the cargo grapple had sustained its hold on the satellite.

"General, we're tumbling." It was Andrea. "Look, there's the horizon, and we're moving up and away from it."

Duke turned to the front window. The deep blue and purple horizon was moving up and away from them. *Damn . . . damn,* he thought. *I need to boost us into a higher orbit . . . buy us some time to figure this thing out.*

"We're losing cabin pressure," Andrea announced.

"How fast?" Duke asked.

"I can't tell. But we're not going to be able to stay up here much longer," she replied.

Duke had already figured that one out for himself. He had to come up with a plan of action and then have a backup. Systematically, he went through all the controls, finding out which ones still operated and which didn't. Andrea was talking, whether to herself or to Willie he couldn't tell. But he was glad. It kept them temporarily occupied.

"The maneuvering thrusters on the Kosmos must have fired. It's the only thing that makes sense. The force from the blast pushed us down like a retro burn and started us spinning." Andrea stopped talking and she surveyed her instruments one more time. "We're starting to enter the upper atmosphere. General, we're coming out of orbit and if we don't react now, we'll either bounce off or reenter sideways and become the biggest shooting star of all time." Her stern look set Duke into motion.

"All right, Andi. Close the bay doors. Willie, get to your seat. We're taking her down." Duke pulled the shoulder harness over his arms and snapped the buckle. Willie was seated and started to prepare for deorbit.

"Are those bay doors locked and secured yet?" Duke went through a mental checklist.

"Cargo bays are closed, but only one lock is secured. The doors must be warped from the fire. I don't think it's going to be a hundred percent." Andrea persistently hit switches and buttons.

"Forget it, Andi. We'll take it as it is. Now, buckle up."

"Still no contact with Houston. Our S-band relay circuits must have been damaged, along with the backup systems." Willie shook his head.

"What about the UHF radio?"

"I've tried it once and didn't get anything." Willie twisted the radio controls back to the UHF-band transmitter. "I'll boost power and try it again. UHF is line-of-sight only. If we're not over a ground station, they'll never hear us."

"Atlantis . . . Atlantis, *this is Houston. Do you copy?"*

Duke froze, his headset filled with static. He could barely make out the voice of Mission Control. "Houston, this is *Atlantis*; we copy." Their intervals of speech overlapped from the interfering static.

"What's . . . on . . . your orbit . . . changed?"

"This is James, Houston; we are coming down . . . mayday . . . I repeat, we are coming down . . . mayday . . . this is *Atlantis* . . ."

Brody Johnston cranked up the volume to maximum. Holding his left hand to his ear, he waved his right hand wildly to quiet the control room. "Say again, *Atlantis*. Say again."

Duke's voice filled the entire room. *"Hou . . . explosion in cargo ba . . . mayday . . . Kosmos sat . . . fire . . . we are forced to deor . . ."* The radio transmission was lost again.

"Brody, what the hell's going on?" Novak, stunned, couldn't believe what he had heard. He observed Soloyov momentarily and then gave his full attention to the capcom.

"Something about an explosion and the satellite." Johnston was working the controls the whole while he was talking.

Novak swallowed hard. "See if you can reestablish radio contact. And contact Tyuratam; maybe they know what the hell is going on."

Duke saw the flashing fire warning light at the same time an acid smell burned his nose.

"Fire warning!" he bellowed, as he checked the fire suppression panel next to his left arm. None of the three avionic bays were on fire. However, the middeck cabin light was flashing.

"Andi, I'm showing a fire in the middeck. Grab an extinguisher and see where the problem is. Willie, let's speed things up. I want this baby on the ground."

"Yes, sir."

Duke hit the four switches marked HE PRESS/VAPOR ISOL. High-pressure helium started filling the two OMS engines.

"Play it back again, and see if you can eliminate some of that static." Novak spun around, looking Soloyov squarely in the eye. "Are you certain there isn't something you forgot to tell us?"

Soloyov stuttered, "I do—do not know any—anything more. I swear." Taking a deep breath, he relaxed and continued, "I am sure our satellite had nothing to do with the fire or explosion, General."

"We're ready, sir." Johnston announced over the loudspeaker for the room to be silent.

"Hous . . . explosion in cargo ba . . . mayday . . . Kosmos sat . . . fire . . . we are forced to deor . . ." Duke's broken message was clear enough so that everyone in Mission Control understood its meaning. Novak spoke firmly to Soloyov.

"I'm sorry, Mr. Soloyov, I'm going to have to ask you to leave. You understand that you would only be in the way here. Once Atlantis is safely on the ground, we'll talk."

Andrea returned with an update. "I couldn't find a fire, General, but there's a lot of smoke down there. The flames must have burned through the outer bulkhead. The smell of acid is real strong. It must be eating into the fuselage. Our cabin pressure is getting critical, too." She buckled back into her seat directly behind Duke and Willie.

"Initiating emergency cabin pressure." Duke hit a button on the left console, reducing their cabin pressure from 14 to 8 psi. Grasping the hand controller, he gently rotated the shuttle. Atlantis swung and was now flying tail first. The blast from the OMS engines stabilized the spinning.

"Willie, call out the data," Duke ordered. Willie, wiping the sweat from his eyes, couldn't think of what info was needed.

"Damn it, Commander! Get with the program. I need your help."

"Ah . . . number one APU tank valve is open. Hydraulic pressure is weak but still in the green."

"Okay," Duke sighed, relieved the fire hadn't damaged the hydraulics, at least not yet. They should be able to control the shuttle once it entered the atmosphere. Willie continued the descent checklist.

"Cabin pressure isn't getting any better. We could have a total breach any time."

"OMS engines are armed . . . everyone hold tight. Five, four, three, two, one." Duke punched the exec button, firing the engines.

* * *

"General, *Atlantis* has a controlled OMS burn. James is bringing her down," Johnston hollered, waving Novak over from seeing Soloyov to the door.

"General! I have NORAD on the phone." The faceless voice boomed out from the chatter.

"Put it up here." Novak pointed to the black phone next to Johnston as he jogged over, picking up the receiver. "Novak here."

"Terrance, this is Van. We're monitoring the situation. Have you figured out what's going on?" The commander of NORAD was watching the events unfold on the control board deep inside Cheyenne Mountain.

"We don't know for sure. We've lost communications, but from the sound of it there was some sort of explosion."

"Is there anything you want us to do?"

"Yeah. Keep monitoring the situation. Our computer simulation shows that at their present course and rate of descent they should be coming down in northern Europe or Norway. We may need your help tracking."

"Understood. I'll keep you posted."

Novak hung up the phone. "Dear God, I can't believe this shit is happening."

"Speed . . . seventeen thousand nine two. Altitude, six hundred eighteen thousand and descending," Willie rattled off the information.

The nose of the orbiter was starting to hit the first few molecules of upper atmosphere and every now and then a blur of pink and red would shoot past the front windows. In the distance, Duke could see the night sky to the west. If at all possible, he wanted to keep *Atlantis* in the daylight.

"Willie, have the NAV computer calculate and identify runways or possible landing sights in the area. We'll need at least ten thousand feet." Duke's eyes swept across the instruments. The attitude direction indicator showed roll 0 degrees, pitch 28 to 38 degrees, and yaw 0 degrees.

"Altitude, 410,000 feet; speed . . . constant. Entering upper atmosphere."

"Damn it, I don't like the feel of this shit. We're coming down too fast. Willie, you got anything yet? I need a place to land this bitch."

"Relax. We'll make it. Let's get through reentry first and see where we come out. If we have to, we'll bail out of this thing." Andrea's confidence radiated through the cabin temporarily.

"We should be entering LOS in thirty seconds," Willie said.

* * *

Johnston watched the computer image of *Atlantis* disappear from his screen. "We just lost contact with them, sir. Last reported position was over east Africa."

Atlantis, reentering the atmosphere, had a buildup of ionization particles surrounding it. All radio signals were blocked.

Some 230,000 feet above Kenya and traveling at 15,000 miles per hour the shuttle's nose and leading edges of the wings had reached a temperature of over 2,800 degrees. The dark pink glow covering the cockpit windows was now disappearing. When the computers registered an air pressure of 20 psi they would automatically shut down the pitch and yaw thrusters. The shuttle's ailerons would then start to control the space plane.

"Where the hell are we, Willie?" Duke asked, not taking his eyes off the HUD.

"One hundred seventy-five thousand feet. NAV says we're over eastern Ethiopia heading inland, to the northwest."

"I'm not slowing her down until you find me a runway." Duke kept the airspeed steady, while Willie worked to locate an adequate strip.

"I show a negative lock on the cargo bay!" Andrea tried to see what was happening with the bay doors, but the harness restricted her movement. "Duke, she won't be able to handle the stress. You'd better land her now!"

"Son of a bitch." Duke saw the flashing red warning light beneath the center CRT. At their present rate of speed, if one of the doors blew open, *Atlantis* would become uncontrollable and could break up in the air.

"But I haven't got anything!" Willie yelled.

"I don't have a choice. I'm taking her down anyway. If we don't find a runway in a few minutes, I want you two to bail out when we hit 20,000 feet."

Duke eased the stick to the left. The Gs built up as *Atlantis* sliced through the upper atmosphere, bleeding off energy. At 120,000 feet, he deployed the speed brakes to fifty-six percent and pitched the nose down. Their speed slowed to Mach 4.35 and falling.

"We're over central Sudan; turn right to a heading of zero seven three. Let's head for the southern end of the Red Sea. All we have to do is spiral down. If we don't find a landing strip, we can put her down in the water," Willie advised.

Duke's eyes went from the HUD to the CRT. It showed a color map of the central portion of the Sudan desert.

"Don't do that!" Andrea declared. "We're coming in too fast. If you start your S-turn now, there is no question those bay doors will open and we'll break up."

"Well, I don't show any other landing sites and we're less than five minutes from touchdown," Willie argued.

"Let's not give up. Willie, keep looking." Duke concentrated on leveling the shuttle at 75,000 feet and slowing her airspeed enough for a safe bailout. He banked the orbiter to the west gradually, then to the north as he bled off more airspeed. Duke now realized there wasn't any way the shuttle was going to make it to the Mediterranean, the Red Sea, or even Egypt for that matter.

"Willie, find me a place to land—an airport, military airfield . . . shit, a highway. I don't give a rat's ass, just find me a place that's flat!"

"Sixty-five thousand feet and descending . . . Mach 3.1," Willie called out. *Atlantis,* losing speed, was three minutes fifty-five seconds from touchdown.

"Roll this thing so I can take a look at what's below us." Willie's eyes went from the NAV computer to the window and back to the NAV computer. *Atlantis* was now over the northern part of Sudan.

"Andrea, get ready to get below and jettison the door. Willie, you've got about thirty seconds to find us something or we jump," Duke ordered, keeping them on a twenty-two-degree glide slope to the surface.

Willie searched the constantly changing NAV computer display. In the left-hand corner of the screen was a small black circle with a red line through it. It was a 10,000-foot runway. *"Hot damn!* I have us a runway. NAV says use only in extreme emergency."

"This is *extreme,* Willie. Where is it?"

Willie pulled against his shoulder restraints, looking out the shuttle's window. He could see the brown, lifeless desert below.

"Turn left, heading two four zero," Willie commanded.

Duke moved the stick left, feeling the shuttle respond sluggishly.

Willie watched the terrain start to change from flat to broken gullies and hills. Then suddenly, "General, I see something. It's an airstrip."

"Confirm the location," Duke said.

Willie's eyes went back to the NAV computer. "This is it. Either you set us down here or let us bail out. We're at thirty-two thousand," Willie warned.

"Watch those cargo bays, Andi. Give me a heading, Willie."

"Turn right, heading one niner eight. You see it? Down there between those two broken ridges."

"Yeah, I see it," Duke said. The *Atlantis* was almost on a direct heading for the runway. Duke studied the thin black line, trying to estimate its length. It looked like 10,000 feet, but it was hard to tell.

Duke looked over the nose of the shuttle into a blur of gray and brown. He banked *Atlantis* north, then to the east. When the HUD read 25,000 feet, he banked the ship 180 degrees, watching his airspeed fall rapidly. He could see the silhouette of two jagged mountain ridges out in front of him. Night was falling here. The darkening sky gave Duke a hell of a time seeing the runway.

"Come on, baby, hold together." He lined up the shuttle's nose with the runway, leveling the orbiter.

"There. Between those ridges." Willie shook his finger, pointing in the direction.

"We've hit the jackpot!" Duke exclaimed, as the black pavement stretched out ahead of them. It was void of any markings and appeared to be abandoned.

"Airspeed 516 knots and dropping. Altitude 9,000 feet." Willie was back to business.

"I'm taking her down," Duke announced.

Atlantis shuddered, suddenly veering sharply to the left. The spacecraft yawed back and forth and its nose pitched up twelve degrees. Duke instinctively pushed the stick to the right and down, trying to compensate.

"It's the right cargo door; it's . . . it's gone," Andrea quavered, being jounced in her seat.

"Hold on, it's going to be rough." *Atlantis* was coming in fast and high. With all his strength, Duke pitched the nose down three degrees. Every knot of airspeed the shuttle lost she flew more like a rock than a plane. She wanted to pitch up to the left and Duke battled the heavy stick, cautiously edging her toward the ground.

Duke, conscious of his airspeed, estimated he had only one or two more minutes of evening light left before he would lose sight of the runway. Feeling his way through the dark with a sleek fighter was one thing, but this battle-ax had a mind of her own.

He pushed the stick forward, the space plane vibrating in protest. The nose of the orbiter lined up at the end of the runway. He placed both hands on the stick and thought of Katie. *If I miss this runway, she'll never believe it,* he thought.

"Willie, get the gear down and locked." Duke didn't dare let go of the stick.

"Okay . . . three down and locked. Five hundred feet. Four hundred feet . . . a little low, Duke."

Duke could barely make out the edge of the black asphalt. Lights flickering in the distant hills distracted him, but he focused back to the runway.

"Seventy-five feet . . . here we go." Duke booted the right rudder pedal gently as *Atlantis* hit the pavement.

"Touchdown!" Willie reached out, deploying the drag chute.

The nose wheel hit the ground, and Duke applied steady pressure on the brakes. The shuttle vibrated, rolling to a stop at the end of the runway.

16

"Praise Allah . . . praise Allah," the guard whispered in amazement at the sight of the giant white plane rolling to stop. The low evening light allowed him to see that its leading edges were still glowing pink from reentry, adding to his bewilderment. He could see long black streaks along its side, as if the plane had been burned during its return to earth. And the upper section of it didn't look right, as if maybe it was gone.

The guard, standing on the fringe of the camp overlooking the runway, stared for a moment longer, not knowing what to do. Then, suddenly, he dropped his rifle and ran toward the main camp, shouting.

Majeed, who was now in charge of the camp's security, lifted his head, putting his fork down at the commotion outside his quarters. The sound of men shouting and running was excited and urgent. Soon the noise was closer and before he could reach the door, it was thrust open.

"Come quickly, Majeed, come quickly." Rilmi, one of the younger men in the camp, was breathing heavily, and Majeed could barely understand him.

Majeed held up his hand. "What is it? What has happened?"

"Come quickly. A giant white plane has just landed on the runway!"

"What! A plane? Is it Libyan?"

"No, no." His eyes wide, he went on, "I have not ever seen a plane like this. I do not know."

Majeed, grabbing his Uzi, rushed out the door.

"Has anyone told Ajami?" he inquired.

"No, he is with Jibril," came the answer from Rilmi.

"Get him. I will meet him at the runway. Go quickly," Majeed shouted, moving briskly ahead.

Down the dark path, between the stone structures, Majeed was careful not to stumble. When he reached the top of the small hill overlook-

157

ing the runway, he paused, sighting the aircraft. Before him was a sight he had only seen in pictures. The white body and black stubby nose were dirty, and waves of heat radiated off the wings. What Majeed guessed to be part of the fuselage was damaged. He couldn't read the lettering on the side of the aircraft, but didn't need to: there was only one country it could belong to.

It had been a day since Kamal had been stripped of his command and led away to the holding area. Feeling strange and confused, he repeatedly went over the events in his mind. He could understand Ajami's suspicions, but he couldn't believe that his friend and leader presumed him to be a traitor. Ajami could turn on anyone; Kamal knew that. But this was the first time he had ever not stood behind Kamal.

The dingy underground room made of reinforced concrete was located in the rear of one of the smaller underground command bunkers. Before being abandoned, it had been used to house communication equipment. Kamal remembered when he and his men had bolted heavy steel bars across its center, cutting the room in half. The walls were almost impregnable. The only light came from the open door at the other end of the room. The passageway connected the bunker, via a tunnel, with the rest of the bunkers and storage rooms buried inside the mountain.

Kamal sat on a worn mattress, leaning against the wall. He was bound by nylon cord around his wrists and ankles. He cursed Ajami for ordering this done. *How can I prove my loyalty when I am a prisoner,* he thought, breathing in the smell of urine and mildew from the air.

"Kamal, I have brought you some food," a voice whispered from the shadows.

He watched as a small-bodied person walked across the floor toward him on tiptoes. As the figure drew nearer, Kamal recognized the young woman, Yari.

"Kamal, I am sorry this has happened to you." She knelt down and slid a plate of food under the rusty bars.

"Yari, it is not safe for you to be here. You should not be in here."

"The men were talking. I heard what happened to you." She wanted to let Kamal know she did not believe the stories about him.

"How did you get in here? Where is the guard?" Kamal's gruffness masked his true concern for her well-being.

"There is something going on at the runway. A plane has landed, and no one knows what it is. He left with the other men to see it," Yari whispered.

Kamal began to question. "No one knows what it is . . ."

"I am worried, Kamal. Will they kill you?" Yari clung to the bars, wanting to help.

"You must not worry about me. I can take care of myself." He softened his tone and looked into her compassionate brown eyes. "Thank you, Yari. Take the plate with you. They must not know you were here." He reached down and took the boiled chicken off the plate. "Now, go on. Go. Out with you."

Yari reached out and stroked Kamal's face through the bars before scurrying from the room.

Duke's stiff fingers unwrapped themselves from around the control stick. He automatically surveyed his crew and cabin.

"You both okay?" The muscles in his arms were trembling from their deorbit, and he tried to shake it off.

"I'm all right, I think." Andrea was rubbing her hand around her limbs, soothing the strain from tension more than anything else.

"Shut down all the electrical systems we can, including environmental controls. We can't risk a fire." Duke guessed the temperature inside the spacecraft was reaching 120 degrees. "Where the hell we land, Willie?"

"The NAV says we're at an abandoned air base in northern Chad, twenty miles south of the Libyan border." Willie wiped his face with a towel Andrea handed him, then read the rest of the data. "According to the charts, Chad's air force hasn't used this base for over five years." Willie looked up at Duke.

Duke's eyes came across the instrumentation again. "Activate the emergency search-and-rescue locator."

Willie did as he was told, hitting the S and R transmitter. A positive response symbol appeared on his NAV screen. *Atlantis'* S-band and UHF radios were down, but at least the S and R transmitter was operating. Now they just had to wait for a NOAA-9 SARSAT, orbiting above them, to pick up the signal.

"No response on S and R." Willie sighed. "Do you smell that? It's acid."

"Yeah, I smell it," Duke said.

They were stranded in a country that had less than friendly relations with the U.S.; however, they weren't enemies. Libya, on the other hand, didn't know the meaning of friendly. NASA had an emergency landing agreement with all countries, but this was DoD's mission and not everyone cooperates with the laws of their government.

"I hope the natives aren't hostile," Duke said, half joking and half serious.

"Looks like we're going to find out. We have company." Willie gestured out the side window at three men walking toward them.

The pale glow of a lantern one of them carried reflected just enough light so that Willie could see wooden rifle stocks. "I think they're carrying guns. What are we going to do, Duke?"

"We don't do anything right now. It's best to let them think no one is on board until we can figure out who they are." Duke turned to Andrea. "Andi, we need to fix that radio. Come on, let's move to the lower deck."

The news had traveled fast. By the time Abu Ajami reached the runway, nearly half of the terrorist camp had gathered around the plane. Some of the men were shining flashlights along its side; others were standing with their weapons pointed, ready to fire. A few kept their distance, fearing the plane was some kind of a trap.

When Ajami heard that an unknown aircraft had landed, his first thought was that his camp was being attacked. Then he crested the hill and saw it. The shuttle looked much different than the images he had seen on CNN while living in southern Lebanon. It was smaller and boxy. And the sides were dirty black, as if the shuttle had been burned. *Why would a space plane land here,* he asked himself.

Ajami's mind swirled with a thousand thoughts as he tried to understand what was taking place. Had Allah delivered this to Ajami? Why else would it be here?

Of course, it was a gift from Allah. He was being repaid for Adib Hamen's misfortune. Righteousness was on his side.

As Ajami approached, he saw one of his men lying doubled up on the ground, crying in pain. Ajami addressed Majeed from behind. "What is the problem with that man? Why is he screaming?"

"He touched part of the plane. His hand is burned," Majeed answered.

Ajami looked the situation over for a few seconds. "Clear these men away from here," he ordered and made a sweeping motion with his hand. "I want them out of the area."

"Yes, my leader. Everyone back to your post or to your quarters," Majeed shouted. He raised his Uzi into the air and pulled the trigger. A burst of automatic machine-gun fire erupted, getting everyone's attention.

Ajami spun around and looked at four men standing next to the nose of the space plane. "You four."

They snapped to attention.

"Set up a perimeter around the plane. Do not let anyone get near it. Understand? No one."

The men nodded and spread out to take up their positions around the orbiter.

"So, what do we have here?" Jibril said, his thin lips curling into a smile as he walked up behind Ajami. Two of his men were standing behind him with their rifles across their chests. Jibril stood with his hands on his hips as the rest of Ajami's men made their way back to the mountainside above the runway.

"Praise Allah's holy name." The Libyan had just noticed the black letters UNITED STATES on the side of the white plane. They were barely visible in the darkness.

"I thought I told you to remain in my quarters. This does not concern you." Ajami's voice cracked with anger.

Jibril ignored the comment. "An American space shuttle," he mumbled to himself. "How did it get here?"

Ajami smirked. "How do you think it got here, you fool. It landed." He was hoping to avoid this.

Ajami caught Majeed's attention in the darkness. "Come with me. You, too, Captain. Leave your men behind. We must talk."

The three men walked about forty feet parallel to the right side of the spacecraft and away from the others.

"Majeed, give me your flashlight," Ajami demanded.

He snapped on the switch of the light and moved the bright beam back and forth along the side of the plane. Up close Ajami estimated its large tail was at least 100 feet high. The black leading edge of the wings now blended into the fast-approaching night. Ajami moved the beam, noticing the dark black smudges along its sides and upper fuselage. The right cargo bay door was completely torn off, exposing a large charred black object. There were deep burn marks in the tiles, and sections of the shuttle's honeycombed superstructure could be seen. The crew cabin looked intact. Ajami focused the light in the window, not seeing anything. He felt his heart starting to pump faster. *What good fortune that the shuttle has been delivered to me,* he thought.

Ajami walked another fifty feet toward the back of the spacecraft. He stopped near the back and focused the beam on the tail section. It was then he realized the black marks along the shuttle's side were not made from reentry but from something else. The damage was too extensive. The lower part of the tail was burned away, and one of the main engines was melted and twisted. The front part of the spacecraft had fared much better.

"It looks as if it is badly damaged, possibly by a fire," Ajami finally said. "There must have been a malfunction."

"Yes, I agree." Jibril rubbed his chin.

"Ajami, do you wish that I escort the captain and his men back to the camp?" Majeed interrupted.

"Do not treat me as an outsider, Majeed. You are only here because my country allows you to be here," Jibril shouted back.

"Enough . . . enough!" Ajami cried out. "We will use this to liberate the Palestinian people. It has been sent to us from Allah." He stepped between the two men with his hands raised. "We can argue about this later. Right now, I am concerned with the Americans. Yes, the Americans. Are you both so stupid to think it landed here on purpose? Have either one of you thought how they are going to react to this? One of their space planes sits in the middle of the desert. I am sure they are searching for it now as we speak. We must hide it and hope they do not know where to look. Then we will have to plan a strategy to use this to our best advantage."

"To our advantage . . . Are you an idiot, Ajami? You should leave it here and abandon this air base at once. Let the Americans come and claim what is theirs," Jibril answered in disbelief, not moving his gaze from the space plane.

"I WILL NOT! This is a gift from Allah, to me, Abu Ajami."

"No, it is not a gift, but a curse. The Americans will come and kill everyone; I told you they know of your operations here. Besides, you do not even have the firepower to challenge them. Everything you have worked for will be destroyed," Jibril protested.

"I may not have the firepower, but your government does. I order you to contact Major Nittal and he will decide for himself. He will understand that Allah has brought us the power we now control." There wasn't any question now: in Allah's eyes he would be the new leader of the Palestinian people. And this American shuttle would be his first step toward defeating the Great Satan.

Jibril was quietly running the scenario through his mind. Ajami was correct; it was not up to him. Major Nittal was in charge of Libya's southeastern defenses and controlled the MiGs and air defenses at the Libyan air base of Aujila to the north. He knew the major's great hatred for the West. Besides, Nittal was a boastful and arrogant little man. He would be willing to challenge the Americans for something that would give him power and favor with Colonel Qaddafi. If Jibril turned tail and ran, the major would have his head.

"Listen to me, Jibril," Ajami said, interrupting his thoughts. "Together we can defend this camp. The Arab world can learn a lot from a machine like this. I want to know what this shuttle is carrying. I will make the United States squirm like a helpless child."

Jibril was listening to every word Ajami was saying. *Maybe it is true . . . We could both benefit from this.*

Both men glanced at each other, remaining silent.

"Majeed, gather a team of men," Ajami finally said. "I want this plane towed into the largest and most fortified bunker . . . number two. Put the camp on maximum alert. I want all the men to take up their defensive positions at once. We need to prepare for intruders."

Without question, Majeed pivoted and headed after the departing guards, shouting orders.

"Contact Nittal. Tell him I need additional air defense missiles, fighter aircraft, tanks, mines, everything they can spare. I want to set up a perimeter around this camp. We need to double, triple our strength. When the Americans come, we will be ready."

THE PENTAGON

Major General Warren E. Clark was just returning from lunch. It was 1:30 in the afternoon and the thought of a quick nap sounded like a good idea as he walked at a steady pace to his Pentagon office. The long, heavy lunch had been a rarity for him. Pentagon colleagues talked him into joining them for a change and were obviously accustomed to consuming the rich, fatty food each day. Though they were all about the same age, mid-fifties, he was at least twenty pounds lighter than the rest of them. *I won't be doing that again too soon,* he told himself.

As he headed up the stairs to the second floor, Clark yawned and then took a couple of breaths, trying to get some oxygen in his system. When he reached his office, he glanced at the oil painting hanging directly on the wall behind his chair. The picture was a gift from one of his old units. An A-10 Thunderbolt II, its cannon blazing away, was approaching an Iraqi tank in the desert.

General Clark wore two hats, of which only one was publicly known. He was the overall commander of the Air Force Special Operation Command, based at Hurlburt Field, Florida. AFSOC was responsible for moving special operations teams, such as the Green Berets, into and out of areas of conflict. His other job was considered a "black" command and only a handful of officers in the Pentagon knew about it. Clark was the leader, and to some degree the driving force, behind the newly formed and highly classified Special Operations Unified Command Team, or SOUCT (pronounced Sock-T).

An air force lieutenant colonel by the name of Brice Madison had first written about the concept of a unified team five years ago while attending the School for Advanced Military Studies. Madison suggested that, with the cold war over, the United States needed to shift some of its focus away from large global battles to smaller encounters that, if gone unchallenged, could eventually erupt into major conflicts. He proposed the idea of developing a highly trained and independent-thinking squadron of air force fighters that could be deployed to an overseas base in less than twelve hours.

Clark had read the paper and liked the idea. However, making changes at the Pentagon was sometimes like trying to turn a supertanker in the length of a football field. Nevertheless, he succeeded. After the Iraqi war, his superiors agreed that a small, hard-hitting force could be used. Clark had spent the last four years getting the SOUCT concept off the drawing board. He had also made sure the team was a team. One of the problems in the Iraqi war had been bringing all of the elements of the military together into one effective fighting unit. Clark thought of it as a football team, one in which the defense practices in Florida, the offense in Montana, and the special teams in California. On Sunday they came together and played. Obviously, the team wouldn't be very effective. And the next time there was a crisis, the United States couldn't count on having six months to prepare for it.

To carry out this innovation, the Pentagon had to reinvent itself. Three staging areas were set up: one at Iráklion Air Base in Crete, one at Okinawa Air Base, and one on Diego Garcia in the Indian Ocean. In addition to these bases, the United States secured agreements with its allies to provide fuel, munitions, communications equipment, food, and lodging at key airfields around the world. If a friendly country or U.S. vital interests were threatened, this allowed an immediate response time. The air force called it global reach.

Each squadron was a highly trained composite wing, a combined unit of air force, army, and marine elements. They consisted of a mix of aircraft including F-117As, A-10 Thunderbolts, F-15Es, and F-16s. Supporting aircraft for SOUCT included two KC-10s and a classified EC-141 Airborne Command Center. In addition, the regional commanders for each SOUCT had the authority to pull what was needed from the other branches of the military. Once deployed, the team could attack and keep an enemy off balance long enough for reinforcements to arrive.

SOUCT was still considered experimental, so Clark was having to spend a lot of time talking to the right people to make sure it maintained its funding. He knew his special ops concept was different from the other branches of the military and he would have a hard time explaining their mission to the lawmakers on the Hill. For the sake of simplicity, Clark broke their responsibilities into categories that included direct action, special reconnaissance, counterterrorism, and unconventional warfare.

"General Clark, I have Chairman Jack Dawson on line three," the office secretary startled him from his lethargy.

"What? Oh, sorry. Thanks." Clark must have walked right past his secretary, not even noticing her. "Clark here."

"It's a good thing you're in town, Warren. I need you in my office ASAP. I need you to bring Special Operation Plan 11084."

Clark thought for a second. SIOP-11084. That was Operation Prairie

Fire. And that meant trouble . . . trouble for the space shuttle. "Prairie Fire?"

"Right. *Atlantis* is down."

The word was flowing down the chain of command very quickly. Mark Collins had received a call on his car phone, from Staffer, to get his ass over to the Pentagon pronto. Jack Dawson needed a CIA Middle East analyst to help piece together data on where the shuttle *Atlantis* might have gone down.

So much for sneaking home early, Collins thought. He was now standing in Mitchell L. Burnell's third-floor Pentagon office. A fifty-seven-year-old retired marine lieutenant colonel, Mitchell was the Defense Intelligence Agency's national intel officer overseeing North Africa and the Middle East. He reported directly to the head of the DIA, an army three star, and coordinated intelligence for the air force, navy, army, and marines. His summaries were well respected around the Pentagon and CIA for their tough, unbiased evaluations of world situations.

Mitchell and Collins had worked together as a select team evaluating raw intelligence, digesting it, and reporting their findings directly to the JCS, DCI, and secretary of defense. They worked well together because neither man worried about being tactful and just told the story the way he saw it.

"We're damned lucky," Mitchell said to Collins, his tone serious. "I just got off the horn with Dawson. He's setting up the meeting in two minutes."

"Thanks." Collins placed the fuzzy gray-and-black satellite photos in his briefcase and left the room. He wished he had a little more time to look the material over. Dawson was sure to be in a shitty mood.

The room was officially known as 2E878, the office of the chairman of the Joint Chiefs of Staff. General Warren Clark, turning left, passed through a series of doorways and made his way through the small reception area into the office. The carpet was a deep chestnut and the chairs matched with a swirling beige and tan southwestern pattern. He was the first person to arrive, and Chairman Jack Dawson was still on the phone.

Dawson put his hand over the mouthpiece. "Sit down, Warren. I'll be right with you."

Clark studied the general while he waited. His appearance didn't fit the stereotyped image of the model JCS. He was somewhat overweight, his hair was rarely combed, and for the most part he looked like an unmade bed.

Everyone knew Dawson loved to talk to the press and never missed an opportunity to testify before Congress. He had a special way of communicating with people and it was only when others saw the man at work that his real talents showed through.

Clark looked out the window to his left, admiring a grand view of the icy blue waves of the Potomac and the national monuments.

". . . I understand that, John, but until I have concrete evidence as to what happened up there and where *Atlantis* is right now, I recommend we don't talk to anyone. *Including* the Russians. I understand Weber's position, but for Christ's sake, give me a chance to piece this thing together. Then we can think this through and come up with a game plan."

Clark could see Dawson's face stiffen. It was clear the secretary of defense, John Turner, was putting pressure on him. Turner was generally low-key and supported the military as long as everything was well thought out. It made Clark wonder where the real pressure was coming from.

"Give me twenty-four hours, John. I don't even know if *Atlantis* is in one piece or not, much less where it is. What are the Russians bawling about, anyway? All they lost was a reconnaissance satellite. I'm missing three astronauts and a $3 billion shuttle! If I don't have any answers in twenty-four hours, then Weber can personally escort every Russian around every facility we have to prove we are not hiding it and pulling one over on them. Are you with me on this, or not?"

There was a short pause.

"Good. I'll see you in about thirty minutes." Dawson hung up the phone and, sighing heavily, turned to Clark. He got right to the point. "Warren, I need your help. It seems the State Department has already decided that the *Atlantis* has crashed and the Russians are hollering foul play." He leaned back in his chair, staring at the ceiling.

"What does the president say?" Clark asked.

"That's another problem. He's in Japan at the Asian Economic Cooperation Conference. Secretary of State Weber has advised him not to fly home. Weber seems to think it may cause some sort of international incident if he reacts too frantically. He's also advising him to contact the countries involved and start asking them to assist in an all-out search. Turner and I have been asked to play this thing down and use the UN if need be. I can't imagine what's on Weber's mind. We know the shuttle is down and I'm worried about the fucking Libyans here, not wheat farmers in Kansas."

Just then Mark Collins tapped on the door and walked into the office.

"General Warren Clark, meet Mark Collins, CIA. Collins is a Middle East intelligence analyst."

The two men shook hands, taking their seats.

Dawson spoke to Collins first, hoping he had something beneficial. "What have you got for me, Mark?"

"I'm going to speak frankly." Collins started by opening his briefcase and removing a plain manila file. "I pulled these six photos off the printer just before I left. They were the last pictures taken by our KH-14 before it moved out of the area." He handed them to Dawson. "It will take a few hours before the National Photo Interpretation Center has time to run them through their computer and clean out the fuzz and blurs."

Dawson lined the six black-and-white photos across the center of his desk. All he and Clark could see were a couple of long fuzzy objects with blotches of black and gray running through the center of each picture. The final one of the series had a faint gray spot on the lower corner of the photo.

Dawson finally looked up at Collins, puzzled. He always wondered about guys who lived in the world of black boxes and computer screens. "Well, I can't figure it out; tell me what the hell these are."

"What I'm showing you is a series of six black-and-white infrared imaging photographs. They start at an altitude of 100,000 feet." Collins pointed to the first photo. "Down to 10,000 feet. This last photo is two mountain ranges running east and west. I believe this faint dark strip is a runway, but I'm not sure . . . and the faint white spot is a very hot heat source. It very well could be *Atlantis* right after it came out of orbit. Or it could be an oil well fire."

"Is the object, whatever it is, intact?"

"It's hard to tell, but I'm willing to bet if that's the shuttle, it came down in one piece."

Dawson leaned back in his chair before speaking. "Let me update you on what I have so far, gentlemen, so you understand my dilemma. NASA can only tell me that *Atlantis* went down somewhere in North Africa or the Mediterranean. We don't have a damned thing off any of our SAR-SATs, and NORAD says they're still looking into the situation and they should be able to narrow it down to a hundred square miles by tomorrow morning. The radar at Ali Ballas is down, and the NSA says their listening posts haven't picked up a damn thing. And to top things off, the DIA is running around with a corncob up their ass telling me to be patient. The only thing I have to go on is what you've brought me. Now, until I hear differently, I'm going with this info."

"Sir, you must realize this is preliminary stuff," Collins said, unfazed. "I'm not even sure what I'm looking at." He knew better than to cave in and tell the general what he wanted to hear. It was better to absorb the pressure and do the right thing. He shook his head. "I can't confirm right now if this is the shuttle or not. Like I said—"

"Where is this?" Dawson interrupted, circling the area with his finger, ignoring Collins's resistance.

"If this is the shuttle, and, like I said, I'm not sure it is, then it went down in a mountainous region of northern Chad. But I'm telling you, sir, I can't be certain about what this really is. We're damned lucky to even have these photos. The satellite that took them was almost out of the area. It was pure blind luck."

Dawson, understanding Collins's desire to be accurate, asked, "Okay. How soon can you confirm this is the *Atlantis?*"

"In two, maybe three hours. As soon as I wash the current stuff through the computer and enhance it."

"When's the next satellite pass?"

"Tomorrow morning."

"Great. Over twelve *fucking* hours." Dawson rubbed his forehead and sat back in his chair.

"Warren, how soon can you get me a team in that region to find out what's going on?" He looked at Clark, not ready to give up.

As usual, Dawson was way ahead of everyone and Clark wasn't going to be left holding anybody's garbage. "What kind of team did you have in mind?"

"Well, you tell me. I would guess a small unit that can sneak in, give us a report, and, if need be, sneak out again if we're wrong."

"I can deploy Pathfinder team Alpha in six hours, General. I just need your order," Clark answered, satisfied that Dawson wasn't wanting to go in irrationally. "If *Atlantis* has landed at this air base, it would be best to have someone on the ground feeding us solid intel."

"Pathfinder?" Dawson asked. He had forgotten he was dealing with the world of special operations; they were just as bad as the black box guys.

"They're a small mobile recon force, assigned with Cobra team sir, stationed at Iráklion Air Base in Crete. Pathfinder is small, fast, and lethal, if need be." Clark, picturing in his mind how to start executing a mission for the situation, added, "We can use Egypt as a jumping-off point."

"All right, you've got it. I'll get Turner to sign the order this afternoon." The chairman's charge-forward type of attitude took both men by surprise as he continued, "General Clark, you're in command of this special operations task force and I want you to report directly to me. At this point, I don't want any of the CINCs involved; they'll just gum up the system if we have to move fast." He paused, gathering his thoughts. "Also, start setting up your operations inside the Special Technical Operations Center here at the Pentagon and begin formulating a plan to recover the *Atlantis* and her crew, dead or alive. That was an air force mission and Duke James was commanding it. I'll be damned if I'm going to sit back and wait for all the red tape before we move." Dawson checked his watch. "You have fifty-five minutes to get things rolling, then I want you both back here. I'm meeting Turner within the hour and I need you with me."

"Yes, sir," Clark said.

Dawson looked at Collins. "Mind if I keep these?" he said, referring to the photos.

"No, sir."

"All right. Let's get to work, gentlemen."

NORTH AMERICAN AEROSPACE DEFENSE COMMAND, COLORADO SPRINGS

Admiral Petersen sat in his office staring at the stack of unopened mail on the edge of his desk, his mind replaying the thought that he could have prevented *Atlantis* possibly being a burning hole somewhere in the desert. NORAD had suddenly become a very somber place, as everyone did their part to try and find the spacecraft. With his door closed, he sat back sipping his coffee, letting the liquid warm his insides. Coffee always seemed to taste better when the weather was turning cold. He tried to get his mind on other things, such as the fishing trip his oldest son had planned for the weekend. The walleyes were biting at Pueblo reservoir, and Petersen had promised his son they wouldn't miss out on the fall action again this year.

"Admiral, Lieutenant Holloway is here to see you." The sound of his assistant's crackling voice over the intercom broke the silence.

"Yes, send her in." He had nearly forgotten about the assignment he had given her and even wondered if it would be of any use now.

"Hello, Admiral." Brenda Holloway thought the admiral looked pale and listless.

"Have a seat, Lieutenant," Petersen said, smiling, trying to be polite. He liked Holloway. She was bright and dedicated, always going the extra mile in everything she did. If Petersen gave her an assignment, she wouldn't do only the minimum required, but would research everything thoroughly, making sure her data was correct and accurate. It was a quality he respected in anyone, not just young officers.

Holloway sat in the chair across from him and set a thick file folder on his desk. "This is the report you requested. It has to do with the Russian Kosmos satellite."

Petersen nodded. He didn't want to make her efforts futile in light of the situation. He listened, trying to look interested.

"The reason I'm here, sir, is because I'm concerned about what I found. I know—ordinarily—under these circumstances—the report would be moot." She spoke haltingly as she pulled out several computer-generated color pictures of the Kosmos satellite. "As you know, we used the Lacrosse radar-imaging satellite to get an electronic image of the exterior and interior of the Kosmos. Well, I used my computer to colorize the data. You instructed me to find out why the satellite was tumbling unevenly." She held up two of the pictures so the admiral could see them. "It seems the Kosmos has some very dense areas where the radar from the Lacrosse couldn't penetrate." Holloway pointed to one end of the satellite. "This large dark blue area in the middle is the reactor core, I'm certain. It's easy to identify. All older Soviet satellites have the same basic makeup. What I can't explain are these other dark blue spots. As you can see, there are ten of them, two rows of five, and each is about a sixth the size of the reactor."

Petersen was quiet as he looked over the pictures. The dark spots were in the same area as the round hatch doors he had questioned the Russian space adviser about two days earlier in Washington. His mind leaped. The Russian had told him the hatches covered empty compartments. It was clear from Holloway's pictures, they weren't empty. He wondered what this meant.

"And now that *Atlantis* has come out of orbit . . . Well, I thought . . ."

"Thought what, Lieutenant?" Petersen's eyes didn't leave the pictures.

"This dark blue color tells me the reactor and these other ten round blotches are made of the same basic materials. They are both very dense and are both heavy metals."

Petersen's eyes lit up like firecrackers. "The color of the reactor— Are you saying they could both be nuclear material? This could be very serious, Lieutenant."

"I know, sir, that's why I brought it to your attention."

"Is there any way you can be sure of this?"

"I'm not an expert, but this would explain why the Kosmos was tumbling unevenly."

"Good work, Lieutenant. Make a copy of this report for me, and fax one to Staffer at the CIA and one to General Dawson at the Pentagon."

"Yes, sir."

Petersen picked up his phone. "Liz, make arrangements for me to be on the next flight to Washington." The fishing trip was going to have to wait again. He hoped his son would understand.

SPECIAL TECHNICAL OPERATIONS CENTER, PENTAGON

As a young lieutenant colonel, Warren Clark had helped draw up many of the conceptual designs that were now the cornerstones of the Special Technical Operations Center, or simply room 2C865. The center was fondly known as the Star Ship *Enterprise,* and the men and women who worked there made sure everyone knew they were members of the Next Generation. The STOC had its own security force and access rules, and each individual of the thirty-two-member team was required to take a lie detector test at least once every thirty days. The technical equipment inside the Special Technical Operations Center allowed the Pentagon and civilian leaders to communicate instantly with special operations, or "black," commando teams anywhere in the world. Special operations units could also receive real-time satellite transmissions and be updated on enemy troop movements directly from the STOC. These sensitive operations teams included navy Seals, marine reconnaissance battalions, the Joint Special Operations Command, and air-sea search and rescue units.

Only five seats were occupied at the monitoring stations; the other three were empty. Eight forty-eight-inch color computer screens, arranged in a half circle, were focused on different parts of the world. Clark squinted in the darkness, his eyes still adjusting to the dim room. The flashing red and green symbols on the computer screens reminded him of air traffic control symbols, when in reality they were transmission codes for teams in the field and NSA listening posts.

Clark stood at the back of the room, trying to get a feel for the place. Being stationed in Florida, he didn't often work directly from the STOC, and this would be the first time he would actually direct an operation from here. He had heard that the Special Technical Operations Center now contained some of the military's largest egos.

"General Clark, welcome. It's nice to meet you in person. I'm Captain William Harris." A short, light-skinned man shook his hand. The navy officer wore a pair of half-frame glasses that rested on the end of his nose. He looked fairly young to be a captain, but the gray, thinning hair swooped up to cover his bald head said differently.

Clark had to bite his bottom lip to keep from laughing. He had worked with this man for over two years, coordinating training missions and sharing intelligence. However, this was the first time he had ever met him. His mental picture couldn't have been more wrong. "It's nice to finally put a face with the name," Clark said. "I wish we were meeting under different circumstances, though." He cleared his throat, switching gears. "We don't have a lot of time, Captain. I'd better get started."

"I already have an office set up for you. Please come this way."

The two men walked through the command center and into a side corridor. Harris flipped on the lights to the general's temporary office. The desk was standard government issue, with a black vinyl top and gun metal gray sides. Resting on it were two phones, a coded fax machine, and a desktop computer. The walls were plain white and barren.

Three large windows in front of the desk, and one in the door, allowed him to see the command floor.

"Two doors down to your right you will find the rest rooms, mess hall, and showers. We operate twenty-four hours a day. Meals are delivered every six hours . . . or you can go to the mess hall and eat when you're hungry. I've instructed my staff to allow you access to anything on this floor and, if you need something, to let us know." Harris's tone was direct and emotionless.

"Thank you, Captain." Clark sat down at his desk. "The CIA will be helping with this also. When we receive any data from Langley, I want it transmitted to my staff at Hurlburt Field and to Iráklion Air Base in Crete."

"To whose attention at Iráklion?" Harris broke in.

For an instant Clark forgot he was dealing with a navy man. "Colonel Brice Madison; he's the field and operations leader for Cobra team." His eyes swept across his desk. "Are these lines secure, Captain?"

"Yes, sir, they are. Anything else?" Harris asked.

"No, that will be all." Clark loosened his tie as he watched Harris leave.

He checked his watch: 1500 hours. It had been twenty minutes since the meeting with Dawson and time was flying. If they were going to get a team on the ground before first light, he would have to work double time. Clark pulled out a small black electronic message keeper from his briefcase and turned it on. He pressed the mode button until it read TELE and maintained pressure on the cursor until he came to the name LT COL BRICE MADISON. He dialed the direct-line number appearing next to the name, connecting him to Madison's office a third of the way around the world.

"Colonel Madison's office."

"This is General Clark. I need to speak with the colonel right away. This is urgent."

"I'm sorry, sir, he's in the field. May I take a message?" Clark guessed it was Madison's personal aide.

"*No* . . . I said it was urgent. I expect you to page him. *NOW.*" Clark closed his eyes, trying to keep his irritation in control.

"Yes, sir. Stand by."

Clark hadn't thought Madison would be in his office, anyway, but he had to start somewhere. He just hoped the thirty-five-year-old lieutenant colonel wasn't in a jet fighter at 30,000 feet or buried waist deep in some swamp on a training mission.

"Madison here."

"This is Clark. We have an emergency. As of twenty minutes ago SIOP-11084 is in operation. The shuttle *Atlantis* is down somewhere in northern Chad. I need your Pathfinder team Alpha in there ASAP."

"Yes, sir."

"You will have some intel data in the next few minutes, outlining where we think she went down."

"Is the shuttle intact, sir?"

"We think so, but it hasn't been confirmed. That's why we need your team in there. Get your men and their aircraft fueled, weapons loaded, and prepare to move out on my order. We're working on getting permission from the Egyptians to use their base at Ali Ballas as a staging area." Clark checked his watch again; every minute was vital.

"I understand, sir, we'll be ready."

As with most things in his life, John Turner liked to keep his third-floor Pentagon office clean, orderly, and simple. The forty-five-year-old secretary of defense prided himself on an open door, open mind policy for looking at ways of improving the world's most powerful military. He had earned a tough bipartisan reputation for asking the right questions and not being afraid to cut defense programs that didn't work or weren't needed. His background in running several large defense contractors had given him a strong ego to deal with just about any situation. Even the secretary's dark black hair was robust, showing just a hint of gray.

Turner heard Dawson's gruff voice in the outer office. "We're a few minutes early."

"That's all right, General Dawson. Mr. Turner is expecting you. You may go right in." Amy, his secretary, stood to open the door.

Dawson, with General Clark following, entered Turner's office and the door was closed. The three men exchanged pleasantries, and the meeting began.

"What's the latest, gentlemen?" Turner asked, leaning forward over a gray notepad.

Dawson spoke first. "Mr. Secretary, thirty minutes ago I spoke with General Novak, our military flight director in Houston. NASA, NSA listening posts, and NORAD have been trying to piece together the last few minutes of telemetry received from *Atlantis*. There is strong evidence that the Kosmos satellite received a micro-burst radio transmission broadcast from a Russian ground station near Antarctica just seconds before the crew reported a fire. Novak believes the transmission activated the Kosmos's maneuvering thrusters, causing them to fire, resulting in *Atlantis*'s reentry."

Turner's face didn't change expression. "So, does Novak think it was intentional?"

"We don't know what to think, sir."

"Any word from the Russians?"

"No. If they do have some answers, they aren't sharing a thing." Dawson continued, "Right now, I honestly don't care who is to blame. We have a much bigger problem." He laid several satellite photos on the desk in front of Turner. "I believe *Atlantis* has come down intact at this abandoned military air base in northern Chad. These are IR photos from our last satellite pass a few hours ago. The base is in a rugged section north of the Depression du Mourdi and is only twenty miles south of the Libyan border. It is just inside what is known as the Aozou Strip, a narrow belt of land claimed by Libya and Chad."

Turner exhaled hard. Dawson didn't have to say any more, the secretary understood.

"There is a strong possibility the crew is alive, but so far we are unable to confirm it. I have ordered one of our special ops Pathfinder teams into the area to get a visual. They should be in place in twelve hours. If *Atlantis* is intact, we will need real-time ground recon in addition to our satellites."

"What else is being done?" Turner asked.

"I have stepped up the readiness of the Eighty-second Airborne, and the Division Ready Brigade is on alert and will move out in eighteen hours." Dawson looked down, referring to his notes, his tone even as he continued, "The carrier *John F. Kennedy* is on station off Libya's northern coast. I have ordered her to step up flight operations to send a strong signal to our Libyan friends. I would also suggest we send in another carrier battle group ASAP. That will take another two days. NASA's quick reaction team is looking at plans to recover the *Atlantis* if we say go. My gut feeling, however, is to keep NASA out of this until we know for sure what's going on. I don't want a bunch of civilians in the way."

"I agree. What are your concerns?" Turner looked at the two men sitting before him.

This time General Clark spoke up. "Mr. Secretary, if this base is truly abandoned, then we shouldn't have any problems. I think it is best, though, if we are prepared for the worst. The Libyans are very unpredictable and they have three large military bases within a hundred miles of where *Atlantis* went down. If they chose to, they could be on top of the shuttle in no time. We have only one unit with enough firepower and readiness to stop the Libyans if this should happen."

Turner sat back and looked General Clark squarely in the eye. "Your Special Ops Unified Command Team . . . SOUCT, correct?"

"Yes, sir. My number one unit, Cobra team, is based at Iráklion Air Base in Crete. They can deploy to Ali Ballas, Egypt, in under six hours and be ready to move out in eight." Clark handed the secretary a map showing that the air base at Ali Ballas was just a few miles east of the Egyptian border and only 223 miles from the desert airstrip. "Supplies, fuel, and additional weapons have already been positioned there. All the pilots have to do is move their aircraft."

Turner was contemplative for a minute. General Clark and Colonel Madison had sold Turner on the idea of SOUCT, a high-tech, highly mobile air and ground combat team. However, all three SOUCT teams were unproven in warfare, and Turner wondered if this was the appropriate time to test them.

"General Dawson, is Cobra team ready for this mission?"

"Yes, sir, I believe it is."

"How long have they been operational?" Turner directed the question to Clark.

"Four months."

"Four months! It takes four years to work the bugs out of any new system or concept. Both of you know that. Why do I feel like I'm being handed a cherry on this one?" Turner folded his arms.

Dawson knew it was his place to answer. "John, if I didn't feel that Cobra was ready, you know I would be the last guy in this room to send them in. Let me remind you, Cobra team's weapons systems have been tested and retested. You have to look at the big picture. We started working on this four years ago and used the last few months to iron out the bugs."

Turner nodded. "Do we have permission from Egypt to use the base?"

"Yes. We received it a few minutes ago," Dawson replied.

Turner thought for a moment before speaking. "Okay, let's do this. I'll authorize the *America* and her battle group to move into the area. Proceed with your plan to deploy the Eighty-second Airborne and the DRB, but only after we have confirmation. Weber is going to have to get permission from Chad before we move in. I'll let you deploy Cobra to Ali Ballas in case you're right and the Libyans get any ideas. As soon as you get verification that *Atlantis* is at that base, contact me and we'll go from there."

17

The dark gray C-141B Starlifter snuck in without the aid of its landing lights at the secluded air base in southwestern Egypt known as Ali Ballas. The Egyptians had built the base five years earlier as a warning to the Libyan government, which was increasingly becoming a menace to the region's stability. Ali Ballas was also used as an early warning center. It controlled a number of radar sights looking west. Two years ago, the United States and Egypt had secretly agreed to stockpile American arms, food, and supplies at the staging area. It was a small, obscure base and its location was of strategic importance, ten miles east of the Libyan border.

The engines of the C-141B were still screaming as Marine Captain Bobby Rodriguez stepped off the back ramp of the four-engine jet transport, followed by the rest of Pathfinder team Alpha. As planned, the pilot didn't power down the engines. He had orders to perform a quick turnaround and be airborne again in less than two minutes.

The night was lit with a half-moon and a few stars shining through the thin layer of clouds above. The thirty-year-old captain rubbed his eyes and blinked a few times before looking around. Well conditioned from daily workouts, Rodriguez stood just over five foot eight. His large neck blended into his broad shoulders and solid arms. Narrow at the waist, he wore a standard marine haircut, which gave him a no-nonsense appearance.

The low-visibility red lights of the transport's interior allowed his vision to adjust quickly to the blackness surrounding the aircraft. Rodriguez could feel the hot exhaust radiating off the transport's engines cut through his loose-fitting desert brown fatigues as he turned away from the C-141B. A blast of cool desert air hit his face, nearly blowing off the black skullcap covering his head.

176

Only three hours earlier, Rodriguez had been sitting with his wife and son in the living room of their apartment near Iráklion Air Base in Crete. A phone call later and a quick conference with his commander and he was somewhere in the middle of no-man's-land.

To the envy of his five-member recon team, Rodriguez was the only one who could fall asleep next to a roaring jet engine and never know it was running. This trip was no exception. The other members kept themselves occupied with endless games of blackjack, cups of coffee, and several dozen Reese's peanut butter cups.

Rodriguez readjusted the sling on his Beretta AR-70 assault rifle and threw his heavy backpack over his shoulder. In the darkness, he could see a faint red light blinking about 300 yards away. The short bursts of light illuminated the area so that he could make out a man standing in front of a large black helicopter. The ominous size of the special forces Sikorsky MH-53J Pave Low III helicopter was easy enough to see. A modified MH-53H, the Pave Low III was one of the largest, most complex choppers ever built. It was designed to fly special forces troops at night or in adverse weather over long distances and at high speeds. Packed with advanced technology, including terrain-following radar and forward-looking infrared sensors, the 73,500-pound helicopter rose twenty-nine feet into the air and was seventy-three feet in length. With a range of over 1,300 miles, the Pave Low III was ideally suited for covert operations. Somehow the sheer size of the chopper made Rodriguez feel better, and flying in it was a hell of a lot better than skimming across the desert in the smaller UH-60 Black Hawk.

Rodriguez started to make his way toward the waiting man just as the blades of the helicopter began circling.

"Where the hell are we, sir?" Master Sergeant Ricky Vasquez shouted over the noise of the jet engines as he came even with the captain.

"You'll know soon enough." Rodriguez turned his head into the wind.

Vasquez yawned, "Well, I have an idea. Smells like the desert. It figures, ragheads again."

"Signal the men to hurry up. It's going to be light in seven hours and we don't have much time."

"Yes, sir."

When Rodriguez had signed up for the Marine Corps after college, he never dreamed he'd become the leader of a specialized Pathfinder force recon team. Then again, he never thought his first assignment would be to spend two months behind enemy lines during the Iraqi war, either. But he did, blowing up bridges, vectoring F-111s to their targets, and assisting in the search and rescue of pilots. Times had changed and so had his team. They were faster, smarter, and even more specialized than before. And even though his men came from three different branches of the military—marines, army, and air force—they were a close-knit brotherhood that relied only on themselves. Their job was simple: sneak in behind enemy lines; remain undetected; and report what the bad guys' strengths and weaknesses were. They would sneak back out of the area and no one would ever know the difference, or, if need be, they could cause just enough havoc to throw the enemy off balance before the main team arrived.

Although Rodriguez was a marine officer, he was officially assigned to the air force. He and each of his team had been handpicked when the Air Force Special Operations Command had been formed, and they had trained together for over three years. Each member rightfully believed he could do just about anything. Rodriguez, however, made sure their confidence was measured and never so much as to make them careless and vulnerable to mistakes. He also made sure the training was comparable to the way they would have to survive in combat. He didn't want any surprises, and his biggest concern was leaving one of his men in the field dead or wounded because of his own irresponsibility.

"Captain Rodriguez, I'm Major White, Air Force Intel. Welcome to Egypt."

Rodriguez snapped him a quick salute.

"Right this way, Captain."

Rodriguez lowered his head and followed the man up the back ramp of the helicopter.

"Please tell your men to buckle up. We'll be on our way shortly."

The blades of the MH-53J Pave Low III were starting to kick up some dust, and the noise became almost unbearable as the last of Rodriguez's men took their seats. The captain listened to the hydraulic motors kick in and close the ramp door, killing most of the noise. Five seconds later, they were airborne, heading west.

Space Shuttle *Atlantis*

"What do you think, Andi? Can it be fixed?" Duke asked.

Andrea crawled down the ladder from the flight deck to the lower crew cabin. She and Willie had removed several of the floor access panels in an attempt to repair the UHF and S-band antennae transmit cables.

"I don't know. I've removed as many access panels as I can, and without going outside it's hard to tell. From the tests I've run so far, there's no question the electrical cables leading to the antennae are all disconnected. That smell is some type of acid, probably nitric. The Russians use it along with hydrazine as booster rocket fuel. I'd say the acid has probably dissolved them." Andrea rubbed her nose because of the foul smell. She adjusted the focus of her flashlight to a wider beam.

Duke peered into the small eight-by-fourteen-inch panel hole, looking at the damage. The inside of the panel had a number of charred black spots. He could see several areas where the acid had also eaten through the insulation and into the fuselage.

"I could splice them back together if we could just find where the break is," Andrea said.

"Shit. That means our SARSAT isn't working." Duke was referring to the shuttle's search and rescue satellite transponder. The shuttle's display board indicated it was working, but the up-link antenna wasn't receiving any power.

"You hear that?" Willie asked.

"More gunfire?"

"No. Listen."

Several sharp metal raps rang throughout the inside of the shuttle.

"Yeah," Duke said, this time hearing the noise.

There were several more raps. Then the sound of a muffled engine could be heard as the latches on the storage drawers began to vibrate.

"Willie, come with me. Andi, you hold tight."

Duke and Willie climbed up the ladder to the flight deck and left Andrea searching for a possible linkup to their world.

National Photo Interpretation Center

Martin Frazier liked working alone in his section of the building. The rest of the room was quiet except for the clicking of the printers and the hum of the huge air conditioners used to keep the computer equipment cool. He watched the light on the mainframe as the computer cycled the raw data one more time. He wanted to make certain the KH-14 photos were completely washed before he dumped the digital images out of the hard drive and onto a disk.

The NPIC was responsible for routinely analyzing thousands of satellite images a day. Their job was to enhance satellite photos and extract the information that was needed. Their high-speed digital computers and processing equipment corrected atmospheric distortions, cleared up out-of-focus images, and eliminated ground clutter.

These photos were taking a little longer than he had planned. The quality of the pictures was just as Collins had described, very poor. Frazier hit the insert button, telling the computer to break the color spectrum down into three sets of four color bands. From there he was able to pick out the early evening shadows around the air base and runway, eliminating them. He combined one of the IR signature photos from another set, merging the two. This enhanced the contrast of the entire photo, and for the first time Frazier was able to make out the structures on the ground along the side of the mountain. He then hit the shift key and turned down the color contrast just a bit.

If I get this right, Collins is going to owe me two tickets to the Redskins, he thought.

As part of the team at the NPIC, this wasn't the first time he had worked with Mark Collins in a crunch. It seemed in the last few years if there was any action in the Middle East, Collins was on top of it.

The picture nearly jumped off the screen. Frazier pressed the data storage button on his keyboard and down-loaded all the data onto a 3.5-inch floppy. A few seconds later, he inserted the disk into a smaller PC in the corner of his office. The computer he had been using couldn't interface with the one that Collins used at the CIA, so he needed the PC to transfer the data to him.

Frazier hit the send button. In ten minutes Collins would have the information on his computer at the CIA.

CIA HEADQUARTERS

Mark Collins felt irritable after a brief hourlong nap on a nearby couch. He rubbed his face and ran his fingers through his oily hair, trying to shake the tired feeling.

The office door was closed and he walked over to sit at his desk. The room was dark except for the light of a brass lamp and the glowing blue computer screen. Collins had piled the CIA files and computer disks he kept in a small fireproof safe behind him. On a chair next to him were a half-eaten Domino's pizza and a six-pack of Coke he had ordered two hours ago.

Collins had prioritized the files, stacking the intelligence summaries squarely in front of him. Each file contained four satellite images along with reports done previously by the CIA's Intelligence side. Collins picked up the top photo and leaned back in his chair, studying it. An older shot, it was taken at a high altitude above 95,000 feet. There were numbers on the bottom reading TR-2/1191-17963, indicating the picture was from a TR-2 reconnaissance bird. This particular photo had been taken after the UN imposed a truce on Chad and Libya several years ago. Collins picked up the corresponding paper. The report stated that a total of five missions were flown at the request of Chad's government and the UN to verify that the Libyan troops were pulling out of the area. It was noted that the Libyans had actually retreated only five miles inside their own border. The cease-fire agreement had merely specified that each country should return to their preconflict positions. The UN had then created a buffer zone along the Aozou Strip, which runs the length of Libya's southern border with Chad and is approximately fifty miles wide.

Collins flipped the picture and paper over, going on to the next photo. It was only six months old. This one had been taken by a CIA-controlled KH-12 satellite. It had been analyzed by someone at the NPIC, evident by three dark circles drawn around what looked like small towns. He skimmed through the report looking for related information. A large number of tanks, MiG fighter aircraft, and heavy artillery were being moved in to three separate bases around the towns of Aujila, Al Jabbubi, and Sawmua, the largest base being Aujila, which was only forty-eight miles from Chad's border.

Collins looked at the photo again. Just by eyeballing, he figured Aujila to be seventy-eight miles from the base where *Atlantis* might have landed. He moved on to the next photo, thinking that was a lot of firepower so close to the shuttle.

"Yeah, I remember this one," he murmured. It was a recon picture of Madadhi. The grainy appearance and lighter gray scale had remained through several washes of the image-enhancement computer.

Collins's mind suddenly switched from the shuttle to the MiG-23 attack. Then it hit him. *A remote air base . . . Of course! If I wanted to fly a MiG-23 and attack an American cruise liner, where would I operate from?* Collins asked himself. *Madadhi Air Base. Could this be where Ajami is operating out of?*

He checked the code number. It revealed that the photo came from an Israeli RF-4C Phantom reconnaissance jet flying at 72,000 feet. He picked up the corresponding report and read on.

1] SUPPLIED BY ISRAELI INTELLIGENCE

2] MOSSAD HAS STRONG REASON TO BELIEVE THAT TERRORISTS HAVE RELOCATED TO THIS BASE IN NORTHERN CHAD. POSSIBLE PALESTINIAN TERRORISTS WANTED BY ISRAELI DEFENSE FORCES FOR THE MURDER OF CAPTURED ISRAELI GROUND TROOPS IN SOUTHERN LEBANON.

3] TERRORISTS ARE BEING SUPPLIED WEAPONS BY MEMBERS OF THE SPECIAL FORCES BRANCH OF THE LIBYAN MILITARY.

Collins saw that the report was dated only five months ago. Just then his computer came to life. Someone was transmitting a document over the network's secure fiber optics modem.

Frazier can move fast when he wants to, Collins thought, as he folded a slice of pizza lengthwise and stuck it in his mouth.

He had requested priority processing from the NPIC on four color photos of the possible landing site of the shuttle. The color monitor of his computer was filling with a detailed three-dimensional picture of the desert. A long black runway ran from the right corner to the center of the screen, and the mountains were now a series of multicolored lines like the ones on a topographic map. The white outline of *Atlantis* could be seen on the end of the runway.

"Well, I'll be . . . There it is." Collins took a sip of his Coke, then picked up a pencil. "Now, if I call this right, Frazier should be phoning me any minute." He took another sip and looked at the phone just as it rang.

"Collins," he answered.

"This is Marty. Are you getting them?"

"Yep. They look good," Collins said, after swallowing a bite of pizza.

"Yeah, some of my best work and in record time. I think you owe me . . . again."

"Let me guess. My tickets to the next Skins' game, just for pushing buttons."

"Bingo," Frazier laughed.

"You got 'em. I gotta go; Clark needs these," Collins said, hanging up the phone.

Special Technical Operations Center, Pentagon

"The Pathfinder team is in the air, General Clark. The pilot needs the location of the drop in ten minutes." Captain Harris was standing over one of the computer screens on the far left side of the Special Technical Operations Center.

"I know that, Captain," Warren Clark said, glancing at his watch. He was to report to Dawson in another hour and so far he was empty-handed. He still didn't have confirmation of where *Atlantis* had come down.

"Where's Collins?" Clark spoke under his breath. He picked up his cup and walked over to the coffee maker.

He had finally figured out why the lighting was only one notch above black and why the room was set up the way it was. No matter where he stood, he could see each of the computer screens, which updated him constantly. Even when getting a cup of coffee. He put his cup under the spout and watched the brown liquid start to trickle down.

"General." Mark Collins entered the room to Clark's left. "I just received the washed photos from the NPIC." He was holding a computer disk.

"Is it what we need?"

"Yes, sir." Collins grinned as he sat down in an empty seat and turned on the computer. He let the machine warm up for only a few seconds before inserting the disk. A couple of taps on the keyboard and a colored three-dimensional image of a twin mountain ridge running east and west slowly appeared on the screen.

"I can't believe we got these photos." He looked up at Clark and Harris, who was now standing next to the general. "Our hunch was right. *Atlantis* did go down in a remote area of northern Chad, and she's intact." He pointed to the screen.

The three men looked as Collins manipulated the keyboard, turning the picture up and down and back and forth.

"There she is," Collins said, after settling on an image looking at the runway from the south at an elevation of approximately 1,500 feet. The small white spot of the shuttle could clearly be seen on the left side of the monitor.

"What are these?" Clark pointed to a series of small squares and oblong shapes at the base of the ridge running north of the runway.

"They look like reinforced bunkers to me, sir, but that's without verification, of course. They're partially buried underground. That's why we didn't see them in the IR photos. They could be for aircraft, or they could be command and control centers." Collins spoke slowly, tapping on the screen. "These buildings here are above ground and made out of metal, probably aluminum."

Clark folded his arms, assessing the situation. "What else?"

Collins tapped a few times on the keys and the picture turned to a pale green and white. "This is an enhanced IR picture." The shuttle was glowing a bright green and could easily be seen. "These spots up in the hills around this area look a lot like campfires or gasoline heaters. These fainter spots are heat from the buildings, possibly lighting of some kind." He looked back up at the general.

"What are you telling me?" Clark frowned.

Collins chose his words carefully. "This air base is called Madadhi by the Libyans, and it looks like *Atlantis* could have a lot of company. It could be in the hands of Abu Ajami." Collins thought out loud.

"Who?"

"Abu Ajami. He's a terrorist and I think he's connected with that MiG-23 that was shot down last week," he said, remembering the radar telemetry taken from the *Kennedy*'s E-2C Hawkeye. The data showed the MiG-23 flying in from the south before it tried to attack the *Song of Flower*.

Clark looked at the computer screen for a few seconds. "Follow up on that and get this information to the Pathfinder team ASAP. Tell them there could be trouble." Clark then turned to Harris. "Captain, I'm going to see General Dawson. Call me if there are any changes."

West of Ali Ballas

Captain Rodriguez listened to the rhythmic thrashing sound as the seven rotor blades of the MH-53J cut into the murky night air. To his right sat Master Sergeant Ricky Vasquez, his twenty-six-year-old sniper. Vasquez had originally been assigned to the Special Operations Command headquarters at Fort Bragg, where he evaluated newly trained Rangers' rifle scores for possible admission into the Weapons Training Battalion, commonly known as sniper school. It was a laid back job until he received new orders and was shipped off to Saudi Arabia. When he returned home, he found his marriage had become one of the casualties of the war. After that he couldn't wait for a chance to get back into the field. When the Air Force Special Operations assignment had been posted at Fort Bragg, Vasquez was the first to volunteer.

Next to Vasquez was the medical officer, Air Force Major Paul Shaw. He was a gentle-looking man and didn't appear to fit in with a rough bunch. But his looks didn't matter. Rodriguez had seen Shaw tear through some of the toughest parts of their training program like it was summer camp.

Directly across from Shaw were the other two members of his team. Sergeant Mickey Lange had two jobs, communications and explosives. He was the youngest member of the team and Rodriguez felt he would have to keep an eye out for him. It wasn't that Lange didn't think things through, but that there were times he seemed to be walking on the edge. Rodriguez hoped that when it came to real crunch time Lange wouldn't screw up.

The last member of the five-man team was First Lieutenant Maximilian Rath, Jr. He was referred to as "the quiet man." Rath was second in command and the scout/spotter for Rodriguez's outfit. It would be Rath's and Vasquie's job to keep the bad guys away from their base camp once they were dug in. When Rath spotted trouble, Vasquez would eliminate it.

Considering the few people interested in joining the military these days, Rodriguez knew he had some of the cream off the top.

"This just in, Captain." Major White, the intelligence officer, emerged from the forward section of the helicopter. He slipped off his green helmet and sat down next to Rodriguez.

"I have some good and bad news. Take a look at this." White handed two long sheets of fax paper to Rodriguez. The fax had come off an IBM high-resolution laser fax machine. Modified to interface with coded UHF radio signals, transmitted via satellite, the resolution of the laser fax was more than five times the quality of the standard office fax. This made it possible to see important details that couldn't be seen otherwise.

Rodriguez tried to steady the fax as he read it. The pale lights of the cabin's exterior combined with the vibrations of the helicopter made it difficult to decipher.

DIRECTLY FROM: GEN. W. CLARK, STOC/PENTAGON VIA DEFENSE SATELLITE
COMMUNICATIONS SYSTEM II
DIRECTLY TO: CAPTAIN ROBERT RODRIGUEZ
23SPET/447/NOVEMBER//*.* - CHANNEL CLOSED - RELAY
      ]PROCEED TO TOUCHDOWN SITE AND ESTABLISH VISUAL CONFIRMATION OF LOCATION
      AND CONDITION OF SHUTTLE ATLANTIS[
      ]POSSIBLE HOSTILES IN THE AREA OF AIR BASE[
      ]EVALUATE FOR RESCUE AND RECOVERY OF CREW AND ORBITER[
      ]SET UP COMMUNICATIONS VIA DSCS EHF CHANNEL FOUR THREE MK TWO SEVEN
      EIGHT. REPORT FOUR HOUR INTERVALS[

The second page contained a detailed satellite map of the area surrounding the shuttle. Rodriguez stared at it for a long time before he spoke. He'd thought for sure they'd turn and go home.

"Son of a bitch . . . *It is Atlantis!*" Rodriguez said loudly enough for the other members of his crew to hear. "How long before we reach the touchdown point?" he asked White.

"That's the bad news, Captain. Our sensors have picked up a Libyan early warning radar sweeping 180 miles northeast of our present location. We're going low level and the ride is going to get real exciting."

"Where are you going to drop us, Major?"

"Well, Captain, we're going to try to get your team within five miles of where *Atlantis* went down. The pilot's going down to twenty feet until we reach the back side of the mountains. We're going to have to maneuver through a series of steep canyons and over one mountain pass." Major White pointed to the middle of the map and then looked up at Rodriguez. "This information is four and a half hours old. The Libyans could be looking for us by now and things could get real hairy. Tell your men to enjoy the ride. Hopefully, we'll have you on the ground in thirty-five, forty minutes."

Rodriguez nodded. "Right . . . enjoy the ride. You just get us down in one piece."

"We're moving," Willie said, putting his hand on the inner fuselage wall. "Feel it?" Both he and Duke were kneeling down on the flight deck. Through the windows they could see the glow of lights below the nose of *Atlantis*.

"Yeah," Duke grunted.

"What the hell do they think they're doing? Maybe we're invited to dinner," Willie joked nervously.

"I'm more concerned about who they are than where they're taking us," Duke replied. He eased himself up between the two front seats, then laid his upper body across the pilot's seat and slowly raised his head until his eyes were even with the bottom of the right side window. Directly below the nose of the shuttle, he saw a large truck. The head-lights cast enough light so that he could see its four wheels spinning up concrete. Standing in front of the truck, directly in the lights, were four men. Three of them were wearing red and white checkered kaffiyehs wrapped around their heads. All four were carrying AK-47s and dressed in brown desert camouflage. The sight confirmed Duke's worst fears. He stayed perfectly still, watching the men move back and forth, waving their arms, and apparently yelling.

The shuttle lurched forward, knocking him off the seat. The truck pulling the shuttle shifted into low gear and was now moving the orbiter off the runway. It swung around, its headlights pointing toward the mountainside. Duke, positioning himself back up, followed with his eyes, trying to get a fix on where they might be towed to help keep his bearings straight. All he could see was a small hill with what looked like three aircraft bunkers cut into the side of the mountain. The center one looked large enough to hold the shuttle.

He cautiously backed away and joined Willie on the floor in the rear of the cabin.

"We're in deep, dark shit," Duke said, rubbing his face.

"What did you see?" Willie asked, starting to feel edgy at Duke's anxiety.

"Four men carrying assault rifles with rags on their heads. It looks like they're towing us to a hangar inside the mountain. I couldn't see anything else other than rocks and sand."

"Who—who do you think they are?" Willie asked.

"I'll give you a hint. They're carrying AK-47s and probably blow up airliners with innocent people on board in their spare time."

"*Fuck.* Terrorists!" Willie exclaimed, lowering his voice unnecessarily, worried they might hear. "What are we going to do?"

"I don't know. But we don't have a lot of options. We can sit in here and wait for help, or try to reason with these people."

"Yeah, right. Three members of the American armed forces are going to reason with a band of hotheaded extremists. I'm sure they're going to be very understanding." Willie laughed cynically.

"You have a better idea?" Duke snapped. "Once they get us inside that hangar, all they'll need is a can opener to pry us out. And you tell me how the hell NASA is going to find us then!"

"That's not what I meant. I meant I agree with you—"

Duke held up his hand. "I know. Sorry. Let's just work out as many plans as we can and stall them . . ." He looked back at Willie.

"Stall them?" Willie squinted, not catching on.

"Yeah. We should check out these new carbon brakes, don't you think?" Duke answered, crawling up to the commander's seat on the left side. He swung his legs around but kept his head back from the window. Then, with all his strength, he pushed down on the upper part of the rudder pedals, applying the brakes. He maintained the pressure, feeling *Atlantis* shudder to a stop.

Ajami watched the BTR-40 grind to a halt. The rear tires of the Soviet-built armored truck were beginning to smoke as they continued to turn on the hard runway but didn't move.

"What is the problem, Majeed?" Ajami shouted.

"I do not know." Majeed walked to the BTR and told the driver to stop. He then made his way to the front landing gear of *Atlantis*. Majeed ducked down, shining his light between the twin tires. He didn't see anything out of the ordinary. He walked back toward the rear of the space plane.

"Put it in gear and try again," he yelled at the driver.

The driver did as he was told and the BTR lurched forward, moving the shuttle nearly two meters before it stopped again.

This time Majeed was ready. He was standing next to the left main gear and saw the heavy disc brake system lock up. He clicked his flashlight off, then ran back to Ajami.

"It is the brakes, Ajami. Someone is engaging them when we start to pull," Majeed reported.

"Good . . . very good. That answers one of my questions."

Majeed didn't understand.

"We do indeed have live Americans on board. This makes this plane even more valuable. And they wish to fight. I will show them who they are fighting."

Ajami backed away from the BTR and lined himself up with the nose of the shuttle. He was not more than twenty meters away when he jacked a live round into his AK, shouldered the rifle, and pointed it at the cockpit windows.

It happened so fast, Duke couldn't react. The first few solid-point bullets didn't shatter the thick Plexiglas windows. They penetrated several inches before stopping. The 160-grain bullets impacted with enough force to blow bits of clear Plexiglas off the back side of the cockpit window. Instantly the interior was showered with small pieces of jagged plastic.

"Duke, get down!" Willie gasped.

Duke covered his face with his forearms and hit the floor. The next burst of fire was more concentrated. The bullets tore into the two center window panels, directly above the center console. A half second later, several bullets broke through and impacted on the wall and ceiling above the two astronauts.

Willie reached out and clutched Duke, pulling him to the rear of the cabin. "You okay, sir?" he asked, grabbing the general by both sides of the head and looking at his face.

Duke exhaled hard and blinked, "Yeah, yeah . . . I'm okay." He was dazed, not sure what was happening.

"Those *bastards* tried to kill you."

"I shouldn't have been so stupid." Duke took a deep breath and tried to regain some of his composure. Then the two men let out a short burst of laughter. "Look, I'm sure Novak's not going to let them just leave us out here. What we need to do now is just buy some time."

"Hey, with the reception you just got, I'd just as soon we wait it out in here." Willie couldn't believe this was happening. He had felt fortunate in the navy to have never had any serious combat emergencies, but now he wondered if maybe it would have prepared him better for this moment.

"Okay. But we need to be ready for anything. We need to think this through." Duke brushed several pieces of Plexiglas out of his hair. "You with me, Willie?"

"I'm with you."

"Let's get below."

"Shine a light up there," Abu Ajami shouted.

Majeed swept his bright beam across the cockpit of the shuttle. The once clear windows were now pockmarked. Several of the thermal tiles directly below the windows were also broken or shattered.

"That will be the last time they try that," Ajami said to Majeed. "Quickly, I want this plane inside and secured in thirty minutes. Where is Captain Jibril?"

"He is at his aircraft radioing for additional equipment."

Good, Ajami thought, as he looked up into the sky and turned his head from side to side. He could feel the power starting to build from deep within him. When the Americans come, he and his men would attack, killing many of the enemy. This was a gift from Allah.

*   *   *

The giant MH-53J Pave Low III chopper swung a few degrees to the west as the pilot, Captain Rachel Grimes, listened to the soft chirping of her RHAW equipment. The signal was growing stronger each time she crested a hill and started down the other side. It wasn't a sound she liked hearing. The airspace around her had been quiet up until twenty minutes ago. Then a Libyan air defense radar had been activated, sweeping her helicopter from the northwest. As each of the powerful E-band radar waves passed over her aircraft, she could hear a faint *beep . . . beep* in her headset. They were looking for her.

Grimes had attended the University of Wisconsin in the air force ROTC program. From there she had gone right to flight school, learning how to fly helicopters and graduating at the top of her class. Eventually she had been transferred to the Twentieth Special Operations Squadron. She commanded one of the most advanced helicopters in the U.S. Air Force. Special forces didn't care if you were a man or a woman; they just wanted the best person for the job.

As the MH-53J skimmed across the desert, Grimes automatically scanned the horizon and the instruments at the same time. She had become accustomed to wearing the heavy night vision goggles and relied on them as a backup for the AN/APO-158 terrain-following radar and AN/AAQ-10 forward-looking infrared system. She also relied on a Litton internal navigation system and a computer-generated map display projection. It was said that if a pilot got lost flying the MH-53J, he or she would be required to step down a notch and start flying fighters.

Grimes was trained for S and R missions over hostile territory, the skilled art of covert insertion and extraction of commando teams right under the enemy's nose. In order to stay off the Libyan radarscope, Grimes had to keep the chopper at an altitude under 200 feet at all times. Flying nap-of-the-earth meant more than just following the terrain into a target area. Each time she flew in and out of Libyan radar coverage, it put more demands on the RHAW. The violent fluctuations in the radar's recorded signal strength had a tendency to cause the RHAW to give false readings. It was a problem that had plagued pilots in the Iraqi war and was still being worked on. The consequence of this, of course, was that the equipment could show that a radar was 200 miles away, when in reality it was over the horizon, ready to lock onto the aircraft.

"Keep your eyes on this, Major," Grimes said to White. She pointed to the newly installed British-developed Ferranti/E-Systems Detection and Tactical Alert of Radar display. "Tell me if it switches from flashing to a solid color or if the dial starts to rotate." The DATAR was a very reliable visual system, covering E- to J-bands, telling the radar's pulse width, transmission rate, and direction. Grimes wanted to keep her focus out in front when flying low-level, especially at night. The ground was more dangerous than any enemy radar.

The MH-53J dipped sharply to the left and nosed up ten degrees, avoiding a large rock outcropping before it swung back to the east, leveling out again and continuing on course. Flying thirty feet above the ground, Grimes forced her eyes to go from the horizon to the radar altimeter every few seconds, then back to the horizon. She didn't trust the automatic flight control system, even if it was linked directly to the terrain-following radar.

Grimes used her left sleeve to wipe the sweat from the crease where her goggles dug into her cheeks. The true airspeed was only eighty knots as she easily maneuvered the 38,000-pound chopper through the rocky valleys and steep canyons.

They were only thirteen minutes away from the touchdown site. She made a mental note to shut down the TFR in three minutes. The last ten minutes of their flight would be flown in electronic silence.

Major White watched the dial on the DATAR jump slightly. The needle jumped one more time before he said anything. "I show another radar sweeping from the north, northeast—no, make that two new radars, Captain." He reeled off the information in monotone. "These two *aren't* E-bands. They're coming from another direction, and moving."

"Can you identify the band?"

"No. They're weaker signals and right on the edge." He blinked, trying to clear his eyes.

"What about the bandwidth? Narrow or wide?"

"They're wide."

"Chances are they're MiGs, Major. With a wide pulse width, it means their radars are searching." If the DATAR showed the beam was narrow, they were getting ready to lock up. They hadn't seen her yet, but that didn't make her feel any better.

"If they're MiGs, they're probably out of the Libyan base at Aujila. It's north of our current position," Grimes added, keeping her head moving right, then left and up and down.

White didn't reply, trusting that she would know what to do.

"Okay, here we go." Grimes took hold of the control stick, disengaging the TFR. She nosed the big chopper down, feeling the Gs build, then leveled out at fifty feet. As Grimes looked left, she saw a small ravine a half mile away. She added pressure to the stick and banked toward the cover.

Ajami watched the heavy twin concrete doors of the bunker slowly close in the center. Several sets of white lights came on, cutting through the dust-filled air. The shuttle nearly filled the interior of the hangar.

The main part of the building was completely covered by the mountain. Only the doors were exposed and even then, right out front, a five-meter-high hill added to its protection. The engineers had left just enough room for an aircraft to turn and maneuver into the bunker itself. There was no way it could be directly attacked. This did little to reassure Ajami.

"Now I want to see who is inside this American space plane," Ajami said to no one in particular.

They had been hovering in the same spot for ten minutes, twenty feet above the warm desert sand. Grimes's NVG showed the jagged tops of the ravine in an eerie green glow above the chopper. The ghostlike shapes of rocks and boulders could easily be distinguished from the cooler dirt. They were hiding from the radars. If the MiGs got a fix on the MH-53J, it would be a fleeting fight and she wouldn't be the winner. She knew her whirling, seventy-nine-foot diameter, seven-blade main rotor wasn't easy to hide, but it could be done.

Grimes watched the fuel gauges and mentally calculated that she still had enough for fifty-five minutes of flight. If her judgment was correct, the MiGs should be out of range by now.

"I'm taking her up, Major."

White's attention went back to the DATAR.

Grimes gently eased the big Sikorsky up and over the edge of the gully. She cocked her head to the right as she listened for the RHAW to pick up the radar and start its warning. There was only one faint *beep* . . . *beep* of the Libyan E-band.

"Scope's clean, except for that E-band."

Grimes smiled to herself. "All right, let's make the drop and get the hell out of here."

She swept the instruments, making sure the TFR was disengaged and the navigational lights were out. A blinking light in the desert could be seen for miles.

"Ten minutes to LZ. Call 'em out." Grimes instructed Major White to guide them to the landing zone.

"Turn left, heading two six four." White watched their airspeed climb. "Hold steady at 120 knots." He felt the chopper roll left and the nose pitch down as they picked up speed.

The next part of the mission was make or break. White flipped on a dim red light positioned above the instrument panel. It cast light into the cockpit, allowing him to see without interfering with Grimes's NVG. Pinned to his flight suit, on the thigh of his right leg, were five black-and-white satellite photos with a superimposed map overlay. The black lines running throughout the picture helped outline the topography of the terrain. White had to find landmarks to pinpoint their position by spotting them visually as they flew by. It was easier said than done.

The chopper's low-drift laser-gyro internal navigational system would get them close, within several miles of the drop point, but that wasn't good enough. Several miles to the Pathfinder team translated to extra hours of travel time.

The superimposed map showed three dirt roads in the area. Their LZ was on the road running east to west and ended at the base of the mountains on the south side of the airstrip. White slipped his NVG over his eyes.

"I need some more altitude, Captain. Take her up to five hundred." A series of small hills was blocking his view.

As the big chopper pitched up, White watched the landscape change before him. The extra altitude added at least ten miles' sighting into the night.

"That's it." He muttered to himself. They were east and south of the LZ. "Take her down. When you hit the road, turn right and follow it until it intersects with another road. Then turn right and head west. That should be it."

"Roger," Grimes said.

White keyed his mike. "Captain Rodriguez, ETA five minutes."

Grimes banked forty degrees to the north and lined up the image of the road so it cut through the center of the cockpit windows. A mile ahead she could see the intersection.

"Two minutes to touchdown," White called out to Rodriguez.

Grimes watched the dirt road narrow and disappear as they climbed up the side of the mountain. She pushed the stick forward and throttled down, forcing the bug-shaped helicopter toward the ground. She leveled the blades and hovered, kicking up dust. Her NVG revealed a level landing spot only a few hundred yards to her right.

She keyed her mike. "Major, tell the team after the wheels touch they have thirty seconds. After that, I'm out of here."

"She's your bird, Captain. I'll relay the message." White unsnapped his harness and disappeared into the back of the helicopter.

Grimes hesitated only a second before banking to the right and setting the big machine down on the level area between the hills of sand and two large boulders. When the wheels hit, the cargo bay door opened and she started to watch the mission clock.

Rodriguez watched the interior lights turn from red to green.

"Let's move it, gentlemen," he shouted, waving them out. Rath and Lange were already outside the helicopter and he doubted if they had even heard him. He turned and gave White a quick salute. "See you in a few days, Major."

"You got it. Good luck, Captain."

Rodriguez turned and ran down the cargo loading ramp into the desert. The turbines on the MH-53J spooled up as the blades lifted the chopper and thundered into the blackness. Pathfinder team Alpha began their trek up the mountain.

DAY
6

WEDNESDAY, SEPTEMBER 22

18

It was the fourth ring before Staffer finally heard the phone. The distinctive tone, combined with a double ring, told him it wasn't his private line. That meant it must be business.

"Ah, damn it, I thought we had this thing under control," he said to himself. He had fallen asleep on the couch. The TV set was still on, airing the local news. The light from the kitchen trickled through the cramped two-bedroom apartment. Staffer yawned and stretched once before rolling off the couch and climbing to his feet. He checked his watch before picking up the phone. It was 12:12 at night.

"This is Staffer." His voice was rough.

"Tom . . . Dawson here. You awake?"

"Am now." Staffer reached for a pack of cigarettes lying next to the lamp. He fumbled with it before taking one out and sticking it between his lips.

"Good. Listen up. I just received a report from Admiral Petersen about the Russian satellite. Have you looked over your copy yet?"

"No, I haven't seen it," Staffer said, trying to remember if he had seen anything on his desk before he left the office.

"I need you involved in this."

"Oh yeah? What's up?" Staffer sucked in a long breath of smoke and sat down on the arm of his couch, exhaling slowly.

"We're not sure. That's why I need to see you ASAP."

"Hey, I hate to pop your bubble, Jack, but I'm not an expert on Russian space systems. Can't this wait until morning?"

"I know you're not, but your man Admiral Petersen is . . . right? And no, this can't wait till morning."

Staffer was starting to wake up. "All right. When and where?"

"In half an hour, my quarters." The line went dead.

197

Tom let the phone fall from his ear. One hour of sleep wasn't going to cut it. He took one more drag of the cigarette before crushing it out in the ashtray. His eyes focused on the ashtray as the last ember of tobacco turned from orange to black and died. *I've gotta quit smoking,* he thought.

Quarters 6 is the official residence of the chairman of the Joint Chiefs. Staffer had been there on several occasions—Christmas parties, Super Bowl Sundays, and other social functions. He generally felt out of place, since he was single and most everyone else was married. This was the first time Jack Dawson had invited him over for business.

The black Cadillac limo pulled up next to the driveway in front of the old, well-kept two-story house. There was a slight drizzle, and Staffer watched his driver prepare to get out and hold the umbrella.

Staffer reached up and patted him on the arm. "That's all right. I won't need it. I'll give you a call when I'm through." He opened the car door, put his head down, and jogged to the marine standing guard by the iron gate.

Gladys Dawson was waiting in the entryway as Staffer reached the door. She was wearing a blue robe and fuzzy slippers. Her snow-white hair and trim figure made her look younger than her years.

"Hello, Gladys. I didn't expect to see you," Staffer said, embracing her hand, a little embarrassed she was dressed for bed.

"Tom, sorry about my attire," she said, looking down. "But Jack's on the phone and asked me to show you in. This way to the study."

Staffer followed her down a short hallway and could hear Dawson's gruff voice before he entered the room.

"Good to see you, Tom . . . and I guess this is good night." With that Gladys turned and left, disappearing up the stairs into their private living quarters.

Staffer gave the room the once-over. It was well decorated with a mixture of aviation and wildlife art. To the left was a row of shelves lined with wooden models of jet aircraft. Staffer assumed they were the aircraft the general had flown while a pilot in the air force. The carpet was a deep forest green, the walls a knotty pine, and the windows trimmed with a masculine fabric. The general was dressed in jeans, white shirt, and a blue sweater with four stars on each shoulder. He was standing next to his desk, talking on the phone. He motioned for Staffer to come in.

". . . when are they due to report?" Dawson asked. He sat down and leaned back in his chair, closing his eyes. "All right, Warren, get some sleep. We'll meet at eight." He hung up the phone.

"Tom, sit down."

Staffer hesitated. On the floor to the right was a large black Lab, sound asleep.

"That's Orion. He's not going to bother you. He's twelve years old, can't hear, and doesn't have any teeth."

"That's what they all say," Staffer joked.

Dawson didn't laugh. "That was Warren Clark. You know him?"

Staffer thought for a second. For some reason Dawson expected him to know every general and admiral in the military. As it turned out, however, he did recall this one.

"Yeah, I know him . . . special ops."

"Right. I have him assigned to the STOC at the Pentagon. He'll be heading up a team to recover *Atlantis*." Dawson reached for his coffee cup. "Clark just told me our Pathfinder recon team is safely on the ground five miles from where the shuttle landed. We should be getting our first report shortly."

Staffer nodded, still not knowing why he was sitting in front of the chairman at 12:45 in the morning.

"This brings me to why you're here." Dawson pushed a folder toward Staffer. "Open it."

Staffer took it off the desk. It contained Admiral Petersen's technical analysis of the Kosmos 3-1660. The report was a quarter of an inch thick and contained colored pictures and colored computer-generated images of the satellite, along with Petersen's written report.

"This was faxed to me from NORAD. Tom, you know Admiral Petersen better than I do. Tell me, how long have you worked with him?"

"Off and on, for about a dozen years," Staffer answered, not looking up from the report.

"Is he qualified for this?"

Staffer glanced up. "Come on, Jack, what's up?"

"Is he qualified for this sort of report? I mean, do you trust him, trust his judgment?"

Staffer thought for a second before answering. *Dawson is being very cautious. Something isn't right.* "Yeah, he's qualified and I trust him. Stop playing with me. What's going on?"

"Tom, hasn't it occurred to you that maybe *Atlantis* went down because something went wrong with that Russian satellite?" Dawson inquired with a frown.

"That's the first thing that crossed everyone's mind." Staffer thumbed through a few more pages of the report, letting out a low breath.

Dawson got up and poured himself and Staffer a cup of black coffee. As he returned to his desk, he said, "There may be more to the satellite than we first thought. If Admiral Petersen is correct, the Russians lied to us. They told Petersen the midsection of the satellite was empty. Well, according to this report, each one of those round access panels has something behind it. But Petersen's not sure what."

"So you want to know if this report is worth pursuing, right?" Staffer looked into Dawson's bloodshot eyes.

"That's right. I don't have time to dick around on a wild-goose chase. But if you have faith in Petersen, I'll get rolling on this."

"Do it. Petersen's one of the best men at satellite ID I know. If he's concerned, I'm concerned," Staffer said confidently.

"That's all I wanted to hear."

"And what about the Russians? If this whole thing happened because of some screwup on their part, they should be accountable."

Dawson rubbed the back of his neck. "I agree, but nothing's been decided yet. Come on, let's get some rest. Tomorrow's going to be a long day."

Il-78 TROOP TRANSPORT

Dimitri Popivich was the only passenger on the Il-78 troop transport as it headed west toward Moscow. The cargo cabin was dark, cold, and filled with the vibrations of a poorly built aircraft. His stomach turned as the fumes from the chemical toilet, mixed with rancid hydraulic fluid, scorched his nostrils.

Popivich was sitting in a most uncomfortable position. His hands were cuffed behind his back and his seat belt was pulled snugly across his lap. The ringing in his ears combined with the sound of the jet engines, adding to his discomfort.

The general had been arrested and hustled off to a nearby stockade. Once there, he was tied to a chair and beaten by two men. At least, he thought it was two. The next thing he knew he was being seated in an empty cargo plane and told he was being transported to Moscow for trial.

Popivich could barely open his eyes. His entire face was a mass of cuts and black-and-blue marks. He was sure if he moved his jaw his lips would crack open and start to bleed again. He had witnessed other people being interrogated by the thugs from the new state police and had admired their methodical and precise beatings. No bones were damaged and if he survived the pain, he would recover.

Dimitri had been puzzled why they didn't ask him any questions, then realized their orders were just to soften him up before arriving in Moscow. He took a long breath and leaned his head against the thinly padded bulkhead.

THE KREMLIN, MOSCOW

Defense Minister Petr Czerlinsky paced back and forth in front of his giant walnut desk. His tobacco-stained fingers were trembling with anger as he held the worn brown file at arm's length.

"Someone should have known." He spoke so softly, at first it was hard for the man, standing ten feet away, to hear what he was saying. "Leonov assured me this would not happen. Now he is dead and I have chaos on my hands!"

"Petr, stop. How could you have known? This man Popivich had always been loyal to the state, to the military. He is a national hero." Ivan Dolezalek, the frail-framed foreign minister, was standing next to the window looking down on Moscow's morning rush hour traffic crawling through a light rain. He was a scrawny man compared to the healthier Czerlinsky, with a fondness for Cuban cigars and French white wine, which he drank a bottle at a time.

Neither Dolezalek nor Czerlinsky knew of the existence of the inner circle or of the truth and real mission of the satellite.

"This may all just be a mistake. We do not even know for certain what has happened," Dolezalek said, his eyes not wavering from the window.

"This is no mistake," Czerlinsky interrupted loudly. "No mistake at all. Leonov and I both had concerns about Popivich's stability." He set the file down and returned to his seat. His cup of tea was cold and untouched. Czerlinsky rested his elbows on the edge of the desktop and placed his chin on his folded hands. He hoped some solution would fill his mind.

"Minister Czerlinsky." It was his secretary. His attention was now directed to the door leading to the outer office. "They are here."

"Good. Tell them I am ready."

Dolezalek feigned a smile and left the office. Czerlinsky glanced over Popivich's file one last time. Possibly Dolezalek was right. The general had always been a good soldier. In fact, so good, the minister wondered if Popivich's judgment could be clouded by passion and sense of duty.

The new Russian defense minister stopped reading. Why couldn't it have gone as planned? He not only felt uneasy about handling the situation but was afraid for his job and his government. He had to evaluate the damage and give a full report to his superiors. Possibly all because of an old-school general who should have been replaced years ago.

Three men entered his office, followed by Dolezalek. Two of them had their hands on each arm of the third man, who had his head down. Czerlinsky couldn't see his face.

"As per your orders, Minister Czerlinsky, I present you with General

Major Dimitri Popivich." One of the men grabbed the general by the back of the coat, uncuffed him, and forced him to sit in front of Czerlinsky. It was then the defense minister saw Popivich's swollen and bruised face.

"Who did this?" Czerlinsky asked, not taking his eyes off the general.

The guards did not answer.

"I said, who did this?"

"In all due respect, Minister Czerlinsky, this man is a murderer. He killed one of your own deputies, Nikolai Leonov."

"*You fools!* I am aware of what he is accused of. But how in mother Russia's name do you expect him to cooperate with us after—after this?" Czerlinsky stood and pounded his fist on the table. "Get out of my office. As far as I am concerned, you are finished." He turned to Dolezalek. "I want an investigation, do you hear me? An investigation. Out with you. Out with all of you."

As the men left the room, Czerlinsky tried to pull himself together. He turned to Popivich. The general appeared to be straining to sit upright. His dark brown wool coat was spotted with drops of water from the cold morning rain.

"General Popivich, I am sorry this has happened to you. I did not authorize it. I hope you are not hurt badly. Please remove your coat."

Popivich didn't move or respond.

"May I get you some hot tea, General?"

"No."

"Are you hungry? May I get you something to eat?"

"No."

"I see." Czerlinsky moved around to the front of his desk so he could get closer to the general. "You have served our country well. Everyone, including myself, admires your great accomplishments. You are the only one to have been awarded Hero of the Soviet Union twice. But that was many years ago."

Popivich tilted his head back. The swelling around his eyes had gone down enough for him to see a little better. "That was when there was a Soviet Union, when there was something to fight for." His speech was slow and dull.

"I see. So you don't approve of what our country is doing?"

"I don't approve of the Americans getting their hands on our most advanced strategic satellite . . . If that is what you mean."

Czerlinsky's jaw tightened as his mood changed from that of reconciliation to anger. "Am I to understand that you alone are the one who decides what is important and what is not important in the defense of this country?"

"Our leaders are not—"

"I am not finished. We asked the Americans for help. They agreed to help us and as I understood from Deputy Leonov you also agreed to cooperate. Now there is evidence the shuttle came out of orbit prematurely because someone under your command fired the control thrusters on the Kosmos satellite. And more distressingly, for some unexplained reason, Leonov is dead. What can you tell me about any of this?" Czerlinsky hoped Popivich would explain everything away, leaving the Russians in the clear.

Popivich looked away, refusing to reply.

Czerlinsky leaned over, placing his face only a few inches away from Popivich's. "General, are you hiding behind fear? If you know something and can clear this up, it is your duty to inform the leaders of our country. Now, tell me. Who fired the thrusters and how did Leonov die?" The minister held his breath waiting for the answer.

"I fired the thrusters. I killed Leonov."

"Why?" Czerlinsky clenched his fist, shouting.

Popivich's face didn't feel the pain as he grinned. "You are a fool, like the rest of the idiots running this country. Kosmos 3-1660 is the most powerful weapon this country ever developed. You should all be applauding me for what I've done."

"What are you saying, Popivich? What is on board the Kosmos?" Czerlinsky shouted, shaking his head. *This man is insane. I never should have let Leonov talk me into this.*

"Leonov knew and now no one will ever know," Popivich muttered.

The defense minister spun around and slammed his fist down on the intercom button. "Send in Minister Dolezalek and the military police," he yelled.

He turned toward the window. The rain had become a fine white mist. Without looking at Popivich, he told the arriving men, "I am placing the general in solitary confinement and charging him with murder and high treason. I want a guard assigned to him full time." He twisted around and caught Popivich's stare. "And, General, I will find out one way or another. Then you will die for this."

19

Rodriguez stopped for an instant, catching his breath. His eyes drifted up to the moon. It was hanging twenty degrees above the horizon and long fingers of clouds cut through its center, blocking most of its precious light. He turned and watched as his men climbed the hill behind him. Besides weapons, additional ammo, and twin canteens, each was carrying a heavy nylon backpack weighing as much as ninety pounds. Sergeant Lange's pack was heavier. He carried their only link to the outside world, a small portable satellite dish that allowed them to communicate directly with the STOC at the Pentagon.

A line of sweat rolled down the side of Rodriguez's face from under his skullcap. He wiped the perspiration off his forehead, trying to keep it out of his eyes. His uniform was already soaked and the miserable memories of the desert were coming back to him. He switched the nine-pound Beretta from his left hand to his right, pointing the muzzle toward the ground. Rodriguez preferred the Italian-made rifle to standard-issue M-16s. The Beretta fired 5.56 NATO ammunition, was well balanced and easy to clean. To help conceal the black barrel and plastic stock of the weapon, he had wrapped it with brown camouflage tape. The rifle now looked more like a plastic toy than an assault rifle, yet it blended into the desert sand perfectly.

Rodriguez glanced around the night sky. The shifting clouds were thinning, and the moon's dim glow was once again leading the way between the rocks and bushes. Each man's night vision goggles dangled around his neck as they continued climbing up a short ravine cut out by a recent rainstorm. The sun would be up in two hours and the team was still a mile from their objective. Fortunately, the low clouds blanketing the eastern horizon would allow them a few more minutes of darkness to get into position.

When Rodriguez reached the top of the hill, he knelt down and took a small map out of his belt. Holding a miniflashlight in his other hand, he swept it back and forth until he found the ridge they were on. Even though the lens was covered with a translucent red cap, he was careful to keep the light low and out of sight.

"Rath," he whispered.

The lieutenant scrambled up next to Rodriguez, placing one knee on a clump of dried dirt as he put his head close to the captain's.

"Let me get about fifty yards ahead of you. Then follow. The air base should be a half mile to the northwest, over that next rock outcrop." Rath nodded that he understood and went down, giving hand signals to the others.

Rodriguez took a deep breath and started for the opening on the downside of the ridge. The terrain was more rugged than what he had expected. He had had instruction at the National Desert Training Center in the Mojave, but that wasn't quite this irregular. These mountains were steep and rocky with large patches of shrubbery. The soil was not the best for good footing, being a mixture of broken shale and sand.

Coming up over the last ridge, he got on his hands and knees, crawling the last few yards up to a cluster of desert cedar trees. He then moved, wiggling on his belly until his shoulders came even with three medium-sized sandstone rocks. *Perfect,* he thought. A brisk wind was blowing and he could feel bits of flying sand strike his face. He had a clear shot of the valley and was well hidden by the terrain coverage.

Rodriguez removed his skullcap, placing it under his left arm. He then pulled out a matte black Litton M911A modular pocket night scope and turned it on. Weighing only 17.6 ounces, the M911A was developed for federal and local law enforcement personnel for drug surveillance. Its compact size, combined with a large 26.8-millimeter objective lens, made it very handy. The unit was powered by two standard 1.5-volt AA batteries and used a phosphor screen and photocathode with multiplied electrons carried by a single fiber-optic tube. The optical image seen through the eyepiece allowed Rodriguez to pick up contrasting bright and dark spots within three miles. The valley was partially lit by the half-moon as he surveyed the ground 3,000 feet below. He set the scope for maximum range and swept the landscape.

Sure as hell, there it was. The jet-black runway spanned out a mile away, running east to west. Rodriguez swung to the right and pointed the scope directly across and below him. He twisted the objective lens in front of the light input window until the greenish yellow blur on the valley floor came into focus. Through the branches of a dead tree, he could see two metal buildings approximately forty feet long and twenty feet high. They were the same ones he had made note of on the fax. Rodriguez swept the night scope left, stopping at the base of the mountain. On the far side of the runway he could clearly see the doors of three large aircraft bunkers that were carved into the side of the mountain. The center bunker was the largest. It was hard to tell at this distance, but it looked as if the sides were twenty feet high. The doors then arced upward like a pyramid, with the pinnacle a hundred feet off the ground. *That son of a bitch is big enough to house a C-5 transport,* Rodriguez thought. A C-5 was the air force's largest transport plane. A small hill, probably man-made, ran in front of the three aircraft bunkers. Rodriguez knew it was built to make it difficult to attack the bunkers from the air.

Rodriguez continued to look west. Parked next to the farthest bunker on his right were five MiG fighters. The aircraft had pointed noses and single cockpit canopies. They were swing wings, but he couldn't make out if they were 23s or 27s.

Rodriguez's gaze followed the edge of the mountain's base. He stopped at what looked like an older troop transport truck. It was parked next to a road a few hundred yards to the west of the last bunker. Three dim lights caught his eye and, focusing, he could see they came from cracks in the side of the mountain. He realized he was looking at rock huts, several rows of them, connecting with what must be a series of pathways. Everything was quiet, with only a few men standing guard in various positions.

Satisfied he had seen most of the significant parts, he put the scope down and referred to his map. The coordinates were slightly off. Rodriguez estimated they were a mile east and a few thousand yards south of the camp instead of three quarters of a mile to the east. The team had an hour for him to pick a place and to set up their surveillance area and radio equipment. Scanning the area with the M911A, he found a suitable spot nearby that would keep them well hidden after the sun came up.

The muffled sound of two rocks being rapped together reached his ears. Rath, the sniper team scout, hiding ten yards away, was signaling a warning. Just then the air filled with the thunderous roar of jet engines. Rodriguez rolled onto his back, searching the sky with the scope. A streak of white light illuminated the sky out of the east. He lowered the M911A as three multiengine transports turned on their landing lights. Rodriguez scratched his cheek, coming back around on his belly, following the planes as they lined up with the runway. Ilyushins, he said to himself; Libyan transport jets.

He eased his way back down to the team. "Okay, we're almost there. A half mile to the west and eight hundred yards down the hill. The main part of the camp is on the other side of the runway. We'll set up, then get some sleep."

Rath checked his watch. "We're scheduled to make our first transmission in forty-five minutes, sir. I don't think we're going to be ready."

"Too bad. I want us secure first. Everyone's had five and drinks. We're not stopping again until we're set up. Clear?"

All the men nodded as Rodriguez put his skullcap back on and slid stealthily out in the lead.

CIA HEADQUARTERS

Retired Naval Captain R. Loran Hogsett was in his office six hours earlier than normal. The last time he was called in to work at 0200 hours was to review the first reports of the coup in the Philippines. That day ended up being a seventy-two-hour marathon fueled by strong coffee and Chinese food. He was already on his fourth cup of coffee, but had no intentions of repeating the Chinese part of it.

Hogsett's office was located one floor below Tom Staffer's at the CIA. The middle-aged ex-sub skipper had been a naval intelligence officer at Patuxent River Naval Station before being brought in to the CIA three years earlier. He was currently serving as the deputy director of Naval Intelligence, overseeing the Russian navy's compliance with the START I and START II treaties. In other words, he was one of the CIA's treaty verification officers, dealing exclusively with the Russian nuclear missile boats.

The Russians generally cut the vessels up into three separate pieces and left them on the dry dock until they were sure a U.S. satellite had photographed them. The same thing was done with the missiles. They were split in four pieces, with the warheads left in the nose cones. Hogsett would review the photos, collect additional data from ground teams, and report his conclusions. It was then decided if the sub or surface ship had been properly disposed of as per the treaty.

This morning Hogsett was working on a different matter.

"Good. I see you got my message." Staffer entered without knocking.

"You're up early. Or, by the looks of you, you haven't been to bed yet." Hogsett looked up, smiling. "Man, you look like shit! I hope she was worth it."

"Right. I haven't had time to go on a date, much less find one. I haven't sat down since I called you." Staffer loosened his yellow tie and plopped down in a chair. The olive green suit only added to the pallor of his face and deepened the dark bags under his eyes.

"Really? Well, I know this girl who—"

"I know, who has a friend who's really nice. No thanks." Staffer chuckled. "The last time you set me up, I ended up looking and feeling worse than I do now."

"Okay, so you didn't drag me out of bed for a hot babe. What do you want me to do with this?" Hogsett gestured to the file sitting on his desk. "I'm not qualified for shuttles, just subs and surfaces ships."

"That's right, and the nuclear weapons on board them." Staffer placed what was quickly being dubbed the Petersen Report in front of Hogsett. "I don't want to give you any preconceived ideas about this, so I'm not going to say anything more. Look it over and evaluate it, then meet me in the tank at eight."

"All right, but I'm thinking you're taking drags off wacky weed instead of those carcinogenics." Hogsett looked wryly at Staffer, somehow knowing it would eventually all come together.

"I'm going up to my office. Buzz me if you need me. Otherwise, I'll see you in a few hours." Staffer was already halfway out the door, checking his pockets for a cigarette pack.

20

SPACE SHUTTLE *Atlantis*

"Wake up, General James." Willie was gently nudging him.

Duke's head rested against the padded storage lockers in front of the middeck. His eyes were closed, and Willie was astonished by his ability to fall asleep under their current situation.

Duke awakened to a throbbing pain in his back. He straightened up until he was flat against the compartments. Sitting on the floor in front of him was a plate of runny yellow powdered eggs and a cup of fruit juice. Andrea and Willie were sitting next to each other three feet away from the ladder leading to the flight deck. Duke glanced at them. By their faces he could tell that his crew wasn't doing well. Each had a stiff expression and looked apprehensive and stressed. *I can't blame them,* he thought. *This waiting is getting to me, too.*

"The eggs are cold, General. It was the best I could do under the circumstances," Andrea said.

"Thanks, I'm sure they'll be fine. How long was I asleep?" Duke asked, rubbing his face. He picked up the plate of food, eating the eggs in two bites. He knew he'd need his strength.

"About an hour," Andrea answered, as she lifted a fork full of the soft, runny mixture into her mouth.

"What time is it?" Duke asked.

"It's morning," Andrea replied, checking her mission watch.

Duke stroked the stubble growing on his face. It had been nearly twenty-four hours since he had shaved and taken a shower. He was annoyingly aware of the dirty oils building on his face and neck and his increasing body odor. The air inside the shuttle was dry and stuffy. If they stayed in *Atlantis* much longer, the tension would become increasingly unbearable.

The lights in the crew compartment were faint, running on one tenth

209

their normal power. The shuttle's computers were down, so Andrea had converted everything to manual override and switched to reserve battery power. This automatically put everything on minimum power output.

Duke took a drink of his juice and set the plastic cup back down. He was starting to feel somewhat revived. "Any luck on the radio?"

"No." Willie looked down. "Afraid not."

Duke took a deep breath. Willie's face was tense and he appeared to be in pain. Duke had never seen his second in command look like this.

He finally spoke up. "What's on your mind, Willie?"

"I just really thought somebody would be here by now, General, that's all." Willie turned his head to the wall. "If this was some airliner, they'd be all over the place." His voice filled with disgust. "Hell, Duke, it's been almost ten hours and we're still sitting here like rats in a cage." He reached out and slammed his fist against the wall.

Duke stood. "Knock it off, Willie. You must know that they are doing everything possible . . . but it's going to take time." His voice was firm yet calm. "Right now, we need to concentrate on staying alive. Keeping each other alive. We don't know exactly who we're dealing with, and we need to go one step at a time. Judging from their clothes and where we're at, they're probably Arabs. Who else would be here in the middle of the desert? What I want you to think about is what we do know, not what we don't know. One, we know NASA has an idea of where we landed. Two, we know whoever is out there has weapons; therefore, we're better off in here. And three, I know someone is on their way to rescue us. They could be out there right now, and we need to be ready to help them."

Willie took a deep breath. "You're right, General. Damn it, I know better. So what should we be doing now?" He wiped the sweat from his eyes with his thumb and index finger, his tone more relaxed.

"Let's clear our heads and start thinking. We were obviously pulled into this hangar . . . bunker . . . whatever it is, to prevent anyone from spotting us. Chances are, however, we're more valuable to them alive than dead." Duke knelt down next to his crew. "They're going to break in sooner or later and, if they do, I want you to remember a few simple rules. First," he looked at Willie, "stay cool. I don't want either one of you to say something that might get us all killed. If anyone speaks English, talk with them; talk about unimportant subjects and try to get them to talk. Let them know we are real people and we know they are human beings, too. I want them to feel and believe we're not a threat." Duke reached up and pulled the stars off his right and then his left shoulders. He then pulled the mission patch off his chest pocket. "They're going to know we're in the military, but let's not rub it in their faces. From now on let's be sure we use our first names only. No rank. Hand me your patches."

They ripped off the Velcro patches, handing them to Duke. He was hiding them in a secured cabinet when a loud thud from the cabin hatch filled the middeck.

"Quiet," he whispered.

After a few seconds they could hear the muffled sounds of conversation followed by a series of reverberant bangs.

"Let's get up to the flight deck." Duke protectively helped Andrea up to her feet. "Remember, we're a team. We need to watch out for each other. Keep your heads down."

PATHFINDER TEAM ALPHA

As usual, Captain Bobby Rodriguez was pleased with what his unit had done in such a short time. The Pathfinder reconnaissance team had secured their position in less than an hour with a minimum of noise and returned the land around them to its natural-looking state.

Their "hide," or observation post, was a simple hole in the ground with only the minimal amount of equipment. They had dug a five-foot-deep crater into the rocky soil directly under the largest tree. Its heavily twisted trunk and a number of the thick branches hanging over the eight by eight concealment would provide additional cover and camouflage. The shelter would also help keep them cool, as well as aiding to preserve the two gallons of drinking water each man had carried in. It was ideal for surveillance from Rodriguez's point of view, even though it wouldn't classify as the perfect OP.

The captain was confident the enemy would literally have to step on them before their position would be revealed. The site he chose was halfway up the mountain, just beneath a rocky ledge, between several large clumps of desert cedar trees. They had a wide field of view that allowed his team to see most of the valley below them. This provided for both security measures and observation of targets. There were only five of them and their best defense now would be spotting trouble before it got to them. If everything went as planned, they would be there, confined in the pit, for two days maximum.

After the hole was dug and the dirt was carefully spread, disposed of in a way no one would notice, a brown-gray netting was stretched over and across the hide. The camo pattern consisted of broken images of rocks and small plants. It had been developed by two Green Berets, members of the Twenty-fourth Infantry Division's Long-Range Surveillance Detachment that had lived behind Iraqi lines for three months during the war. The material also duplicated the fluctuating reflected sunlight on the surfaces of the desert-scene camouflage. The netting was nearly indestructible but maintained an ultralight weight.

Rodriguez and his team used a series of one-inch-diameter black PVC pipes to support the corners and middle section of the netting. A heavy nylon rope was pulled across the top for added support. The front and sides of the netting were then raised barely six inches above ground level. This was done to allow a 280-degree frontal view of everything around them and to avoid noticeable movement from anyone on watch inside the OP.

A simple tunnel was then carved out to allow the team an emergency exit from the hide. They could crawl out the back and escape up the side of the hill, using large boulders and rocks along the way for cover.

Rodriguez checked his watch. The other men were exhausted, sitting in various positions against the far dirt wall. Except the communications man. Sergeant Lange was behind schedule and should have been finished burying the radio antenna twenty minutes ago.

Rodriguez stood so he could see outside the hide. The sun had been up for at least fifteen minutes and was starting to burn through the light morning haze hugging the ground. He put a pair of 8×30 Steiner binoculars to his eyes, surveying the buildings and airstrip below. He scanned slowly, giving verbal descriptions for Rath to write down. Every minute detail was noted and logged. In the daylight he could clearly make out the tops of the aircraft bunkers cut into the mountainside. They appeared to be of Western design and were likely to be reinforced. The heavy bunker doors had been built in four large sections, allowing aircraft to move in and out of them. The doors looked to be several feet thick and made of concrete. That meant that whoever was controlling the base had to have access to electrical power in order to move them.

The two aluminum hangars were painted a desert beige in an attempt to match the surrounding landscape. *Poor camouflage,* Rodriguez thought. The runway looked narrow, yet it was extremely long. Rodriguez guessed it to be 10,000 to 12,000 feet.

The three Il-76 transports were parked on the far side of the runway. Their cargo bays were closed, and Rodriguez could see they were refueling. On their tails were the green squares of Libyan markings with a large green circle on the side of the fuselage. He could hear the low rumble of the engines warming up. Rodriguez looked farther west and spotted the five MiGs next to one of the hangars, their canopies open. He could now tell by the rounded radomes they were MiG-23s. He brought his binoculars back to the east, and as he did he started counting the men around the aircraft. He stopped at fifteen; they were all carrying rifles. Four of them were dressed in khaki uniforms, but he couldn't tell if they were Libyan military. The rest were dressed in civilian clothes.

"That's it," Sergeant Mickey Lange whispered. He secured the last plastic connector on the Eyring low-profile antenna (ELPAC) cable. He made sure the gold-plated connectors were lined up perfectly before he snapped them together. The foil-shielded cable had been strung out before daylight and buried at least three inches deep in dirt and sand. It had taken a little longer than planned to meticulously conceal the 200-foot cable, twisting it among the rocks and terrain. He was careful, remembering that during his training several surveillance teams were discovered because the enemy had spotted the radio antenna exposed on top of the ground.

"I count fifteen men in the open," Rodriguez said. "Shoot, I wish they hadn't unloaded before we were settled." He turned to Lange. "How much longer before we're up and running?"

"I'm done," Lange answered, hurriedly unwrapping a piece of masking tape from the PVC boot of the cable, used to keep debris out, and plugging it into a gray box the size of a milk carton. He then pushed two smaller power cables into a laptop computer. Lange pulled the classified communications code disk from a secure pocket on his fatigues and shoved it into the slot. A green LED light signified that the communications software was loading onto the hard drive. COMMUNICATIONS SETUP flashed on the screen. Lange ran the power-on diagnostic test, typing P>/ SELF TEST and striking enter. The screen flashed 00 READY.

Rodriguez waited by his side until Lange nodded. "Okay, go."

"Start by transmitting our location for GPS and give our status. Let General Clark know we've counted fifteen armed men so far. Five Libyan MiG-23s are on the ground, and three Libyan IL-76 transports have unloaded unknown cargo and are being refueled right now," Rodriguez ordered.

"Yes, sir." Lange's first item of business was to turn on the Navigation System with Time and Ranging Global Positioning System, or NAVSTAR GPS. The GPS consisted of two parts, a constellation of twenty-one orbiting satellites and a ground-control section to manage them. The satellites circled the earth twice a day. Their orbital tracks were systematized in a way to keep four satellites above the horizon at all times. The ground-control section confirmed the precise position and synchronization of each satellite in relation to the earth and each other. It then uploaded position and time rectifications, independently moving the satellites.

The GPS receiver, in the laptop computer, used a form of triangulation, so that if the team moved from their position to another it would still be able to get a fix on the satellites. The receiver homed in on the transmissions and received what was called an almanac. The almanac notified the receiver where each satellite was located every minute of the day. The receiver then interfaced with the almanac to determine which satellites were in optimum position to plot the team's location. The receiver needed at least three satellites for a two-dimensional bearing on latitude and longitude and all four satellites for a three-dimensional bearing. The correct time in each GPS satellite was critical. They were equipped with an internal clock accurate to one second every 300,000 years.

Lange typed up the message Rodriguez had given him, watching the words appear on the gray, back-lit screen. When it was complete, he pressed the down-load button, sending the electronic codes of each word into the electronic message unit microprocessor. The EMU was an alphanumeric device containing four megabytes of memory that automatically encrypted the message. With two keystrokes, Lange instantly compressed the message, and the unit's PRC-319 transmitter sent a burst transmission on 288 MHz. The narrow-band classified military frequency was used as an up-down link by USAF communications satellites. The defense communications satellite parked directly over them relayed the micro-burst transmission to the NSA in Maryland, where it was decoded and transferred to the STOC at the Pentagon.

MADADHI AIR BASE

Abu Ajami sat alone in a darkened room, located in the rear of the underground pilot's quarters, no bigger than a broom closet. He could feel it starting to happen; he had waited too long. Curled into a tight ball on his cot, he felt his body beginning to shake uncontrollably, his mind drifting, slipping away into visions of the past and dreams of the future. *Allah help me . . . give me strength.* With Kamal in the holding cell, Ajami had failed to take his medication.

He rose, his legs trembling. Sitting on the wooden desk in the corner was a black bag. Inside was a clear injectable drug called Phenothixene, an antipsychotic that would keep his delusions of persecution and grandeur in check. A single injection lasted thirty days. His doctor in Tunis had told him what symptoms would occur if he failed to take the drug, things such as constantly worrying about the time and never remembering it. The concept of night and day would begin to blend into one and he would be consumed by insomnia. In days he would be reduced to a directionless state, unable to focus on tasks as simple as bathing and shaving. Fortunately, he had been diagnosed before he had ever experienced a complete breakdown. And he would not allow himself to suffer one now. Not now, when Allah had finally given him the power to free his people.

Ajami tapped the brown glass bottle containing the Phenothixene, turning it upside down. He inserted the quarter-inch-long needle, extracting 2 cc of the drug into the syringe. Pointing the needle straight up, he squeezed to remove any air. Some of the liquid squirted out. Ajami's heart skipped a beat. Something was wrong. The color of the drug didn't appear right. Only one other man knew about his medication . . . *Kamal, the traitor.*

"No!" He smashed the small bottle against the concrete wall, along with the filled syringe. *Kamal is trying to poison me.* He removed three other bottles and broke them, watching the medication run down the wall.

Ajami tried to clear his clouded mind. He grabbed the medical bag, searching its contents. At the bottom was a small plastic prescription bottle. It was sealed and inside were two dozen blue and yellow Phenothixene tablets, his reserve supply of medication. He removed one and swallowed it. The tablet would calm him for approximately eight hours. Then he would need another.

The inside of the bunker complex reminded Majeed of a tomb. The man-made walls were dull concrete, with sections of reinforced steel exposed every few feet. The complex smelled of mold and human waste. The tunnels leading from room to room were lit with only a single light bulb spaced twenty feet apart, and Majeed could see where pieces of the ceiling had fallen to the floor.

Majeed turned right and entered the pilots' crew quarters. The room was large, measuring fifty by a hundred feet with a ten-foot ceiling. The left side of the chamber was lined with two rows of metal bunk beds. The mattresses had been removed, leaving their wiry frames bare. The right side was lined with tables, chairs, and lockers. The room had been designed to hold forty pilots as well as their flight gear.

Majeed walked to the back of the quarters. He knocked twice on the door, then waited. This was Ajami's place of seclusion when his men occupied the bunker complex.

"Who is it?" Ajami shouted.

"Majeed."

"Enter."

Majeed opened the door and walked in. Ajami was sitting on the center of his bed, with his knees pulled to his chest and his hands wrapped around his legs. Ajami's fine black hair was pulled back and tucked neatly behind his ears. His eyes were wide yet calm.

"I have received new information. American news agencies are reporting that one of their shuttles may have malfunctioned. They are saying that it left orbit, but there are no other details." Majeed shifted the sling holding his Uzi from one shoulder to another.

"Remove the Americans at once!" Ajami demanded. His voice was tight and strained.

"It is being done." Majeed caught Ajami's eyes as he turned and exited the room. For an instant he thought he saw the frightened look of a desperate man.

SPECIAL TECHNICAL OPERATIONS CENTER, PENTAGON

Captain William Harris straightened his back and stretched his legs. At the same time his computer beeped twice and the screen went blank. Harris jumped at the sudden noise; it was the Pathfinder team in the desert. The transmission was being sent via an underground fiber-optic cable from the NSA. The team was using the satellite linkup, and all their transmissions were decoded by the computers at the NSA before being retransmitted to the Pentagon. The entire process took less than thirty seconds, and for all practical purposes it was real-time information.

He watched the message appear across the screen:

```
NOVEMBER/WHISKEY/ROMEO 7721V89
TO:            STOC/COMMAND
FROM:          PATHFINDER TEAM — ALPHA
SITUATION:     TEAM DUG IN AND SECURE. SURVEILLANCE OPERATIONS COMMENCING,
               COUNT 15 ARMED MEN. 3 11-76 LIBYAN TRANSPORTS. 5 MIG-23 LIBYAN
               FIGHTERS. CAMP APPEARS TO BE HOSTILE. NO SIGN OF ATLANTIS OR
               CREW.
NEXT CONTACT:  FOUR HOURS — 15:30 HOURS.
```

Harris pressed the save button, transferring the data onto a backup disk in the H drive. He then pressed the print button. The dot matrix printer next to him clicked off the short message from the team. He ripped it off the printer and headed toward General Warren Clark's office.

As instructed, he knocked on the door twice and entered. General Clark was lying face down on the dark green cot next to the wall.

Clark rolled over and sat up. "What is it?" he yawned.

"General, this just came in from Alpha team. They are on the ground, dug in and safe." Harris held out the paper.

Clark took it and, while reading the message, rubbed the back of his neck. "Confirm their transmission." He looked at his watch, calculating what time it was in Egypt. Madison and Cobra team should be touching down at Ali Ballas within the hour.

"Contact Colonel Madison. I want to know when Cobra team will be ready to move out."

"Yes, sir."

"All right . . . keep me informed of anything else." Clark stood. He had to get on the phone to Dawson.

* * *

The Palestinian kept his hands steady as the bright blue and white flames of the cutting torch melted away the aluminum frame of the shuttle's hatch. His dirty black welding helmet was getting heavy and the eighteen-year-old could feel sweat rolling down his back. The silicon tiles on the outside had to be chipped away before he started to cut into the metal skin of the plane. He moved the torch from the area he was cutting and turned off the acetylene and oxygen mixture, killing the flame. He lifted the visor on the helmet and reached for a hammer and chisel. Another man, next to him, was chipping away the tiles on the right side of the hatch.

"How much longer?" Majeed called from below the crudely built wooden platform the two men were standing on.

"This is very difficult. The metal is of very high quality."

"I said, how much longer?" Majeed asked, growing restless. Four armed men were standing behind him with automatic rifles in their hands and pistols tucked in their belts.

"I would say we are halfway finished. It will be another fifteen, twenty minutes."

Rodriguez read the confirming message as it appeared on the computer screen.

"Okay, Sergeant, switch to standby." Rodriguez didn't want any unnecessary radio transmissions giving away their location. Just then he heard a low thunder in the background. His eyes met Rath's.

"Yeah, I hear them," Rath answered and went to look out the front of the OP. He motioned to Shaw that he was relieved and took over the watch. Rodriguez joined him.

Lieutenant Rath tilted his head to the right. "Those are choppers, all right." The sound of their rotors cutting through the heavy morning air was very distinctive.

"There to the left, just off the deck at nine o'clock."

Rodriguez counted four Mil Mi-8 sweeping in from the west, the transport helicopters slowly making their way across the runway in front of them. Each chopper swung around and then touched down one right after the other, kicking up large clouds of dust.

"More equipment," Rath said.

"Yeah, they're getting ready for something." Rodriguez looked over at his second in command. "I don't like the way this is starting to look. I want you and Vasquez to move out. Set up a position above us. When you dig in, contact me and then take two-hour intervals of rest and stay alert. If they're expecting company, I don't want to be the first uninvited guests."

"Yes, sir." Rath signaled to the team's other sniper, Ricky Vasquez. Each man slipped into what is known as a gilly suit, which was nothing more than a bunch of brown and gray strips of cloth sewn together. They placed the suits over their heads and shoulders, helping to break up their outlines and silhouettes. The suits were bulky but lightweight and relatively cool to wear. Vasquez grabbed his backpack and scoped heavy-barrel bolt-action rifle. The two exited out the back of the OP and silently climbed up the hill.

Rodriguez addressed the other two members of the team. "Lange . . . Shaw, try to get some sleep. I'll take this watch. Lange, I'll wake you in two hours."

Libyan Lieutenant Shmuel Mizrahi waited for the blades of the Mil Mi-8 to stop moving before he stepped off the brown camouflaged chopper. He could taste the desert dust in his mouth as he slipped on his sunglasses and walked toward the first underground bunker.

"Lieutenant Mizrahi?" One of the terrorists approached him.

"Yes."

"This way. Captain Jibril and Ajami are waiting for you."

"I know the way." Mizrahi looked straight ahead as he and the other man neared the doorway. Two Palestinian guards stood on each side of the entrance.

Mizrahi was not a stranger to the camp. He had been stationed there when it had been an active Libyan air base for two years. He'd flown against the French-backed Chadian air force. It had been a long and bloody campaign, and the Libyan air force had not fared well. Mizrahi, however, had masterminded a plan and repainted his squadron's French-built Libyan F-1A Mirage fighters in French combat colors. They were to fly right into the Chadian's home base at N'Djamena. The French and Chadian forces would never know what hit them. The plan had not been a success and there were some unfortunate losses. While still 100 kilometers from the Chadian capital, their flight had been discovered and challenged by French ground controllers. Their IFF transponder codes didn't match the computer codes the controllers were using. Mizrahi's four F-1As were engaged by French Super Etendards. Two of his wingmen were shot down, but Mizrahi managed to down one of the Etendards. Thus it was hailed as a victory, and Mizrahi had been promoted to first lieutenant.

Mizrahi let the Palestinian cross in front of him as they entered the main underground tunnel connecting the bunkers and storage rooms. He guessed they were headed toward the old command and control center, which was straight ahead, the first entrance on the left. The concrete walls were still a deep shade of gray, as he remembered, and the tunnel still poorly lit. He could hear the distant echoes of voices and the thud of his flight boots. The only thing that had changed was the smell. The stench now reminded him of a highway rest room.

They walked a hundred or so meters and the Palestinian turned into a room with a large map of the Middle East on the far wall. Sitting at a table was his commanding officer, Captain Faisal Jibril.

"Reporting as ordered, sir." Mizrahi saluted and stood at attention.

Jibril rose to his feet. "Lieutenant, welcome." He looked at Ajami. "This is Ajami, the camp's leader."

Mizrahi nodded in his direction.

Jibril got right to the point. "Were you able to secure the additional equipment I've requested?"

"Yes, sir. Everything is on the way. In twenty-four hours this will be the most secure area in northern Africa."

"And air defenses," Ajami demanded. "What about the air defenses I need?"

Mizrahi hesitated.

"You may speak freely," Jibril said.

"Three SA-6 systems will be here shortly. My men will have them operational by nightfall. I am also airlifting two of our SA-8 mobiles. They, too, will be operational by nightfall," Mizrahi reported, not looking at the Palestinian.

Ajami paid no attention to the lieutenant's insolence. "This is a start, Jibril. But I need more. I must give Majeed instructions on where to place the defenses." He turned, leaving the two men alone.

Jibril walked over and closed the metal door. "What about the ground troops I requested?" he asked in a low tone, still afraid of being overheard.

"Major Nittal agrees with you; Ajami is not to be trusted. There will be twenty T-72 tanks with a company of ground troops and their support vehicles here in twenty-four hours. He has already given the order."

"And Qaddafi . . . what is he saying?" Jibril asked.

"Qaddafi is still hiding in the desert. Nittal has taken charge of this operation," Mizrahi answered, still at attention.

Of course, Jibril thought. Nittal is not a fool. He will use this to win Qaddafi's praise. No wonder he is cooperating with me.

"What else needs to be done?" Jibril asked.

"Sir, this base is not fit for defensive operations. I have flown in six technical engineers to help bring the base up to proper standards. My first concern is that the underground fuel storage tanks have been contaminated with groundwater. I also suggest we step up round-the-clock foot and air security patrols . . . we can use the helicopters."

"I agree. Do it," Jibril grunted. "Anything else?"

"Yes, sir . . . May I see it? The space shuttle. I would like to see it."
The lieutenant's expression had not changed, but there was a hint of
eagerness in his voice.

"In time, in time. Right now, it is most important you set up operations immediately. We all know it is just a matter of time before the
Americans will be here."

"Yes, sir," Mizrahi answered and left the room.

"That should do it," the welder said, as he turned off the cutting torch
and took off his helmet. His eyes stung from the heat and salt of his
sweat.

"Are you through?" Majeed asked.

"Yes. The hatch is cut open." He could tell by Majeed's stare he
should gather his tools and get out of the way.

Majeed, with his eyes on the hatch door, directed one of the security
guards standing next to him: "Go and inform Ajami we are entering the
plane. Let's go." He climbed the stairs with two of the guards following.

"Stand back," he said, kicking the hatch on the shuttle three times.
The door gave a little with each blow. On the fifth try it fell into the
shuttle. Majeed stepped back to the side, expecting a blast of gunfire to
erupt from within.

When nothing happened, he motioned, whispering, "Follow me . . .
and no shooting, we want them alive."

He crouched down, turning on his flashlight. Cautiously he crawled
into the plane.

The interior was dark and the air was heavy with human odor. He
straightened up, sweeping the beam of light across the interior. It suddenly hit him: he was inside an American shuttle, but he couldn't let the
awe of the moment distract him from his duties. The walls were padded
and everything appeared to be in disarray. Majeed, seeing a ladder leading up to another level, shouted in Arabic: "Surrender yourselves! You
have no escape, no place to run. If you surrender, it will be easier on all
of us."

There was no answer. Majeed switched off the flashlight, letting his
eyes adjust to the low light. There was light filtering down from the port
hole directly above. He reached for the first rung of the ladder, repeating
more calmly, "Surrender yourselves. I know you are up there; it would
only be a matter of time before my men find you." After moments of
silence he realized they would not understand him and repeated his
demands in English.

*   *   *

"What should we do?" Andrea whispered to Duke, her voice panicked.

"Nothing. We're going to do as he says and come out slowly with our hands in the air. Remember, we're not a threat. We have to let them know that." Duke looked at Andrea and then at Willie, waiting for a reaction. "Willie, you with me?"

"Yeah . . . I'm with you. Dead or alive."

"Remember. Remain cool and do as they say," Duke said slowly.

Majeed pointed his flashlight at the descending man. He could feel his heartbeat quicken as his grip tightened on his pistol. The two guards standing behind him held up their AK-47s. He repeated his order to the soldiers not to shoot. The American hesitated, then came into view. Majeed could see that his hands were in the air.

"Don't shoot. We are unarmed," Duke spoke as firmly as he could.

Majeed motioned with his pistol for the American to stand clear of the ladder. He could see two others waiting to climb down.

"Come on down, Andi. It's okay," Duke called up reassuringly, keeping his eyes on the man he believed to be in charge. Andrea, with Willie in tow, came down the stairs. They took their places next to Duke.

"Search them," Majeed demanded, then put his arm out. "No, wait. I will do it. You go upstairs and make sure there is no one else." He looked at Andrea first, then back at Duke. The other guard stepped back at an opposite angle, moving his rifle back and forth across the group. Majeed placed his pistol in his holster, then very thoroughly and smoothly ran his hands around each one.

"They are unarmed," he said. Retrieving his gun, he motioned toward the opening.

Keeping their hands in the air, they moved single file to the hatch.

Ricky Vasquez was careful to step only on rocks as he climbed up the mountain above the main OP. Footprints could linger in the desert dirt for days. Following closely behind him, utilizing the same rocks, was his spotter, First Lieutenant Rath.

"Vasquie . . . to the right, fifty yards and below the largest boulder. See it?" Rath whispered.

"Yeah, I see it. Looks good." Vasquez switched his rifle from his left hand to his right and continued.

Both men headed to the cluster of rocks next to a dried brown bush. The rocks would provide shade and the bush would help conceal their weapons from the rays of sunlight. To a sniper, the sun could be a fatal enemy. One flicker of reflected light could give their position away.

When Vasquez and Rath first met, they couldn't have seemed more different. Coming from dissimilar backgrounds, it took an entire month before they could even tolerate each other and two more months before they began to trust one another. They soon discovered, however, that they liked the same food, beer, and football teams. That had been three years ago. Now they were closer than most brothers. A bond had materialized. They even thought alike. When behind enemy lines, knowing your partner's next move could save both your lives.

Vasquez moved in behind the largest boulder, lying on his stomach facing north, toward the main part of the camp. Rath moved in next to him, taking out his 24-power SLR Redfield spotting scope. Vasquez put his 7×50 binoculars to his eyes. Immediately they started to search the area around them and the OP for any enemy foot patrols. Their first search was fast, aimed at identifying obvious threats. It took less than a minute.

"Clean."

"Clean," Rath agreed. "Go to secondary." With the first part of the search over, the two men went to part two. This was where the true art of observation came into play. Rath, with his powerful spotting scope, would make a detailed search of everything 1,000 yards and farther out. Vasquez, using his binoculars, would search everything closer in. They would each make mental notes of possible enemy hides, rocks, ditches, and vegetation. They would also locate the likely paths for any patrols in the area. Because they were in the desert and cover was limited, this search lasted only ten minutes.

"Secure," Vasquez muttered.

"Secure . . . I've spotted about thirty men, but they're all on the opposite side of the airstrip." Rath looked at his sniper. "You know that'll change quick."

"Yeah." Vasquez carefully moved a dead weed over his unfolded bipod, mounted on the foregrip of his rifle. "I can get a clear shot of anyone moving up from below."

"Okay, Vasquie, I'm on deck for the first watch; you get some sleep."

"Yes, sir." He rolled over on his side and placed his sniper camo hat over his face. Rath keyed his radio headset. "Rushmore . . . Icebox . . . in position. Area secure."

"Roger, Icebox."

The reception was good. Rath, contented, repositioned himself so he was more comfortable. The desert, starting to warm up, was alive with the faint noises of insects looking for a place to rest to avoid the scalding heat. He resisted the temptation to take a drink from his water jug.

Instead, Rath evaluated their situation. First, the positives. The enemy was dug in and fortified, operating out of hardened bunkers. They weren't mobile, and he and Vasquez would know where their strong points were. He estimated their position was 1,800 yards away from the bunkers. It wouldn't be easy, but Vasquez had the uncanny ability to drop a man at 2,000 yards. On the negative side, there was a lot of enemy personnel at this base and the Libyans were bringing in more firepower. Rath wiped the sweat away from his eyebrow and continued scanning the area around him.

Ajami entered the bunker to see the three Americans kneeling with their faces toward the wall. Majeed was walking behind them while two men stood with their guns focused on them. Ajami came closer and Majeed backed away.

"Have they resisted?" Ajami asked.

"No, my leader."

"They are cowards," Jibril spoke out, coming into the bunker.

"I doubt that anyone who flies into space is a coward," Ajami replied, bringing his attention to the astronauts. "Make them stand and turn around. I want to see their faces."

Majeed walked over to the woman, motioning her to stand along with the other two men.

Ajami stared into their eyes, then looked them over. Their light-colored flight suits were dirty and soiled. He had never felt as he did at this moment. Here, in his possession, was the grand prize. The wonderful power of it made him smile. He shook off the warm feeling, alarmed that he might have exposed his true thoughts.

He walked up to Willie first. Removing his pistol, he placed the barrel under the man's chin. He snapped the safety off, watching the American's eyes blink with fear.

"He's just playing with you, Willie," Andrea breathed, angered by the intimidation tactic.

"Shut up," Ajami said in perfect English. "I did not give you permission to speak." He pushed the pistol further into Willie's throat but turned and looked at Andrea. "A woman . . . a *woman* defends your honor. Is she one of your Western whores you are so fond of?"

Willie tried to swallow, waiting for a bullet to rip into his head at any second.

"Leave him alone," Duke James demanded, snapping his head around and looking right at Ajami.

Ajami lowered the pistol, walked over, and stood in front of him. They were nearly the same height. Their eyes met, boring into one another. Neither flinched or made a move.

"So . . . you are the leader of the space plane."

Duke remained still, not answering.

Ajami raised his gun and jammed it up under Duke's chin, forcing his head up. "You will be the one I kill first."

Duke slightly turned up his mouth, keeping his eyes on Ajami.

"Why are you here?" Ajami asked, averting his gaze, shifting it back and forth. His eyes became frenzied, like that of an animal.

"Our shuttle malfunctioned and we were forced to land," Duke said slowly.

"Stop! Enough of your babbling. I will determine what sort of mission you were on. Majeed, take them to the holding cell. Keep their hands and feet bound. I will deal with them later. First, I must know what they are carrying on their plane."

"Yes, my leader."

21

With his bound hands Duke grabbed two of the rusty cell bars and tried shaking them. The one-inch-thick steel bars didn't move. They were firmly anchored into each side of the wall with large bolts.

Duke surveyed the room, soaking in the details. From the size of the bunker *Atlantis* was in and the distance they had walked, he estimated they were at least a hundred yards underground, maybe more. The walls of the cells were made of concrete like the rest of the bunker, and the room they were in was dirty and unlit. A pile of broken tables, chairs, and other junk was near the front of the room. Light filtered in from the corner doorway twenty feet away. The rearmost third of the holding area, where the two cells were located, spanned the width of the rectangular chamber. Duke and his crew were in the right cell with a straw bed and metal bucket, which was to be used to relieve themselves. The other cell contained the same items except there was a large Arab man sitting with his back to them. The man had not moved and was quiet.

Willie lifted his hands, trying to loosen the rope wrapped around his wrists. He got up and walked over next to Duke. "If we had only been able to get a radio message out . . . or something to let them know where we are," he whispered.

"I have to believe they're on the way, Willie. What I'm more concerned with is keeping us alive until then. The man they call Ajami must be the leader," Duke said, studying the figure in the next cell.

"Did you see his eyes? He's a madman," Willie stated, remembering the gun shoved under his chin.

"Yeah, I saw them. I also saw something else, though. He's mad, but he was scared, too." Duke nodded toward the Arab in the cell next to them. "What do you think?"

"I think he's in here to listen to every word we say," Willie answered flatly.

"Yeah, me, too."

Duke and Willie walked back over and sat down next to Andrea on the bed. The waiting game was about to begin.

Pathfinder Team Alpha: Icebox

Lieutenant Rath was lying flat on a rock cliff overlooking the valley. Vasquez was behind him, in the shade, asleep.

Rath adjusted the focus on his spotting scope as he moved it slowly left to right. He could see, through the distorted hot air, groups of armed men starting to walk from the center of camp into the surrounding hills. Several of the men were wearing military uniforms, while others were in civilian clothing. Three groups of two started moving across the runway toward their positions.

"Foot patrols," he sighed aloud. It was preferable they would only have to hide from helicopters, but they remained parked next to the bunkers. Soldiers on foot was an entirely different defense. He focused the scope on the men and keyed his communication mike. Under his hat Rath was wearing a miniature radio headset with an earpiece connected to a small microphone, which was coiled around to the front of his mouth. The device allowed him to communicate with the OP up to three miles away using EHF radio bursts. The radio and receiver contained a microcomputer that constantly varied the transmissions between frequencies, making it impossible for the enemy to listen in.

"Rushmore . . . this is Icebox. Bad guys heading our way," he whispered into the mike.

"Roger, Icebox. We see 'em." It was Sergeant Lange.

Rath tried to adjust his position on the hard ground. He was finding it harder to concentrate as the temperature climbed higher and languor set in. He turned his attention to his watch. In thirty minutes they would be approaching the vicinity of the OP. He looked back through the spotting scope as the first group of men started to climb into the hills to his left.

The Pentagon

The crisis team meeting had been moved up three hours. It was now 0455 hours. Tom Staffer had managed to rustle up a third cup of strong black coffee from the cleaning lady. She always carried a thermos with her, he had discovered on one of his other late night work jaunts. He felt a little better. A short nap, a hot shower, and two cold cinnamon rolls could do wonders. The meeting was to be held in the Tank. It was a soundproof room on the second floor of the Pentagon where the Joint Chiefs held their weekly meetings. Staffer assumed that Admiral Petersen had caught an earlier flight in from Colorado Springs, enabling Dawson to hurry things along. His assumption was confirmed as he entered the Tank, closing the heavy metal door.

"Good morning, Tom. Have a seat and we'll get started. Everyone's been introduced." Jack Dawson looked around, waiting for anyone to speak up if they hadn't. He was sitting at the end of the rectangular table.

Staffer's eyes went up to the clock hanging on the back wall. He was five minutes early but still the last person to arrive. Sitting to the right of General Dawson was John Turner, the secretary of defense, General Warren Clark, and Mark Collins from the CIA. On the left was Loran Hogsett, Staffer's intelligence officer, and Admiral Petersen from NORAD. Behind Dawson were several large wall maps of the Middle East and a dry erase board. Even in the computer age, Dawson still preferred wall maps and chalkboards.

"General Clark, would you give us a brief update, please," Dawson began.

"Yes, sir. We've received two reports from our Pathfinder team on the ground. They confirm the air base is active with Libyan transport aircraft and there are currently five MiG-23s on the ground. The complete visual count of men in the camp at this time is up to thirty-two. With the additional transports coming in, we don't know what that will do to the numbers. I am speculating the orbiter and crew are being held in an underground aircraft bunker. The problem is, from the background info we have on this base, there are three bunkers and presently can't be positive which one she's in." Clark finished speaking, setting his notes back down on top of his file.

"Collins, what's the latest satellite data?" Dawson asked.

"Our last KH-14 pass confirms most of what General Clark just reported. The NPIC is doing a detailed IR and photo examination, trying to pinpoint the base's power and water supply source. They probably have some type of electrical generators. The National Security Agency has only detected scattered radio signals coming into or out of the base, nothing we've been able to listen in on. I finished reviewing a series of IR photos, and the Libyan military base to the north seems quiet. I'm seeing aircraft engines to automobiles, but nothing out of the ordinary. If they're preparing for something, I don't see it." Collins folded his arms and leaned back in his chair.

Secretary Turner frowned, looking around the room and ending his search on Dawson. "With each passing minute, General, this thing is getting out of control. Shouldn't we be doing something?"

"We are. That's why we're here, Mr. Turner." Dawson turned to Loran Hogsett and grinned, trying to break some of the tension in the room. "Loran, Mr. Staffer informs me you've had a chance to review the Lacrosse satellite pictures."

"Yes, sir, I have."

"Good. What can you tell us?"

"Well, realizing I normally analyze nuc boats, not satellites . . ." Everyone chuckled a little. "The Russians told us the ten canisters in question on the Kosmos were empty. Admiral Petersen's photos show a different story." He opened a file and removed the radar-enhanced pictures of the Kosmos. "Admiral, what radar power setting was the Lacrosse programmed at when these images were taken?"

"Maximum power with a narrow beam."

"And the range?"

"The first pass was about fifty miles but at an angle of fifteen degrees. The second and third passes were farther away." Petersen scanned his notes to make certain he was correct. "The third pass we were able to get a straightforward radar shot less than five degrees off center. What you have are the radar images. I brought along a series you haven't seen . . . these are standard pictures of the Kosmos taken from one of our recon ships." Petersen extended the photos to the man next to him.

Hogsett slipped on his glasses and the room fell silent as the ex-sub skipper scrutinized each picture.

"Ah, shit, I was afraid of this," he moaned, then looked at Dawson and Staffer. "We have big trouble, gentlemen."

"Explain," Dawson said, sitting up, his attention seized.

"The Lacrosse's radar is powerful enough to penetrate the hulls of some of the best-built nuclear submarines in the world. Besides giving us a good idea of what a sub's superstructure design looks like, it can easily distinguish the size and number of nuclear warheads while the missile—"

"What the fuck does that have to do with—" Turner interrupted, impatient with all the talk.

"Mr. Turner, the Kosmos is carrying ten large nuclear warheads."

"What?" Dawson rose from his chair, dropping the photos to the table.

"I brought these other images for comparison. This one is a radar impression taken from the same Lacrosse C bird at 280 miles above Severodvinsk shipyards in the Arctic six months ago. It's a good shot. The picture is crisp and clean. It shows a Russian Delta-class sub in dry dock. This Delta IV is relatively new, built in the late eighties. It carried sixteen SS-N-23; they're liquid-fueled MIRVs with three warheads each. From these pictures, you can see that the outer hull is lime green, indicating it's made of a high-quality carbon steel with a rubber tile outer covering. This dark blue cube in the rear is the reactor core, and just behind the tower are two rows of dark blue blotches . . . the sub's nuclear warheads." Hogsett moved his pencil over the photos, pointing out the areas. "These blotches are reflectors, impenetrable metallic buffers surrounding the weapons' cores to keep the neutrons from escaping. The casings are so dense our radar can't penetrate them. The Kosmos's blotches are the same color, shape, and density."

Turner ran his fingers through his hair. "This is inexcusable! We not only have a downed shuttle, now you're telling me there are nuclear warheads on board it? And it's at an air base controlled by the damn Libyans?" Turner's face was flushed with anger as his eyes bore in on Dawson, then Hogsett. "You damn well better be sure about what you're saying."

"John, sit down. This is a shock to all of us. Hogsett isn't to blame. If you want to bite someone's head off, wait till you catch up with Weber. He's the one that pushed this through."

"I hate to add to the hysteria, but there's more. It's not just the Libyans we need to be worried about," Collins jumped in, relieved the mood had escalated so he could voice his concerns without being the only bearer of bad news. "I'm concerned this base is a training camp for a terrorist organization—" He stopped. Everyone in the room was staring at him.

"Well, go on, Mark." Dawson motioned with his hand.

"This is a CIA intel report written a few months ago. It contains several high-altitude photographs of the air base, taken by an Israeli RF-4. The reconnaissance data is vague, but the Israelis speculate this is an underground operation." He handed the CIA brief to Turner.

Staffer's mind jumped as pieces of the puzzle came together. "That's it! The MiG-23 the navy shot down a week ago . . . Is it possible it may have flown out of this base?"

"That's what I believe . . . that this base is fully operational and commanded by a man called Abu Ajami," Collins said, looking around the room.

Turner studied the brief a moment longer, then handed it to Dawson. "Hogsett, do you have any idea what kind of nuclear weapons we are dealing with?"

"I would guess these warheads are comparable to our own W-78s used on the Mark 12A MIRV system. That would make it a typical three-stage thermonuclear explosive. Very dangerous and very powerful."

"Estimate how powerful," Turner prodded.

"Knowing the Soviets, probably a yield of ten to twenty megatons. Enough to level a large city and then some."

"How difficult would it be to remove these nukes?" General Dawson asked, while writing on a yellow notepad on the table in front of him.

Hogsett removed his glasses. "It depends on the type of arming sub-system the Soviets used when they built this thing. If they were using a barometric switch . . ." he paused, making sure he had his facts straight and that everyone knew what he was talking about. "A barometric switch is basically a titanium-reinforced glass tube. It breaks under the high G stress of reentering the atmosphere and arms the warhead. If anyone tries to remove a warhead, they had better know what they're doing. If that tube breaks, it's over with. Even if each warhead is deactivated by using the right sequence, there's still a chance the system's sensing equipment will issue a self-destruct signal, detonating it. Without direct help from the Russians, I'd say the Libyans' chances of removing one of the weapons safely is fifty-fifty. At best," Hogsett added.

"Staffer, I want you and Hogsett to compile this information into a nice neat little packet. I want to be able to hit the Russians over the head with it. I don't know what kind of game they're playing, but I'm going to find out." Turner's eyes met Dawson's, knowing they both had the same question. "If the Libyans or terrorists do remove one of those warheads, what then?"

"I don't even want to think about the possibilities. They could sit on it for a while. Put it on top of one of their new rockets or cram it down our throats," Hogsett answered.

Turner starting tapping on the table. "I want to hear an airtight recommendation for attacking the base and for recovering the shuttle, those Russian weapons, and the crew. I have a meeting scheduled at the White House in two hours and I'm not walking out of here without a plan in hand. *For Christ's sake,* how the hell did this happen!" The secretary breathed heavily, regaining his composure.

Dawson rose from his chair and walked over to the maps behind him. His mind was piecing things together. "We know we are dealing with a remote air base controlled by the Libyans. Hogsett's correct. All the Libyans have to do is remove one warhead and they'll have us by the balls." He swiveled around, addressing General Clark. "Is your air ops team up and ready in Ali Ballas?" Dawson pointed to the Egyptian base on the map for Turner's sake.

"Yes, and they'll be ready to move in six hours." Clark's tone was matter of fact.

"Good." Dawson rubbed his chin. "Mr. Secretary, under the circumstances, I'm going to recommend the following. Since General Clark's Cobra team is based here at Ali Ballas, we can order them in just before dawn . . . seventeen hours from now. They have the muscle to neutralize air defenses, including MiG cover, and any armor on the ground."

He paused for a moment, wanting to make sure Turner understood. "The F-117As, A-10s, and F-16s can attack ground targets while the F-15s sweep the sky of enemy MiGs. The F-15Es can take out the base's communications equipment and power supply." Dawson pointed to the area between the three Libyan military bases and Madadhi, then continued, "Staffer, I want you and the CIA to provide General Clark with current satellite imagery. We're going to need real-time data once this thing starts." He walked over next to his seat. "General Clark, tell your Pathfinder team we need to know in which bunker the shuttle is located. I don't give a shit how they find out, but we need to know. After that we can finalize a recovery plan."

"Yes, sir."

"Anything else, gentlemen?" Dawson asked.

"Yes, General," Tom Staffer sounded off. "I get the feeling you're discounting the terrorist threat. If it is Abu Ajami running this camp, it could be a more dangerous situation than you realize. These terrorists may be more threatening than the Libyans. They're not as predictable."

"What are you suggesting?"

"I think it would be a good idea to have Collins on the ground in Ali Ballas to help advise your team. He's studied Middle East terrorist groups and knows them better than anyone else in the CIA. Maybe in the end they won't need him, but it wouldn't hurt."

Dawson looked at Collins, then back at Staffer. "Do it. I'll have an F-15B fueled and ready to go at Langley Air Base in one hour. Now, let's get moving."

Staffer looked at Collins. "You have one hour. Pack your bags."

PATHFINDER TEAM ALPHA

"Incoming transmission, sir," Sergeant Lange said in a low voice. The other two men, Rodriguez and Shaw, were huddled near the front of the observation post.

Rodriguez crouched down and watched as a message from the Special Technical Operation Center in the Pentagon flashed up on the communication computer screen.

NOV/BEV/CCDZ/SWQWVV 7721V89

TO:	PATHFINDER TEAM -- ALPHA
FROM:	STOC/COMMAND **URGENT**
1]	FIND LOCATION AND STATUS OF ORBITER AND CREW.
2]	INTELLIGENCE BELIEVES SHUTTLE IN ONE OF THE UNDERGROUND AIRCRAFT BUNKERS.
3]	RELAY AT ONCE WHEN VERIFICATION IS MADE. END

"How in the *hell* do they expect us to do that?" Lange asked, looking up.

"I don't know. But it sounds like shit is going to hit the fan pretty damn soon. Acknowledge the transmission."

"Yes, sir."

Rodriguez moved back up to the front of the OP. It was now mid-morning and he could feel a light breeze sneaking in underneath the netting. There was a rustle through the leaves of a nearby tree as the wind blew up from the valley below. The air felt good, hitting his face as he lifted his head above ground level to scan the broken landscape with his binoculars. Rodriguez had lost sight of the foot patrols making their way up as they climbed into the gullies below him.

He heard the hiss in his headset, then Rath's voice. *"Rushmore . . . Icebox. Do you still have a visual?"*

"Negative, Icebox."

"I see two men . . . three hundred meters at twelve o'clock."

Rodriguez looked directly beneath the OP, straining to pick up any movement. He saw one of the men and then the other emerge from behind a large rock and disappear again. They were following each other in single file. It was obvious by the way they were walking they hadn't been well trained for scouting and surveillance. They should have been spread out. It was not only safer but would allow more ground coverage in less time. A good sniper could take them both out instantaneously.

A few seconds later, Rodriguez watched the men move out of the gully into a flat area vacant of any rocks and underbrush.

"Icebox . . . I see the bad guys." Rodriguez aimed his binoculars directly at the two figures.

"Advise, Rushmore . . ."

Rodriguez didn't answer right away. Instead he patiently studied the men. They were moving slowly but deliberately as they continued toward the OP. He guessed they would be on top of the hide in fifteen to twenty minutes. *One of them could answer some very important questions. I could kill two birds with one stone.*

The two men had stopped and were talking to each other. Rodriguez thought through his plan. He looked for any signs that would tell him which man would break under pressure first. "Icebox, do you see a good spot to drop one, repeat, *one?*"

Rath meticulously traced the course of the gully until it seemed to branch out into five deeply cut fingers a hundred meters from where the men were now standing. *"Yes . . . one o'clock . . . 175 meters out."*

Rodriguez tried to see exactly where Rath was looking, but his view was partially blocked by several dry shrubs. *A good hiding place,* he thought.

"Icebox, I'm going out. When I'm in position, drop the old one. I'll get the other."

"They're on the move again."

"Roger, I'm moving." Rodriguez grabbed his rifle and motioned to Lange. They snuck out the back end of the OP, starting down the side of the mountain on their bellies.

Ghassan Musa put the heavy AK-47 over his left shoulder as he stayed within a dozen feet of the older man called Salahat. A drop of sweat rolled off his brow and down the side of his face.

"I will thank Allah when we reach the top of this mountain," Ghassan said, taking another step.

"It will be much easier to search the mountain when we walk down than it was going up," Salahat said over his shoulder encouragingly. "The sooner we reach the top, the sooner we can rest." He put his head down and unknowingly continued straight toward the end of the gully and the OP.

Rath reached his booted foot out and nudged his companion twice.

"Vasquie . . . grab your rifle and get your ass over here. We have company," Rath whispered, just loud enough for his sniper to hear.

Vasquez rolled over and crawled so he was shoulder to shoulder with his spotter.

"You awake?" Rath questioned with a smirk.

"Shit, you know I smelled a kill . . . where?"

"Two men . . . one o'clock, 250 meters down from the OP. I see one and the other should be right behind him."

"Okay, what's the plan?" Vasquez reached into his pocket and pulled out a sandwich of cheese crackers with a half inch of peanut butter between them. He ate it in two bites. Then, as Rath relayed the orders, he screwed a matte black twenty-four-inch silencer onto the end of his M40A2 sniper rifle. He rested the heavy stainless steel barrel of the .308 caliber weapon on his left forearm. "Let's see," he said to himself, "two hundred and fifty meters . . . six power should do it." Vasquez turned the notched black ring on his 3×9 Leopold variable III scope to 6 and put it to his right eye.

"One o'clock. The old one's in front, light brown shirt, next to that clump of trees."

"Got him," Vasquez uttered, as he saw the two men through his scope. He removed three rounds of 7.62-millimeter ammunition, holding them firmly in his right hand. While keeping his eye on the lead man, Vasquez took the three cartridges and tapped them noiselessly on the side of his rifle to make sure the gunpowder was uniformly packed in each. Unlike every other sniper in the USMC, Vasquez didn't use the standard Lake City M118 match ammo issued to him. Instead, he used a special round he handloaded, consisting of a Hornady .30 caliber 168-grain match hollow point bullet, Winchester competition brass, and 51.3 grains of IMR 4831 gunpowder. The powder in each cartridge was weighed to exact standards, and each bullet was seated to within 0.0005 of an inch. It had taken Vasquez six months to perfect this load, but it was time well spent. The handloaded cartridges increased his accuracy over ten percent at 500 meters. That translated into more successful hits on a target than anyone else on his former rifle team.

He quietly opened the bolt of the rifle and slipped two of the rounds in the magazine and the other one into the chamber.

"Ready," Vasquez lipped as he closed the bolt and clicked on the safety.

Rodriguez and Lange were creeping along, half on their bellies, half on their knees, not making very good time. The trick was to move fast, of course, but it being midmorning they were hampered by the situation. Rodriguez didn't like the odds. At the rate they were moving, they would arrive at the end of the gully only a few minutes before the foot patrol. He didn't have much of an option now; they were committed.

Rodriguez spoke nervously into his mike. "Rath, talk to me. Are we going to make it?"

"They're still in the gully . . . but it looks like they've slowed up some." Rath refocused his spotting scope, following up to the captain. *"There's a narrow hill sixty meters just ahead. If you get in behind it, you could crawl right up to the underbrush. They'll never see you."*

Rodriguez stopped just long enough to search the terrain with his eyes. He didn't see what Rath was talking about but was sure he would find it once he got to it.

"Roger. We're moving again."

"Salahat . . . wait," Ghassan paused in midstride.

"What is it?" Salahat turned back to look at the younger man. "Did you see something?"

Ghassan didn't move as he looked and listened to everything around him. A sudden sense of danger and apprehension came over him.

"What is it?" Salahat asked again.

"Someone is watching us . . . we are too close together." Ghassan's attention went to the broken landscape above them, looking for anything unusual.

Salahat scanned the area in front of him, then spoke. "Did you see something or just hear it?"

"I am not so sure." Ghassan lowered his rifle to a more ready posture and took a cautious step to the right.

Salahat nodded. "We probably frightened a lost jerboa. We'll follow this ravine until it ends, then spread out if it will make you feel better."

"All right," Ghassan agreed, keeping his eyes on the rugged mountain.

Rath watched Rodriguez and Lange as they crawled into the underbrush. Their desert camouflage blended well into the surroundings. Rath picked out a perfect place for a two-man ambush.

"ETA, two to three minutes," The spotter informed both the captain and the sniper. Rodriguez clicked his mike twice, acknowledging the transmission.

"Okay, Vasquie, you're up next," Rath said as he backed away from Vasquez. "Wind out of the west at five knots, 265 meters." Rath spoke from behind his sniper, eliminating any chances of visually distracting him.

Vasquez sucked in a deep breath and let it out slowly as he tried to relax. At such short range he wouldn't have to adjust his scope. His rifle was zeroed at 200 meters.

Vasquez concentrated on the cross hairs. He had not shot at a living target since the Iraqi war. The two men were now clearly in view. All he had to do was wait for them to get closer to the end of the ravine and take out his target. The sniper's skill would be proven if the man died the instant the bullet struck him.

Vasquez slid the safety knob off with his thumb, feeling the warm metal snap forward. He brought the tip of his forefinger on the edge of the trigger and aimed the cross hairs a few inches in front of the old man's head. He just had to wait for the right moment, allowing lead time for the bullet to travel the distance. Behind him, Rath signaled to Captain Rodriguez that everything was ready.

The shot had to be perfect. The segment of the brain controlling all motor reflexes was located just behind the eyes, running from temple to temple. For a successful kill, Vasquez would have to hit roughly a two-inch-diameter target. If he missed by even a few inches, the man could live up to eight to ten seconds, enough time to retaliate or shout out a warning.

Vasquez watched the target move closer to where Rodriguez was hiding. He flexed his fingers, then felt for the exact position on the trigger. Taking in another deep breath, he let out half of it, concentrating on the center of the cross hairs. He slowly applied pressure to the 2.5-pound trigger, releasing the rest of his breath between heartbeats.

"Sweet dreams," he said, and the rifle jumped back against his shoul-

der. The muffled sound of the racing bullet leaving the end of the silencer filled his ear.

Rodriguez kept a steady gaze as the side of the older man's head exploded into a mass of red mist and bone fragments. The 168-grain hollow point bullet impacted just behind his right eye. He died instantly.
Rodriguez knew they had only seconds to react.

"Ahhh," was all Ghassan could mutter as his friend fell to the ground
with a hard thump, not moving. He moved a few steps forward, reaching to help him up, then stopped. He stared blankly at the bloody pieces
strewn about. He looked left and right, not knowing where the bullet
had come from.

It was all the time Rodriguez and Lange needed. Rodriguez lunged
from behind the brush, straight for Ghassan. He mashed the butt of his
rifle into the side of the man's head, cutting a wide gash into it. Lange
stood guard, pointing his M-16 at the terrorist.

Ghassan blacked out, striking the dirt face first.

Rodriguez crouched down. "Icebox, keep us covered." He looked at
Lange. "Get down, Sergeant . . . sweep the area." Rodriguez was talking as he disarmed the terrorist, cuffing his hands behind his back.

THE KREMLIN, MOSCOW

The fortified basement room, located thirty meters underground on the
north side of the Kremlin, had not been used for five years. A cold room
with only one entrance, the KGB had utilized the chamber to extract
confessions from enemies of the state. The bullet-pocked wall showed
evidence that many of the confessors had been shot promptly after telling the KGB what it wanted to here.

General Dimitri Popivich sat, hands and feet tied, in a wooden chair
near the center of the barren room. He sat with his head down, gazing at
the rust-covered drain. A bright spotlight hung from the ceiling, focused
on his face.

"I will not tolerate you lying to me again, General Popivich!" Petr
Czerlinsky's face was ruby red with fury. "I just got off the phone with
the secretary of defense for the United States. We have managed to piece
this incident together and it seems your plan failed. The American shuttle was not destroyed as you had hoped. It has landed . . . in northern
Chad. The Americans believe the Libyans now have control of it."

Popivich's stony expression didn't change.

"You want the old ways, I will give them to you. Guard, hand me your belt." Czerlinsky firmly took hold of the four-inch-wide, heavy leather belt, striking the general.

"Now, I will ask you one more time. What do you know of the nuclear warheads on Kosmos 3-1660?"

Popivich tasted blood in his mouth but said nothing.

Czerlinsky, frustrated, hit Popivich repeatedly until he was sure he had broken the old man's jaw.

"Do you not know what you have done? Your mission has failed and you alone have put your countrymen in danger." He sighed, scooting a chair next to the weakened man. "Your country needs you now. Be the soldier you are and tell me so the Americans will not retaliate against us. Are there nuclear weapons?" He shook the general by the arms until the man's eyes met his.

Popivich's eyelids closed. "Yes . . ."

PATHFINDER TEAM ALPHA: ICEBOX

"Whiskey one, Whiskey one . . . inbound . . . inbound." Rath sent the radio warning. He was looking at a twin-engine prop plane banking out of the east.

"Of all the damned luck. Hide your asses," Vasquez uttered, unheard by the members of his team crawling around in the foreground, trying to carry two bodies. The sniper adjusted his grip on the rifle as the Libyan aircraft landed in the middle of the runway.

Rath watched through his spotting scope. The gray-and-white six-passenger airplane powered down, turned, and taxied toward the bunkers, away from them. The aircraft came to a stop, its engines still running. The side door opened and the stowaway stairs fell to the ground. Then one man exited the plane. He was dressed in a dark blue business suit and was carrying a black briefcase. The man was greeted by one of the terrorists and led away.

The spotter heard the sound of the engines' power increasing. The aircraft turned back in the direction of the runway and in a matter of minutes was airborne again.

"November, november." The danger had passed. Rath's teammates continued their trek to the OP.

22

MADADHI AIR BASE

It had been four years—four years and three months, to be exact—since Huda Ziad had last visited the desolate base in the desert. The memory lingered fresh in his mind. The Chadian army had been only twenty kilometers to the south and advancing. Colonel Qaddafi's worst fears were coming true: his enemies were winning the war. As head of Libya's chemical weapons program, Ziad's mission at that time was to arm several MiG-27s with a mixture of deadly nerve gas. One evening, when the winds were blowing in the right direction, the jets took off. Two days later, with twenty percent of the Chadian army dead or dying, Libya went back on the offensive.

Ziad stepped away from the transport plane and walked toward the aircraft bunkers. A gust of hot wind hit his face, reminding him how much he hated the desert. A gun-carrying terrorist approached him.

"My name is Majeed. This way."

Ziad followed, not wasting any words on a subordinate trained to obey orders. A tall man with a thin and crooked nose, his features were severe, leaving one to wonder if he had ever smiled or been a young child. Ziad was one of Libya's foremost technical experts on military weapons and delivery systems. Trained by the Japanese firm of Nihon Seikojo, he had had a hand in designing everything from Libya's military computer network to its air traffic control system. Before moving to Libya in the late seventies, he had been a university professor in Syria for twenty years. He had taught graduate students advanced courses in physics, mathematics, and political science. The university had forced him to resign his position because of allegations he had plotted the murder of one of his young male lovers, a German student, allegations he could not disprove.

Ziad and Majeed passed through the last set of guards and entered the bunker to the overpowering sight of *Atlantis*. It nearly took the breath out of him.

"I am Captain Jibril."

Ziad set his briefcase down and removed his jacket, not acknowledging the Libyan officer. His eyes were fixed on the shuttle.

Jibril ignored the man's arrogance. "This way."

Ziad stood for a second, examining the outside of the spacecraft. His eyes went to the cockpit windows; they were shattered and broken. Other than a few small smudge marks, the front section of the spacecraft looked to be intact. He walked around to the right side of the shuttle. The yellow overhead lights of the bunker made it easy to see the long black burn marks and the large sections of heat-resistant tiles that had burned away. The right wing of the plane wasn't damaged, and the terrorists had built a wooden scaffolding up and around the nose section leading to both sides of the wing roots. Ziad climbed the ladder, onto the scaffolding, and crawled up to the edge of the cargo bay. Standing there, he examined the burned contents. One of the cargo bay doors was gone. It looked as if it had been torn away, leaving jagged fingers of twisted aluminum where the hinges once were. Yet it was the inside of the bay that caught his attention. A badly burned, octagon-shaped object filled the center of the shuttle bay. Ziad assumed it was a satellite and estimated it to be thirty-five feet in length and fourteen feet in diameter. He could see several round spheres that looked like antennae, although they were scorched and melted in several areas. The satellite, along with the interior fuselage of the cargo bay, was severely charred. Sections of insulation were dangling from the sides, and Ziad could see several areas were molten aluminum had cooled and solidified.

Ziad crouched down to get closer to the satellite. He could see perforations covering its outer skin. He wondered what the satellite had been used for.

He stood and looked around the bunker. The terrorists had built a machine-gun nest near the nose of the shuttle and were constructing several more around the plane.

"Where is Ajami?" Ziad asked. He had been briefed by Major Nittal and had expected the terrorist leader to greet him.

"Ajami rests. I am in command here," Jibril answered.

Majeed made a guttural noise in his throat, but only stared at the captain.

"I was told I would have you at my service, Captain. Bring me a cutting torch and clear this bunker at once," Ziad ordered.

Jibril hesitated a moment, his jaw tightening. Then he pivoted around to the sight of Majeed's amused smile.

"Leave here at once."

* * *

"Come in," Ajami moaned. He was alone and sleeping, although the room was bathed in yellow light.

"I apologize for waking you. Ziad has sent me. He has found something of importance inside the cargo bay of the space plane. You are to come quickly." Majeed spoke rapidly. He was leery of how his leader would react to being awakened and then ordered to report without delay.

"What . . . what has he found?" Ajami was almost shouting.

"He would not say, only to tell you that it was of great significance." Majeed observed Ajami's pale face. The sides were blotched with dirt and his eyelids were pink. The man had not shaven and looked ill.

"Where is Ziad now?" Ajami asked, this time with greater control.

"He is waiting for you in the bunker." Majeed backed out of the way as Ajami stumbled from his bed and toward the door.

"Find Captain Jibril. Bring him to the bunker."

Ajami made his way through a series of tunnels before he arrived at the aircraft bunker. He walked past the guards and climbed up the wobbly scaffolding on the left side of the shuttle. He then dropped himself down inside the cramped cargo bay where Huda Ziad was standing.

"I have found something of magnificent interest." Ziad's face and arms were covered in black soot as he skipped the amenities. In his left hand he was holding a metal saw and behind him was a cutting torch.

"What have you found?" Ajami asked eagerly.

"This object is a satellite and it has been badly damaged." He pointed to the burned and melted down-link antenna. "It is still warm from a very hot fire. Come here. Let me show you something else."

Ziad had cut a large segment of the satellite's aluminum outer skin away from the lower section. It was big enough so he could see the interior of the satellite. He turned on his flashlight and panned it left and right across several round cylinders, stopping at the base of the closest one.

"This is a rocket motor attached to what looks like a medium-range missile. So far I have found four of them, but I believe there are more." Ziad pointed to the round access panels along the side of the satellite. He gazed back at Ajami and then moved the flashlight toward the top of the missile. "Affixed to the top of each missile is a warhead."

"A *warhead* . . . What kind of warhead?" Ajami asked, unconsciously running his hand along the satellite, as though it were a thoroughbred racehorse.

"Until I see it, I won't know for sure. But let me ask you this. If you were going to put a missile into space, what kind of warhead would you put on it?"

Ajami's insides somersaulted. "A nuclear warhead."

"That is what I believe."

Ajami's attention returned to the gray-and-white missile. "Can you remove one?"

Ziad shook his head. "A nuclear missile is a very complicated thing. I have some training on conventional surface-to-surface systems, but not for this. It could be very dangerous."

"Do you have any idea what I could do with a nuclear warhead?" The terrorist's face was alive with marvel. To him, the danger was minimal compared to the power he could possess.

"I believe Colonel Qaddafi would be better—"

"No." Ajami put up his hand. "I want you to get me one of those warheads. After that, the Libyans can do whatever they want with the rest of them." Ajami didn't vary his stare from Ziad's small eyes. He could not trust the Libyans. "Name the price for your labor and silence. I do not want Jibril to know of my plan."

Ziad looked back at the half-exposed missile, studying it and deciding if he could pull it off. The lower section was the solid fuel motor, fairly basic. However, the fuel was very toxic, killing instantly if it was not handled properly. The warhead would be mounted to what is called a bus. It would contain the system's electronic brain, target settings, arming and autodisarming switch, and the reentry system programmer. He had to remove the warhead and the bus from the rocket motor. The hard part would be removing the warhead from the bus.

Ziad's eyes met Ajami's. "My price is . . . one hundred thousand American dollars and a passport to the United States."

Ajami continued to gaze into Ziad's eyes. That amount of money would be nothing compared to the turning point of the holy war.

"You will get what you ask for when I have my warhead," Ajami said.

"At least four warheads, maybe more." Ajami had met Captain Jibril as he was exiting the bunker. They were both now walking toward the holding cells.

"This is not good news. I am surprised the Americans have not already attacked. A shuttle is one thing, nuclear weapons are something different," Jibril said.

"That is why you must give me more equipment," Ajami reasoned. "I must have the means to defend this camp."

"Stop and listen to what you are saying." Jibril halted midstride, grabbing Ajami by his right arm. "You are not thinking this through. The shuttle is no longer of importance. We must remove the warheads and transport them to a secure, well-equipped base as soon as we can. Let them come and get their shuttle, but it will be too late. We will have abandoned the base and taken the warheads with us."

Ajami knew this was becoming a game of time. He had to race against retrieving his bomb before the Libyans took the power away from him and the arrival of the Americans.

"Yes, you are right. But I must have more equipment to defend this base until we remove the bombs," Ajami lied, as they entered the holding cell. The two guards from the outer door followed them in. Ajami removed his pistol and motioned for the guard to open the astronauts' cell door.

"Stand against the wall," he ordered.

"Do as he says," Duke whispered, getting up off the floor.

"We know what you were transporting in your shuttle bay. We know of the nuclear weapons aboard your space plane. I want those weapons and you are going to help me." Ajami's voice exuded his contempt.

"What? There aren't any weapons on the shuttle," Duke replied calmly, believing the man was fishing for information.

"*Liar!*" Ajami shouted. "I have seen them." He looked over each American. "Which of you knows about this? You. Start talking." He pointed his pistol at Willie.

"I don't know anything about nuclear weapons."

"I am going to kill you. I will not tolerate lying." Ajami raised his pistol, pointing it to the ceiling. He squeezed the trigger, sending a bullet into the hard concrete where it broke apart, showering the area with bits of hot lead. "Let me explain to you who I am. I am Abu Ajami, the true leader of Palestine. I alone have been chosen by Allah to free our people. The weapons on your space plane have been sent to me by Allah." Ajami snapped his head around, looking at everyone in the room. "You are liars . . . all liars. Now tell me what I must know."

"I can't tell you something I know nothing about," Willie said firmly.

Ajami swung his hand around, hitting him in the face with the butt of his pistol.

"Willie!" Duke shouted, as his second in command fell to the floor.

Willie wiped blood from his mouth as he stood. "I'm all right, General," he said without thinking.

Ajami smiled, turning to Duke. "General . . . So this was a military mission. And now I have your weapons." He looked at one of the guards. "Take this man to the hangar." Two guards, one on each side, escorted Willie out.

Ajami turned back to Duke, expecting to see fear, but Duke met him squarely in the eye.

Ajami looked at Duke's stern face for several seconds. *He does not fear me,* Ajami thought, as he turned abruptly and left the cell.

Duke stood rigid as the terrorists left.

"I'm afraid for Willie," Andrea spoke up.

"Shit. What the hell are they talking about? Nuclear weapons?" Duke was baffled.

"My guess is our new friends, the Russians, may have tried to slip one by us." Andrea sat on the floor, her back against the wall.

Duke walked over, deliberately looking into the other cell. The man was not more than five feet away. "What is your name?" he boldly asked.

"Kamal." The Palestinian was sitting on his bed, staring at the ground.

"What are they going to do with him?"

Kamal turned, laughing. "They will make him talk."

"And what if he can't answer their questions?" Duke demanded.

"Then they will kill him and come for one of you next."

Duke had been watching this man, Kamal. He didn't seem like a stupid person. As a matter of fact, his English was good and he showed no fear of the guards when they entered the room. If anything, it seemed the guards made it a point to stay away from him. Duke had wondered if the man could be a plant, put in the cell to learn what he could about the Americans. But if that was the case, why hadn't he tried to ask them any questions? Duke knew if they were going to get out of here alive, they would need help.

"Why are you here? What was your crime?" Duke asked, lowering his tone.

Kamal didn't answer.

"I get the feeling that everyone placed in a holding cell eventually dies one way or another . . . which includes you. Am I correct?"

Again Kamal was quiet.

"If you want to live, we can help each other."

Kamal fought back the urge to smile. "How can you help me?"

"When our countrymen arrive, all hell is going to break loose. You know the way out of here, I don't."

"So how does that help me?"

"Because . . . when they save us, I will tell them to save you. You can walk away a free man."

"We will be dead long before any of your soldiers ever reach this part of the complex. I should not be talking to you; you are a stupid American." Kamal turned away.

Willie's arms were numb from the dirty nylon ropes cutting deep into the upper parts of his arms. The two guards had put him in the new restraints and now a burning pain sliced through the center of his back from the strain on his shoulders being pulled together from behind.

Next to the shuttle loomed a crane with a hoist and pulley system. It had been used by the Libyans to remove aircraft engines from their fighters during the war. Several terrorists pushed Willie closer to the crane. They then hooked his tied hands to the end of the hoist and raised him several feet off the ground. Willie nearly passed out from the pain.

"American . . . how many warheads?" Ajami asked, jabbing his ribs with his pistol.

"I told you. I don't know anything about this. This is a Russian satellite. We took it out of orbit. That is all I know." Willie struggled to speak, his shoulders dislocated.

Ziad looked at Ajami, speaking in Arabic. "Perhaps he does not know. Ask him if one of the others knows anything."

"He is lying." Ajami turned back toward Willie. "Is this warhead armed? Can it be transported? If you tell, I will not kill you and the others."

"I told you, I don't know . . . I know nothing about this . . . We were on a simple satellite rescue mission. Then there was this explosion and . . . and a fire. That is all I know." Willie's head drooped wearily, confused thoughts running through his mind.

"I believe he tells the truth," Ziad said.

Ajami motioned to one of the guards. He raised the butt of his rifle, hitting Willie in the face, shattering his cheekbone.

"He lies! Everyone lies!" Ajami shouted.

Rodriguez forced his prisoner down and through the back entrance of the OP, making as little noise as possible. He then hog-tied the man, placing him out of the way in one of the corners. A moment later Lange appeared.

"Any problems?" Rodriguez gulped down some warm water from his canteen and handed it to his sweating team member.

"No. I covered the body and our tracks." Lange took a swallow, letting it trickle down his throat. "He definitely wasn't Libyan army, but he was in good health. Teeth and body fat were normal, no lice or sign of disease. He didn't have anything on him other than ammo, his weapons, and two liters of water. I'd say they're well taken care of."

"I was afraid of that. Anything else?"

"He was married."

Rodriguez let out a long breath. "Keep that to yourself. Vasquez doesn't need to know."

Lange signaled his understanding.

All these facts worried Rodriguez. It told him the men at the base were not just a loose band of misfits. Chances were increasing they were dealing with professionals, and that raised the stakes. These guys would have had some training, were already being armed with more equipment, and would probably want to fight until the bloody end.

"Lange, type up we have acquired a prisoner. Bunker info for the shuttle will be following soon. Then you and I will have a nice little chat with our guest."

"I'm looking forward to it, sir."

Rodriguez cocked the hammer on his Glock nine-millimeter pistol, pointing it directly at the head of his prisoner. Lange slowly removed the tape from the man's mouth.

"Do you understand English?" he asked.

The man's eyes were blank and wide.

Lange asked again, this time more forcibly. The man nodded, his frightened eyes shifting from Lange's face to the pistol and back again.

"I'm sure you know the rules to this game, but let me go over them." Lange breathed in, then began: "If you yell out, we kill you. If you try to escape, we kill you. If you don't cooperate, we kill you. Do you understand me, or should we just kill you?"

The prisoner nodded yes.

Rodriguez turned his head away from Lange so he could roll his eyes. He saw Shaw silently chuckling at his post.

"Good. What is your name?"

"Ghassan . . . Musa . . ."

"All right, Ghassan. Are you thirsty? Would you like some water?"

Ghassan nodded yes. His dark brown eyes seemed to soften.

"Good. You will get some when you answer some very simple questions for me."

"What do you want with me? I do not—"

Lange slapped his hand over the man's mouth, bringing his head down close to the prisoner and raising his eyes up to the captain. "I suggest you lower your voice, Ghassan, or my friend here . . . well, he will blow your head off. You see, he really enjoys killing people." His tone was soft as he whispered, "He was the one who killed your friend. I watched him do it, and he was smiling. He wanted to kill you, too, but I stopped him. I told him you looked like a smart guy, that you would have some answers. Understand?"

Lange took his hand away after the man nodded.

"I only have a few questions to ask you. How many men are at your air base?" Lange lifted up, grinning reassuringly.

"I do not know."

"Yes, you do. How many do you think, then?"

"I am only a foot soldier. That is all. I do not know those things," Ghassan responded.

"Were those Libyan transports I saw landing last night?" Lange inquired, knowing the answer to his question.

A hundred thoughts ran through Ghassan's mind all at once.

"What transports? What are you talking about?" Ghassan stammered.

Lange shrugged, turning to Rodriguez. "He's giving me the runaround, sir. I guess I was wrong about him."

"Do you want to die slow or quick?" Rodriguez smirked as he pulled out his field knife, holding it in front of Ghassan's face with his left hand. Its shining five-inch blade reflected some of the low light of the OP. His other hand still gripped the Glock. Without warning, Rodriguez slashed his knife across the terrorist's cheek, just below his eye. The sharp blade cut a deep gash into the soft skin.

Ghassan didn't move. He could feel the blood running down his face. He knew he deserved to die for getting captured, and it would either be done by the Americans or his own men.

He spit in Rodriguez's face, shouting in Arabic, "I will die with honor!" Lange punched him in the jaw. Then they both turned to Shaw.

"I don't think anyone could have heard. Rath says we're still clear, too."

"Shaw, get your syringe. This raghead doesn't realize he's going to give us the info we want one way or another." Rodriguez wiped his face and stood to take over the observation post.

Lange put some fresh tape over the man's mouth as Shaw retrieved his medical bag. Then, after filling the syringe, he stood in front of the soldier.

"Roll up his sleeve," Shaw instructed.

Yari was in a restricted area of the complex and she knew it. She walked at a normal pace down the dreary tunnel. She had tucked her shoulder-length hair neatly inside a brown ball cap and was wearing bulky fatigues to hide her feminine features. Her heart was beating wildly in her chest.

The afternoon meal would be served shortly. If her timing was right, she could reach the holding area before a new guard was posted. Over the past few days she had frequented the tunnels at various times, making certain most of the men posted in the area had seen her. If one of the men did happen to challenge her presence, however, she had planned to answer that she was lost.

The young woman slowed, reaching the end of the main passageway. One hundred yards to the right was the entrance to the holding area. She knelt down and peered around the corner. No one was standing guard. Yari quietly slipped down the tunnel and entered the dim, sour-smelling room. She stopped short in front of the cells for a second. She had never seen Americans before.

At once Kamal knew who it was. "Yari, what are you doing?" he asked anxiously. "I told you not to come here. It is too dangerous."

Yari tiptoed up to the door of Kamal's cell. "I have brought you more food and clean water."

"You cannot keep coming here. They will kill you if they find you feeding a prisoner." Kamal's voice was stern, filled with angry concern.

The two astronauts studied the scene taking place and looked at each other. The hushed voices and fearful glances from the woman told the story.

"I know their ways and I am always careful. They will not find me." She unbuttoned her shirt and pulled out a cloth bag. She handed the package to Kamal, her touch lingering on his hand. "Inside is a—"

"Someone's coming," Andrea whispered.

"Quickly, Yari . . . hide." Kamal's chapped dirty finger pointed to a pile of broken wooden chairs and tables stored near the front of the chamber.

Yari fleeted across the room and wiggled in behind the mildewy heap of debris. She felt the sticky sensation of a spider's web across her face.

Guards appeared at the doorway. Two of them were holding a person up under his arms. He was slumped over, his feet dragging behind him. A third guard was standing directly behind them carrying an AK-47.

Duke and Andrea rose to their feet, knowing it must be Willie. Kamal shoved the bag Yari had given him under the mattress.

"Stand back," one of the men said in English before he opened the cell door. They tossed Willie's limp body into the enclosure. Duke reached out to catch him from the fall, but he landed with a heavy thud.

Two of the guards left as one resumed the post outside the door.

Duke picked him up as Andrea rushed over, moaning, "Oh, Willie."

The pilot's face was barely recognizable. It was a mass of blood, cuts, and bruises. His lips were split in several places and one of his eyes was swollen shut. Duke placed him gently on the mattress, his outrage sur-facing. "This fucking filthy bed isn't fit for a dog!"

Willie murmured, attempting to open his eyes to the blurry sight of Duke and Andrea kneeling next to him. "Oh God, what train hit me . . ."

"Shh, Willie." Andrea ran her hand across his forehead, trying to soothe him.

"Andi, check and see if he has anything broken. Willie, where does it hurt?"

"They broke a few ribs. My face hurts all over . . . I think my nose. I can't breathe . . ." Willie began hyperventilating, only increasing his pain.

"You have to hold on, Willie. I won't let them take you again," Duke assured him.

"But I saw it . . . I saw a warhead, Duke . . . I saw one."

"Willie, are you sure?" Duke glanced at Andrea.

"They showed me one inside the satellite. It's a fucking Russian nuke . . ." Willie coughed, blood drizzling from his mouth. Andrea tore a strip of material from her flight suit, wiping his chin.

Duke let out a long breath. "What did you tell them?"

"I couldn't hold out, Duke. I'm sorry . . . I couldn't hold out. I let you both down." The wounded man's sobs were broken with coughs.

"Willie, it's all right. I need to know what you told them. It could be important."

"I told them everything I knew . . . the mission . . . our ranks . . . everything. But it wasn't good enough. They don't believe me, anyway. They think we all know about the nukes. They want to know how to arm it . . . disarm it . . . I don't know."

Duke saw that Kamal was standing next to the heavy metal bars separating the two cells. He had listened to their every word. Duke met the man's stare, then glanced back in the direction of the woman. She had scooted out from the pile and was cowering in the shadows.

Duke shouted for the guard to come in. He spoke with authority, and the soldier did as he was ordered.

"Bring me some bandages and clean water. My friend is hurt and needs attention."

He was giving Yari a chance for escape. Kamal motioned with his eyes for her to leave now. She glanced at him, then disappeared through the doorway.

"You are a prisoner. You will receive nothing." The guard walked away from the cell door and returned to his post.

Kamal turned, addressing Duke. "Any chances you had of escaping are gone. I know Ajami. He will not allow anyone to walk out of this camp alive with what is now his."

Duke detected a slight amount of concern emanating from the imprisoned man.

"Well, your Ajami won't have a choice. In a few hours there will be enough men and firepower raining down on this shit hole to kill every living thing for a hundred miles."

"Including you," Kamal snorted.

"Including me and you. There is no way my country is going to let nuclear weapons fall into the hands of terrorists," Andrea shouted.

"Okay, Andi . . . calm down. We need to think over the situation again. This puts a different light on things." Duke went over and rested a hand on Andrea's shoulder, keeping his gaze on Kamal. "And you, are you prepared to die?"

"I have been prepared to die all my life. I am of no value. Ajami is a great leader. By the time your soldiers come, he will be a hundred miles away with what Allah has given him."

"Well, we'll see soon enough, won't we," Duke replied, bending down next to the other crew members.

Kamal shuffled away from the bars. He had said too much and knew it, but forgave himself because his days were numbered. The only reason he was still alive was because Ajami had other things on his mind.

Kamal felt around under his mattress for the cloth bag Yari had snuck in to him. He reached inside, feeling several pieces of bread and dried dates, and pulled out a plastic bottle of water. But something else weighed down the bottom. He grasped it with his tied hands and withdrew a rusty .45 caliber automatic pistol. Turning his back on the foreigners and keeping the weapon close to his chest, Kamal removed the magazine. He ran his thumb over the top of a dirty .45 caliber bullet. Now he just had to wait for the right time. Kamal placed the pistol under his mattress.

The OP was quiet. Shaw had jotted down the translated information Lange had extracted from the prisoner and relayed it to STOC. The shuttle was in the center bunker. The prisoner was now lying in the corner, soundly sleeping off the barbiturate. The men had resumed their shifts and were back to their routine business.

The low *thump, thump, thump* of helicopters moving up from the airstrip below filled the air.

"There . . . left ten o'clock coming off the deck, Mi-24 gunships." Rodriguez watched as several two-tone choppers methodically twisted their way up from a few thousand yards to the west. He didn't take his binoculars off the two aircraft.

"More transports, Captain, coming in from the east. I count two . . . three . . . four." Lange had risen at the sound and was surveying the eastern sky as the big Il-76s lined up.

Rodriguez let out a slow breath. "More troops and equipment. *Damn!*"

23

The sharp whine of jet engines pierced his ears as Air Force Lieutenant Colonel Brice Madison watched the last two fighters of his Cobra team bank to the left and line up with the runway as they flew in out of the east. Whiffs of blue smoke exploded out from under the rear landing gear as the F-15Es touched down. Their nose gear hit a few seconds later and the fully loaded, dirty-gray fighter bombers turned and taxied toward the hangar area several hundred yards away.

"That's it," Madison said to himself. He always felt better after all the Echo models arrived safely. They were the backbone of his air-to-ground assault element. He pulled in a lungful of fresh air as he walked briskly back toward the main hangar behind him. The air felt good, even if it was hot and dry.

Madison was apprehensive. The base was remote all right, almost too remote. It was barely big enough for all his aircraft, and the ground crews were already complaining about their quarters, no air conditioning. At a temp of 105 degrees, that was bad news.

Colonel Madison was sort of an oddity in the USAF. He looked the part of a standard fighter jock, with short-cropped hair, a small athletic build, and a commanding presence he had picked up while attending the academy. He was married, with two small children, and enjoyed bird hunting whenever he could get away for a weekend. Yet that was where the similarity ended from the standard blue suit/jet jock officer. Madison didn't share the military's total trust in high technology, especially in weapons systems that were fresh off the drawing boards. As a matter fact, in many instances Madison was on the opposite side of many of his old school commanders.

Madison's fast track had started when he became one of the youngest instructors at the Tactical Fighter Training Center at Nellis Air Base in

Nevada. It was there that he was able to define his theory on air-to-air and air-to-ground combat. He then applied his theories to different scenarios and computer models of how post–cold war conflicts could be fought. The cornerstone of Madison's battle plans was a four-stage sequence known as OODA: observing the enemy; orienting his team to the difficulty of the mission, terrain, and type of enemy they were about to face; deciding when and how to move; and, lastly, acting on their decisions. Madison also stressed the relevance of getting inside the enemy's head. If a pilot or a soldier could predict his enemy's next move, he could defeat him every time.

Madison had worked and studied hard after leaving the academy. He was rewarded by being chosen to join a select team of officers pulled from all branches of the military. They tagged themselves the Jedi Knights. They were a group of professionals who shared ideas on tactics and strategy. It didn't take long before Madison's superiors were looking to him and the rest of the Knights for a fresh perspective on tough military situations.

It had been from Madison's previous theories that Cobra team was established four years earlier. The young lieutenant colonel was now in command of a tight band of highly trained pilots. They were skilled in flying everything from the low-tech and ugly A-10 Thunderbolts to the sleek state-of-the-art F-117A Stealth fighters. The team was backed up with a highly mobile and effective ground assault force trained in quick-strike, hard-hitting tactics. It was rumored that Cobra team had the firepower and training to engage and stop a full armored division, inflicting thirty percent casualties, in less than six hours. Madison wasn't sure how accurate that was, but his men boasted they were better.

"Status report," Madison barked, as he neared his command center, a converted C-141 Starlifter. The big jet was parked next to one of the light brown aluminum hangars. Two auxiliary power units were running at full force, supplying it with electricity.

Chief Master Sergeant Melvin Howard, a fat-faced Swedish American, wiped the sweat from around his neck before answering. "Things are shaping up better than I expected, sir. Communications are up and running. We established a satcom up-link with the STOC ten minutes ago. We have fuel, food, and plenty of fresh water. I'm waiting for the last C-17, and that should round out our ordnance supply. It should be here within the hour. Damn, is it hot." Howard paused to catch his breath. "I've got to hand it to the Egyptians, Colonel. This base may look like shit, but they did a damned good job equipping it."

"Were you able to secure the additional Paveways and Mavericks I requested?" Madison ignored Howard's trivial chatter and walked toward the ladder leading to the main deck of the Starlifter. He saw that an Egyptian army officer was standing guard at the bottom of the stairs.

"Yes, sir." Howard hurried to keep up with his commanding officer.

"Good. I want each maintenance crew stuck on their aircraft like panty hose to Madonna's ass. Every bird in this squadron better be at a hundred percent and ready to fly in less than four hours. That means every INS better be up and running as of right now. If we have to move, I don't want to wait for some greaser who's had his thumb up his butt. Is that clear?"

"Yes, sir." Howard saluted and moved rapidly away from the fiery colonel. Madison just put a big monkey on his back. His job would be on the line if every aircraft wasn't up and running perfectly in the specified time.

Madison reached the base of the metal stairs and climbed up. Within seconds he was inside the dark, cool, air-conditioned control center of Cobra team's flying command post. He removed his dark glasses, sticking them in his right breast pocket, and surveyed the interior.

The immense T-tailed C-141 originally had been designed and built as a heavy four-engine cargo and troop transport. Two months after Cobra team had been formed, the air force completely gutted and rebuilt one of its older Starlifters, giving it the designation of EC-141, Airborne Command. The airframe had been modified to withstand the added stress of a large radome located two-thirds of the way down the fuselage. A second ground-targeting surveillance radar, incorporating the same features as used by the E-8C J-STAR's system, was attached to the bottom section of the fuselage. Just ahead of the wings was a twenty-four-foot canoe-shaped faring. It contained a Norden-built phased-array multimode radar. The concept was to combine the best features of E-3 AWAC and USAF/Army E-8A J-STAR systems into a flying mobile command center crammed full of the latest in ultra-high-speed computers, electronics, and satellite communications equipment. The classified EC-141 was a thoroughbred that gave Madison a total situational awareness of everything happening on the ground and in the air out to a 200-mile radius around a combat area.

Madison stepped down the center aisle toward the rear of the aircraft. The left side of the transport was lined with several technicians seated behind multicolored tactical information displays that included semi-active radar and passive infrared sensors. The right side consisted of an array of backup systems, including communications and large computer-generated maps of the area. Near the rear of the plane was the direct down-link to the Central Imagery Office at the CIA. The reconnaissance data gathered from several CIA-controlled KH-14 digital-imaging and Lacrosse B and C radar satellites could be received directly. This aided Madison's, his pilots', and the planning staff's ability to have an advantage, staying on top of the ever-changing battlefield activity once a mission began.

"Colonel," Master Sergeant Jason Oliveri said. He looked up from his computer display. "All combat aircraft have arrived."

Madison nodded. At the same time the phone rang. He sat down before he picked up the yellow receiver.

"Colonel Madison here."

"Colonel, General Clark." The general's tone was grave. "We have a new development . . ."

"Yes, sir."

"I'll get right to the point. We just received word from the Russians confirming that nuclear-tipped missiles are inside the satellite on board *Atlantis*. There's a damn good chance the Libyans and terrorists have discovered them."

"Ah, shit . . ." Madison cocked his head to the right as he listened, "Nukes and terrorists, sir? Did I hear you right?"

"That's right, Brice. We've learned that the base is controlled by a radical PLO terrorist group backed by the Libyans. We don't know who they are or how much firepower they have. Our concern right now is to make sure they don't get their hands on one of those nukes. The CIA is sending you a terrorist specialist. His name is Mark Collins. He'll be able to help piece some of this together."

"In all due respect, sir, I've got a mission to plan and execute. I don't have time to screw around baby-sitting the CIA."

"Damn it, Madison. I'm not going to argue with you about this. Staffer tells me Collins is good, and I trust Staffer's judgment. He won't be in the way. Use him if you can. Understood?" It wasn't really a request.

"Understood," Madison replied, hanging up the phone.

"Problems, sir?" Oliveri asked, standing in front of the colonel's desk.

"Nothing we can't handle. Only nukes, terrorists, and, worst of all, the CIA." Madison's sarcasm was dry and Oliveri listened while the colonel repeated what he had just learned from Clark.

"Well, that explains this transmission from Langley. This specialist will be here in half an hour." Oliveri referenced the piece of fax paper he was holding.

"When he gets here, you deal with him. Right now, I want to meet all the flight leads in hangar one. We have a hell of a lot of planning to do. Get on the horn to STOC. Get every shred of information they have on this base and the surrounding area—everything." Madison took out a yellow notepad and started to scribble some notes. The planning had begun.

Captain Jibril was alone in his aircraft, seated behind the radio equipment. "Major Nittal, Ajami is demanding to know when the remaining defenses will be in place." He let off on the radio mike switch.

*"I am assembling them now. We have something more to discuss. It is
not wise to trust Ajami. To protect our interests, you must not let him
keep control of the shuttle or the warheads. Ajami's only loyalty is to his
cause. We may become his first victims,"* Nittal warned.

"There are over fifty terrorists here. I need ground troops to support
me."

"You will have what you need. Contact me again in a few hours."

Jibril listened as the radio transmission went dead.

There was a new guard standing outside the doorway, and Duke had
mentally timed their rotations. His body was growing weak and he
struggled to keep his mind alert. Their food and water rations had ended
when the terrorists realized they had been on a military mission. Andrea
and Willie were asleep on either side of him, both curled up on the
squalid mattress. In the next cell over Kamal remained stationary on his
bed.

The inside of the holding area seemed darker, filled with the noticeable mixture of foul odors. Duke's mind wandered, doubting they
would ever see the sun again, as he leaned his head up against the
concrete wall. He wasn't sure if he could face the thought of Katie and
the kids living the rest of their lives without him. Duke knew his wife
was a strong woman and would manage well with their children. It was
his feeling of loss that bothered him at this moment.

STAGING AREA, ALI BALLAS, EGYPT

Mark Collins stepped out of the two-seat F-15B trainer's cockpit and
climbed down the aluminum ladder. He now knew what a sardine felt
like after traveling across the Atlantic in a can. His legs were cramped
and he was sweaty and hungry. They made the trip in eight hours and
had refueled in the air four times. The hot sun felt good.

Collins grasped his duffle bag and briefcase, thinking, *What the hell
have I gotten myself into? I should be home with my wife, drinking a
beer.*

"Mr. Collins, right this way, sir," a smart-looking staff sergeant said.

Collins, squinting, slipped on his sunglasses and followed. They
walked several hundred feet, through the nearest hangar, until they
reached a room crammed with pilots and support people.

"Sergeant Oliveri will be here in a few minutes," the man said, turning
to leave.

"Excuse me, but I've been instructed to talk with Colonel Madison
only." Collins set his briefcase on a nearby desk.

"I'm sorry, sir. I'm following the colonel's orders. I would suggest you sit here and wait for Sergeant Oliveri." The sergeant walked away.

Collins took the advice. Somehow he'd known he'd get the run-around. One of these days those ego jockeys were going to learn that without solid intel from the CIA they'd be grounded.

PATHFINDER TEAM ALPHA: RUSHMORE

Six hours had passed since the latest Libyan transports had landed. It was evening and a smattering of fluffy low clouds were rolling across the desert sky. The sun would be setting in a few more hours, bringing on the cold ebony night.

"Sir, they're unloading." Lange was on watch. He threw a wadded up candy wrapper at his sleeping captain's nose.

"ZSU-23s . . . that's the third one. The other two have already moved out of the area." Lange was looking at and talking about a ZSU-23-4 quad, self-propelled antiair gun. They were easy to identify, by the four liquid-cooled twenty-three-millimeter guns and black oval micro-wave target-acquisition and fire control radar dome. The ZSU was capable of firing over a thousand rounds a minute, was highly mobile, and effective against low-flying aircraft. The Libyans normally deployed four of them with each tank and rifle regiment, sixteen to a division. Rodriguez forced himself out of his deep sleep and brushed his left hand over his nose.

He moved over, next to Shaw. There were only four transports parked on the east end of the runway. Two hours ago there had been seven.

"Where are the other three Ilyushins?" Rodriguez asked.

"They took off about an hour ago, sir." Lange smiled. "I thought I'd let you sleep."

"Thanks." Rodriguez rubbed his face. "I must have really been out of it. I didn't hear a thing." He raised his binoculars, yawning.

Both men were thinking the same thing. Where there are ZSUs, there are tanks. In this case, they must be on the way.

As two more ZSUs rolled off the third Il-76, the back cargo bay of the second opened. A desert brown camouflaged, low-profile, six-wheeled vehicle slowly made its way off the ramp, turned, and parked a few hundred yards away from the transports.

"Shit. When did the Libyans get their hands on Geckos?" Gecko was the NATO code name for an SA-8 missile system. Rodriguez counted as three more of the boxy transport vehicles drove off and parked next to the first one. Each truck carried four white air-to-air missiles, along with a single large tracking antenna and two smaller acquisition and fire con-trol radars.

The cargo doors on the last transport opened and, within minutes, two mobile SA-6 launch vehicles rolled off, swung right, and headed toward the west end of the runway.

"Get this to STOC ASAP," Rodriguez ordered, then keyed his mike. "Icebox . . . this is Rushmore, do you copy?"

"Icebox here," Vasquez answered.

"Can you see where they're moving those SAMs and triple As?"

"It looks like they're using the artillery to reinforce both ends of the runway and the SAMs east of the mountains."

"All right . . . Rushmore out."

24

Captain Jibril stood at the doorway to the command and control center before entering. Less than twenty-four hours earlier, the room had been empty and looked large. Now it seemed meager, nearly full of communications and early warning equipment. On the far wall were several maps of the surrounding area, and to his right was a radar scope that had been installed only hours ago. He watched it sweep methodically back and forth as the technician fine-tuned the controls. It gave him little comfort to know they were now linked directly with the early warning station south of Aujila. Only their southern flank was exposed, and Jibril's plan was to fill that gap with SA-8s and SA-6s.

"Status report," Jibril demanded, as he entered the room.

Lieutenant Mizrahi snapped to attention. "Our foot patrols are returning from the field now, Captain. They report nothing out of the ordinary. I have ordered two Mi-24 helicopters to fly in a search pattern around the base. Major Nittal reports ten more MiG-23s and four MiG-29s are now operational. All pilots are on full alert."

Jibril felt satisfied. With this much aircraft under his command the Libyans could control the sky for several hours. That should be long enough to remove all the nuclear weapons and store them safely.

SPECIAL TECHNICAL OPERATIONS CENTER, PENTAGON

"This just in, sir, from Rodriguez." Captain Harris handed General Clark the latest transmission from the Pathfinder team Alpha.

"They're building a wall around this thing like there's no tomorrow." For the first time Clark was starting to doubt if Cobra team had the resources to recover *Atlantis* and the nukes.

257

"Get me Madison on the horn." He walked back and forth between the computer terminals. Seconds later Harris handed him the phone.

"Madison . . . Alpha is reporting additional aircraft and equipment flying into the target area. We're going to have to move that time up. What's the soonest you can have a plan ready and move out?"

"I need more time and information, sir. I need a better understanding of my enemy, the layout of the base, and their air defense systems . . ."

"You should be receiving the updated information on the base you need right now. As far as knowing your enemy goes, hasn't Mark Collins arrived yet?" Clark could feel the anxiety in Madison's voice. He knew the first real stint was always the toughest.

"No, sir. And frankly, I don't have time to hold some CIA's—"

"Madison! You listen to me. He may be the only one who can help you. Collins knows about the terrorist leader in charge of the base. If you want to get inside these guys' heads, like you say, then get your *ass* in gear and talk with Collins. This show is going on the road soon, and you'd better be ready. Is that understood, Colonel?" Clark could be the heavy if he had to be.

"Yes, sir."

Madison hung up the phone. "I want all flight leads assembled at 2000 hours in ready room one. And have someone find out if Mark Collins has landed. I want to talk with him," Madison shouted out to his assistant, then folded his arms. He didn't like thinking the general might believe he had cold feet.

Tom Staffer hurried into Jack Dawson's Pentagon office, closing the door behind him. His brain was feeling somewhat like mush. For the last six hours he had been helping to analyze every shred of information the CIA had on Madadhi Air Base and the southern Libyan defenses. He wished they had more data.

Staffer was relatively pleased by how well things were going on the CIA's end. Information was flowing to Ali Ballas and Collins was now on the ground. Staffer's biggest concern now was whether Cobra could get the job done. The Libyans had advanced aircraft stationed at Aujila, and no one knew if they would use them.

Through the large window on the left he could see the overcast evening sky. The thick clouds were starting to break up, and several gray patches of sky could be seen.

"Jack, sorry I'm late."

Dawson was facing the opposite direction, away from the front of his desk. He looked over his shoulder and motioned for Staffer to join him.

In the corner next to one of the bookshelves was a medium-sized television screen with a black box on top containing a round video camera lens. A red indicator light told Staffer the Defense Video Link Network was operating. The secure video system allowed the members of the National Security Council to communicate with each other all over Washington. All around the world, for that matter. A DVLN system operated over standard phone lines and used a coded video camera signal with voice link so that cabinet members could be seen as they talked. The system was nothing more than an advanced version of an AT&T video conference network used by most Fortune 500 companies. Each member of the NSC had access to the system either in their home or office. Air Force One carried a satellite up-link and down-link permitting the president to converse with each person directly, even at 40,000 feet over the Pacific Ocean.

"Speed it up, Tom; we're fifty seconds away from transmission."

Staffer straightened his tie and pulled up a chair next to the JCS and sat down. "I take it everything went well with Turner and the vice president."

"I'm not sure. I just got off the phone with Secretary Weber. The little gnat tried to climb all over me. He's talked with Chad's military leader, explaining our operation. They've agreed to stay out of the area until its over. The president canceled the rest of his meetings and is now on his way back to Washington. Weber says the old man's pissed because the Japanese are asking all sorts of questions. And now he has to come up with an explanation of why the president's cutting his trip short. We all know he's really mad at himself for fucking up with the Russians. At any rate, I'm sure the networks will be picking up some kind of a story in a few hours from now."

"Well, by the time they figure out what's happening, this thing should be over." Staffer knew that on secret military operations the networks generally ran four to six hours behind events.

"We'll see." Dawson sat up, seeing the video screen flicker on as the speaker filled with static.

"This is Air Force One . . . stand by for the president of the United States." There was a voice but no picture.

Seconds later Staffer and Dawson saw the image of the president appear on the screen. He was dressed in a white shirt, no tie, and sport jacket, seated behind a large walnut desk. Staffer could tell he was sitting in the upper section of the Boeing VC-25A, a converted 747. The presidential seal was hanging in the background on the dark brown paneling. The president looked tanned and relaxed.

"Gentlemen, Secretary Turner has just informed me of the situation. I'll tell you the same thing I told him. I want every one of those warheads recovered. Every single one."

"We're working on it, Mr. President," Dawson replied swiftly.

"Jack, Turner tells me you intend to use Cobra team to recover the shuttle and her crew."

"Yes, Mr. President," Dawson answered.

"We haven't used them before. Wouldn't a more experienced and larger force be more appropriate?"

"No, sir. We don't have anyone else who can move out as rapidly, and Cobra is specialized, with more than enough air cover and firepower to support our ground attack."

The president paused only a moment. "Okay, Jack, I'm going to trust you on this one. I've told Turner to transfer two more carrier battle groups into the Med. He'll also see to it that everything is at your disposal to make sure that the base is secured ASAP. Tom, I want the CIA to supply Cobra with every shred of intelligence you have when you get it."

"It's already being done, sir."

"Jack, how soon before Cobra moves in?" The president rested his left elbow on the arm of his chair.

"If everything goes as planned, this will all be over with before you touch down." Dawson didn't want to be committed to a specific time. It was better to have some leeway.

"I'm briefing several senior members of Congress in the next few minutes. I want bipartisan support for this operation, and I especially don't want any leaks from the press. I'll stay in tune to things from here until I land."

"Yes, Mr. President." The two men watched the screen grow dark.

Dawson turned a somber face to Staffer and spoke grimly. "Tom, Turner asked me to draw up a backup plan. The president has approved it, and I think you should be brought into the loop now. I'm going to need the CIA to update the crews with real-time intel if we give them the final go-ahead."

Staffer swiveled in his chair. "Well, let's have it."

"In three hours two B-1B Lancers will be taking off from McConnell Air Force Base. If Cobra team doesn't secure Madadhi by 0300 tomorrow, the president has given Turner the authority to destroy the base, along with *Atlantis* and everyone in it."

Staffer let out a long breath. He knew the president was being prudent. The Libyans couldn't be allowed to recover the nuclear warheads. "Does Clark know about this?"

"No, and we're not going to tell him until after the operation begins. He already has enough on his plate."

"I see," Staffer said. "I hope it doesn't come to that. A lot of Americans could die."

"I know. But chances are, a lot more innocent people would die if we don't terminate it here and now. You know what kind of men we're dealing with and I can't take time to argue the morals of the decision. We've got to set this thing in motion."

Captain Harris's eyes stung as he stared at the thirty-six-inch color computer screen. He was a bit out of practice, but it was coming back to him. Hell, with Collins gone he really didn't have a choice. Harris was beginning to feel a bit edgy and grimy from working twenty-four hours straight, currently studying a photo taken on the KH-14's morning pass 245 miles above the North African desert. The sky was clear and there was very little surface wind to distort the scene. The Keyhole had been able to obtain a series of very clean, sharp pictures. It used a rubber mirror to remove most of the atmospheric distortion before the images were broadcast to the CIA and the NRO, but there was still no substitute for clear weather.

The fourth photo he studied, however, had been shot at precisely 0553.14, two minutes after sunup. Long shadows were cast across the landscape. Harris played with the software's filtering program to eliminate most of the murky spots and was fairly successful. He zoomed into a narrow section of the air base on the north side of the runway. A large stubby outcrop protruded several hundred yards. The particular area had caught his attention when he examined some of the KH-14's IR photos taken twelve hours earlier. They revealed unusual warm spots on the surface, suggesting something was there.

"General Clark, take a look at this."

Clark walked over behind him and looked at the screen.

"I think I've found it, sir, even without the blueprints." Harris breathed in, then rubbed his weary eyes.

Clark smiled, instantly knowing he had found the base's power supply.

Harris tapped a function key several times, zooming in on the area. In the center of the screen a fuzzy image of a short eight-inch-diameter pipe sticking out of the ground less than two feet high was evident. "Look here, General. It's an exhaust pipe, I'm betting for diesel fuel. This would explain why this warm spot shows up in the evening and in the morning. They're recharging their batteries, just like the Iraqis." He tapped a few more keys and instantly changed the screen from an aerial photo to an IR image. The screen flashed to images of green, gray, and black. "I'm starting to see a pattern. They're using electric generators powered by diesel engines. A German design."

"Target it," Clark ordered. "That will be one of the first areas Madison's men should hit."

Harris widened the photo to show the ground around the exhaust pipe. "Now, wait a minute, take a look at this area." Coiled in a mass under poor-quality camouflage were several long black aircraft refueling hoses. Only fifty yards away were two Il-76 transports. "This is also the base's refueling area. They must have kerosene stored underground right next to those generators. If we take their power out, then the fuel goes up along with it. And . . ."

"Yeah, I know. And chances are the shuttle crew goes up with the fuel." It was a hard-learned lesson. The Iraqis had kept the American pilots they had captured housed right next to their underground storage tanks of jet, gasoline, and diesel fuel. Clark would be a fool to think these guys weren't doing the same thing. "Get that information to Madison and tell him of our concerns. He'll have to make the call, not me."

"Yes, sir." Harris glanced at his watch. "Frazier and his team at the NPIC should be faxing their data pretty soon and we'll know where the air defenses are."

"I hope you're right," Clark said under his breath. "I hope you're right."

Kamal sat in the corner of his cell, careful he was out of sight from the Americans. His stomach growled with hunger, but he cautiously saved the rest of the food Yari had brought him.

He worked the slide of the older .45 automatic pistol back and forth discreetly. He could feel pieces of its plating break free in his hand. The gun was in bad shape. Its outer surface was red from rust and dirt. It appeared to have been buried for several years. He doubted if it would work and wondered where Yari had gotten it.

The former security officer's thoughts turned to Majeed taking over his command. Kamal knew if he had had a prisoner such as himself, the man would have been tortured and shot the very same day. *Majeed will surely be Ajami's downfall,* Kamal thought, as he hid the pistol under his blanket. He also knew by Ajami's actions that his leader had failed to take his medication. It would now only be a matter of time before Ajami regressed into uncontrolled fits of anger and delusions.

STAGING AREA, ALI BALLAS, EGYPT

Mark Collins sat in the rear section of Cobra team's command post. Although the EC-141 was sitting on the ground in the hot desert sun, its interior was cool. The sound of chattering technicians checking and rechecking their equipment mingled with the atmosphere. The men behind the computer consoles were calm and businesslike.

Madison was said to be an extreme perfectionist. Observing the command post, this statement came to life. Everything was in its proper place, down to the paper clips and pencils. The trash cans even gleamed.

Collins had never met the man but picked out the colonel the moment he stormed in. Madison's intense eyes and stature gave him away even though he was wearing a green flight suit just like the rest of his pilots.

"Mark Collins, I'm Colonel Madison. You have some information for me." The colonel was abrupt and sat down behind a small metal desk, crossing his legs.

"Yes, sir." Collins didn't bother to hold out his hand. He wasn't expecting a warm reception.

"I have a briefing with my flight leads in thirty minutes, so make this fast."

Collins opened his briefcase, debating if this was the time to put the colonel in his place. He was here for a reason, not a vacation.

"I've already read your intelligence reports on this terrorist, Abu Ajami, the Black Prince or whatever the CIA calls him, Mr. Collins. I don't know what more you could possibly add. You're worried about a handful of terrorists; I'm more concerned with the fucking Libyans."

"Ajami is not your ordinary—"

"He's a raghead, isn't he?" Madison snorted.

"Your arrogance is going to make a jackass out of you." Collins stopped making sure he had the colonel's attention. "We're dealing with too many unknowns here. Shit, you've seen what a couple hundred pounds of explosive can do to the World Trade Center. Do you have any idea what Ajami could do to New York with a twenty-megaton nuclear bomb? It would be a big mistake to discount these terrorists as just another bunch of armed thugs." He threw the report in Madison's lap.

Madison stiffened. "Mr. Collins, our mission is to secure Madadhi and ensure that none of those nuclear weapons leave that base. That means destroy their air and ground power in the first few hours. Once that's done, I'm confident Lieutenant Ghere and his attack team can clear those bunkers in minutes, terrorists or no terrorists."

Collins didn't say a word as the two men continued to stare at each other. "I've studied this man, have you?"

Madison didn't answer the question.

Collins continued. "He's dangerous because he is so unpredictable, Colonel. I know Ajami won't play down your capabilities . . . he's smarter than that."

"Okay, go on."

"I think once your men hit the ground and assault those bunkers, you'd better be ready for anything," Collins answered back. "The Libyans may be protecting and providing for this base, but chances are Ajami is in charge of it. That means he controls the shuttle, its crew, and, right now, those warheads."

"You know this for a fact, that this man controls the shuttle and crew?" Madison couldn't take the chance Collins was correct.

Collins retorted. "Of course I can't say I know for sure. But I know a hell of a lot more about terrorist operations than you do. Ajami is not the type of man to would let the Libyans walk in and take over his camp."

Madison sat back in his chair, his thoughts churning. "What else can you tell me?"

"I've been poring over every file we have on the man for the last five days. He's a genuine head case. The Mossad believes he's on medication to control his paranoia."

The colonel stood up, placing his arms on the desk, and stared across at Collins. "Okay, is that all the good news you've got?"

"Well, there is one other thing I need to let you know. I may have thrown a hornet's nest into this camp. After the MiG attempt on the liner, I wanted to try and smoke Ajami out. I started some suppositions, through an informant, that we were able to intercept the MiG because of a leak in his camp." Collins grew rigid, prepared for the backlash this would create with Madison.

"Well, I wouldn't expect anything less from the CIA but to add grease to the fire, now would I?"

Collins smiled at the familiar phrase. "Then you'll understand why I have to go along. If you made the bed wrong, then you have to fix it. I know this man and if you get into a hostage situation, you'll need me there."

"Now, wait a minute. I'm not going to—"

"But, colonel, you and I both know how vital it is to have someone on the ground who can get inside this man's head. I'm the logical choice and I do know how to handle an M-16 . . . qualified expert."

Madison couldn't believe the balls on this young man. He didn't have time for a drawn-out argument and decided he was the CIA's responsibility, not his.

"All right, Mr. Collins. Contact your people. If it's fine with them, then check in with Ghere. He'll issue some fatigues, a helmet, and flak jacket. As for giving you a loaded weapon, you'll have to convince Ghere of that."

"Thank you, sir." Collins turned to leave, thinking that Christine, his wife, would shoot him herself if she knew what he had gotten himself into.

"Oh, and Collins, I think you know that old adage really is 'You made your bed, now lie in it.' I want you to remember that when all hell is breaking loose around you."

25

Jibril could feel the icy stare of the man before he even saw him.

"Yes, Major Nittal, I understand." Jibril hung up the phone and turned to face Ajami. He saw Majeed standing behind him. "My government wants to know when the warheads will be ready to transport. Each hour we wait is an hour too long. They are losing confidence in your ability to keep your word."

Ajami looked past the captain as his eyes scanned the command center. He was very pleased. The room was alive with men and equipment. To his surprise, Jibril and the Libyans were keeping up their end of the bargain.

"This is my operation. I will let you know when it is time." Ajami's tone was low, barely audible.

"I heard that one of the foot patrols didn't report in . . . is there trouble?" Jibril asked.

Majeed, standing next to Ajami, spoke out. "That is none of your concern. It is not uncommon for men to desert once a battle begins. The traitors will be found."

Ajami's mind was on bigger things. He folded his arms. "The defenses you promised . . . where are they?"

"Everything is in place." Jibril pointed to a large round table in the center of the room. Resting on it was a detailed map of Madadhi Air Base and the surrounding area. There were red and blue spots on the map, showing the locations of the air defenses. "Would you care to check for yourself?"

Ajami walked over to the map and examined the defenses' positions. "Are they operational?"

Jibril bore his eyes into the man, tired of his incessant badgering. "My friend, you need not concern yourself with my duties, either. They will be operating by nightfall," he replied, not wanting to give away his true feelings. *I will be relieved when I can finally eliminate this madman,* he thought, smiling serenely.

Duke stood as three men entered the holding area. He could tell that the taller silhouette in the back was Ajami.

"Bring the same American." Ajami's voice had a more ominous tone to it this time. When he walked into the light, Duke noticed there were dark circles under his eyes and the pupils appeared to be dilated.

"Duke, don't let them take me," Willie pleaded, as two Palestinian guards opened the cell door and looked in his direction.

"He doesn't know anything. Take me instead." Duke stepped in front of the guards.

"Ah . . . the leader fights for his men. You prefer to go in his place, brave American?" Ajami asked, as he put himself between the men, face to face with Duke.

"How about if you get rid of Mutt and Jeff here and we just go out back? We can settle this man to man. Or are you afraid?" Duke drew up what energy he had left and swelled his chest.

Ajami's eyes lit with fire at Duke's words.

"You stupid American. You think that power is proven by beating a man like I did your friend over there?" he asked mockingly, disgusted by this apparent lack of understanding. "This man does not respect you, nor did he obey you. He has shamed you and still you let him live. Even if I were to fight you, your honor would not be restored. A true warrior never talks with the enemy."

"You mean talk with a worthy enemy." Duke reached out with his bound hands in a flash, pulling Ajami to him. "Listen, you *shit*. Half the men under your control wish you were dead. And I'm—" Duke's words were stopped short as one of the soldiers clubbed him on the back of the head.

As Willie was hauled away and Andrea went to Duke, Ajami turned to see Kamal staring at him. Their eyes met.

Kamal spoke solemnly. "He is right, my leader. There are a lot of men who would wish to see you dead. But you must know I am not one of them. I have helped to keep you alive all these years, a loyal servant, and now you turn your back on me."

"Kamal, I have spent many hours meditating on how you could have betrayed me, and I have not found an answer. I came to trust you too much. Allah has sent me a warning through you and I will heed it." Ajami exited, making his way to the safety of his quarters.

Ajami entered his room and closed the door, locking it. He removed his pistol, making sure it was loaded. He cocked the hammer, pointing it toward the door, as he sat on the corner of his bed. *When they come, I will kill them, every one of them. These men will never have the chance. Allah is my leader. He will protect me. This gift is from Allah for my greatness.*

Ajami looked through the black metal sites of his pistol, his finger brushing the trigger.

An hour had passed with Willie hanging from the crane again near the left wingtip of the shuttle, his back against the wall. Two Palestinian guards were on either side of him. The interior of the large aircraft bunker was filled with light blue smoke, the yellowish overhead lights cutting through it. Willie could smell burnt plastic and rubber. He lifted his swollen head and saw the bright flickering light of a cutting torch on top of the shuttle's cargo bay. He guessed they were trying to remove the outer skin of the satellite.

Willie drew in a slow breath, feeling the sharp, piercing pain as his rib cage expanded. His hands were numb and cold from the lack of circulation, and he was drifting into and out of consciousness. He doubted he would live through another round of interrogation. He had told them everything he knew, but it wasn't enough. Willie attempted to wiggle his fingers to get the blood flowing as he dropped his head and passed out again from the pain.

STAGING AREA, ALI BALLAS, EGYPT

The briefing room was hot, cramped, and filled with cigarette smoke. Two exposed seventy-watt light bulbs hung from the ceiling, casting an amber glow on the flight leaders. Madison could tell by their conversation that the pilots were psyched and ready to go. He tried to listen to several conversations at once to get a read on what was being discussed.

Seated before him were the best pilots in the air force, the backbone of Cobra team, the flight leaders of each cell. Madison would rely a great deal on each man's expertise, experience, and judgment in planning and executing this operation.

"All right, men, let's get started." Madison waited until the room fell quiet before he began.

The wall behind him was divided into three uneven sections. Half of the wall was covered with a large black-and-white computer-enhanced satellite photo covering a 400-mile radius around Madadhi Air Base. The other half of the wall was split evenly with maps of the area between the Libyan airfield at Aujila and a close-up of Madadhi.

"H hour is 0430 tomorrow. Colonel Randell, you and your team of

F-117s, call sign Vader, will be the first to lift off. Your primary target will be the early warning radar south of Aujila." Madison pointed to the spot on the map. "The station there provides radar cover over Madadhi and also controls any Libyan aircraft that may enter the airspace during the operation. A Pave Low chopper reported picking up E-band radar waves last night when they dropped the Pathfinder team. Since then, air force intel has identified the radar site. The latest satellite pass also gave us the exact locations of three additional SAM sites that have become operational in the last eight hours." Madison stopped, looking back at Randell. "Because of the number of targets, your squad of Stealths will have to fly separately instead of in pairs. I will leave it up to you to assign the individual targets." He placed a copy of the target map in front of the colonel.

Randell, lighting a cigarette, took the sheet and blew the smoke out of his nose.

"Murphy and Whitehead, your F-15Es will go in after Randell. Whitehead, you'll be flight leader for Mercury package. Plan to come in low and take out anything that tries to sneak in under our radar coverage. Currently, the Libyans have a number of aircraft on the ground at Madadhi. I want them all destroyed ASAP. Murphy, you're in charge of Cadillac group. I want you and your fifteens on top; catch anything that comes in high. I am going to leave it up to the both of you to configure your fighters for both air-to-air and air-to-ground."

Madison looked at Lieutenant Leonard Tobin. His was the group of pilots slated to fly the F-16 Wild Weasels. They were kindly referred to as the "beer boys," call sign Corona. The Weasel drivers were the youngest men in Cobra and had one of the deadliest jobs: killing active SAM sites. "The sixteens will be right behind the F-15Es. If you Eagle drivers run into any SAM threats, vector the Wild Weasels for support. Tobin, tell your men to be heads up. We may need you in the air-to-air role." He handed the young, dark-haired lieutenant a series of satellite photos. "Each one of these sights is mobile, so you'll get one more update before you take off."

Madison turned to Captain Gaines Bristol, the A-10 flight lead. "I want the A-10s to wait and enter the area along with the ground support only after every threat has been knocked out. Bristol, my gut tells me there will be a lot of small ground targets to clean up. Make sure your aircraft are fully loaded. When it's clear, the C-17 containing Lieutenant Ghere and his team will land." Madison scanned the room. "Any questions or comments?"

There were none, and Ghere, the leader of the Sky Fire ground team, jumped into the discussion.

"I would like to point out this is not going to be like any hostage rescue mission we've practiced. We need to keep in mind that surprise is not on our side. These men know we are coming and are waiting for us. After studying the satellite photos, I've decided the best plan of attack would be straight on. The A-10s need to support us when we hit the ground, to wipe up any resistance on that mountain above the bunker."

"All right, men. I want this operation over by 0700 . . . three hours max. Anything else?" Madison looked around at each team leader.

No one said a word.

"Meet with your teams and get the last-minute details worked out. Latest intel will be supplied to each of you an hour before takeoff. Dismissed."

PATHFINDER TEAM ALPHA

Rath crawled into the OP through the back entrance. Vasquez followed right behind him. The sun was touching the horizon and a chill nipped the air. Both men were tired, thirsty, and hungry.

"Good work, Lieutenant . . . Sergeant," Rodriguez said. "Our guest was very cooperative, with a little persuasion." He nodded toward the captured terrorist.

"When's the cavalry coming?" Rath asked.

"We just got word . . . Madison's ordered an attack to begin at 0430 tomorrow."

"It's about time! Another twelve hours in this hellhole and I'd attack single-handed." Vasquez stretched his achy muscles under the coverage of the netting.

"You two get some rest. I want both of you on the hunt again at 0400."

Rath nodded and Vasquez, with his mouth full of peanut butter and crackers, muttered, "You got it, Captain."

Ziad turned off the cutting torch and with his gloved right hand peeled away the last bit of hot aluminum skin from the side of the satellite. He felt the tension in his body ease a little. He was still alive. None of the missiles' solid rocket motors had caught fire and exploded, as he feared might happen.

Ziad unclipped the flashlight from his belt and turned it on. He had methodically cut and removed an eighteen-inch-wide by twenty-seven-foot-long section of the satellite's outer skin, where he assessed the remaining warheads to be located. The inside of the Kosmos was exposed, and he could see how much damage the fire had caused. As he crawled back and forth, he didn't like what he saw. The interior was a charred and melted mess. The fire had spread throughout the core of the satellite, making it impossible to understand the system's wiring and safety characteristics.

He climbed down from the shuttle to where Ajami waited for the news. "Most of the warheads are damaged, but there are two that appear to be accessible." He wiped the sweat from his forehead with his sleeve, leaving a greasy mark. "I am sure the only thing that kept the warheads intact were the graphite and fiberglass heat shields under their nose cones." Ziad rubbed his brow with his fingers.

"How soon can you have one removed?" Ajami asked.

"It will take a while to remove a nose cone. That must be done first. Then I will have to disconnect the wiring from the main missile body to the warhead bus. I can then remove the shield. It depends. Three, maybe four hours."

Ajami examined Ziad's face. He felt as if the entire bunker complex was closing in on him. Every dream, every goal, in his life was within reach if he could just get one of the warheads. In one mighty blow he could kill the evil controlling his people. Ajami ran his fingers through his black hair. His plan would fall apart if they didn't hurry.

"And what of Jibril? You must be certain he does not suspect what we are doing," Ziad said with concern in his voice.

"I will handle Jibril. You just get your job done and we will both have what we deserve." Ajami turned and walked out of the bunker, heading toward his chamber. He needed to find Majeed. He would use him to keep Jibril away from the missiles. Majeed would interrogate the woman prisoner and Jibril would oversee it. That would keep the Libyan away from the warheads until he could secure one. He turned around and picked up his pace, walking down the tunnel toward the command center.

26

Major Hiyam Nittal had not eaten in over twenty-four hours. He was once again studying the American tactics during the Iraqi war. Nittal speculated that the Americans would first hit while it was dark. It would be a fast and furious attack, and his forces would have little time to react. Libyan naval intelligence was reporting the carrier *Kennedy* had stepped up operations in the Mediterranean and the USS *America,* along with its battle group, would enter the waters off their northern coast in fourteen hours.

Nittal was standing in the underground command center between the early warning radar and communications equipment. As was the case on most hot evenings, the room was filled with the redolence of the sweaty technicians working the equipment's controls. He walked up behind the men monitoring the computer terminals that linked them directly to the radar station scanning the skies to the south of Aujila.

"The scope is clear. There is no air traffic in the area." The technician gave the info to the major automatically.

"What power level are they operating on?" Nittal asked.

"533 kilowatts . . . eighty-two percent power, sir."

"That fool," Nittal muttered to himself. "Why is he not following my orders? Contact Sergeant Isma'il at once. Order him to increase his radar power to 100 percent."

"Yes, sir," the technician reached for a phone.

"Is the backup radar in the area?" Nittal asked First Lieutenant Shazli. The short, dark-bearded man was sitting behind a blank computer monitor.

"Yes, Major, as per your orders, the new radar is concealed under camouflaged netting and is standing by fifteen kilometers south of the current station." Shazli was now looking at the major. His computer

271

screen had been tied into another radar system just hours earlier. How-ever, since the radar was not operating, his radar scope was clear. Nittal just looked at the junior officer.

"Should I give the order to bring the PRV-9 on-line?"

"No. Order them to warm up their electronic systems only. Instruct the crew that under no circumstances are they to activate the radar until I give the order," Nittal barked.

"Yes, sir." The lieutenant picked up his phone. Seconds later, his blue-screened radarscope was warming up along with the electrical equip-ment of the second station. All the radar crew would have to do is raise the antenna and activate it.

"Major, it is Captain Jibril. He says it is urgent." One of the Libyan communications officers was holding a black phone, an uninterrupted link to Jibril's command center at Madadhi.

Nittal took the phone. "Yes, what is it?"

"Ajami has deceived us and is planning an escape with the warheads. Ziad is working with him," Jibril informed his commanding officer.

"What proof do you have?" Nittal asked.

"I was outside the bunker entrance. I heard him talking with Ziad. They are planning to steal a warhead and flee the base."

"Ajami should never have been trusted. What do you propose now?"

"The bunker where the shuttle is located has been heavily fortified by Ajami and his men. I must wait for the reinforcements. If need be, I will kill Ajami. But I am sure I will meet opposition from his men. I will wait until Ziad removes the weapons, then dispose of him as well," Jibril said, then added, "We must act now."

Nittal looked at the digital clock on the far wall. It was now 2200 hours. His heavy armor fast-attack company would be moving out within the hour.

"I have already issued the order. They can move only so fast. They should reach your position by dawn. It would be best if you hold off until the support troops reach you. If Ajami or any of his men suspect our intentions, they could delay us long enough for the Americans to arrive. Keep me posted." He hung up the phone. "Curse Ajami, he is a madman! I should never have allowed him to rise to this position.

"Lieutenant, give the order for Major Wazir and his troops to acceler-ate their operation."

MADADHI AIR BASE

Duke James could sense it. The interior air of the bunker had cooled several degrees, telling him night had finally come to the desert. He stood near the cell door, listening to every sound as it echoed down the tunnel twenty feet in front of him. He could hear footsteps and voices and see the shadows of men moving past the doorway. Duke knew that when help arrived it would come under the cover of darkness. He tried to reassure himself the U.S. military was out there planning their assault.

Duke let his mind roam to images of his wife and children, to the time when they had moved to Houston. He remembered the excitement and anxiety they had shared during his astronaut training, and how he loved to hold his wife, sitting by a warm, glowing fire in their home. Duke wondered how Katie was handling this, what she had told the kids. His mind drifted to Willie, wondering if his friend was still alive. *When I get out of here, I'm going to kill that bastard Ajami,* he thought.

Andrea touched Duke's arm. "Thinking about Willie?" she asked softly.

Duke turned and looked into her eyes. They were scared and tired. "Yeah . . . my family . . . and Willie."

"Good God, I hope he's still alive." Andrea rested against Duke.

"He's tougher than you think, Andi."

"I can't hold out much longer."

"Yes, you can. Just try to stay focused on getting out of here." He tried to be positive. The dark figures of two men caught his attention. "Stand back," Duke said, pushing Andrea behind him.

Majeed approached the cell as Jibril stood in the shadows in back of him. He stood for a second before unlocking the cell door. Majeed opened it halfway and swung his Uzi around, pointing it toward Duke and Andrea.

"American, come with me," Majeed grunted.

Duke hesitated, then moved toward the open door.

"Not you. The woman." Majeed motioned with the barrel of his weapon.

"No," Duke said quietly, but with authority. "She stays with me."

Majeed swung the cell door open and stepped in. His Uzi was leveled at Duke's head. "The woman comes with me."

Andrea stepped out from behind Duke. "It's all right, Duke. We don't have a choice."

Majeed reached over and grabbed a handful of her hair, pulling her out of the cell. "You are a smart man. A woman isn't worth dying for."

"If you lay one hand on her—"

"Shut up." Majeed said, clicking off the safety of his Uzi. The muzzle of the gun was only a yard away from Duke's head. Majeed backed out of the cell, slamming the door behind him. He took Andrea by the arm and the three exited the holding area.

"You will *never* see her alive again," Kamal said, standing next to the bars separating him from Duke. "I know what they do to women. She will die a painful death."

Duke turned away, now alone in the cell. His anger boiled inside him.

DAY
7

THURSDAY, SEPTEMBER 23

27

STAGING AREA, ALI BALLAS, EGYPT

Colonel Kirk ("Masterblaster") Randell watched as Cobra team's airborne command post lifted off the runway and into the sky. It was followed by two KC-10 Extender tankers. He watched the big lumbering aircraft's blinking red and green wingtip directional lights until they disappeared into the distance.

The colonel had received his written execute orders two hours earlier. He suited up, ate, then made his way to the hangar to his waiting jet. The forty-two-year-old former F-4 Phantom jock looked at the horizon to the west before he stepped from the ladder and slid into the cockpit of his single-seat, twin-engine F-117A Stealth fighter. There was a thin line of clouds hanging below the half-moon. Otherwise, the night sky was clear, filled with the sparkle of stars.

Randell's five-foot-nine frame fit snugly behind the faint yet distinctly colored multifunction displays of his aircraft. He had had his maintenance crew paint "The Evil Enchantress" under his name printed on the side.

If flying the big jet had taught the father of four anything, it was patience. The Stealth was like his wife of twenty years: he loved her, but she could be very temperamental, and he had learned to baby both. He took his time strapping himself into the ejection seat comfortably, preparing for the short flight into Libya. Next he placed the cold rubber oxygen mask around his face, checking the systems; it was up and running.

Before joining Cobra team, Randell had been part of the 4450th Tactical Group. Based at Tonopah, Nevada, they were known as the Grim Reapers. He still wore the Reapers' numberless squadron patch on his lower right sleeve. Randell had more or less been told he had to volunteer for the USAF's newest elite fighting team. He was torn with the feeling that in taking the job he knew he would not see his family as much as he wished. However, flying the Stealth would give him the opportunity to do what he loved: sneaking in behind enemy lines and being the first one to hit a target. It was a sensation very few men in the air force would ever feel.

Kirk Randell would be the Stealths' flight leader for tonight's mission. The four F-117As would be using the call sign Vader, after Darth Vader in the movie *Star Wars,* and Randell would be flying Vader One. Using *Star War* characters as call signs for the F-117As had started during the war with Iraq, and it was now a tradition.

The Stealths would each take off at precise intervals, then link up before refueling. Together they would head for the KC-10 tankers that would be orbiting just inside Chadian airspace in southern Egypt. After they topped off their fuel tanks, Randell would break north on a separate programmed path to his target, the early warning radar station at Aujila. The other three F-117As would hit the SAM sites around Madadhi Air Base, then turn and head back to Ali Ballas. With the EWR and SAM sites out of action, the F-15Es would follow thirty minutes later, taking out any aircraft on the ground and in the sky. The F-16s and A-10s would then streak in and hit the remaining ground targets as the F-15Es patrolled the skies above them. Madison's EC-141 airborne command center would control both the air and ground operations, being the fighters' eyes and ears.

Randell mentally ran through his strategy as the jagged-edged cockpit canopy of the F-117A closed around him. He heard it lock into place, shutting out the low rumble of the APUs as they struggled to start his engines.

MADADHI AIR BASE

Andrea's face exhibited her defiance. "I'm not going to tell you anything, *because I don't know anything."*

Majeed and Jibril were alone with her. Her arms and legs were tied as she stood in the pilots' briefing room, located directly down the tunnel from the holding area. Andrea faced a large wall map of the surrounding area as the two men tried to intimidate her. Only it wasn't as she had expected. Sure, she had been pushed around a bit, even slapped, but nothing like Willie. It was as if the one called Majeed were holding back.

Majeed paced, asking the same questions over and over again.

"One more time . . . what do you know about the weapons in the satellite?" Majeed drilled.

"Nothing. I don't know anything about weapons."

Jibril stood in the corner. He had consented to oversee the interrogation of the woman astronaut by Majeed. Yet his instincts told him that Ajami wanted to keep him away from the hangar. Majeed, who knew how to speak English, had been talking for quite some time. Jibril wasn't certain if Majeed had learned anything new, but he doubted it.

Jibril focused his attention on the scene before him. "Is that the best you can do, Majeed?" He laughed. "I believe you are putting her to sleep."

Andrea did indeed appear to be languid. Her big blue eyes were partially covered by droopy lids and long lashes.

"I will handle this my own way, Captain," Majeed sneered back, irritated at having to work in front of the cocky little man. "What is your job on the plane?"

"Mission specialist," Andrea answered.

"Mission specialist . . . very good. So you are an intelligent woman." Andrea glanced up at him. *What did that mean,* she wondered.

"She knows nothing. I am returning her to the holding area," Majeed said, moving to take hold of her arm.

"You are a fool, Majeed. You have not learned anything because you have not hurt her." Jibril stood and abruptly hit Andrea across the face with the back of his hand. "Now, ask her your question." He raised his hand a second time, indicating he would strike her again if she did not cooperate.

Majeed jumped at the smaller Libyan, knocking him back a few steps. He then grabbed the man's throat, pushing him backward until they hit the wall. "This is *my* prisoner. *I* am in charge of what is done here. If you hit her again, I will kill you."

Jibril tried to speak, but couldn't with the grip the Palestinian maintained on him. The fire in Majeed's eyes caused him to nod his head in agreement without fighting back. Majeed let him loose, the disgust evident in his gestures.

"I told you she knows nothing. I will return her to the holding area now."

"Ah, you want something else from her perhaps," Jibril rasped, rubbing his neck. "You need not play those games with American women, my friend; they have no *'ird* to protect."

Majeed took hold of Andrea's arm, ignoring him, and escorted her out of the room. They walked through the empty tunnels back to the holding cells. Majeed handed her a piece of cloth, keeping his eyes straight ahead. Andrea dabbed at the blood trickling from her cut lip, gazing up at him. She thought it unusual but believed he had saved her from being beaten further and wondered why.

"Things are not always the way they seem," Majeed said softly, not altering his stare, as they walked past the guard back into the holding area.

TWENTY-TWO KILOMETERS SOUTH OF AUJILA, LIBYA

"Inform Nittal we are now at full power," Master Sergeant Isma'il said, confused by the order. Isma'il knew the P-35M system was most efficient when operating at eighty-two percent. However, a good officer didn't question the orders of his commanders, especially Nittal's. "I want everyone alert," Isma'il bellowed. "Everyone!"

Atif Hamza, a middle-aged Libyan, sat perfectly still and upright as he scanned the wide-view, two-color Soviet-designed radarscope. The narrow cinder block building, housing the four men and radar equipment, was void of activity except for the commanding officer's chain-smoking. Hamza tried to overlook the annoyance of the smoke. His attention never wavered from the center of the screen. As senior technician, he had just returned from Syria, where he had spent three weeks training on the P-35M system. His grades had been good, and his commander now regarded him as the best man to find and distinguish long-range targets.

"Hamza, I want to be alerted if anything out of the ordinary appears on your radarscope." The officer took another drag from his cigarette and exhaled in the air above the man's head.

"Yes, sir," he answered, feeling pressured to spot something as his eyes watered from the smoke. He coughed and waved his hand, hoping that would alert Isma'il to the more present interference in the air.

F-117A VADER ONE

Randell watched and waited for the last F-117A to finish refueling and break from the KC-10's boom. The fighter drifted away from the tanker to 10,000 feet below. He keyed his open mike three quick times, giving the signal to the other aircraft they were ready to proceed, the mission was a go. Randell listened for the three other Stealth pilots' responses of double clicks. Each pilot then turned off his aircraft's external navigational lights and the black jets faded into the inky night. One at a time, they nosed over, banking toward their targets. The Vader flight would be the first coil of the Cobra strike.

EC-141 QUEEN BEE

The EC-141 was heading south at 182 degrees, climbing toward its cruising altitude of 38,000 feet, its speed 480 knots. The big aircraft was on the southbound leg of a tight oval flight pattern ten miles inside Libyan airspace. Although the interior was illuminated by the dancing multi-colored lights, the mood was all business and no cheer.

"Okay, what do we have here?" Second Lieutenant Victor Garnsey, the electronic warfare officer, asked under his breath. He adjusted his glasses and watched the bright red numbers of his AN/APR-38 RHAW system jump on the left side of the instrument panel. The Libyans had just boosted the power output of their long-range search radar south of Aujila. The question was, had they spotted something, or was their timing just preparing for the inevitable? His gaze drifted back to the warning panel. The frequency of the radar had stayed the same, ranging from 2,900 to 2,990 MHz, but his training told him the added strength in the signal was a threat.

He keyed his mike. "Colonel Madison, we have a problem." As he spoke, he typed a set of commands triggering the AN/ALQ-131C noise/deception and jamming pods. He put the system on standby, his finger hovering over the button.

Madison rose from his chair and walked to the center of the aircraft to stand behind Lieutenant Garnsey.

"The Libyans just boosted their power level, sir. The signal is weak, but we're too damn close."

"Have they spotted us?" Madison asked.

"It's possible, sir."

"What's Vader's flight status?" the colonel asked the man next to Garnsey.

"Refueling is complete. They're on their way to the targets," Master Sergeant Jason Oliveri, the mission's air boss, answered from his seat behind the computer console. "ETA to first target . . . thirty minutes, sir."

"All right, let's back off and tell the KC-10s to follow in behind us. Order the Strike Eagles to hold tight. I want to see what happens after the Stealths go in."

"Those F-15s are scheduled to take off in ten minutes, sir. Delaying them would throw the entire mission off." Oliveri's tone was respectful as he pointed out the effect of the colonel's decision.

"I know that, Oliveri." Madison didn't like having to explain himself, but he wanted the young man to understand his tactics. "If the Stealths don't eliminate the SAMs and that radar, I'll send in a couple of Eagles at a time to saturate the target. But I won't send in all those birds to get plucked out of the sky."

The air boss picked up a phone, contacting the cockpit. "Bring us back across the Egyptian border."

F-117A VADER ONE

It whispered to him when he crossed the border and banked northwest at 8,300 feet. Now a steady drumlike throbbing sounded in his helmet. The Libyan E-band early warning and search radar filled the sky with pulsing radio waves, hunting for aircraft. Randell turned the volume down. The unearthly noise distracted him.

He activated the FLIR (Forward Looking Infrared) system and tightened his grip on the stick, nosing his aircraft over into a thirty-degree dive. Four minutes later, the triangle-shaped jet was 8,000 feet lower. The F-117A surged as Randell forced her nose up. He felt the subtle pressure of 2.5 Gs roll over his body. Leveling the fighter at 300 feet, he centered the stick and nudged the dual throttles forward a half inch, nursing a few more pounds of thrust out of her engines. The neon green numbers of the Stealth's airspeed indicator, on the left side of the HUD, climbed to 392 knots. The bleak desert flashed below.

Randell used his thumb to routinely push an actuator button on the throttle handle. The multifunction display's right side instantly changed to a computer-generated 3-D moving map showing his present location and the programmed flight path he would take to the target. Prior to leaving the ground, Randell had entered the exact latitude and longitude of his takeoff location into the Stealth's INS. Each checkpoint of his course of attack was then inserted, as well as the precise position of the target. The solid white line zigzagging toward the radar site indicated he was now seventy-four kilometers inside Libya on a heading of 248.

Randell designated his next checkpoint to give a specific latitude and longitude readout. The Honeywell H-423/E cold ring laser gyro had an accuracy of less than 0.220 nautical miles per hour, and the Stealth's backup computer compensated for the difference. In a flash the computer told him he was right on schedule and a quick check of the instruments verified the The Evil Enchantress was operating perfectly.

The jet banked left and then right as the autopilot changed course.

SPECIAL TECHNICAL OPERATIONS CENTER, PENTAGON

Harris was waiting by the color photofax machine. He knew what it was before it finished printing, and wondered what could be done about it. In the center of the photo was a ZSU-23-4 antiaircraft gun. It was camouflaged fairly well, resting in a shallow ditch on the south end of the runway, but an NPIC analyst had spotted it just minutes ago. He wondered why he hadn't seen it himself. He placed the photo on his computer scanner, transferring the image into digital form. The picture then appeared on the high-resolution computer screen.

"General, take a look at this." He showed the picture to Clark. "I don't know how I missed it."

"Okay. Let Madison and Rodriguez know about it," was all Clark said.

Harris heard the dot matrix printer. He ripped off the message and read it. "Word just in, General. The F-117s have refueled and are heading toward their targets."

Clark reached for the phone. "Everything is set, Mr. Secretary. Madison reports the Stealths are on the way," Clark informed Turner at the White House situation room.

"All right. I'll let the president know," the secretary of defense said, hanging up.

Clark caught the flicker of concern in Dawson's eyes. "I know what you're thinking, Jack. Don't worry. If anyone can pull this off, it's Madison."

"I'll be in my office. Keep me posted." Dawson left the operations center.

PATHFINDER TEAM ALPHA

"It's time," Rodriguez whispered to Rath inside the pitch-black OP.

"I know." Rath sat up. He was incredibly tired and still hadn't fallen into a restful sleep.

Rodriguez turned on a dim red hand-held light, illuminating the far corner of the observation post. "We received this from STOC. It seems the ragheads managed to sneak a gun in under our noses."

Rath reached for a water bottle and removed the cap. He then pulled out three dextroamphetamines from his breast pocket and popped them into his mouth. He washed them down in one big gulp. The strong stimulants would bring him back to life in minutes.

"What's the problem?" Rath asked, as he took the satellite faxphoto from Rodriguez.

"There's a ZSU-23 on the east end of the runway. The spy boys at Langley picked it out about ten minutes ago." Rodriguez pointed to its location. "You and Vasquie have thirty minutes to get into position and take it out."

"That's an armor antiaircraft gun! Thirty minutes will be cutting it close." Rath placed his NVGs on his head, hitting the switch to turn them on.

"Don't screw up, 'cause precisely at 0435 an F-117A is going to take out this mobile Gainful." Rodriguez was now pointing to an SA-6 mobile SAM less than 300 yards away from the ZSU-23. The black outline of the

BTR-60PB armored SAM launch vehicle could easily be seen as it sat between several large boulders in a ravine. "That triple-A gun needs to be taken out in time, or it could mean big trouble for that fighter."

Rath studied the photo for a few seconds. His pulse rate quickened as the amphetamines started to kick in, making him feel pumped and ready to go. He and Vasquez would have to cover three quarters of a mile to get into position. They'd better move fast.

Rath heard the click as Vasquez snapped his AN/PVS-4 starlight scope onto his rifle. Vasquez tightened the lug bolts, securing the scope. His expression told Rath he was primed.

"Okay, let's go, Vasquie. See you right after the fireworks, Captain." He and Vasquez slipped out into the darkness.

TWENTY-TWO KILOMETERS SOUTH OF AUJILA, LIBYA

Hamza rubbed his eyes. He had been sitting at his station for seven hours without a break, and it was becoming difficult to concentrate solely on the empty radarscope. He hoped several Chadian jet fighters would streak across the sky, just to relieve the boredom.

Sergeant Isma'il stood to crush out another cigarette on the concrete floor, alerting Hazma to end his wishful thinking.

"Headquarters is demanding to know the status of your equipment."

"As before . . . everything is operating perfectly."

"And your power level?" Isma'il grunted.

"As you have ordered, sir, 100 percent."

"Very well then, carry on."

Hamza continued to stare at the blank scope and wondered why his commander was in such a cantankerous mood.

Several sparkling yellow flecks of light flashed past on the left side of his cockpit. *Campfires,* Randell told himself. Travelers along one of the desert roadways must have stopped for the night.

He brought his attention back to the RHAW equipment. The E-band radar was still operating in the same frequency range. The good news did little to ease his worries of the operator discovering he was out there.

Randell coaxed the Stealth up past 1,500 feet on a heading of 301. He gently banked the fighter right and left to break up his faint frontal radar signature. It was a tactic all F-117A pilots used to confuse a wary radar operator.

Reducing airspeed to 340 knots, he listened to the soft hum of the engines spool down. He checked his timing. He would hit the radar site three minutes before the other three Stealths started their target runs on the SAM emplacements around Madadhi.

Randell's breathing increased as he switched the computer from navigation to weapons delivery mode. He then triggered the target's position on the INS, verifying it. The Evil Enchantress drifted up to 2,000 feet before kicking into autopilot again. The MFD revealed an IR-generated black-and-white television picture of the surrounding landscape. Randell pulled back on the throttles, dropping his airspeed further, below 280 knots. He scanned the HUD and FLIR MFD.

The terrain encircling the radar complex was fairly void of vegetation, so the radar command center should be easy to spot. Two dirt roads crossed to the south of the narrow building and a power line was to the north. It was an ideal target compared to the hardened underground bunkers he had practiced destroying in the simulator. As he flew closer, Randell aligned the contour features with those on the satellite photo strapped to his left knee. He picked up the main road leading him northwest to the subtle outline of the building in the distance. Two vehicles outside the south end of the structure had been parked for a while, he noted, because their engine compartments lacked the glowing white of heat.

The sand and rocks around the building had cooled much quicker than the insulated command center. Consequently, the concrete structure appeared in a pale ivory on the IR screen. To the southeast of the building, a third of a kilometer away, Randell saw the rotating antenna of the radar. He was now approaching from the southeast at 2,010 feet.

Two minutes from weapons release, Randell double-checked that the navigational lights were off. He tugged at his restraints, making sure he was firmly strapped into the Stealth's ejection seat. He flicked the master button to arm. Then he began to manipulate the fingertip target designator, located on the closest throttle handle, maneuvering the targeting cross hairs over the terrain toward the target. It took Randell a mere thirty seconds to center the thin white cross hairs on top of the building. This process was known as designated munitions point of impact, or DMPI. Because of the size and relative softness of the target, Randell decided to use only one bomb.

By pushing and then releasing the TD switch, he instructed the computer as to the precise location of the target. A tenth of a second later, the F-117's invisible laser designator began to blast the center of the building with a narrow laser beam at DMPI.

Randell swept the HUD with his eyes. The symbology displayed the need to correct his flight path two degrees left to compensate for crosswinds. With his fingertips, he gently eased the stick left, moving exactly on target. He lowered his head to the center MFD. The Evil Enchantress had passed the max range point of the flight, and his GBU-27 would now have enough energy to impact the target.

Holding his breath, he pressed his thumb on the red button on top of the Stealth's control stick. He felt the aircraft's sudden resistance when the weapons bay doors snapped open. The 2,000-pound laser-guided weapon fell quickly, upon release from its shackles. Immediately the doors closed.

The penetrating bomb cleared the aircraft, and the detector unit picked up the reflecting laser light pulsing from the rooftop of the command center. A hardened electronic computer microprocessor and digital autopilot fed a steady stream of commands to the four canards. The fins worked in unison, directing the bomb toward the laser target.

For an instant Hamza saw a speck appear on his radar screen. He typed in a set of commands, trying to focus on the electronic return, but with no success. Like undressing in front of a windowshade with the light on, The Evil Enchantress exposed herself only for the brief moment her bay doors opened.

Hamza glanced at his commanding officer from the corner of his eye. While he debated if the blip was worth mentioning, the room filled with the sudden thunderous roar of the one-ton bomb crashing through the ceiling of the structure. Hamza's next sensation was that of the fire and heat accompanied by a bright burning light surrounding his body.

Randell the Masterblaster watched the blur of the bomb enter the top of the building on his MFD. The thick metal outer skin of the explosive was designed to penetrate several meters of steel and concrete before exploding. Because of this, the GBU didn't detonate on impact. Rather, it was a full two seconds before the bomb vaporized the command center into a raging inferno. A charred and burning crater, twenty feet wide and ten feet deep, took the place of the radar center.

"Target one destroyed," Randell muttered to himself. He jammed both throttles forward. The Stealth's airspeed increased rapidly as he exited the area to the west, jinking right and left. Several kilometers to the north he saw the orange tracers of an antiaircraft gun filling the sky with twenty-three-millimeter armor-piercing rounds. He hit the chaff button, expelling several bundles of radar-breaking foil. To the south, another gunner was sweeping the night sky in a wide arc, doing his best to bring down the unseen bandit.

"You snooze, you lose," Randell called out into his oxygen mask. Now seven kilometers out, he put the Stealth in a hard 5 G turn and sped to the southwest. He grunted, tightening his stomach and leg muscles, as the Gs built. He followed the symbology on the HUD as he banked the fighter back to the southeast a full 180 degrees. The Evil Enchantress, returning to the scene of her crime, was flying back toward the demolished command center.

As Randell came wings level, he pointed the nose of the aircraft toward the wire mesh radar antenna still rotating and broadcasting. With the cross hairs over the antenna, he clicked the TD button and released it, locking the laser onto the base of the unit. Again his eyes went to the HUD, double-checking the symbology before crushing the red launch button down with his thumb. The second GBU-27 sailed out of the weapons bay. He kept his eyes on the MFD until the bomb smashed into the antenna's base, dispersing it in a ball of fire.

"California dreamin' . . . California dreamin'," Randell said, as he keyed his mike. His coded message to Madison confirmed that both targets had been destroyed.

Randell put The Evil Enchantress into a gradual climb toward her cruising level of 12,000 feet. He unhinged his oxygen mask and wiped the sweat from around his eyes.

28

The night was hushed, with only a breath of wind out of the east. Rath and Vasquez crouched down behind two small mounds of dirt. At the base of a ravine they had followed out of their mountain OP, the men had stopped to get their bearings. Even after years of training Rath was still amazed how his perspective changed when looking at the world through his NVGs. He recalled one of his instructors telling him that the essence of special ops equated to being a hawk by day and an owl by night, two silent and deadly predators.

Before moving forward, Rath glanced back over his shoulder at the main part of the air base a mile or so behind him, across the runway. At ground level he couldn't see as well as when in the higher OP, but the outlines of the parked aircraft were easy to distinguish. The lights around the enemy bunkers were out, yet he sensed movement.

Vasquez tapped him on the shoulder. "Right 100 meters. That will put us in range."

Rath readjusted his backpack, then started the trek across the last stretch of ground. They moved like creatures of the night.

EC-141 Queen Bee

The radar warning light on Garnsey's threat panel blinked off just before he received the call from the lead F-117A.

"First target kill confirmed, sir. Vader One just took out the radar site at Aujila. He's headed home."

"Right on time and no problems." Madison held his sentry position behind the electronic warfare officer, looking at the computer screen. It illuminated a bright blue outline of each country's borders and the loca-

288

tion of the EC-141 circling above southern Egypt and northern Sudan. In his mind, Madison pictured the other three F-117As on their target runs.

"Give the order to move us back across the Libyan border. I want us in sensor range of Madadhi as soon as possible." Colonel Madison grinned, looking at his air boss, Oliveri. "Get those 15s airborne."

AUJILA, LIBYA, SOUTHEASTERN COMMAND CENTER

Major Hiyam Nittal emerged from his office.

"There was nothing on the scope. I was monitoring the data being broadcast from the P-35M. I didn't see a thing. Now it is gone, sir. There is nothing there." His radar screen was empty and black. "I've checked the electronic relay—voice communications, everything. All lines are dead." The radar technician's voice sounded his alarm.

"*Shabah,*" one of the men in the background whispered. It was the Arabic word for ghost, the Saudi's nickname given to the F-117As during the war.

"Just as I thought," Nittal said aloud. "What about the PRV-9 radar station? Did they hit that?" he quizzed Lieutenant Shazli.

"No, sir. The crew reports no damage."

Nittal regretted having to sacrifice the first radar station, but he had speculated the Americans would use their Stealth fighters for an initial attack. Now, if only the Americans in charge of the rescue would continue as Nittal anticipated. Jibril and his men would have to absorb the opening air attack. After the American aircraft had spent most of their weapons and fuel, he would order every plane at Aujila to strike. His ground troops could then move in and take control of the air base from Ajami and his men. By the time the Americans regrouped, he would be in control of the warheads.

"Advise the reserve radar station to stand by." Nittal picked up the phone. "Patch me to Jibril at once."

Vasquez quietly worked the action on his M40A2 rifle, loading the chamber with an armor-piercing round. He then brought the gun to his shoulder and laid the stock over a football-sized boulder. It would be a steady platform from which to fire. He touched the switch, turning on the night-vision scope, and brought it up to his eye.

Rath was lying next to him flat on his stomach. He, too, was looking through an AN/PVS-4 starlight scope, only his was on a tripod. The two men began their finely honed method of target location.

"Ten o'clock, 200 meters. I see the outline of a T-72 track," Rath whispered, referring to the low-profile tracked vehicle that carried the radar and four twenty-three-millimeter guns.

"Yeah, I see it, too."

Rath contemplated the situation. The gun, commonly known as a Shilka, was pointing away from them at a forty-degree angle. He could see the radar dish protruding from the top of the chassis, and on both fenders were thirty-gallon drums of diesel fuel.

Vasquez finally asked the question that had been bugging him for the last half hour. "What's your plan?"

"We're going to shut this thing down."

"Well, that's a fucking good plan, Lieutenant," Vasquez said. "A .308 bullet won't penetrate the armor of a ZSU-23."

Rath kept his eye on the self-propelled AAA gun. "That's not what I had in mind, *dipshit*. Do you see the dish on top of the turret? That's the gun's radar, its eyes. When I give the order, punch a hole through it," Rath commanded. "With a little luck, and if you're as good a shot as you say, we'll knock it out."

Vasquez turned the eyepiece focusing ring on his scope, brightening the fluorescent picture. He placed the scope's cross hairs on the center of the dish. "I have it . . . dead center."

F-117A VADER TWO

Major Patrick Finney's attention went from the HUD to the RHAW sensor, then back again. The thirty-four-year-old, 210-pound ex–Air Force Academy linebacker was a twenty-three-mission veteran of the Iraqi war. He watched the HUD's symbols as the autopilot swung his Stealth fighter four degrees to the north to a new heading of 211, altitude 2,100 feet. He had been in the air for forty-five minutes and the computer indicated he was three minutes twenty-four seconds from weapons release, five seconds behind schedule.

"Damn it," he said aloud into the empty cockpit. Five seconds was too much. He edged the throttles forward, watching both RPM meters increase slightly. *Hell, even one second behind is too much.*

Finney reviewed his plan. It called for him to drop his weapons at the same time as the other two fighters flying to the north. Precision bombing has always been practiced by the F-117As. In the skies over Baghdad, during his previous missions, Finney's wingman had made the mistake of releasing his bombs ten seconds behind schedule. As a result, three fifty-seven-millimeter antiaircraft rounds had been able to estimate his location and hit the left side of his aircraft, nearly ripping off the wing and tail fin. With the grace of God, the pilot was able to limp back across the Saudi border and land at an emergency airstrip.

A turmoil began to boil inside Finney because the RHAW equipment wasn't picking up the enemy's radar signals. Intel had stated that each SA-6 site had at least one ZSU-23-4 supporting it. However, the radar warning equipment wasn't sensing any strong J-band microwave emissions.

The max range symbology appeared on the MFD. His total concentration was now on the FLIR.

"Come on, baby, where are you?" He searched the IR picture. The SA-6 mobile missile site was evading him and his time was running out. A hot steel target should be easy pickings.

Finney referenced the satellite photo on his knee, hoping to sight a clue. "Man, it should be right there." The photo was of two small shadows, bushes, on one side and a large outcrop of rocks on the other side of the SA-6. When he looked back at the MFD, all he could see was the outcrop and bushes. The SAM wasn't there.

The sons of bitches had moved it. The satellite photo was twelve hours old and the SA-6 was gone. He nosed the Stealth up a few degrees and clicked his mike. "California riot . . . no joy."

Rath tripped a firefly, a small infrared strobe light the size of a cigarette lighter, tossing it into an open space in front of him and Vasquez. The strobe was only visible to IR systems and should steer the F-117A pilots clear of their position. The lieutenant hoped the Libyans weren't also using any IR sensors.

"On my mark, Vasquie . . . three . . . two . . . one . . . now," Rath whispered.

Vasquez squeezed the trigger, concentrating on the mark. His rifle lunged and for a moment both their night-vision scopes blacked out from the sniper's muzzle flash.

"Bull's-eye," Vasquez said, putting his eye back on the scope.

Captain Jibril slammed the phone down. "Lieutenant Mizrahi, scramble your pilots. The radar station at Aujila has been destroyed."

Mizrahi instantly became active. Several of his pilots were already sitting in their MiG-23s. He hit the alert button on his desk.

To the north, the sky lit up in a shower of sparks and fire. Rath knew what it was, an F-117A had just hit its target, probably an SA-8 missile site. At the same time, from midway up the mountain across the runway, three bright flashes snaked their way into the sky. They were hand-held SA-7 SAMs looking for the heat emissions of an enemy aircraft. The color of their frosty blue rocket blooms was a unique characteristic of the solid rocket motors. A split second later, brilliant streaks of small arms and triple-A fire erupted from around the SAM site now burning. The Libyans were responding by shooting randomly into the air at their unseen enemy.

"Get ready, Vasquie. Let's hope this guy ate his Wheaties this morning." Rath put his head down and covered it with his arms. He was expecting a violent shock wave to pass over him as one of the Stealth's 2,000-pound bombs took out an SA-6 site somewhere in the distance. After thirty seconds he was still waiting.

"Something's wrong," Rath said, looking up, then checking his watch. "The target should have been destroyed by now." He heard a whining noise followed by the deep whisper of moving air. There was only one aircraft in the world that made that sound. An F-117A had just passed over them. He keyed his mike.

"Rushmore, this is Icebox. We have a negative boom on number one target."

"Roger, Icebox, stay on your target," came Rodriguez's answer.

"Vasquie, take out those fuel tanks on the back of the Shilka," Rath ordered. One well-placed bullet would cause the diesel fuel to explode.

Vasquez opened the action of his rifle and slipped in an Ultra-high Explosive round. The UHE was essentially a specially designed 168-grain match hollow point that had been filled with a mixture of ultrafine ammonia nitrate and a liquefied propane gel. Ammonia nitrate pellets were ground into a powder, then combined with the supercooled propane forced inside the hollow interior bullet. It was then sealed under extremely high pressure. The single bullet had the explosive power of a quarter stick of TNT at a maximum range of 500 meters.

Vasquez steadied the cross hairs on the left fuel tank. He took a deep breath, released half of it, and relaxed, squeezing the trigger. The silenced rifle made a muffled noise as both men waited for the rear portion of the chassis to explode. Nothing happened.

"Again," Rath ordered.

Vasquez jacked in another UHE round, waited for his scope to clear, and shot again, this time at the right tank. Again nothing happened. He reached out uneasily and touched Rath on the arm. "Lieutenant, I know I nailed both of those fuel tanks."

Rath didn't question his sniper. It was an easy shot for Vasquez and the chances of him missing were nil.

"Cover me," Rath said, as he placed his NVGs back on his head. Vasquez chambered another round. The spotter stood in a hunched position and started out across the flat ground toward the ZSU-23.

* * *

The sound of the commotion brought Duke out of his light sleep. He sat up in time to see a half dozen men flash past the outside of the cell.

"Andrea, get up," he whispered. "The cavalry is here."

"Oh, thank God." She sat up on the mattress, roused from a fitful sleep. "I was beginning to think they weren't going to come." She sobbed softly, bringing her slender hands to her face, wiping away the spilling tears.

Duke knelt down and helped her to stand. "Yeah, they're here, but remember what I said. This is the most dangerous time for us. Do as they say and we'll make it."

They could get killed by either the Libyans, the terrorists, or their rescuers. It wouldn't be the first time hostages were killed in the heat of battle.

Finney felt the Gs bleed off as his fighter came out of a tight turn. He centered the control stick and dropped the nose, picking up a few knots of airspeed. He leveled off at 5,000 feet on a heading back toward Madadhi, ten kilometers to the east. He banked the Stealth left and right, trying to get a visual of the ground below. He could make out a few burning fires in the distance. The other Stealths had hit their targets.

Finney switched his computer system from nav mode back to target mode and waited. The FLIR showed the black contour of the airstrip below him. He also saw three large transport aircraft, six helicopters, and five MiGs parked along the left side of the runway.

He throttled back, reducing his airspeed, and centered the white targeting cross hair where the target should have been. He then clicked the field of view switch, enlarging the IR picture of the MFD. He clicked it again twice.

"There it is," he breathed, having just spotted a very small black square in the lower left side of the IR display. To the southwest of it was a bright IR strobe light. *The Pathfinder team,* he thought.

He moved the cross hairs over the new target and magnified the picture. From 5,000 feet, the boxy characteristic outline of a launch vehicle looked like an SA-6 mobile SAM. The strobe had reassured him the Pathfinder team was out of the target area and now he wouldn't go home empty-handed.

The "in range" symbol appeared on the screen, and he tapped the red button on top of the control stick. A single GBU-27 glided out from beneath the fighter.

Rath was fifty meters from the ZSU-23, on his hands and knees, hiding behind a dried bush. He swept the area with his NVGs, perceiving that something wasn't right. It didn't make sense that there weren't any people climbing out of the turret. Vasquez had put three holes into the vehicle. It would have caused some type of malfunction, if it didn't disable the radar system altogether. Looking closer, Rath noticed that the bottom of the vehicle appeared to be flat rather than three dimensional. He spotted the track treads, but they were faked. Rath realized he was looking at a decoy. The Libyans had set up a steel and wooden platform that, from the air, looked just like a ZSU-23.

A hissing whistle streaked above Rath. He felt a wave of panic pump through his veins as he heard it.

"God help me!" he screamed, instinctively burying his face in the cool sand. He covered his head with his arms, cursing. *How could I be so fucking stupid,* he thought.

The whistling shrilled in his ears until the ground around him buckled with a violent shock wave. Rath's body was jostled and tumbled about fiercely. The 2,000-pound bomb vaporized the ZSU-23 decoy.

"No, you stupid idiots! Keep those lights off!" Lieutenant Shmuel Mizrahi screamed as the pilots exited the bunker onto the flight line. Several of the ground crews were using flashlights rather than the hand-held glow sticks.

Two of the MiG-23s were already warming their engines as Mizrahi watched the other pilots crawl into the cockpits and strap in.

"I want every aircraft in the air at once," he yelled at the top of his voice to the ground personnel. Behind him he heard the whine of a Mi-24 Hind attack helicopter as its engine started.

AUJILA, LIBYA, SOUTHEASTERN COMMAND CENTER

Lieutenant Shazli relayed the information to Major Nittal. "Jibril reports the attack has begun. Two of the SA-8 sites have been destroyed. He is scrambling his aircraft and requesting that more air support be sent now."

Nittal's eyes flickered. "Contact the backup station; tell them we are ready to start transmitting. Wait to send in the air support. I will see what plan of attack the American's are taking first."

STAGING AREA, ALI BALLAS, EGYPT

"Canopy clear," Captain Thomas Delattre called out as the 270-pound acrylic bubble of his F-15E was lowered into place on the cockpit rails.

The crystal clear windscreen slid forward two inches, sealing the sandy-haired captain and his weapons system officer, second Lieutenant Nick Baxley, into their Strike Eagle.

Delattre and his WSO had been recruited by Cobra team nine months ago. They both fit the personal leadership profile Madison was looking for. The two men worked well as a team, each having close identical traits of self-discipline, smarts, and an excessive drive to win. But that wasn't all. Delattre was considered a bit of a rogue officer, a free thinker. He had nearly been kicked out of the air force during flight school. Twice he had been caught engaging in mock dogfights during training missions, which was strictly against the rules. During the last instance the pilot he was flying against flew into the ground, killing himself and destroying a T-38. Delattre lied, saying the other pilot was in trouble and he was just following him. He felt they had both known the chances they were taking and the other pilot's error was what had killed him. It was unthinkable to him that he would never fly again. In the end, Delattre was let off with a disciplinary mark on his permanent record. Everyone in his class knew the truth, including his instructors. However, Delattre's raw flying ability and desire to overcome adversity propelled him above most of the other pilots in the air force. It was a trait Madison wanted every man under his command to have.

Delattre released the brakes of his fully loaded F-15E and steered the aircraft toward the end of the runway. It would be thirty minutes until the sun came up, which would give him and the other seven F-15Es the advantage of darkness and surprise. Two bright rows of lights flashed down each side of the runway as Delattre put the dark gray nose of the fighter bomber on the center line and stopped. He was the last of Cobra team's eight Strike Eagles to get airborne.

Lieutenant Baxley, the backseater, continued his preflight checks. His office consisted of four CRTs displaying imagery and combat data aligned side by side in a neat row on top of the instrument panel. He repositioned the moving map display, a reproduction of the flight data on the HUD, to the far left side so it was adjacent to the radar output and horizontal situation indicator. The HSI gave him course and heading information.

"All set, Captain," Baxley called out.

Delattre snapped his mask into place and scanned the instruments one last time. He then looked at the takeoff control lights on his right side. The light switched from red to yellow and finally to green. Without breaking radio silence, he advanced the throttles with his Nomex-gloved left hand until he felt the jolt of the afterburners kicking in. His ground speed climbed past 160 knots, and he drew back on the stick. Over 58,000 pounds of engine thrust lifted the fighter off the runway into the black night sky.

Pathfinder Team Alpha: Icebox

"Lieutenant . . ." Vasquez gently turned Rath's head and placed his fingertips on the carotid artery, feeling for a pulse. "Rath, can you hear me?"

Vasquez could feel a heartbeat, very faint. The nearby fire from the burning ZSU-23 decoy cast enough light so he could see that blood was dripping out of both of Rath's ears. He began brushing the dirt and debris from the lieutenant's arms, back, and legs. "Rath, come on, man, can you hear me?"

"Ahhh . . ." Rath moaned, rolling over. He brought his hands up to his head. The pounding was so intense he couldn't focus.

"Try to get up; we've got to get back to the OP." Vasquez strung the lieutenant's backpack on his right arm and held his rifle tight, then helped lift him with his left. They were in a bad way, out in the open like this, with the fires lighting up the area; although now he was more worried about the F-117A returning than the Libyans.

Rath moaned again, opening his eyes. "Shit, Vasquie, go on without me. I can't move."

"Shut up! We're getting the hell out of here, together." Vasquez held Rath firmly, then pulled him along with his feet dragging behind. The safety of the OP sat waiting up on the other side of the mountain.

29

"First reports coming in, General," Captain Harris stated from the communications center. "The F-117As destroyed three SA-8s and one ZSU-23. The pilots report light resistance. All aircraft are accounted for and are returning to base."

"What about the SA-6s?" Clark snapped.

"No reports of SA-6s being knocked out."

"Not good." General Clark folded his arms and looked at the ceiling. He wished he was with Madison, in the thick of things.

Harris didn't say a word as he sipped his coffee, listening. Pilots, particularly pilots that flew the black jet, he had learned, always hit their targets. At least that's what they reported to their commanders. That was why bomb damage assessment was so damn difficult. Now it was up to him to either confirm or negate the Stealth pilots' accounts of what happened over the battlefield.

He studied the real-time IR photos from the morning's KH-14 pass as they started appearing on his computer screen. First, he clicked up an aerial shot of Madadhi Air Base from 10,000 feet.

"That's odd," he said after several seconds. It showed only two bright spots, hot burning areas where the heat was intense enough to melt metal. He also saw several warm spots. It didn't compute with what the pilots were reporting. The delivery systems on the F-117A had all been upgraded since the war, making them even more accurate. If the F-117A reports were right, they should have been able to destroy more air defenses than that. Harris made a note of it and moved on. He wanted to get a clearer understanding of what was happening before he opened his mouth.

Harris used the computer mouse to instruct the software to broaden the field of view and move to an altitude of 50,000 feet. He then moved the picture north, putting the Libyan air base of Aujila in the center of the screen. He tapped on the keyboard several more times, zooming in on the military base.

"General Clark, you better come take a look at this."

Clark knelt down next to him so that he was eye level with the computer screen.

Harris pointed to the bottom of the monitor. There was a row of green hot spots moving southward along a two-lane paved highway.

"This could be trouble. And frankly, I didn't think they'd have the balls to do it." Harris zoomed in on the IR images and explained. "These are very unique IR signatures. I count fourteen heavy tanks, along with six personnel carriers and three, maybe four, antiaircraft guns. They're bunched together." He pointed at the last two vehicles. "These are mobile SAMs. By their size, probably SA-6s. The entire convoy is traveling at a high rate of speed, forty, forty-five miles an hour. By the size of their heat signatures, I'd say the tanks are T-55s or T-72s. With the Libyans it could be a combination of both."

"They're heading toward Madadhi?" the general questioned, not quite accepting the info.

"That'd be my guess, sir." Harris didn't take his eyes off the computer.

"How long before they could reach the base?"

"Not more than an hour."

Clark thought about the situation. He had expected the Libyans to put up some kind of a fight, then turn tail and run. He didn't believe they would try and reinforce the base after the rescue operation had begun. Fourteen tanks could be serious trouble; Madison would have to divert his A-10s away from other ground targets around Madadhi. And he needed those Warthogs to provide air support for the C-17 when it landed with Major Ghere and the ground assault team.

"That's not all, General." Harris recalled the aerial photo from above Madadhi. "I would say less than half the air defenses around the base were destroyed by the Stealths."

"Are you sure?" Clark's face showed his disbelief.

"Well it's going to take some time for the boys at NPIC to analyze the multispectral imagery and get it back to me. But take a look at this." He pointed to the hot spots. "These two indicate the only direct hits on hard metal structures. They're confirmed kills. The bright color is created when a magnesium chassis is burning. These other dull spots are bomb craters. The pilots may have hit something, but it wasn't a hard target."

"What's in the air right now?" Clark asked.

"Madison reports the Stealths are headed back to Egypt and the F-15s are due to begin their runs in fifteen minutes, sir."

"What about the A-10s and F-16s?"

"A-10s will fly in twelve minutes, the sixteens ten minutes after that."

Harris didn't need to explain that because of the A-10s' slower speed they would need more time to get to the area. The F-16s would follow, overtaking the Warthogs.

"Get this new information to Madison. Those fifteens better know what they're in for, and I want those tanks removed from the equation before they become a big problem." He spoke directly to Harris, then turned to watch the data relay screens.

PATHFINDER TEAM ALPHA

Vasquez more or less dropped Rath into the OP. The man's ears were ringing, but his head had cleared enough to remember what had happened.

Rodriguez turned on the muted red light, anxiously waiting to see or hear from his men. "Son of a bitch," he muttered, looking at Rath's appearance. "What the hell happened out there?"

Vasquez stumbled in with all their equipment. He smiled up at their team leader, saying, "He just about got his nuts blown off by one of our Stealths." Rath, still wobbly, was wiping dirt from his face and eyes. Shaw had joined him with his medical bag, checking Rath over.

"Are you all right?" Rodriguez asked.

"Yeah . . . I think so," Rath answered quietly, more embarrassed than anything else.

"How about you, Vasquie?"

"Me? I'm just really hungry," he said, shoving more peanut butter crackers in his mouth.

"Listen, Captain . . . we have trouble . . . ouch! Shaw, quit poking at me, this is important. The Libyans have deployed decoys. Fake SAMs and 23 MMs. I got close enough to ID one." Rath spoke excitedly, causing Rodriguez to look at Vasquez, who shook his head in agreement to verify it wasn't delirious talk.

The sudden roar of jet engines in the distance caught their attention.

"Listen . . . those are MiGs," Vasquez said, jumping up next to Lange to look out the front of the OP.

Rodriguez joined the two men, asking, "How many?"

"Two . . . three . . . I count four," Lange answered. "And I also hear choppers." The well-defined sound of an Eastern Bloc turbofan spooling up, mixed with the piercing sound of rotor blades, filled the air.

Rodriguez held his NVGs to his face. He could make out the muted green shapes of men running to their aircraft. The rotors on one of the Mi-24 helicopters rotated in momentum. He waited until he saw a second and a third Mi-24 prepare for lift-off.

"Okay, let's get back to business," Rodriguez ordered. "Lange, get on the horn to Queen Bee. Tell them the MiGs and the Mi-24s are taking off and about the air defense decoys. The pilots should expect heavy resistance."

Lange typed the message, coded it, and blasted it to the EC-141 and the STOC.

Libyan Second Lieutenant Al-Huni raised the landing gear on his MiG-23MF, picking up a few extra knots of airspeed as his camouflaged fighter bomber cleaned up, straining for the black early morning sky. Behind him, three more of the swing-wing fighters lifted off, each at ten-second intervals. The fifth and last MiG's engine wouldn't start. It sat on the ground next to the westernmost bunker.

Al-Huni was the only son of a prestigious Libyan businessman. His father had paid the proper government bureaucrats and made sure the appropriate gifts were delivered to high Libyan military officials before Al-Huni had celebrated his tenth birthday. This was all done so that some day he could enter flight school, become a fighter pilot, and learn the military system. After his years of service he was to join his father in the brokering of weapons to Middle Eastern countries. Surprisingly, after two years of training, the short, awkwardly built man was the best pilot of the MiG-23 squad assigned to engage the Americans.

Al-Huni had practiced engaging air-to-air targets at night as part of his instruction in Syria only four months ago. There he had learned that flying at night was tough and demanding, more so than the day missions. However, former East German pilots being employed by the Syrians had taught him how to use the darkness to his advantage.

The pilot concentrated on the HUD as he pitched the nose up five degrees, continuing his climb. He tuned his radio to a frequency of 315.25 and pulled back on his throttles to allow his wingman to catch up. At 240 knots he swept the wings back and leveled at 500 meters.

"Come on, where is that ground control radar?" he spouted into his mike. Without the guidance of a ground radar, Al-Huni would be forced to turn on his air-to-air radar in order to find the American targets in front of him. That would also give away his position. He banked to the northeast at a heading of 037.

"Lead aircraft . . . four two seven. Respond." The raspy voice of the ground control intercept officer crackled through his helmet.

"This is aircraft four two seven . . . transmission confirmed." A new ground radar started broadcasting to the north. A wave of relief rushed through him.

"Two targets at 3,000 meters and climbing. Turn to a heading of one one three and engage."

"Roger," Al-Huni radioed. He skimmed over the SOS-3-4 radar warning and detection equipment. It showed that the enemy aircraft were flying with their radars turned off. The IFF symbology was also clear.

The Libyan pilot had studied American tactics. At their current altitude, he speculated they were either F-15s or EF-111 electronic jammers. He hoped they were the larger, less maneuverable EF-111s; F-15s were a formidable opponent. He scanned his instruments again, then glanced outside the cockpit. The black sky was turning a royal blue. In a few minutes it would be light enough to see miles around him.

PRV-9 EARLY WARNING RADAR, SOUTH OF AUJILA

Only two men were at the controls inside the desert brown command and communications van. Camouflage netting draped over its exterior broke up the outline of the container-shaped vehicle. Ten meters away, also sheathed in camo and linked by a thick copper ground cable, a five-meter-wide surveillance antenna rotated once every three to four seconds. The inside of the van was basic and even at this early hour was stuffy.

The backup early warning system had been purchased from the Syrians two years before and had just been taken out of storage three weeks earlier. Both men were surprised the system was operating at all.

"I want another systems check," the chief master sergeant ordered, his concentration not leaving the palpitating deep blue scope.

Seconds later, his second in command responded: "I don't see any problems, sir. The radar is operating within parameters."

EC-141 QUEEN BEE

Colonel Brice Madison read the data as it appeared on the tactical information screen. The Pathfinder team was reporting that the Libyans were using SAM and triple-A decoys and launching their aircraft. Satellite photos were helpful, but they told only part of the story. Without ELINT no one could be sure which SAM sites were operational and which weren't.

"Contact the fifteens. Air defenses are going to be heavy," Madison warned.

"This just came in from STOC, sir. Ground troops are moving in from the north." The tactical information officer handed a two-page fax to Madison. The colonel used his miniature penlight to read the transmission. The first page gave a brief description of the ground forces, and the second page was a detailed map of the area between Madadhi Air Base and Aujila, Libya, showing the roadways and terrain. Captain Harris, providing valuable info, had circled a bridge thirty miles north of Madadhi that crossed a deep canyon. If Madison's team could take out the bridge, the Libyan armored column would have a hell of a time crossing. It should slow them down long enough for the A-10s to cut them to pieces. Harris estimated that the Libyans would reach the bridge in thirty minutes, just after sunup. Madison studied the fax, planning their next move.

Lieutenant Victor Garnsey, the electronics threat officer, sounded off the instant he saw the new data. "Trouble . . . I have a new radar threat . . . bearing 023." The EC-141's RHAW equipment identified and categorized the new ground radar operating at 2.56 GHz. "It's a powerful E-band . . . south of Aujila . . . ground control and early warning. They probably see us, sir."

"What the fuck?" Madison swore.

"Pop up . . . I show three . . . four bogeys . . . loose formation, altitude 1,900 to 1,300, speed 380 knots and closing in on the Eagles," Sergeant Oliveri chattered. "It's the MiG-23 Floggers from Madadhi." They were on the outer edge of his radar's range limit.

Madison listened intently. The bogeys were at low altitude on an interception course for the Strike Eagles. The lead group of four F-15Es, Mercury package, was at 15,000 feet, twelve minutes to the east of Madadhi. The other group, Cadillac package, was three minutes behind at 13,000 feet.

In five minutes the lead package of F-15Es would be going low level on their planned run to take out the Libyan aircraft on the ground. The second group were to climb and conduct a combat air patrol, in the event the Libyans launched fighter aircraft out of the north and tried coming in behind them.

Madison took a large pinch of Red Man tobacco out of its foil pouch, stuffing it between his gum and lip. Chewing it helped him think. The damn Libyans had a backup radar. Now he would be forced to split his limited resources, something he didn't want to do. Madison cursed himself for being too cautious. Thirty minutes earlier he had delayed the F-15s takeoff, giving the Libyans the needed time to launch their aircraft.

"Contact Mercury one and two. I want those MiGs brought down. Then divert Mercury three and four north to take out that new radar. Where's Delattre?"

"Flying trailer, sir . . . position four of Cadillac group," Oliveri relayed, as he pointed to the blips on the radar screen. An IFF number told which aircraft was Captain Delattre's F-15.

"What's his weapons mix?" The colonel's mind raced to a plan of action.

A tap on the computer keys and Oliveri had the info displayed before him. "Two AMRAAMs, two GBU-10B Paveways, and four Sidewinders."

"Perfect. Divert him north to a heading of 010 . . . his orders to follow." Madison stood stiffly, his legs spread and hands placed on his hips.

"Yes, sir." Oliveri immediately keyed his mike. "Mercury one and two, I show four bogeys at a spread of 230 to 250 degrees. Center aircraft is bearing two four three. Engage and splash. Mercury three and four, break to three four niner. We have a new ground radar threat. Repeat. New radar threat."

The pilots responded, and Oliveri watched the jets break formation and head in their designated directions on his radarscope.

"Cadillac one, two, and three, maintain current heading and climb to flight level 24,000. Cadillac four, break to zero one zero at 5,000. Will advise of your new target." Oliveri loved the challenge of working the F-15Es. It was one jet that could just about do it all.

Major Roger S. Whitehead, flying Mercury one, watched as the glowing orange tailpipes of Mercury three and four disappeared to the north. His radar warning equipment told him he was now being watched by both friendly and enemy radar. The thirty-year-old pilot from Atlanta wondered how the Libyan's ground radar was back on the air. Unlike the F-117A Stealths, his F-15E showed up on a radarscope like a snowstorm in July. It was the only complaint he had about the much-coveted jet.

Out of the corner of his eye he sighted his wingman pulling up tight on his left wingtip. They climbed through 18,000 feet and leveled out.

"Okay, let's brighten their day, Stoner," Whitehead said to his back-seater.

Major J. B. Stone toggled the switch on his instrument panel, turning on the Strike Eagle's powerful AN/APG-70 synthetic aperture radar. He set the antenna to air-to-air scan mode and tilted the antenna down to a forty-five-degree angle. The radar began sweeping the sky in front of them, searching for aircraft. It had the capability to detect and lock onto enemy targets over 130 miles away.

"Radar contact. Four targets bearing two three seven," Stone called out. "Altitude, 2,000 feet and descending. Separation, twenty-degree spread." The enemy aircraft were bunched in a loose group heading toward them from the southwest.

"We got 'em, too," Whitehead's wingman radioed.

Multiple bogeys was not what he had been expecting. His F-15E was loaded with three CBU-87 general-purpose cluster bombs, which he was to use on parked aircraft at Madadhi. At least his fighter also carried two AIM-7 Sparrows and four AIM-9M Sidewinder air-to-air missiles, as well

as an M161A1 Vulcan twenty-millimeter cannon. If they got into a
high-G furball, he would have to drop the cluster bombs in order to turn
with his target. Whitehead punched the microphone button on the throttle. "We'll take the two on the north, you guys get the two on the south."

"Roger, Lead. The two south suckers are dead meat." Mercury two
broke hard left and streaked away to the south, descending.

Whitehead keyed the internal mike. "Stoner, let's make this easy. No
screwing around. One missile, one bogey." He then jammed his throttles
into afterburner. Whitehead put his nose on the lead target as his F-15E
broke through 600 knots. They were closing at over 1,100 mph on the
closest bogey.

The high-pitched warning tone stabbed into his ears, causing Al-Huni to
tighten his jaw with pain.

"F-15s!" he shouted, recognizing the computer-generated RHAW tone
of the American interceptor's radar. "Break formation. Execute the eva-
sion and attack sequence," Al-Huni radioed the other three MiG-23s.
They were supposed to be hunting the invaders, not vice versa. Someone had turned the tables.

The MiG-23s breaking their flight pattern and going low level individ-
ually would be on their own. The older planes could turn with the
Eagles below 2,000 feet. But in order to engage the Americans, Al-Huni
and his team would attempt to stay low enough to confuse the Americans' powerful radar, allowing them a chance to outmaneuver the swift
F-15s.

Al-Huni pushed the black nose of his fighter down, feeling a couple
of negative Gs bite into his shoulder harness, and headed for the
ground. His airspeed increased to 570 knots before he hauled back on
the stick and leveled out 100 meters above the desert. As the Gs fell off,
he banked hard to the right and dropped the nose of the MiG a few
more degrees, until he was only thirty meters off the deck. He was
heading south at 540 knots, flying on a perpendicular course to the lead
American fighter. He steadily added power until he felt the kick of the
afterburners.

Stone watched his radarscope as one of the targets broke off and turned
away from them. *Must not be his day,* he thought. He looked back to the
closest bogey on the scope, fast approaching them.

"Bandit one . . . forty-two miles and closing. Bandit two is low and
level . . . heading away," Stone called out from his position behind his
pilot.

"First things first," Whitehead said, making up his mind to kill the closest bandit. He adjusted his oxygen mask and then flipped the Strike Eagle over, heading for the ground inverted. The pressure of the dive kept them both pinned in their seats.

The black ground had given way to a dull gray and he could make out a few subtle features of the terrain below. If the enemy wasn't going to come up to play, he would take the battle to them. He watched the HUD click off the altitude and airspeed as they passed through 10,000 feet, descending rapidly.

"BVR . . . weapons select." Stone reminded his pilot that the target was beyond visual range, which meant he needed to choose a radar homing missile.

Whitehead selected an AIM-7 Sparrow and righted the F-15E as Stone started calling out the radar data.

"Target now thirty-seven miles and closing. Altitude, 1,300 feet and climbing. Still heading straight for us."

"He wants to play chicken." Whitehead admired the courage of the Libyan pilot. Or possibly he didn't know what he was facing.

Whitehead veered the fighter ten degrees to the north, taking his nose off a direct intercept course for the bogey. The forty-five-degree spread of the radar cone continued to illuminate the bandit. He hoped the MiG-23 pilot would think he wasn't flying directly toward him. Then Whitehead could draw him in closer, getting a quick, easy kill. It was a tactic he often used at Red Flag to defeat inexperienced F-16 fliers.

Al-Huni waited until the pounding sound of the enemy radar had faded in his headset before he put his fighter into a hard 5 G slicing turn and headed back in the opposite direction, north. His airspeed dropped as he came out of the turn and backed the throttle off to full military power. The MiG floated back up to 100 meters, straight and level.

"Flight leader . . . four two seven. Engage target!" The GCI officer screamed his order.

This is a suicide mission, Al-Huni thought, as he reached over and turned off his radio. He had flown a mission like this over and over again in his mind. He throttled back again, pivoting his wings out to a setting of twenty-six degrees, and popped his air brakes, reducing the airspeed to below 340 knots. He watched the compass swing around as he headed back toward the air base.

"Come on, you bastard . . . *follow me.*"

"This is too easy," Stone said, as his radar locked up on the closest MiG. "Radar lock. Twenty-nine miles, altitude 2,000 feet. Still closing."

The targeting cursor on Whitehead's HUD flashed three times and the tone in his helmet became even, telling him that a positive radar lock had been achieved. He put his thumb on the release button, resting it there.

"Now or never, man. He's going to bolt on us," Stone moaned a warning.

At twenty-four miles, Whitehead turned the Strike Eagle back on a head-on course for the target and watched the G meter return to 1.0. He pressed the weapons release button. The F-15E shuddered slightly as the 510-pound missile blasted off the port-side wing root rail in a flash of white sparks and fire.

The Libyan GCI officer called a warning, but it was too late. The pilot's glory turned to death in a fraction of a second. He wrapped both hands around the stick and with all his strength pulled it back. The nose of the MiG was thrust up and the radar lock of the Sparrow had a perfect bull's-eye. Traveling at Mach 3, the speeding missile slammed into the belly of the plane. Crushed into his seat with the force of 6 abrupt Gs, the pilot never saw what hit him.

Al-Huni saw the warning symbol on his HUD flash red, and the Sirena 3 radar warning receiver jumped to life as a G-band, continuous-wave acquisition radar painted his fighter. In a flash, the warning sounded again as an H-band radar locked on also.

"Oh no . . ." He flipped on the IFF transponder, telling the nearby SA-6 site he was a friendly. Seconds later both warnings stopped as the SAM's ground crew shut down the radar.

"That was too close." He made a mental note of the SA-6's location.

Al-Huni looked up in time to see a distant fireball in his rearview mirror.

"Allah save him," he whispered, hoping the man had ejected in time. Rage started to burn inside him. The naive pilot, just out of flight school, had trusted the ground control officer, following his orders. In Al-Huni's mind, Libyan GCI officers were a worthless lot of men, nothing more than cowards who didn't care about their pilots and knew nothing about air-to-air tactics. In combat, the only man he trusted was himself.

Al-Huni's eyes swept across the instruments, checking that everything was operating normally. He slid the MiG up to a new altitude of 200 meters, stroking the throttles forward. Madadhi Air Base loomed in the distance, only fourteen kilometers away.

"Now it is my turn," he said into his oxygen mask, as he picked up airspeed, heading back to the base.

* * *

"Splash one MiG," came the call from Mercury two. They had just downed their first target eight miles to the south of Whitehead and Stone.

Whitehead sucked in a deep breath. Adrenalin was pumping into his veins as he broke left to a new heading of 194 and leveled out at 7,000 feet to get his bearings. The radar showed the last MiG was eighteen miles below him, only a couple hundred feet off the deck, heading away.

"Come on, Stoner. I need radar lock on this guy," he urged.

"There's too much clutter. He must be dropping chaff. Get us in closer," Stone complained. He knew what was happening. The chaff, combined with the fine sand of the desert, mixed in with hard rocks and dirt, was absorbing and reflecting portions of his radar emissions. He narrowed the beam width, which at the same time tightened his radar's targeting cone, hoping to achieve a lock.

Whitehead grunted as he again pushed the big fighter over and headed for the deck, closing the distance. He brushed the weapons select button with his thumb, making sure it was still set on AIM-7 Sparrows.

"Close enough." Ten kilometers east of Madadhi field, Al-Huni chopped the throttles, punched the chaff button, and broke hard back to the east, heading 102 degrees. His strategy was to accelerate back toward the American at high speed, laying out a narrow corridor of chaff. If he could keep moving and change his course often, he might stop them from locking onto his fighter. Then he could come in under them and fire a salvo of two AA-7 radar-guided missiles.

He turned on his J-band High-Lark 2 radar, setting it for a full-power, wide-angle sweep. He moved the antenna up to a forty-degree slant to scan the sky above him. Glancing at the HUD, he hoped his radar would pick up the American aircraft. It didn't. He put the MiG into afterburner and dropped the nose, staying below eighty meters.

The eastern sky had lightened enough for Al-Huni to visually search for the American fighter above him. He saw nothing. Yet the constant pulsing in his helmet said the Americans were out there, looking for him. He punched the chaff button again and watched his airspeed climb past 500 knots.

Whitehead and Stone shot through 5,000 feet in their F-15E. Whitehead drew back on the stick as the Mach meter fluttered just below 0.98.

Stone watched the radar return symbology on the left CRT. "Bogey coming around, changing course. Now heading 105 . . . fifteen miles and closing, speed increasing. Heading right for us. I don't like this shit. Suicide junkies make me nervous."

"Then hurry and get me a lock, Stoner!" Whitehead shouted.

"Enemy radar . . . J-band. It's a High Lark. He's looking for us. Thirteen miles . . ." Stone rattled on. "A little bit closer . . . Come on, baby, do your stuff. There! Lock bearing one zero four."

Whitehead saw the lock symbol take shape on his HUD. The rectangle was fading in and out, then flashed, verifying a lockup. He tapped the launch button with his thumb and watched the missile speed away.

Al-Huni flinched at the flash of the launch. It would take forty-five seconds for the missile to reach him.

"Fast and lower," he thought aloud. The single 27,500-pound thrust afterburning turbofan was producing maximum power, pushing his fighter past 670 knots. With his fingertips he gently held the stick, making sure the MiG didn't climb above eighty meters or start drifting dangerously lower.

Within fifteen seconds a bright speck, the missile's exhaust, emerged ahead of him. Al-Huni fought the natural urge to break and run, knowing his timing had to be flawless. Salty sweat rolled down his forehead, stinging his right eye. He blinked rapidly, not taking his hands from the control stick or throttle, concentrating on the HUD.

A silver smoke trail appeared behind the speeding Sparrow. He estimated twenty seconds to impact. His airspeed had topped out at 745 knots.

Al-Huni held his breath and struck the chaff button three quick times. He popped open the air brakes. The MiG seemingly halted, suspended, throwing him against his shoulder restraints. He hit the chaff button again and brought his fighter out of afterburner, snapping the stick back. Because of the high speed, the MiG's elevators didn't respond as quickly as he had hoped. The nose struggled to come up as the aircraft slowed.

"Come on . . . come on," he grunted with the building Gs.

At 590 knots the MiG suddenly shot straight up. He jammed the throttle forward, putting the MiG-23 back into afterburner, and hit the chaff button repeatedly to empty the dispenser.

Unknown to Stone, the Sparrow's seeker head was looking at a series of strong radar returns caused by the exploding chaff. The MiG-23 had changed its flight pattern and radar signature. With its nose pointed straight at the missile, it generated a smaller return for the missile to stay locked onto. The Sparrow's software was programmed to adjust course automatically and attack the most distinct radar return.

The speeding AIM-7 Sparrow pitched down and flew a direct line for the boiling cloud of chaff a half mile below.

Al-Huni held his breath as the deadly projectile twisted past his windscreen. It entered the churning ball of chaff and exploded several hundred meters away. He let out a sigh, then jumped slightly as his radar abruptly locked onto the target above him.

He squeezed the trigger on the stick once, counted to three, and squeezed it again, sending two semi-active radar-homing AA-7 missiles toward the unseen target. His gamble had worked; he was on the offensive.

"We missed!" Whitehead yelled.

"Enemy radar lock. Break left!" Stone shouted.

Out of the corner of his eye, Whitehead saw the first missile a split second before he slammed the stick hard left and forward, throwing his F-15E into a turbulent 6 G diving turn. His heavy bomb load put added drag and stress on the airframe as it strained to come across the missile's beam, trading altitude for airspeed.

The basic missile break-lock maneuver was too little and too late. The first AA-7 missed the Eagle by less than fifty yards, its proximity fuse detonating the warhead harmlessly behind them. The second AA-7 corrected itself and smashed into the port tail fin, bursting.

"Holy shit!" Stone wailed. The F-15E rocked as if it had been hit by a train.

"Son of a bitch. We're hit!" The F-15E's flight computers counterbalanced the aerodynamic changes caused by the explosion, keeping the fighter in the air. Whitehead's training took over automatically as he hit the emergency jettison button, releasing the bombs on the right side of the fighter, then dropped the centerline external fuel tank. His attention subsequently went to the instrument panel. No red warning lights, yet. He throttled back and gently pulled the stick toward him, bringing the stricken fighter out of its dive, careful not to pull more than 2 Gs. The controls were stiff but still responsive. He leveled out and turned, looking back over the aircraft.

The right tail was nearly gone. Deep pockmarks in the aluminum skin from flying pieces of metal covered most of the rear. He turned back to look at the HUD, as the dark brown and green Libyan MiG-23 streaked past in the distance, climbing.

Whitehead felt his insides move up his throat. If the Libyan got above him, he was dead.

"Stoner, can you see if we're on fire?" Whitehead wanted a visual even though the warning light was not flashing. He pushed the throttles forward and the stick back, trying to stay level and keep the Libyan in sight. The Strike Eagle responded a little sluggishly.

"No fire, Major, but there's a hell of a lot of damage."

"Queen Bee . . . this is Mercury one. I repeat, Mercury one. We've been hit and need backup. We are in a furball." Just then his instrument panel lit up, indicating his right engine was out.

EC-141 QUEEN BEE

Oliveri had watched the series of events unfold on the radar screen before him.

"Mercury one. Back up in five. Repeat, back up in five." He keyed his mike again and contacted the three F-15Es of Cadillac package orbiting above. A second later the lead aircraft banked away, heading toward Mercury one's position.

Oliveri's concentration shifted to the left side of the screen as the blip, representing Mercury two, made a small S-turn and slid in behind the red triangle depicting the MiG-23. The pilot was now in a position to launch on its second target. The triangle dissipated from the screen in one blink of his eye.

As he broke through 6,000 feet, Al-Huni snapped his fighter upside down and leveled out. His G suit hissed with expanding air as it pressed his perspiration-soaked uniform against his skin.

He looked over his shoulder and could see the F-15 below him, black smoke pouring out of its right engine and its starboard tail gone. The missile had hit the fighter but hadn't done enough damage to bring it down.

Suddenly the American's engine stopped smoking and the Eagle nosed up, heading toward him. Al-Huni felt panicked to finish it off quickly. He put the MiG into a sharp turn, pushing its nose down directly for the American. He flipped the weapons switch to guns and rested his finger on the trigger.

The shock wave of the explosion had momentarily shut down the starboard engine. The RPMs on the engine continued to increase as the compressor blades spooled up again. Whitehead didn't have any rudder control, and the stick would move only a fraction of an inch forward or backward, giving him limited control. By the way the F-15E handled, he figured, correctly, that the right tail plane was gone.

He moved the throttles forward just short of the afterburner groove and watched his airspeed climb. At 420 knots he started to point his nose at the MiG. He needed airspeed so he could maneuver.

"Come on, sweetheart, come on." Whitehead clicked the weapons select switch to AIM-9M Sidewinders. *One pass, one kill,* he thought. "Good Lord, just give me one more pass."

As the MiG pushed over, gravity helped the little fighter pick up valuable airspeed. Al-Huni swept his wings back to a full seventy-two degrees and clicked the engine into idle. With the MiG plummeting, he centered the HUD-mounted gun sight and pressed the trigger. The GSh-23L twin-barreled twenty-three-millimeter cannon erupted, sending red tracer rounds toward the F-15E. They missed, passing by a wide margin.

Al-Huni had lost most of his ability to turn with the American plane when he put his wings back for speed. He tried to compensate but was gaining airspeed too rapidly for the control surfaces of the MiG to react. He opened the air brakes, but it was too late. The American fighter sped past him 500 meters away. Al-Huni cursed his plane.

"Big mistake, fucker." Whitehead grimaced, pushing hard on his stick to follow the Libyan. "I've got your ass now." The Strike Eagle would pull only 4 Gs, but it was enough to swing in behind the MiG.

Whitehead banked around to the north, keeping his eyes locked on the bogey. The enemy fighter was only two miles ahead of him on a direct route for the ground. Whitehead needed to close the distance so the heat-seeking head of the Sidewinder could lock up. When the enemy pilot started to pull out of his dive, he would fire.

"Breaking through 2,000 feet," Stone called out. The spice-colored desert was quickly coming up at them, and he could see the MiG clearly slicing through the cool morning air below.

At 450 knots Whitehead heard the initial chirping sound of his Sidewinder missiles attempting to lock up on the hot tail pipe of the MiG. The enemy fighter was now a mile and a half below, still accelerating.

"Lock up, baby . . . lock up," he coaxed. He watched the MiG pitch deftly up and down as the enemy pilot tried to lose some of his airspeed more quickly. The Libyan would have to pull up at any second or risk plowing into the desert.

*   *   *

With only 135 meters of altitude remaining, Al-Huni made his move. He popped three infrared flares and curved to the right. His compass told him he was now heading back over the SA-6 site.

The operator in the command van had routinely shut down his radar. This was done intermittently to avoid detection from American HARMs, high-speed antiradiation missiles. Al-Huni turned his IFF switch on and off and popped three more flares.

"Where is that SAM?"

The chirping had turned to a rattle sound as the AIM-9M locked up on the infrared heat source of the MiG's engine. Whitehead was careful not to overstress his fighter. He was still above and behind the Libyan at 1,000 feet. Something told him this would be his last opportunity to kill this stubborn opponent.

The tone was loud and even. An instant later, two Sidewinders left the starboard side of the F-15E on an uninterrupted course for the MiG.

Al-Huni was looking over his shoulder when the missiles left the rail. The instant he saw the flash and smoke, he hit the flare button again and broke southeast, but it was too late.

As the first missile hit his fighter, he pulled himself into a tight ball and armed the ejection seat. The MiG shook and started to yaw and pitch wildly. The second missile entered the burning hole created by the first and vaporized the back half of the aircraft as the canopy blew off and the ejection seat ignited, pushing him out of the crippled fighter with the force of 6 Gs. A bright flash told him his MiG had exploded only seconds after he had punched out of the aircraft.

Al-Huni hung from his parachute. His face and arms were cut and bleeding. The cool air revived him as his MiG hit the ground a couple thousand meters away. He watched the bluish black smoke bellow from the wreckage, and he thanked Allah he would live to fly again.

Major Whitehead banked to the north and keyed his mike. "Splash number two. Mercury one is RTB."

"Spike . . . spike . . . two o'clock!" Stone yelled. "Over the fence." An enemy SAM site had activated its radar, and they were being painted by its pulsing electronic beams. "Break hard right!"

The experienced radar operator had chosen to keep his radar turned off until hearing the sound of jet engines above his command and control van. His equipment had picked up the MiG-23's IFF signal, steering the H-band tracking radar away from it. This had enabled the SA-6 site to surprise the American fighter.

Whitehead slammed the stick right, turning into the radar. The F-15E's ALQ-135 electronic countermeasure system powered to life, analyzing the threat as an acquisition and tracking radar transmitting on 6.70 GHz. It proceeded to broadcast a steady stream of H-band radar waves back at the transmitter, attempting to jam it.

For a few seconds the jamming succeeded, allowing Whitehead and Stone to gain altitude and airspeed. The SA-6 radar, close and powerful, operating only 2,000 yards away, dominated the E model's countermeasures. The SAM launch warning light flickered on as the radar band frequency changed to an I-band and locked on to their fighter. It was a tracking and fire control radar signifying that a launch was only seconds away.

"Four thousand feet . . . forty-five . . ." Whitehead whispered under his breath. "Lock up. Those bastards have us in their sights." The warning light flashed on.

At 5,000 feet, the pilot nosed over. *No use pushing my luck,* he thought. He banked to the northeast as the countermeasures automatically ejected several bundles of chaff, attempting to break the enemy radar lock.

"Launch. Two missiles four o'clock. *I don't see them,"* Stone hollered, straining to see over his left and then right shoulder to get a visual on the deadly SAMs.

The SA-6s had lifted off one at a time and streaked into the gray morning sky. Both missiles had launched from the same TEL (transporter-erector-launcher) so that they were in a tight formation several hundred yards apart.

The only way Whitehead was going to defeat the SA-6s was if he could spot and turn into them, confusing the radar. He continued to bank the fighter around until he caught sight of their fiery exhaust trails. The SAMs were gaining altitude, snaking their way toward him.

Whitehead broke left, losing track of the SAMs. Seconds later, he again got a visual on the lead missile coming up toward him. It was going to be close.

* * *

The SA-6 accelerated incredibly fast. The ZUR 9M9 solid-fuel rocket motor generated 8,600 kilograms of thrust in its 240-second engine life. On a cold day with heavy air, the 1,200-pound SAM could reach a speed of Mach 1.5 in eighteen seconds. The 9M9 was designed for low cost and optimum performance with very little maintenance, making it ideal for desert warfare.

"Break now!" Stone called.

A half mile away the lead SAM accelerated on an intercept course. The pilot flipped the fighter on her side and nosed over, slamming into a forty-five-degree angle. Both men were smashed against the side of the cockpit wall, the aircraft struggling to push over and outmaneuver the SA-6.

The lead missile attempted to correct, but Whitehead had timed it perfectly. Its radar seeker head was no longer picking up a strong reflecting radar return. The internal computer instructed the guidance system to go into automatic acquisition mode. The SAM swung left and right, trying to find a new target, as it disappeared into the distance.

The second SAM was still locked onto the spiraling F-15E. As the radar return of the Strike Eagle changed, so did the missile's flight path. It was too close and would pass within lethal range no matter what the pilot tried to do.

"More power," Whitehead protested. With all his strength he shoved the stick down, striving to dive in under the second missile.

His damaged aircraft couldn't turn or pick up airspeed fast enough. The SAM exploded thirty yards from the fighter on the left side, engulfing the Strike Eagle in a white-hot ball of flames and turbulence. The port side engine died and a portion of the left wingtip ripped off. Blasting bits of metal hit the cockpit canopy, shattering it. The controls froze solid.

The jet somersaulted and Whitehead saw the sky and ground blur into one picture at the same time. The F-15E righted herself and went into a slow left-hand turn toward the ground. As his senses cleared, he reacted to the situation.

"Stoner, get ready to eject," Whitehead ordered. His fingers felt the stick lighten up as the backup hydraulic system kicked in.

"Ready," Stone shouted over the whistle of air rushing in through the holes cut into the windscreen.

"Hold tight . . ." Whitehead paused. The Eagle was starting to come back to life as they spun toward the ground. One engine was running and their airspeed was at 240 knots and climbing. If they waited to eject, they would have a better chance of surviving. Every mile they hobbled toward the Egyptian border brought them closer to an easier and more successful SAR.

At 1,000 feet, Whitehead jerked the stick toward him and felt his Strike Eagle shake and yaw out of the dive. He came level at 300 feet and watched his airspeed hover near 290 knots before creeping up again. At 300 knots, he put the nose up two degrees and added power.

"You hurt, Stoner?" Whitehead asked, feeling some relief.

"A little beat up, but I'm okay."

"I think we can make it. You with me?"

"Yeah, I'm with ya."

At 1,500 feet Whitehead leveled out and keyed his mike. "Queen Bee, Mercury one. We've been hit again . . . heavily damaged. Current heading 135 and level. One engine is out. Controls sluggish, but we're coming home." Whitehead heard the pulsing sound of the radar fade as they retreated from the area.

"Yeah, we're coming home," Stone repeated, sighing.

30

"Four MiGs down!" Mizrahi shouted. "The Americans will roll through this base as if it were nothing." He turned to Captain Jibril, who was standing next to him in the communications and command bunker. The two men were looking at an amber computer display terminal, a direct linkup with the Libyan radar to the north of them. "Do you not have any suggestions?"

Jibril was quiet. When he did speak, he didn't look at his second in command. "Our only goal is to keep the Americans away long enough for our ground forces to get here. Then we will get the weapons and retreat into our own base."

"And what happened to our additional air cover?"

"There is nothing I can do about that. Either Nittal sends it or he doesn't."

Majeed was standing in the doorway leading to the main bunker containing *Atlantis*. He examined the area before entering. Wooden scaffolding still surrounded the front section of the shuttle and Ziad was on top of the space plane, looking down at him. His once white shirt was now black and blotched with sweat. Several guards were standing near the nose of the shuttle with their AKs trained on him, while several others were placing claymore mines around the American spacecraft.

To Majeed's left was a machine-gun nest, sandbags stacked five feet high in a neat semicircle. A heavy 7.62-millimeter PK GPMG belt-fed machine gun sat ready in the middle of the sandbags.

"Where is Ajami?" Majeed asked Ziad, who had stopped working and was now staring at him.

"Where do you think he is? Meditating in his quarters."

316

Majeed watched as the last of the mines were put into place around *Atlantis*. Each mine was carefully concealed and positioned to do the maximum amount of damage to an intruder. The thin, kidney-shaped mines were set to detonate at a thirty-degree angle off the ground, sending their 700 stainless steel ball bearings out at a ninety-degree angle. This allowed them a clean kill of anything out to a distance of 150 feet.

Majeed was curious and took a few more steps toward the shuttle.

One of the guards lowered his AK-47, pointing it directly at Majeed. "What is the meaning of this?" Majeed asked.

"Ajami gave orders to keep everyone out of this area," the guard said, his eyes fixed and gun ready to fire.

"This is ridiculous! I am in charge of security here. Why was I not told of that order?" Majeed protested.

"The order included you. We are just doing what we were told."

Majeed gazed over at a BTR-40 armored truck parked next to the shuttle. "What is that doing in here? Are you taking one of the bombs somewhere?"

Ziad glanced down, annoyed, from his work. "You are distracting me. Why don't you go and ask Ajami yourself."

Majeed stood pensive for a moment, then slowly stepped closer. The two other guards raised their rifles, pointing them at Majeed's head as he froze in his tracks.

"Do not force us to kill you, Majeed. Ajami's orders were clear . . . *no one.*"

He looked into each man's eyes. There was no doubt they would shoot him. Ajami had personally picked the staunch guards himself.

Ziad laughed. "Ha! You're in charge of security? Ajami must think differently. Now, go away and leave me to my work."

Majeed exited the bunker. Ajami was up to something, and he intended to find out what it was.

EC-141 QUEEN BEE

The EC-141 leveled off at an altitude of 35,000 feet. With the threat of the MiGs gone, Madison had ordered his pilots to move closer to their objectives. They were now orbiting forty-five miles inside Chadian airspace. The two KC-10 tankers maintained their sheltered position off their left wing at the same altitude. Two F-16s were patrolling above them, ready to take on any intruders coming into the area.

Oliveri scanned the large computer screen in front of him. It showed that Madadhi Air Base was 180 miles to the southwest. The EC-141's early warning radar was close enough to Madadhi that he had a clear picture of everything in the sky around them right down to treetop level.

The EC-141 command center was not only designed and patterned after the AWAC's block 30/35 system, it also incorporated the same ground-targeting surveillance radar used by the E-8C J-STAR's system. Enemy ground movements were detected by radar data generated from the maneuverable, side-to-side scanning synthetic aperture antenna. This real-time information was then processed by four high-speed computers capable of completing 600 million operations per second. Madison could see what was happening in each area of the operation without delay.

At a range inside 180 miles, the system was proficient at differentiating and identifying tracked or wheeled vehicles moving along dirt or paved roads at high speed. It located and detected portions of tracks or tires that were on the ground and stationary. Comparing that to the fast-moving parts of the vehicle in question, it could be exact enough to trail targets as small as a motorcycle traveling sixty miles an hour.

Oliveri flipped the standard gray switch on the center of his console, activating the EC-141's system ground-scanning radar. The wide-area surveillance and moving target indicator known as WAS/MTI appeared on the screen next to the air data display. All air and ground activity around Madadhi was now being watched by him.

Oliveri followed two blips as they swung around the back of the mountain, north of the airstrip, and disappeared into one of the deep ravines. The computer first identified them as medium-sized helicopters, then classified them as Mi-24s. He speculated that the choppers were trying to hide and tapped on the keyboard to store the data. Of the six attack helicopters, he at least knew where two of them had landed.

"I want an update on the fifteens." Madison had walked over directly behind Oliveri and was analyzing the scope.

"Mercury three and four at 600 feet, ninety miles from second ground radar target . . . twelve minutes south . . . speed 580 knots, heading 345. Cadillac four is at 5,000 feet, speed 420 knots, still heading 010."

The colonel nodded. "Give me a big picture of the ground." He fought the urge to stuff another wad of tobacco in his mouth as he prioritized things in his head. Predominantly he had to take out that new ground radar and stop the ground troops from reaching Madadhi.

Oliveri typed instructions on his computer keyboard. The computer display flickered slightly before showing the ground data. A black-and-white map of the entire area of the WAS/MTI's coverage was now on the main screen.

"Zoom in on this area." Madison pointed to a discreet bend in the road to the north leading into Madadhi Air Base. The name AL KISAWA appeared next to it.

Again Oliveri punched keys and the computer's software focused in on the immediate area around Al Kisawa. Both men could see the fuzzy outline of a single-lane road cutting through the center of the screen. A third of the way down the computer monitor, the ground became broken where a deep ravine cut through the desert.

"Okay, let's look at this closer." Madison pointed to where the bridge should be located.

A hazy image of a medium-sized overpass traversing a narrow section of the steep canyon came into view. Seconds later the SAR (synthetic aperture radar) and computers clarified the picture. A black-and-white image, with photo quality, of the bridge permitted both men to see details as fine as grapefruit-sized rocks scattered along the roadway leading to it.

The overpass was constructed of two heavy concrete slabs several meters thick with large steel pillars supporting each end. One large round concrete support, fifty feet high, aided in sustaining the center section. When the Libyans constructed it, they had in mind the heavy military equipment that would use the roadway and bridge to enter northern Chad.

"That's it. Give me another overhead." As the picture transformed, Madison could see the shapes of tanks and personnel carriers moving down the dirt road. "How long before they reach the bridge?"

"Seven to eight minutes." Oliveri's experience prompted the close guess after watching the speed of their travel on his scope.

"Take a picture and send it to Delattre along with an INS update. I want that bridge out of commission in five minutes."

Oliveri did as he was told, and a half minute later the new data was on its way to Cadillac four's navigation and tactical computers.

"The Pathfinder team is reporting all Mi-24 choppers are airborne and have flown out of the area," Oliveri said.

"Do you confirm that?" Madison asked.

"I spotted two choppers earlier, setting down to the north," Oliveri responded.

"And the other four?"

"I haven't found them, sir. Starting the search now." He punched in the code SSM: MI-24 FIND/LOCK. The sector search mode appeared on his screen. The computer automatically concentrated on a smaller 7.7-square-mile area, hunting for the radar signatures of the other four Mi-24 choppers. When the computer found them, it would store the data and alert Oliveri to their location.

Well, if the choppers aren't flying, they aren't a threat right now, Madison thought.

"Our A-10s have lifted off," Oliveri announced, not looking up.

PRV-9 Early Warning Radar Station

"There must be twenty aircraft out there." The sergeant looked at the center portion of his technician's scope. He had been watching two low-level enemy blips heading straight for their location. At a distance, they were easy to keep track of, but as the two aircraft got closer they dropped lower to avoid detection. He opened up the direct communications channel to the command center in Aujila. For a brief moment the two targets appeared once more before disappearing behind a series of hills sixty-five kilometers away.

"Multiple targets to the southeast. I am still showing two—I repeat, two—targets bearing 176. They are on a direct intercept course for this station. Requesting air support now."

"Stand by." It was the same answer he had been getting for the last ten minutes. The sergeant looked over at his technician. They were both starting to get worried.

Captain Thomas Delattre, flying Cadillac four, was eighteen miles southeast of Al Kisawa.

"Confirm the transmission," Delattre ordered.

His backseater, Lieutenant Baxley, pressed a button, sending a coded signal back to the EC-141 authenticating the new orders and computer relay.

"What's up, Nick?" Delattre asked, as he pulled his oxygen mask away from his face.

"Our new job is a bridge. Eighteen miles to the north. Take a new heading of 254."

Baxley felt the Strike Eagle bank slightly as he analyzed the radar data that had been transmitted from the EC-141. His number two CRT showed a clear generated image of the bridge. From the picture he could tell that the Libyans had built the bridge by blasting through the rock ledges on both sides. After plowing the roadways through, they strengthened the structure with the heavy concrete pillars and slabs.

"Hope you like 'em tight and quick, Tommy, this one's going to be a rough squeeze," Baxley called up to his pilot.

The EC-141 was also reporting that ZSU-23s and SA-6s were accompanying a large number of tanks and personnel carriers moving down from the north. They would have to beat them to the bridge.

"There isn't any hole I can't get through, boy, but let me have a look." Delattre's center CRT filled with a facsimile of the radar image. "All right . . . I'm taking her up. Get a picture, then we'll blast it."

As the throttles went forward, the Gs pressed on their bodies as the aircraft pushed up. The sleek Strike Eagle soared to the proper altitude. At 12,000 feet, Delattre leveled the fighter. His WSO began picking out the bridge with the F-15E's synthetic aperture radar.

Baxley watched the CRT display containing radar data. He moved the cursor back and forth until he had it centered on the target. As the resolution sharpened with each pass of the beam, he locked the image into the flight computer, instructing it to guide the pilot to the target.

"Got it, Captain."

That was Delattre's cue. He flipped the fighter over and pointed the nose down at a thirty-degree angle to the ground. He watched the Strike Eagle's airspeed climb past 580 knots.

Major Simia Wazir tried to spit the foul-tasting dust out of his mouth, but it didn't do any good when traveling at 45 kph. As soon as he did, another gust of wind blew puffs of dirt from the broken, rocky route toward Madadhi back into his face. He would have to put up with it as long as he preferred to ride with his head and shoulders above the T-72's turret.

The major, a seasoned commander of the Fifty-fourth Armored Battalion, was no stranger to this part of southern Libya. He had been to Madadhi several times, the last being when the Libyan army had pulled out of northern Chad. He and his squad of twenty-five T-72s had been the last to leave. It was a memory any tanker would cherish for a lifetime. They had defeated Chad's best tank company, easily killing them at will as they pushed south. Wazir's team had had the highest kill percentage of the conflict, utilizing the terrain and smoke to conceal their movements.

Now Wazir's orders were to regain control of Madadhi Air Base from a group of terrorists and fight off a possible American ground attack. He moved his company forward with great confidence, anxious for a worthy challenge. He was sure he would be promoted when the mission was complete.

The terrain in front of him evolved from rolling sand and rocks to steep hills and boulders. They were approaching Al Kisawa, a small village with a population of fewer than fifty people. Four kilometers south of the village was the bridge and thirty-eight kilometers farther was Madadhi. The major checked his watch. They would be at the air base in half an hour.

"Stop at the top of the next hill," Wazir shouted into the turret at his driver. He swiveled around and surveyed the area. In the dusty distance he could see the rest of his company in close trail.

* * *

"Navigational FLIR on," Delattre grunted out loud, instructing Baxley to bring up the forward-looking infrared sensor and the LANTIRN (low-altitude navigation and targeting, infrared, for night) system.

As Baxley switched to scan, Delattre leveled the fighter at 500 feet, pointing its nose toward the northwest. The F-15E bounced up and down as it cut through the tepid morning air. Unlike the F-111F Delattre had piloted before, the Strike Eagle was not as pleasant to fly at low level. It was a trade-off he tolerated gladly, though, for the advanced weapons system and maneuverability in a dogfight.

"Four minutes to target," Baxley called out from the back seat. Delattre nudged the throttles forward, increasing his airspeed to 400 knots. He hoped to be on and off the target before the tanks would be in range to be a real threat. The steering prompt moved on the HUD as he guided the aircraft around a long narrow section of broken hills and back into the open again. The desert streaked by in a blur. He pulled back on the stick, picked up 200 feet of altitude and leveled out at 710 feet.

The added altitude gave him time to glance down at the lower left multifunction display without worrying about broadsiding an incline. The instrumentation told him that both his 2,000-pound GBU-10Bs were armed and ready.

One ought to do it, he told himself. If Delattre could, he wanted to save the other 2,000 pounder for another target.

Wazir clicked off the radio and raised his 10×50 binoculars, following the road until it reached the bridge 500 meters below him. The road narrowed into a single lane, forcing each of his vehicles to slow down and cross the bridge one at a time. One ZSU would cross first to stand guard against any possible ambushes. Then the tanks and other vehicles would follow, spaced apart, with the second ZSU bringing up the rear.

The major scanned the airspace, looking for any hints of enemy aircraft. After a few moments, he lowered the glasses, satisfied that everything was clear. The dirty gray sky had turned a light blue, telling him the sun would be up in minutes.

"Damn, we should have moved out sooner," he muttered under his breath. Nittal reported that an air strike had taken out their early warning radar and there were more aircraft in the area. The Americans were slithering around out there, and the last few kilometers into Madadhi would be the most dangerous.

Wazir clicked his radio back on. "I want two ZSU-23s up here with me at once."

He heard the rumble of the two tracked antiaircraft guns as they came up even with his tank.

"Set up with one of you on each side of the road and activate your radars. Be alert and don't let anything get past you!"

Each Shilka commander saluted and ordered their drivers to proceed.

"Three minutes to target," Baxley sounded off. "Targeting pod on." The lieutenant activated the weapons' high-resolution tracking FLIR located under the fuselage. A targeting correlator appeared in the center of the infrared CRT, indicating that the laser designator was on. He glanced back at the full-color moving map CRT, noting the pilot was right on course. Baxley didn't let his eyes wander outside the cockpit, keeping all his concentration on the instruments.

Delattre crested another hill and watched his altitude creep up to 900 feet. He leveled the aircraft and blinked hard in the low light, clearing his vision.

"Anybody lookin' at us?" Delattre scanned the radar warning receiver.

"Negative, all my lights are clean," Baxley answered.

"This is another milk run. Here we go." Delattre banked northeast for a few seconds and then back to the west. The bridge ran north and south, so in order to get the main support section he would have to come in out of the east. At 2,000 feet he leveled on a heading of 256.

"Ten miles from target . . . one minute forty seconds," Baxley rattled off the routine data.

The second ZSU-23-4 moved into position and locked its tracks on the east corner of the bridge. The gun operator swung the four-barrel twenty-three-millimeter cannons to the east and pointed them up at a forty-five-degree angle. The ZSU-23's commander gave the order for the radar observer to bring up his radar and start searching for targets.

"Let's move," Wazir shouted over the radio. His tank lurched forward as the driver started down the hill.

Oliveri watched his radar screen aboard the EC-141 as one of the tracked vehicles moved across the bridge and stopped on the opposite side. The F-15E wasn't going to make it in time. The ground threats were already at the bridge.

He keyed his mike. "Cadillac four . . . Queen Bee, heads up. I'm showing threats at the bridge."

* * *

Both of them heard the warning from the EC-141.

"Okay, where is it?" Baxley shouted. "I should be seeing the bridge by now."

"It's all right, kid, just take your time. It ain't going anywhere," Delattre reassured him.

"Thermal crossover." Baxley cursed the IR screen. It was not as clean as he had expected. The LANTIRN system had been designed for use primarily at night, when the sky was dark and cold. Since the ground and small rocks lose heat rapidly at night, it's easy to pick up larger, warmer targets. However, the new day's temp was rising, warming the air and ground around the bridge quickly. His IR image was blending the air, ground, and structure of the bridge together.

He checked their location: seven miles from the target and closing at 490 knots. He tried to wait patiently, not taking his eyes off the screen.

"Holy horseshit, there they are." Baxley transferred the IR image to his pilot's HUD. At six miles, the F-15's sensor had picked up a line of hot spots moving down the road toward the bridge. "I show two ground targets, one on the south side of the bridge and the other on the north. You see them?"

"I see them." Delattre didn't voice any concerns to the younger man.

"No radar threat," Baxley said, thankful his pilot was a cool hand. At four miles, Baxley spotted it. "There it is, man. Target lock. Turn right two degrees."

As their radars came on and the circuits began warming, the ZSU-23-4 radar operators simultaneously eyed the target. It was streaking in from the east at a high rate of speed.

"Target bearing one four seven . . . altitude 600 meters. *Fire . . . fire!*" came the excited and rushed commands. There was scarcely enough time to target it, move the four-barrel gun turret, and begin firing. The complete sequence took a minimum of thirty seconds.

"Enemy radar . . . eleven o'clock," Baxley warned, hearing the radar tone fill his helmet. The F-15E's threat equipment, operating in the search mode, instantly identified the ZSU. The pitch of the warning tone told him it hadn't locked up yet. "Off right . . . off right!" he shouted.

"Hit the music. We're going for it. Closing on target." Delattre, determined, pressed the throttles to the stops until both engines kicked into afterburner. Both men were flattened back into their seats.

Baxley flipped the radar jammer on, momentarily shutting down the two smaller J-bands painting their fighter. He immediately centered the laser on the concrete pillar in the middle, supporting the bridge. With a touch of his hand he instructed the computer to lock on.

"Lockup," he called, waiting.

When the cursor flashed, Delattre released the laser-guided explosive. The dark green bomb separated from the aircraft on a rapid descent, following the thirty-inch reflected beam of the invisible laser.

"Knock, knock, suckers," Baxley announced, smiling under his oxygen mask. He looked out the left side of the cockpit. He could see the bridge below and the two triple-A guns attempting to target them.

A cloud of oily black diesel exhaust billowed out from behind Wazir's T-72 tank. It was half of the way across the overpass. Behind him, a second tank was barreling onto the bridge. Four others pulled into position behind them, followed by another ZSU. The drivers were carefully staggering their positions, leaving a minimum of five meters between them.

The Shilkas' moving gun turrets caught the major's attention. The sky crackled with the roar of jet engines.

"Move this thing . . . *NOW!*" Wazir shouted. "Get off the bridge!" His face flushed red with a mixture of anger and fear. He dropped into the center of the tank, not taking the time to close the hatch above him. He covered his ears from the shrill whistling of the laser-guided projectile cutting through the air at Mach 0.95.

The driver held the accelerator pedal to the floor. The speeding forty-ton chassis rambled off the bridge a fraction of a second before the laser-guided BLU-109 bomb struck the left edge of the main concrete pillar. The hardened steel nose sliced into the softer concrete, crumbling the middle segment into a thunderous ball of fire and smoke. The explosion toppled the second tank completely off its tracks into the canyon below, crushing its crew on impact.

The distinct force of the powerful shock wave passed over Wazir's tank, tossing the crew around like popcorn. The major, still standing, hit his head on the interior steel wall and fell to the floor dazed.

Dull-witted, with a bleeding three-inch gash above his right eye, Wazir waited for the sound of the jet aircraft to fade away before he moved. Then he wormed up slowly to glance outside the turret. The smoke and debris were clearing with the morning breeze. A jagged ten-foot section of concrete had been blasted out of the left side of the bridge, along with the main pillar, roughly cutting a third of it away. Twisted steel reinforcements protruded out of the center and several bomb fragments were burning.

The amazing thing was that the bridge remained standing. The Libyan engineers had designed it to take a direct hit and survive, and they would be proud that they had succeeded.

Wazir shakily keyed his mike. "Move out. I want every vehicle across this thing at once."

F-15E Mercury Three and Four

Fourteen miles south of the Libyan PRV-9 early warning radar, the lead pilot habitually checked his altitude, airspeed, and fuel status. The two fighters were northbound in loose formation, cruising at 3,500 feet a quarter mile apart. They had been flying unopposed with a clear sky and no other aircraft in the area. It was a bizarre feeling for both pilots, as if the Libyans didn't care that two American fighters were penetrating their airspace. Both had expected to fight their way to the target and then have to fight their way back out of the area.

The WSO flying in Mercury four saw the faint infrared images first. "I show two IR targets. Bearing three five two, about two hundred yards south of the nearest hill. It's a weak read, but it's our target, all right."

"Good job. This mother's mine," the pilot announced. He was rightfully possessive of the target. It was his backseater that had spotted the lukewarm IR signature of the radar site first. Under the rules of engagement he would be the first to attack it.

"Four . . . this is three. We confirm your contact," came the call from the flight leader. *"We have it also. Roll in on my wing. I'm going in first. You can follow."*

"Ah, *shit!*" Mercury four clicked his mike twice to verify he understood the transmission, but he didn't have to like it. His WSO had found the damn thing. Why should some lieutenant colonel take his fun away killing it? He chalked it up as one of the hazards of only being a captain.

The lead Strike Eagle did a slow turning roll to the left and lined up the target on his HUD. Mercury four pulled up tight on his wing. They were two minutes from weapons release.

PRV-9 Early Warning Radar, South of Aujila

The technical sergeant looked at his commanding officer, not believing how stupid the man was. "One minute fifty seconds, sir. Those targets are closing fast and still no sign of air support."

The lieutenant didn't respond.

"I don't see any air cover coming out of the north."

"It will be here. Watch the targets."

The sergeant squirmed in his seat.

"The air cover will be here." The lieutenant's voice was weak. He was careful not to look the man in the eye.

The technician's right leg came around the chair and he seriously considered bolting from the room as a last-minute effort to save his life.

"You have your orders. Stay at your post."

The sergeant had been manning the radar for the last forty minutes, watching the two blips snake their way toward his station.

"I'm getting the hell out of here," the sergeant finally said nervously.

"I said, stay at your post. That is an order."

"You stay at your post, Lieutenant. I do not wish to die." The man jumped from his chair and lunged out the door of the control van before the Libyan officer could even reach for his pistol.

The lieutenant, wiping the sweat from his forehead, took the man's seat, looking at his watch. Fifteen seconds passed as his eyes drifted from the sweeping beam of the radarscope back to his watch. The sergeant could be right; he was about to die. Another ten seconds passed and he thought, *Nittal has lied to me.* Five more seconds passed while his thoughts raced on.

"There is nothing I can do to protect the radar," he rationalized.

The lieutenant found himself running across the desert eighty meters from the radar's control center. He hesitated and turned to a bright flash of light illuminating the sky around him. A violent wave of air and flying debris knocked him to the ground as he realized the sergeant's cowardice had saved his life.

Delattre came out of a steep climb and leveled at 3,400, heading to the southwest. He throttled back into idle and opened the air brake, slowing the big aircraft to 280 knots. He then rolled the F-15E on its side so they could both see the bridge below them two miles away.

"Sierra hotel! We nailed it, sir," Baxley said, unsnapping his mask. "Whew! You went through that baby so quick, they didn't know we were coming till we were already gone!"

Delattre wiped the perspiration off the side of his face and leaned his head against the back of the ejection seat. The mushroomed smoke was clearing and he studied the target area. It became apparent it wasn't what he wanted to see. He had expected an entire section of the bridge to be gone. It wasn't. A portion of the bridge was still connecting both sides of the canyon. Then he noticed a small dark object moving on it. His heart missed a beat.

"My ass, we nailed it! Son of a bitch, those tanks are still moving across the thing! We hit it, but we didn't kill it."

Baxley knew his pilot's tone of voice. They were going back to finish the job. "There's two triple As down there, sir, and they aren't going to let us slide in so easily this time," he objected.

Delattre didn't hear him. He was already concentrating on turning the fighter. Adding power, he thrusted the nose down, picking up airspeed as he dropped through 1,500 feet.

Delattre knew the ZSUs would be ready for him. He checked his weapons display, showing only one Paveway remained, then thought about his options. He could come in high and attack the bridge from above 10,000 feet, avoiding the threat altogether. But if he missed, the Libyan ground units would cross and move into Madadhi, reinforcing the air base. He couldn't allow that to happen. If he came in below 10,000 feet, the ZSU-23 operators would have plenty of time to look at, target, and kill him. The four-barrel cannons could spit out over 1,000 rounds a minute, putting up a wall of flying steel no fighter in the world could overcome. His only other option was to go low-level, below 200 feet, and hope the ZSUs' tracking radars would be confused trying to filter out the ground clutter. His only risks were flying into the ground and coming up against a skilled cannon operator who was having a lucky day. He cursed himself for not using both laser bombs the first time, then shook off the error, saying, "Fuck it. I'll get it this time."

In forty-five seconds Delattre had put five miles between him and the target area. He drew the stick back, pulling a steady 5 Gs, and turned back to the east.

"Batten down the hatches, Baxley."

The backseater breathed deeply, tugging at his shoulder harness and lap belt, and reported, "Fifty-five seconds to target."

Only one of the ZSUs maintained its original position at the southern end of the bridge. The other had moved. Wazir had ordered the second antiaircraft gun to climb a couple hundred meters up the nearest hill. It now sat on a rocky ledge overlooking the canyon, a perfect place to take aim at a low-level aircraft.

Wazir watched the fourth T-72 roll off the end of the bridge. He had instructed them to come across one at a time now. At the other end, another tank revved its engines, rumbling forward.

The bridge's superstructure was becoming extremely unstable with each heavy tank. The major could hear the distant thunder of a high-performance aircraft. He used his binoculars to scan the sky around them. The American would be back. Only this time he hoped the surprise would be his.

* * *

Delattre dropped below 300 feet, keeping his aircraft's speed pegged on 480 knots. The F-15E crested a hill and pushed over as he guided it through the sky. He worked the stick as the stress of several negative Gs reminded him of how fast they were traveling.

"Weapons armed," Baxley reported. "Three miles and closing."

Neither man paid attention to the details of the surroundings flashing by outside the cockpit. Delattre concentrated on his HUD and the feel of his fighter. His whole being took on the contours of the terrain with the jet flying to the left of the canyon, weaving right and then left. He watched his altitude dip below 250 feet as the radar threat warning light flashed on.

"I see it. I'm jamming," Baxley said, wrapped in his duties. "Thirty-five seconds to target."

The ZSUs' radars would have a difficult time distinguishing them below 200 feet. The trick was that Baxley would have only a few seconds to lock the laser onto the bridge and Delattre would have to release the bomb before they were out of range.

As Delattre passed over a large hill, he banked left and down the other side. Each man felt the nylon restraints pull him into his seat. He turned a few degrees south and then north, skirting the top of a narrow rock outcrop. The warning tone from the threat panel cut in and out as they cut through the two enemy radar beams. Twenty-three seconds from weapons drop, they broke into the open and the bridge came into view. Delattre banked sharply to the right, inching the stick down until the HUD read 160 feet. They were flying directly toward the bridge.

Wazir lost sight of the American fighter dropping below the horizon. He had spotted it approaching out of the west, hugging the contour of the terrain. Its dark gray camouflage wasn't easy to spot against the light morning sky.

"Where are you?" he questioned out loud.

The unanticipated blaring, ripping sound needed no explanation. The number two ZSU, located on the hillside, had thundered to life. Wazir watched the red tracer rounds of the cannon cartridge twist through the air to the west. He could tell that the operator had not waited long enough. He was shooting too high and ahead of the enemy aircraft.

Delattre didn't react to the first few bursts of triple-A fire screaming into the sky ahead of him. They would miss by a wide margin.

"Increase the jamming," he calmly ordered.

"We're at max," Baxley countered, hitting the chaff button. "Laser on. Here we go."

The bridge was in the center of the F-15E's HUD. At their extremely low flight level the Strike Eagle bounced up and down, varying its altitude twenty feet at a time. Another burst of cannon fire filled the air in the distance ahead. Instinctively, Delattre knew it was from the same site.

"Negative laser lock. Give me some altitude."

"No way, we'd be sitting ducks."

"Then break off, Captain! I need altitude," Baxley shouted in protest.

Delattre didn't have a choice. He would give his WSO what he needed. With his fighter traveling at 560 knots 145 feet above the ravine, he pulled back on the stick. He watched the HUD, 170 . . . 180 . . . 190. The bridge was growing closer with every beat of his heart.

The radar operator's screen was filled with ground clutter as he tried to pick up the target. The American was jamming his radar, and his antenna was pointed toward the ground. He decided to rotate the emitter skyward and hope the target crossed his path.

He pushed the power boost button to increase the amount of electricity flowing through the antenna. It eliminated most, but not all, of the jamming. As the antenna came up fifteen degrees, the scope began to clear. He could see a soft reflection of an aircraft.

At 330 feet, ten seconds from the target, Baxley's instruments indicated they had laser lock on the bridge. "Lockup," he cried out tensely.

Delattre silently moved the throttles forward just short of afterburner. Worries of triple-A threats and hand-held SAMs crossed his mind. His IR signature was big enough without turning his F-15E into a flaming rocket. He jinked the aircraft right and left, trying to nullify the enemy radar's tracking solution.

"Eighteen hundred meters and closing." The gunner on the number one ZSU swiveled his guns to the west, ready to depress the dual triggers in preparation to fire. The targeting cursor flashed to red. His radar was locked up.

The third volley of gunfire streaked across the nose of the F-15E. Delattre winced slightly. The red tracers were bright and fast.

"Seven seconds." Baxley called off. "Three degrees right—I got a second radar! They're locked on us!"

Through the HUD, Delattre could now see the lingering smoke from their first attack.

"Where's that other gun?" he barked, not expecting a response, but was answered with a round from the second ZSU as it let loose.

Delattre saw the flashes, followed by tracers, burst over the canopy. He dropped the nose of the F-15E, recovering and leveling his plane at 290 feet, keeping the bridge centered in his HUD. Out of the corner of his eye, he witnessed several rounds coming up toward them as the fighter escaped their battering. The second gun, closest to the bridge, adjusted its aim, sending a salvo straight for them. Delattre swallowed, not removing his eyes from the bridge, taking in the vibration of several cannon rounds impacting his aircraft's right wing and tail. The fighter yawed left and right, pitching up with the force of the exploding rounds under its wingtip.

"Two . . . one . . . weapon's release." Delattre pickled the GBU.

The number one and two guns were firing continuously, permeating the sky above the bridge with a flood of armor-piercing bullets. Radar lock had proved to be useless; the enemy fighter was traveling too fast to follow. Desperation took its place.

Wazir swore as the American F-15E passed over the bridge at only 300 feet. Through the roar of the engines and firing guns a low-pitched whistling sound escalated. He climbed back inside his tank, this time closing the hatch behind him. The whistling ended a half second before the bridge exploded and collapsed.

The jolt from the blast rocked the low-flying F-15E. Delattre's helmet smacked the canopy as one more round tore into the underside of his Strike Eagle.

"We have a fuel leak, auxiliary tank." Baxley scanned the instruments looking for additional damage to the flight controls or avionics.

Delattre automatically hit the jettison switch, separating the tank from his aircraft. Breaking through 5,000 feet, he felt the aircraft's vibration in the stick. It wanted to yaw to the right. The fist-sized holes in the right wing and vertical tail were putting added drag on the airframe. At least the controls were responsive and they weren't losing any hydraulic fluid.

At 10,000 feet, Delattre leveled and turned to a heading of 157.

"Queen Bee . . . Cadillac four, bridge destroyed. Fuel at bingo. Heading for tanker."

"Roger that, Cadillac four. Change your heading to one four niner."

Delattre adjusted his heading, then hit autopilot and unhinged his mask. He was beat up, but not out of the fight.

31

"The last F-117A is touching down now, sir," Captain William Harris reported. "A-10s are thirty minutes from their target, and the EC-141 is reporting no other aircraft in the area."

"And the ground movements?" General Clark questioned anxiously.

"One of the F-15Es reports the bridge at Al Kisawa is destroyed. And another reports the second ground radar has been nixed, too." Harris was reading the data as it appeared on his screen.

"Well, that was easy. Tom, I was expecting more than this. Weren't you?" General Clark asked, relieved.

Staffer crushed out his cigarette, exhaling the smoke while he stood. "Yeah, I was."

"It's not a lot of resistance considering what's at stake. It makes me wonder why they're not putting more aircraft into the air."

"You're forgetting about the helicopters," Staffer added.

"No, I'm not. They're gone also, except for two that have set down close by in the mountains. By God, we have to assume the Libyans and terrorists both know about the warheads, don't we? Could they really be waiting for a main assault on the ground?" Clark folded his arms in contemplation. "Or maybe this Ajami isn't going to be as tough as Collins thought."

"Maybe," Staffer answered. "Or maybe not."

STAGING AREA, ALI BALLAS, EGYPT

The darkened interior of the C-17 transport was virtually noiseless as the big aircraft rolled down the runway to the west. The pilot steadily added power until, twenty seconds later, the nose of the four-engine transport

333

lifted off the runway, followed by the main gear. The subtle vibrations of the aircraft in flight gave Mark Collins his first serious doubts about his insistence on going on the rescue mission. He tightened his lap belt as he looked around the cargo area of the C-17. Madison may have been right, he really wasn't cut out for this. Boot camp was a distant memory, but he didn't recall there ever being any men like the ones surrounding him now in his platoon, or in the military in general.

Sitting along each side of the bulkheads, in the front half of the C-17's cargo bay, were the members of Cobra team's ground rescue squad. The squad consisted of thirty-two of the toughest, mean-eyed men Collins had ever seen. As their leader, First Lieutenant Alvin W. Ghere, known as No Fear Ghere by his men, had explained to him during the briefing, each man had been pulled from the best of the marines, Airborne, and Green Beret units from around the world. They all were well versed in jungle, desert, and arctic operations. Being assigned to Cobra wasn't voluntary; it was mandatory. Yet all the men appeared to relish this line of work. They were of average height, only a few being over six foot tall, although each one looked as if he could win an iron-man competition. What really fascinated Collins was the way they seemed to communicate with each other. They didn't say anything, only looked at each other in varying expressions.

Resting on Collins's lap was a fully loaded M-16 and strapped to his waist was a Beretta nine-millimeter automatic with several loaded magazines for his assault rifle and pistol. Neither one of the weapons had serial numbers. He was wearing a lightweight Kevlar flak jacket under his chocolate chip, desert brown fatigues. His boots were dull brown, and the soles had been ground down to hide the real size of his foot. On his right shoulder was a gray-and-black low-visibility American flag with black tape covering it. He was not to remove the tape until they entered the bunker complex. One of the other team members had helped camouflage his face with brown and black greasepaint.

Twenty minutes later, as the transport leveled, Collins relaxed a little. He was seated across from Lieutenant Ghere, Cobra team's ground attack commander. Unlike the business professional type that Collins was used to working with in the CIA, Ghere fit the stereotyped image of a Rambo warrior. He was square jawed, didn't have a neck, and shaved his head. His hands were humongous and his forehead had a half inch of thick bone protruding over his eyes.

The second half of the transport was filled with the team's ground equipment, the most impressive being the single M2 Bradley fighting vehicle fastened securely to the floor of the aircraft. Collins also counted four HMMWVs (high-mobility multipurpose wheeled vehicles) known as Hummers. Directly behind the Hummers were two fast-attack vehicles. They looked like dune buggies. Strapped next to the FAVs were a half dozen brown Kawasaki KLR-250 motorcycles. Painted on the side of the fuselage in bright orange letters was "Send us in to kick some or send us home to get some." It seemed appropriate for this bunch.

MADADHI AIR BASE

Ajami stood on the edge of the shuttle's cargo bay looking down at the satellite. The area between the Kosmos and directly behind the crew compartment, about ten feet, was littered with twisted pieces of metal. Ziad had cut away several large sections of the satellite's protective skin, exposing the nearest missile.

Kneeling down, Ajami examined the internal workings more closely. Ziad had removed the round access door directly over the missile, revealing the main body of the compact ICBM. It was white with black smudge marks from the fire. But that's not what caught his attention. Resting on top of the satellite was the missile's nose cone. When Ajami looked further into the satellite he saw it, the gray-colored graphite skin of the nuclear warhead.

"You must hurry." Ajami spoke with an urgency that made Ziad uncomfortable. "This should have been done hours ago."

"You cannot rush this. If I make one mistake, we could all die."

"If you do not succeed, we will all die, anyway." Ajami felt sure the Libyans were plotting to kill him along with most of his men. His mind drifted to the arising problems outside. The Americans were going to be attacking the bunker any minute. He needed to get his bomb out safely to ensure his power and command. This was now the most important thing in his life. He hadn't slept or eaten in forty-eight hours. His body was becoming weak and his mind dull.

What time is it . . . what day is it? Ajami brushed the hair out of his eyes as another swell of uneasiness swept through him. He had spent his entire adult life planning for an operation like this. It was necessary he stay in control to guarantee there would be no mistakes.

But the warhead was fast becoming a faraway dream, not the weapon of promise to destroy his enemies. The voice inside his head was no longer whispering, but instead yelling for him to leave the camp at once without the bomb. *I can't lose control of my base. Allah guide me, I beg you.*

Ziad climbed down inside the burned cavity of the Kosmos satellite. He had cleared away enough of the debris so that he could crawl in under the nose cone of the missile. Ziad had determined there were nine nut and bolt assemblies, one inch in diameter, holding the warhead and guidance system to the top of the rocket motor. He had spent the last four hours cutting through each one and was now gently working a metal saw over the last stainless steel bolt. The quality of the Russian metal was unusually high, making the process frustrating and time consuming. If his calculations were correct, however, this would be the last major obstacle to removing the bomb.

After a few minutes, Ziad heard a snap as he cut through the last bolt. The bomb shifted a few inches, relieving the pressure on the protective outer cone.

"It is loose," he shouted from under the bomb. "*Quickly,* bring me the chain."

Several men below pushed the crane next to the cargo bay of the shuttle, swinging it over the satellite. They then lowered the cable from the pulley that was attached to a length of heavy chain. Ziad jumped on top of the satellite as Ajami reached up and grabbed the chain, making sure it didn't hit the outside of the warhead.

"Connect it here and here," Ziad said, excitedly showing Ajami where to attach the steel hooks on the lead sections of the chain.

Ajami did as he was instructed, putting the chain around the base of the bomb and connecting the hooks to two small holes in the lower part of the graphite skin.

"Now raise it up . . . slowly . . . slowly," Ziad cautioned. The men working the crane hauled back on the wire cable. The block and tackle strained under the pressure of the 1,800-pound warhead. Very deliberately, the bomb started to rise out of the shuttle, then suddenly stopped.

"Hold up . . . stop!" Ziad shouted. He jumped from the satellite back into the cargo bay and crawled in under the warhead. There was barely enough room for him to shift his body.

"What is the problem?" Ajami anxiously called down. Ziad was busily checking a bundle of wires leading out of the warhead's bus to the main missile assembly and didn't answer. He guessed it was part of the guidance system gas spin jet, which was still attached to the aluminum shroud separating the reentry vehicle from the propulsion system. The wires would have to be cut. If the bomb did have a self-destruct, it would be located in the warhead section, not the rocket motor. At least, he hoped that was the case.

Ajami, waiting now impatiently, called down once more, "What is the problem, Ziad?"

Grabbing a pair of wire cutters and his flashlight, Ziad used all his strength to squirm in between the outer shell of the bomb and the thick aluminum skin on top of the rocket. He turned on the flashlight and smiled. The Russian engineer who had designed the system was either lazy or very intelligent. All the wires, and there looked to be several dozen of them, leading from the rocket motor to the warhead were in a nice, neat group. All he had to do was get close enough to cut them and the warhead was free. They could then lower it to the ground. His mission was almost complete.

Ziad used all the strength in his legs to push himself closer. The bomb rocked somewhat, pinning him against the rocket motor. *Careful,* he cautioned himself. He opened the pliers and cut the first wire, then the second.

Pathfinder Team Alpha

Standing in the OP, Rodriguez scanned the opposite side of the runway and didn't like what he was seeing. Or rather, what he wasn't seeing. It bothered him that, after the initial attacks, things had quieted so hastily. The choppers and all but one of the MiGs had lifted off, leaving the three large transports. Moments after that, the base had come alive with men running every which way. Minutes later two of the transports started their engines and took off to the east, leaving one behind. The final transport had been towed into the easternmost bunker and the door closed, leaving the MiG parked outside. But that was half an hour ago, and now that the sun was up, he couldn't see anyone moving around the bunkers.

"Any time now," Lange whispered, looking at his watch. "This silence is too eerie for me."

An F-15E streaked in out of the east only a hundred feet off the deck and Lange jumped, having spooked himself. The pilot had come in under the radar coverage of the SA-6 and SA-8 sites. Two triple-A gun emplacements opened fire but missed the speeding jet by several hundred feet.

"Mark 'em," Rodriguez called out, oblivious to the communications officer's childish behavior.

"I got 'em," Lange answered, marking where each site was located on their area map.

The pilot popped several infrared flares, dropped his ordnance, and pulled up in a vertical climb, leaving the area as fast as he had come.

"Shit, they were ready for him," Lange said, spotting long, thin smoke trails. On the hillside, over the center bunker, two hand-held SA-16 heat-seeking missiles launched at the American intruder. The two tactical SAMs created a snakelike hissing sound as their stubby fins cut through the air. The first SAM went straight for one of the flares, exploding as it neared it. The second missile followed the American fighter for a moment before wavering off to the south.

"Come on, blast 'em back," Rodriguez cheered as he watched a barrel-shaped bomb leave the underside of the F-15E and continue in a straight path. As it neared the ground, it opened, spewing out a wide trail of soup can–sized bomblets over the ground in front of the bunkers. The CBU-87 had been designed to attack parked aircraft on the ground and troops dug into a concentrated area. Each individual bomblet had enough explosives to destroy a small car.

Both men watched the bright flashes as the explosives detonated on impact in a rectangular pattern. Seconds later the parked MiG-23 erupted in flames as the shrapnel cutting into its fuel tanks ignited.

"Queen Bee, this is Alpha. Tell that fifteen driver he nailed the MiG."

"Roger. Can you get us a visual on enemy troop casualties?" came the callback.

"Negative. We're too far away to get a read on that. But there's a hell of a lot of triple-A and SAMs still active down here," Rodriguez radioed.

"Roger that, Alpha. Are you guys in position to give us some help on that one?"

"Can do, Queen Bee. What'd you have in mind?"

"We have six A-10s inbound in fifteen minutes. We need your eyes to vector them to the targets."

Rodriguez paused before he answered. "This area is still too hot with SAMs. Those Hogs are too slow and low."

"Wild Weasels in five, Alpha."

"Understood. Then we'll vector the Warthogs and do a little damage on our own."

"Queen Bee out." The radio operator on board the EC-141 had just told him that they still had a few surprises for the SAMs on the ground.

"What do you make out of it?" Lange asked.

"I still don't like it. Those bastards have buried themselves under the ground. We're going to have to dig them out. Rath, are you and Vasquie fit to go hunting? There's a couple of SA-16 positions above the center aircraft bunker causing our birds some problems. If they show their faces, I need someone who can hit 'em between the eyes."

"I think we can manage that," Rath answered, smiling at his sniper. Like cats on the prowl, the two men slipped out of the OP.

32

Ziad used his other hand for support as he reached for the last wire. Several drops of perspiration rolled down the side of his outstretched arm, and he suddenly felt overwhelmed with weariness and thirst. With just his forefinger and thumb he opened the pliers and snipped the last copper wire.

"I am finished," he shouted, a little weakly. "Raise it up."

He tried to help push the heavy warhead assembly away from him as it started to move up, but it was too awkward. The confined area restricted him from any secure grips, and the last thirty hours of work had worn him down. Ziad put his head back, relieved that the bomb was finally free. He decided to wait to climb out of the satellite once the warhead was swung away from the rocket. He shut his eyes to relax as the crane moaned under the strain of the bomb's weight.

The popping sound of a hook snapping loose from its hold on the warhead brought his eyes open, but there wasn't time or room for Ziad to roll out of the way. The warhead fell several feet, crushing down on his head and chest. He tried to scream out but couldn't. Unable to breathe, the engineer blacked out and died.

Ajami watched on helplessly in horror as his power seemingly slipped through his hands. "*Stop!* Give me some slack," he shouted, and jumped over next to the bomb assembly. Working as fast as he could, Ajami quickly reattached the remaining chain hooks onto the bottom of the bomb and motioned for the men operating the crane to hoist it up again. The warhead lifted unsteadily on the straining hooks. Ajami shoved it clear of Ziad's body.

"Okay, that's enough," he yelled. The bomb was lowered none too soon onto the satellite in the shuttle. The crane wasn't sturdy enough to lift the heavy warhead. Ajami felt for a pulse on the mangled man's neck, but there wasn't one.

F-16C CORONA TWENTY-ONE

"Corona twenty-one, area is SAM hot. Radar and IR." The call came from the EC-141.

Before answering, the pilot verified he had just crossed the final way point.

"Ah, roger that, Queen Bee. I copy." The lead F-16C Wild Weasel, Corona twenty-one, piloted by Second Lieutenant Leonard Tobin, approached the forward edge of battle area at 10,000 feet, twenty-seven miles southeast of Madadhi. Unlike the standard NATO Wild Weasel configuration, which consisted of an F-4G Phantom and an F-16C flying together, Cobra team used only F-16Cs. The single-seat fighter was both faster and more maneuverable than the Phantoms. Each of the six Weasels were trained to act alone, relying on their sophisticated AN/APR-38 radar homing and warning system along with two AGM-88B HARM "fire-and-forget" high-speed antiradiation missiles. In addition to the HARMs, each F-16 had wingtip-mounted AIM-9M Sidewinders for self-defense. Also uncharacteristic of their NATO brothers, which were discouraged from mixing it up in the air-to-air role, the F-16 Weasels of Cobra team didn't have a choice. Because of the limited number of aircraft, each fighter was required to perform several different roles.

"Corona package, this is Flight Lead. We are cleared to engage. Area is hot. Let's do our stuff and stay alert," Tobin warned. "Sixty seconds to attack pattern Voodoo." This gave each of the fighters permission to fire his weapons when ready and instructions to check over the instruments one last time. The Weasel mission demanded that all systems were operating perfectly. Each pilot was under strict orders to break off and return to base even if only a computer was malfunctioning. "Let's turn and burn, gentlemen."

PATHFINDER TEAM ALPHA: ICEBOX

It is said that a sniper's worst enemy was the daylight, and Vasquez agreed. He and Rath owned the night. But during the day he had to play by the light's rules, working around it.

Dressed in their desert camouflage, the two methodically picked their way down the side of the mountain. Rath was in the lead and used every large rock and bush for cover as they slithered their way over to a small pile of fallen shale several hundred yards from the runway. It wasn't the best place to set up a sniper hide, but it was the best available to them under the circumstances.

As they neared their goal, Vasquez crawled past his scout, carefully placing his rifle on the ground in front of him. Rath stayed in the shadows and removed his binoculars and laser range finder, checking the lenses for dirt and dust. Without a word, they scanned their environment, making sure it was clear of any enemy patrol troops that might have snuck up unknowingly.

"Clean," Vasquez whispered, picking up his rifle.

"Clean," Rath answered. It was time to report in. "Rushmore . . . Icebox. We're in position."

"Read you, Icebox. Keep an open channel."

"Roger." Rath turned the volume down on his radio.

"I need a distance, Lieutenant." Vasquez removed six .308 rounds, holding them in his left hand.

"Eight hundred forty-seven meters." The digital readout on the bottom of the single-reflex hand laser range finder was accurate up to two-tenths of a yard at 1,000 meters. "Mark the center bunker."

Vasquez unscrewed the elevation cap on the side of his scope and dialed it up to 900 meters. "Wind?" he asked.

"Looks like eight to ten knots out of the east." This time Rath was observing nothing more than several pieces of dried grass a hundred meters ahead of them. They were barely moving.

"Set," Vasquez said, as he worked the action of his rifle, loading it.

Flying the Wild Weasel mission was like playing a deadly game of cat and mouse, and Tobin savored every minute of it. Rather than flying around the SAMs using brute speed and powerful ECM packages like the F-15Es, Tobin and his team of SAM killers came in low at a moderate rate of speed. It was their goal to get the SAM operators to light up so they could obtain a precise and accurate kill. The pilots liked to think of themselves as being more refined and gracious. They gave the SAMs a chance, then knocked the shit out of them, where the fifteens were just savagely aggressive.

Tobin banked to the southwest at 600 feet, concealing his position behind an extended slender hill as long as he could. During their preflight briefing the latest satellite data had given them the locations of four SAM sites on the east side of Madadhi. Yet that was not his main objective. Tobin was on the hunt for the SAMs that hadn't been spotted by the boys at Langley. It seemed that the Libyans had learned many lessons from the Iraqi war, one of them being effective camouflage and concealment.

Tobin popped up to 1,200 feet and throttled back, using his eyes to sweep the desert below him. His threat warning equipment was silent.

"Now, don't be rude, you should come out and greet your guests," he called into his empty cockpit.

Vasquez saw a twinkle of light flash through his rifle scope. Possibly the sunlight reflecting off a gun barrel or a wristwatch. It was all he needed to focus in on an area. He studied it for over a minute. Then he saw movement as someone stirred.

Smooth move, Ex-Lax. Sure enough, there was a man walking. No, make that two men. Vasquez could see their heads. They were looking into the sky. What Vasquez had seen was the glimmer of the sun's rays mirroring off their spotting glasses. He watched them for a few more seconds as they sat down in a shaded area.

"Center bunker . . . fifty yards up and twenty yards to the left. Next to the largest boulder. I see two ragheads. Verify," the sniper whispered.

"I see them. Those could be our boys. Can you take them?"

"Not both. The way they're sitting I would only be able to get one before the other took cover."

Rath didn't have to think over his answer. "Okay, Vasquie, we wait. I want them both."

Mark Collins felt his stomach roll over. *This sure isn't like flying first class.* His flak jacket was biting into his rib cage as a line of sweat rolled down into his right eye. *I think I'm going to throw up,* he thought.

"You okay, Collins?" Ghere asked. "You look a little pale."

"Ahh . . . I'm fine, Lieutenant. The ride's just a little bumpy, that's all."

Ghere chuckled. "You think this is bumpy. Wait until we go low level. It'll knock your eyes out."

Collins smiled. *Just great.*

The SA-8 was hidden under several layers of cotton and nylon camouflage webbing. The brown, white, and black woven material was cut in different directions with clumps of dried grass and large dead weeds sticking out of it. The radar operator and fire control officer were quite positive of the job they had done concealing their site the night before. The launch vehicle of their SA-8 tactical SAM blended into the desert so well it was difficult, to say the least, to spot it even twenty yards away.

The SAM team's routine was simple. They activated their surveillance radar for thirty seconds, allowing it to sweep the sky around them. If nothing came up on the scope, they would shut it down for another thirty seconds, starting the process over again.

"Negative contact," Karni Sela, the radar operator, advised, switching the radar to standby. The pale green scope began to fade. The problem with mindless routines was they got boring in no time at all.

"Corona twenty-three. Magnum." One of the other F-16s had just fired a HARM at a SAM site somewhere to the north. He waited for the confirmed kill call.

A minute later. *"Corona twenty-three . . . Colorado dreamin'."* The code word signaled a kill.

"Good job, Twenty-three," Tobin radioed back.

Tobin looked at the threat panel below his HUD. The instruments remained clean, no enemy radars were sweeping the sky in front of him. He pulled the nose of his fighter up, gaining a few hundred feet in altitude, thinking maybe he wasn't high enough.

As his F-16 broke through 2,000 feet, the AN/APR-38 package picked up the first weak electronic traces of a radar in the distance.

"There you are. Guess who's coming to dinner." His supercooled, superconducting navigational computer instantly plotted a course to the target area. Tobin approached the target slowly. When the operators spotted him, he wanted them to think he was something other than a fast-turning fighter.

"Contact," Sela said. A target was on the outside edge of his radar coverage, not yet within the range of his missiles.

"Target type?" his commander asked.

Sela waited, wondering why fire control officers always asked this stupid question. He simulated actions of trying to identify the incoming aircraft, knowing his system didn't have the capability. Without dispute, he simply answered, "Target type unknown. Altitude 930 meters, speed only 320 knots. It's coming toward us."

"Shut down the radar."

"Yes, sir." Sela did as he was told.

"Very amusing," Tobin remarked as the signal died. "Are you going to pretend you're not at home?"

Keeping an exact heading of 203, Tobin added forward pressure on the throttle and nosed over for the ground. He watched his altitude fall, 1,600 . . . 1,300 . . . 800.

At 500 feet he slammed the throttle back into neutral and at the same time pulled the stick back, forcing his small fighter up and away from the ground. The F-16 protested with the seething force of 7.5 Gs, slamming him back into his seat. Tobin grunted under the pressure, watching as the HUD clicked off the fast-changing flight data. When he bottomed out at 150 feet, the aircraft leveled, airspeed 400 knots. Tobin felt the strain of the Gs bleed off as he swung in behind a long incline, hiding his presence from the SAM site.

"Two can play this game," he thought out loud.

"What do you mean, it is *gone?*" the launch officer demanded, now doubting his subordinate had even seen a target to begin with.

Sela searched his scope, looking for the target. He watched the lime green beam sweep in a counterclockwise direction, but nothing was there.

"Negative contact, sir," Sela replied, taking the heat. *You idiot, you shouldn't have shut down the radar,* he thought.

Zigzagging toward the radar, Tobin estimated he had traveled over ten miles. He kept his fighter below 300 feet, making sure he didn't cross into the line of sight of the SAM's radar. He waited another thirty seconds before showing his face.

A flick of his wrist sent the side stick control straight back. The F-16 shot straight up this time with the force of only 6 Gs, the fighter's altitude and airspeed mounting swiftly. He moved the stick right, spinning the fighter as it climbed. A spinning F-16 would show up on a radar screen like a lighthouse in the night. Whoever was out there looking for him would now get their chance.

"New target . . . bearing zero seven one," Sela called out, trying to hide the relief in his voice. The middle-aged sergeant could breathe easier again.

"Distance."

"Eighteen kilometers."

"Get me a lockup!" the commander, still irritated, shouted.

The SAM system included a totally self-supported package containing both surveillance and tracking radars. The six high-speed missiles were housed in protective fiberglass containers, keeping sand and dust away from their guidance systems.

The launch officer swiveled the housings to the north, ready for launch, then instructed the computers to trigger two of the missiles' internal guidance systems. The digital tactical display told him the target was still too far away to lock up and fire on. He waited, his finger hovering above the launch buttons.

The F-16C Wild Weasel's APR-38 automatically identified the type of radar as a surveillance operating at 7.35 GHz. It switched into a fully automatic mode, prioritizing the radar threat posed by the SA-8. The computer informed him the electronic emissions coming from the site were not designed to lock onto a target, just spot it.

"Now," Tobin told himself. Rolling the fighter over, he made a long, sweeping turn while maintaining 3,800 feet. The enemy radar signal was strong and painting him from the southwest.

The F-16 came wings level and Tobin's eyes brushed over the instruments, checking the HARM. It was ready to launch. The next few minutes were critical. One stupid mistake and it could be over for him.

A warning tone sounded in his headset a second before a red radar threat light started flashing below his HUD. The radar frequency had changed to 13.67 GHz. The SAM site had switched radar frequencies from search to tracking mode.

"Yeah, that's right, baby, lock up. *Here I am*." He adjusted his grip on the throttle, keeping his fighter at 380 knots. He pointed the nose toward the SAM site as the APR-38 computer identified the radar's frequency, azimuth, and location, storing the data in its memory. The system then dumped the information into the port side HARM missile's homing and tracking computers. The "fire when ready" symbol flashed on the HUD.

"Radar lock. Bearing zero nine seven," Sela read off the data from the radarscope, still eyeballing the target.

"Range to target?"

"Sixteen kilometers," Sela answered.

The bearded Libyan launch officer was growing impatient. The tarrying target was not in range. "Electronic countermeasures?"

"None in the area."

"Good. He must not know we are here."

"Thirteen kilometers," Sela called out. "Eleven—" Sela didn't finish. The transport shook as two semiactive radar SA-8s left their housings, leaving a trail of yellow sparks and fire.

"Corona twenty-one. Magnum," Tobin radioed his launch. The AGM-88B HARM missile left the underwing rail of the F-16 in a blaze with silver smoke. The internal electronic seeker head was locked onto the solid stream of radio waves flowing from the SA-8 site.

"Warning . . . warning," the computer sounded.

"Ah, shit." Tobin muttered. His eyes went to the launch threat warning light as it winked from a flashing to a solid red. The SA-8 radar was locked on his fighter.

"Launch warning . . . launch warning," the computer sounded again.

"Yeah, yeah . . . I know, Bitchin' Betty," he retorted to the recorded voice. Accelerating to Mach 2 in only seconds, the HARM climbed into the distance, disappearing.

Five and a quarter miles away the two SA-8s were airborne at 1,000 feet. Their solid fuel boosters had burned out, completing their job of pushing the missiles out of their protective containers to a speed near Mach 2 in three seconds. The two missiles, flying seconds apart, continued to accelerate as the sustainer stage of their propulsion systems ignited, sending the missiles past Mach 2.85 in a burst of white flames.

Each enemy missile was fitted with a double-beacon transponder located on the rear fuselage. The rearward-facing antenna was sending and receiving a steady stream of targeting telemetry as the SA-8s' computer systems guided the SAMs. The three forward fins pivoted left and right, steering each missile toward the radar return of the F-16.

Tobin wasn't going to wait around. He trusted the "fire and forget" missile's capabilities to hit the target. He couldn't afford to worry about anything but the SA-8s. The SAMs were small and extremely maneuverable, making them difficult to see and avoid. His best defense was to head for the deck and try to break the radar lock on his fighter.

Banking left, Tobin tossed the fighter over, kicking into afterburner. The F-16's single General Electric F129 turbofan spooled up, generating over 29,000 pounds of thrust in only seconds. The Gs increased with speed as he broke through 2,000 feet at 450 knots. The warning light remained a solid red. He swept the skies around him looking for any traces of the SAMs.

By now Sela knew they were dealing with a fighter. The blip on his scope turned and accelerated too fast for a large transport or any mid-size fixed-wing aircraft.

"Target is descending through 500 meters. Range, nine kilometers bearing one one eight," he called out.

Again the launch officer hit the fire button, sending two more missiles into the air.

* * *

Two thousand feet above the SAM site and four miles to the northeast, the AGM-88B HARM pushed over as its Thiokol dual-thrust, solid-propellent rocket motor shut down. The missile was now in a terminal dive using the inertia from its rocket booster to push it to the target. Its programmable digital microprocessors had a positive location lock on the SAM site. Even if the SA-8 shut down its radar, the missile would follow a computer-generated flight path, which was constantly being updated in its avionics package, allowing the HARM to destroy the radar site.

Tobin snapped his head right and left, trying to get a visual on the SAMs. The F-16's ECM equipment automatically kicked in, trying to jam the up-link or down-link receivers of each missile.

Unknown to him, the SA-8's electronic counter-countermeasures package sensed the electronic jamming coming from the F-16 and reprogrammed the injunction emitter. The guidance antenna converted the up-link signals to a stronger I-band frequency, shutting down any chance to jam the signal for a few more minutes.

Lieutenant Tobin put the fighter in a hard right-hand 5.5 G turn, spinning as he descended through 1,100 feet. As the F-16 banked to the southwest, two flickers of light caught his attention. Then he lost sight of them. The rocket motor of each missile had just burned out.

Tobin turned into the flight path of the missiles cutting in front of him. "I wanted to come for dinner, not be dinner!" he yelled, trying not to panic.

Sela followed the two missiles approaching their target. "First flight, thirty seconds to impact."

The launch officer sat motionless at his station.

"Twenty-five seconds to impact."

"Warning . . . warning," Bitchin' Betty nagged Tobin relentlessly. Fifteen hundred yards above, diving toward him at two times the speed of sound, he saw the lead SAM. Tobin had only one chance, and he did it without thinking. Kicking the nimble fighter back into afterburner, he went into a maximum 9.3 G turn, pivoting his fighter into the deadly missile's flight path, trying to dive in under it.

The maneuver was so abrupt and violent Tobin had to fight to keep from blacking out from the pressure. The G forces crushed his upper chest, forcing the air out of him and making it impossible to move his arms or head. His G suit hissed and the air bladders inside his helmet and around his waist and legs expanded, trying to prevent every drop of blood from leaving his upper body. As his vision narrowed, Tobin moaned, tightening his stomach and leg muscles with all his strength. He saw the first missile dart over his aircraft.

The SA-8 was fitted with a thirty-six-pound high-explosive fragmentation warhead. Like most SAM systems developed by the former Soviet Union, it was designed with a proximity fuse and alternate command detonation program. As the SA-8 passed within fifty-five feet of the F-16, it exploded. The resulting fireball filled the air with a thousand marble-sized steel ball bearings.

The AGM-88B made a slight midcourse correction before colliding with the SA-8 site. The HARM impacted the lower left side between the tracking and surveillance antennae. Because of its speed, Mach 2.54, the missile ripped through the two-inch steel plating surrounding the site, a fraction of a second before it turned the interior into a burning pile of liquid steel and black fire.

The radio up-link and down-link to each SAM were subsequently shut down, blinding each of the missiles. Both Sela and the launch officer died instantly, unaware of the fact that they had ever been in any danger.

Tobin's cockpit filled with a brilliant glare, and the F-16 shuddered as the shock waves rippled around its airframe. With the radar warning light on the threat panel blinking off, Bitchin' Betty was silenced.

The F-16 came wings level at 500 feet and Tobin filled his lungs with cool oxygen. He looked directly at the instruments, first going to the engine's RPM readout, then checking for fire warning lights. The second missile in pursuit had exploded far enough behind his aircraft that none of the erupting projectiles penetrated its aluminum skin.

In the distance, Tobin could see two more SAMs rocket straight up out of control. With the radar gone, they could no longer track on a target.

"Corona twenty-one . . . Colorado dreamin'." His unsteady voice radioed a confirmed kill. The action left him a bit frenzied. However, the thrill of the kill took over and he brought his fighter out of afterburner, heading back toward Madadhi, gaining altitude. He had one more HARM and he planned to use it.

33

Jibril watched another communication's channel flicker off as the radio link to the easternmost SA-8 site died. Disillusioned, he began to pace the floor behind the computer terminals. What had started out as a simple plan was transforming into a military debacle. Though it was through no fault of his own, Jibril was sure he would pay for it with his career.

"Patch me in to Nittal at once," Jibril said, finally deciding he had nothing to lose. When the coded communications link was open, he picked up the phone. "Are you monitoring our current situation?"

"Yes, Jibril, I am," Nittal answered coolly.

"Then you are aware I am down to minimal air defenses. All of the MiGs you sent me have been blasted from the sky."

"Where are the warheads?" Nittal asked, as if the aircraft were of no great loss or relevance.

"The state of this air base has not changed. Ajami and his men still control the three aircraft bunkers, along with the shuttle and the bombs. And until I get some air cover and ground troops, nothing is going to change." Jibril became flustered by the man's lack of priority. "Now, either you give me some support or I'm calling everything off!"

"I, too, have been fighting my own battles, Jibril. All of the early warning radar stations in the area are down and—"

"Shut up, Nittal! I am tired of your stupidity! I want action, or those choppers will be ordered to land in minutes to evacuate my men." He wasn't going to sit there while his men and equipment got obliterated.

Nittal breathed heavily in deliberation. Jibril's threat of evacuation would be a major setback for his plan. He knew the American aircraft would be most vulnerable after expending most of their fuel and weapons, just before their ground troops landed. Nittal could then deploy his

349

second flight of MiGs, along with his tanks to clean up, sending the cowards into retreat. If Jibril deserted the base now, the air defenses would collapse, allowing the Americans to acquire a strong foothold before Nittal was ready to attack. The captain was vital to him for the sole purpose of keeping the superpower off balance. Then there was the problem of Ajami and the bombs.

"You must not leave the base. I am aware of what you need, and I know I have been of little help to you." Nittal went on to justify his actions. "However, if I had sent our MiGs into combat when you first requested, they would have been chewed up by the Americans in minutes."

"So what are you proposing?" Jibril shouted.

"The MiGs will be airborne in minutes. Every fighter at this base, including my MiG-29s. They are armed, fueled, and ready to fly."

"And my ground support?"

"An American air strike has cut off most of the ground forces moving south to reinforce you. Major Wazir and six T-72 tanks have survived and are on the way to assist you. Can you and your men hold out for another thirty minutes?"

Jibril's skepticism lessened with the current information. "Yes . . . we can hold out. You have thirty minutes. That is all." Jibril hung up the phone. He knew he was expendable, but at this point he held a bargaining chip with his position.

EC-141 QUEEN BEE

Orbiting 123 miles east of Madadhi, the command and control aircraft came out of a long, arcing turn.

"Confirmed Corona two one. Proceed to next target area." Oliveri motioned with his hand, holding up one finger. "Colonel Madison, I have confirmation. One more SAM site is destroyed. Lead elements of the Weasels are approaching Madadhi now."

"Do we have a clean flight path for the follow-on packages?" Madison was referring to the slower-moving A-10s and the C-17.

"Yes, sir. Right to the edge of the runway."

"Any other aircraft in the area?" Madison felt poised, with everything starting to fall into place.

"No, sir."

"Excellent." Madison picked up the phone linking him with STOC. As he gave his report to the Pentagon, Oliveri turned back to his computer screen. Three F-15Es, from Cadillac package, were at 18,000 feet, circling above the base, flying combat air patrol. The KC-10s had moved closer and were eighty miles from the hot zone at 22,000. Two more

F-15Es, these two from Mercury package, had joined in formation behind the KC-10s, one of them taking on fuel. Cadillac four, Delattre's fighter, was at low level, getting ready to turn west and hook up with the Extender for his turn to refuel.

To the east of the base, the F-16s were clearing away the remaining SAMs. Oliveri watched the scope as the pilots crisscrossed through the sky, trying to entice the SAM operators to bring up their radars and fire on them. Twenty-five miles farther to the east the six A-10s were in a tight formation at 10,000 feet. To conserve fuel, they were traveling below 300 knots. Their orders instructed them to stay clear of the area until Oliveri gave the go-ahead. Lastly, at 18,000 feet, on the edge of the screen, Oliveri spotted the large C-17.

The sector search mode symbol began to flash in the upper part of the computer screen. Mi-24 helicopters appeared next to it.

Oliveri dumped the data into the memory banks. He zoomed in on a 7.7-square-mile area in the mountains north of Madadhi. The SAR/FTI had located the position of two more Mi-24 attack helicopters, twenty-three miles northwest of the base. The radar picture picked out the two choppers in a narrow gully, sheltered by several high, rocky cliffs on the west and south. *No wonder it took so long,* Oliveri thought. Analyzing the picture, he was amazed his sensors had even spotted them. The Libyan pilots had done a descent job of concealing their birds. If the EC-141 had been fifty miles farther east, his equipment would never have picked up their radar image.

Oliveri returned the screen to its original mode. "Four down, two to go."

WHITE HOUSE SITUATION ROOM

It was late night in Washington as John Turner, the secretary of defense, surrounded by several staff personnel, watched the latest battle data appear on the big TV screen in front of them.

"Sir, I have a personal message from General Dawson." A clean-cut naval ensign handed Turner a folded piece of paper.

The secretary of defense flipped it open, reading to himself and shaking his head. The message indicated that the B-1Bs had just reported in. They were over the Mediterranean.

Turner looked at the ensign. "Have my car brought around. I'm going to the Pentagon." He glanced back over at the screen, not wanting to consider the decision he might have to make.

Aujila, Libya, Southeastern Command

Nittal exited the underground bunker to be enveloped in the dry desert air. It was an abrupt change from the cool, recycled air of the command center.

"Briefing complete, sir. The first aircraft will be airborne in two minutes," the air wing commander said, continuing, "The MiG-23s will lead the attack, followed by the twenty-nines."

"Very good." Nittal shielded his eyes from the sun as he looked left and right. He stopped, looking directly ahead at a series of a dozen hardened concrete hangars, each housing two to three fighters. The base was alive with the sound of jet engines and men working their various stations.

Several hundred feet away two MiG-23s pulled out, taxiing to the edge of the runway. They were followed by two other sets of aircraft. The MiGs' desert brown camouflage contrasted with the light blue morning sky.

Nittal watched the fighters light their afterburners and glide into the air. He had saved his best for last.

Second Lieutenant Fahmi Qasmi had never been in combat, but he regarded himself as one of the finest fighter pilots in the Middle East. Including Israel. He was short and somewhat chubby for a fighter pilot, yet could do things with a MiG only his commanders dreamed were possible. Flying came easily to him, a gift, and because of his natural skill behind the stick, he had been permitted to train with the best instructor pilots in North Korea, Iran, and France.

Three months ago, Qasmi had been sent from his training base near Sardalas, in western Libya, to serve under Nittal's command. It was not an assignment he much cared for. He missed the lively nights in the bright, flashy city. The food was plentiful, and the women who worked the streets selling themselves for a profit enjoyed his status and regular visits. He gladly paid the price for an evening of decadent entertainment.

Since being stationed at Aujila, Qasmi felt he had been caged like an animal. Not only were they too far from the city, but he was restricted to flying his MiG solely during the night. He was convinced that Nittal was obsessed with base security for no apparent reason. In Qasmi's opinion, it was impossible to keep all military activity out of the watchful eyes of American reconnaissance satellites and there was no sense in sacrificing valuable training time.

Qasmi shifted his heavy helmet as he ran one final radio check. His fueled and battle-ready MiG-29 was then pulled from the hangar. The sun's rays flooded the cockpit, forcing him to squint as he inspected the instruments. Several hundred meters away three more of the two-tone MiGs were also being pulled out onto the taxiway. The MiG-29s, or Allah's Power, as they were referred to by the ground crew, were the finest aircraft in Libya's inventory. Only two years old, the planes were a match for anything the West could put into the air.

Qasmi pulled his fighter into the lead position, waiting for the others to follow. They had five minutes before takeoff to join in the battle, time enough for the MiG-23s ahead of them to deplete the Americans' weapons.

EC-141 QUEEN BEE

At first Oliveri couldn't believe his eyes. He didn't want to. The upper portion of his square radar screen had lit up with four new red triangles, enemy blips. He focused on them for a few seconds to be certain the electronic readouts, which were not always perfect, were not deceiving him momentarily.

"Colonel Madison, we have trouble," Oliveri called out, loud enough for everyone to hear.

At once, Madison was looking over his air boss's shoulder.

"I show four . . . six . . . eight new targets at low altitude and airspeed. They're taking off from the Libyan base in the north."

Madison studied the screen for a moment before speaking. "Aujila! Those aircraft are taking off from Aujila. Damn it all to hell!" Madison's crimson face matched his heated emotions.

"I now show *twelve* targets heading one seven three. Altitude 2,000 feet and climbing, speed 360 knots and increasing. Range 192 miles," Oliveri reported.

"What's the status of our aircraft?"

"I have three F-15Es armed with AMRAAMs and Sidewinders refueled at ready. One more of the same in a few minutes. We can always pull sixteens off the Weasel mission to support the F-15s," the controller suggested.

Madison took a deep breath, letting it out slowly. "I want a wall in front of those enemy fighters. Put the F-15Es out in front and back them up with the sixteens. Whatever air defenses remain at Madadhi will have to be taken out by the A-10s."

Oliveri's gaze, now glued to the screen, picked up four more targets. Sixteen enemy fighters were now headed toward Madadhi.

34

Delattre slid the sun visor down over his eyes and watched the refueling boom retract back toward the KC-10, leaving a white trail of evaporating kerosene in its wake. As he slackened his grip on the stick, his fighter floated away from the huge tanker. The pilot banked to the north with full tanks of fuel, listening to the radio chatter in his helmet.

"Cadillac Lead, this is Queen Bee. Do you copy?" the EC-141 radioed.

"Copy, Queen Bee . . . this is Cadillac Lead," Lieutenant Colonel Shawn L. Murphy flying the number one F-15E of Cadillac package, called back.

"Lead, we have a Scarlet situation. Repeat, Scarlet situation. Radar contact on sixteen targets. They're fighters. Bearing due north." Oliveri's matter-of-fact tone then gave the inevitable order. *"Cadillac package to engage and splash."*

A Scarlet situation was not good news. The code word was only used to indicate that their combat situation could deteriorate extremely fast.

Delattre quickly ran the math in his head. Each of the four Strike Eagles carried six air-to-air missiles, four AIM-9M Sidewinders and two AIM-120 AMRAAMs per aircraft, for a total of twenty-four. *Queen Bee must be in dreamland,* he thought. *There's no way we could kill all sixteen in one pass.* Twenty-four missiles against sixteen targets didn't work in live combat.

Colonel Murphy obviously agreed, radioing, *"We're going to need some backup. I only have twenty-four missiles."*

"Roger, Lead. You'll have backup. Blow through 'em and the F-16s will follow and clean up the leftovers," Oliveri said. *"Cadillac package, take a heading of zero one niner. Bogeys at angels 8, speed 400 knots and increasing. All aircraft go to Squawk Mayday."* Each pilot was

354

instructed to switch the IFF signal to emergency position boosting power output.

Colonel Murphy turned the Hazeldyne APX-76 IFF transponder to the proper setting and swept the sky around him. He could see his number two and three aircraft flying off his right and left wing each several hundred yards away. *Where's Delattre?* he wondered.

"Cadillac four, report your current position," he radioed.

"Cadillac four . . . eighty miles south. Just off the tanker and heading north."

"Hurry and get your ass up here."

"Roger. On my way."

Delattre jammed the throttles into afterburner, turning his fighter into a winged rocket. Fifteen seconds later, the F-15 broke through Mach 1 at 6,000 feet above the sandy floor of the desert.

"Hold on. We're going back for more," Delattre said to Baxley.

As the three-ship formation dropped through 18,000 feet, Murphy's WSO called out, "Radar contact bearing zero one seven. Altitude 12,000 feet and climbing. Range ninety-seven miles . . . 980 knots and closing."

"Roger, Lead. Two is a copy."

"Three copies."

The Libyans were fast approaching and if Murphy wanted to get the upper hand, his squad should fire first. They would have to go head to head with only three aircraft. Delattre, in Cadillac four, would have to sort things out when he entered the area.

Each of the E model's radars looked at four separate formations of aircraft flying at staggered altitudes and speeds. Murphy realized that if the Libyans forced the Americans into attacking one or two of the four ship formations at a time, it would leave the other MiGs free to penetrate the Americans' air defense zone. Once this was done, any one of them could take out the command and control structure, in this case the EC-141. If they succeeded in taking out the EC-141, the rest of the force would be blind and deaf.

Before reacting, the colonel forced himself to thoroughly study the blips on his radar screen, watching the flight paths of the enemy aircraft. Murphy was going to have to break formation and order his pilots to fight separately. His insides screamed that it was against the rules of engagement. Each F-15E would have to attack one four-ship group, leaving the last configuration of MiGs for Delattre or the F-16s, whoever arrived first.

"Range eighty-seven miles," his WSO reported. "Closure at 1,147 knots."

Murphy tugged on his oxygen mask before speaking. "This is Cadillac Lead. Weapons cleared. Three go right . . . two go left . . . break."

The two other F-15Es snapped into opposite hard banking turns toward their targets.

"Lock up the AMRAAMS," Murphy ordered.

"Yes, sir." His backseater, a first lieutenant named Hank Bowes, did as he was told, manipulating the radar controls, trying to get a lockup. He switched the radar from a supersearch to a vertical scan mode, instructing the computers to lock onto the first aircraft to enter the target cone.

Murphy scrutinized the vertical situation display on the upper left side of his instrument panel. The lead group of fighters was below him to the left, five degrees. The VSD gave a distinct picture of what was happening ahead of his fighter, along with alphanumeric target data such as IFF codes, aspect angle, closure rate, the enemy's ground speed, and altitude. When a target aircraft came into range, the colonel could transfer the data to the HUD, where the symbology would reference steering data and weapons information.

"Lockup one," Bowes announced. "Lockup . . . two." The F-15E's big APG-70 radar was powerful and sophisticated enough to track twenty-four targets while simultaneously locking onto and attacking six others. "I'm getting some clutter," Bowes warned. The Libyans were trying to jam his radar by ejecting large bundles of radar-breaking chaff.

"Their radars shouldn't be able to see us this far out." Murphy looked over his shoulder and then back at the HUD, watching his airspeed increase. At 570 knots, he opened the air brakes, slowing his aircraft slightly.

"Three degrees right bank. Give me some more airspeed." Bowes wasn't the pilot, but in his own mind he commanded the fighter.

"Situation?" was all Colonel Brice Madison asked.

"Cadillac's taking them head on," Oliveri responded, keeping his eyes on his scope.

"That damn Irishman had better not get himself killed," Madison muttered, thinking of his friend Murphy.

"The fifteens are coming in from above and closing at 1,230 knots . . . distance 62 miles. Too far for missile lock." The air boss proceeded to keep the colonel informed of the unfolding events.

Madison returned his attention to the computer screen. If Murphy played it cool, and chances were he would, he would wait until the Libyans were forty miles away before cutting loose with his AMRAAMs.

At 2,000 feet Qasmi turned on his MiG-29's radar to standby and nosed up ten degrees, gaining altitude quickly. He was sure the Americans' AWAC surveillance aircraft was already tracking his position. But he thought it foolish to give them an added advantage with his radar blasting at full power.

"Arm your weapons," he ordered his wingmen. "Break on my command only."

The radar return was oblong and extremely strong. He had seen it before. Several targets flying in close formation, trying to confuse his sensors. He waited for several passes of the radar so the computers had enough data to break out the return and identify the number of targets. In fourteen seconds he had his answer.

"Four new contacts bearing zero two one."

Madison knelt down next to Oliveri. "Shit! That makes twenty altogether."

"These have a different radar cross section and they're moving faster. Speed 470 knots and climbing." Oliveri looked at his commanding officer. "There's a good chance they're MiG-29s."

Madison, stunned, dropped his gaze to the floor for a moment before responding. "Tell the pilots to move us on the back side of the track and lower our altitude to 18,000. If any of those MiGs get within forty-five miles of here, order them to take this bitch down to the deck quick."

"Yes, sir." Oliveri felt his adrenalin surge.

"And radio the C-17." The colonel stood, but kept his voice low. "Put them in a holding pattern until this is sorted. The last thing I need is a couple of MiGs using our ground team for target practice."

CADILLAC LEAD

"Forty-three miles. I have a strong radar return and lock." Bowes downloaded the targeting data into his two AIM-120 internal tracking and guidance computers. *Strange,* Bowes thought. *If the Libyans did know the Americans were out in front of them, they didn't show it.* Their flight path hadn't changed in the last few minutes. They were continuing to fly straight and level.

"Forty miles . . . a little more clutter."

"Queen Bee, this is Cadillac Lead. Start the buzzer." Murphy requested that the EC-141 start jamming the Libyans' communications channels.

The moment the launch signal flashed, Murphy squeezed the weapons release button, sending the first missiles on their way. He pulled the fighter up and away from the dual smoke trails twisting away into the distance.

"Lead . . . fox one, fox one," Murphy radioed, telling his wingmen he had just launched two radar-guided missiles.

"Cadillac two . . . fox one, fox one." The second Strike Eagle had launched his AMRAAMs.

"Cadillac three . . . fox one, fox one."

Six AIM-120s were airborne, their semiactive radar seeker heads following the reflected electronic signals coming off each individual target.

Oliveri watched the red computer-generated lines representing the missiles migrate away from each F-15E at Mach 4. The computer's telemetry told him that each of the missiles was operating normally as each one locked onto its target. He observed the first AIM-120, within nineteen miles of its target, adjust with a midcourse correction, weaving ten degrees right and then five degrees back to left.

"Go active . . . go active," Oliveri quietly coached, anticipating the small, internal radar head's switch from semiactive to terminal homing.

"I show two active missiles. Let's blow and go, man." Bowes powered down the APG-70 radar to fifty percent power. No use in frying them. "Break high and away."

Murphy broke high to the left. The AMRAAMs were now on their own, being guided by their internal active radar.

Traveling at 2,800 mph, the first missile detonated a few feet above the lead MiG-23 pilot's cockpit. It ripped it to shreds in a blaring burst. The force disintegrated the nose section, and the debris breaking loose floated downward. The central portion of the airframe tumbled end over end, spewing fire and smoke.

Out of the corner of his eye, the pilot flying the number two MiG saw the explosion as his flight leader vanished in an orange ball of flames. He reacted by pushing his stick left as the second missile erupted below and to the right of him. The aircraft rumbled and shook as fragments of the warhead tore into the wings and tail section. His first thought was to save the aircraft, as he worked the rudder and stick, trying to steady the fighter. However, the hydraulic lines were cut in several places and, as the pressure went to zero, the stick froze. The fire warning light came on and the disabled MiG tossed over, nosing down toward the ground. It entered a flat, counterclockwise spin.

The pilot wrapped both hands around the ejection handle, straightened his back, and armed the firing mechanism. He yanked the ejection cord between his legs, blowing himself safely out of the stricken MiG-23.

One hundred and sixty-five miles away, in the heart of the EC-141 combat control center, Oliveri and Madison watched with silent moral support for the flying Eagles.

"Splash one. Splash two." Two blips faded from Oliveri's screen, victims of Cadillac's AMRAAMs. He watched as four more of the advanced missiles streaked toward their targets to the east.

Seconds later, missiles three and four hit their marks, remarkably bringing the number of downed fighters to four. His attention shifted to the left side of the screen.

"Come on, let's go for six," he implored.

Missiles five and six, fired from Cadillac three, were the last to reach their target area. The fifth AIM-120, which was tracking a MiG on the western part of the formation, abruptly swerved to the west and pushed over for the ground, disappearing off the radarscope. It had missed its target by several thousand yards. The targeting telemetry told Oliveri the radar seeker head had malfunctioned, losing contact with the MiG.

The sixth missile was still on course, actively tracking. At 2,000 feet above the enemy fighter, the AMRAAM went into a 10 G right-hand turn and started to dive. It slammed into the MiG from above, turning the high-tech fighter into pieces of flying wreckage and killing the pilot on impact.

"Twenty-seven miles and closing. Weapons check," Bowes said, watching his radar screen as two of the remaining targets started to swing left away from them.

Murphy switched from the radar-guided AMRAAMs to his four AIM-9M Sidewinder heat seekers. The targeting cursor on his HUD led him to where the Libyans were banking away from him. He checked his airspeed and altitude, putting the nose back on the targets. The Sidewinders didn't have the range of the AMRAAM. He would have to close in several miles in order to get a lockup. His plan was to take one of the MiGs out with a surprise frontal shot, come around, and kill the one left from behind.

"Seventeen miles," Bowes said.

Murphy's entire body tightened with his adrenalin pulsing strongly.

Second Lieutenant Qasmi activated his NO-193 radar. He positioned the multimode pulse-Doppler to scan at thirty pulses a minute up to an altitude of 15,000 meters. As the radar came on-line, he saw what he was looking for in a matter of seconds. A large number of planes filled the airspace ahead of him. He was on a direct course.

Qasmi zoomed the scope out to a maximum beam width of sixty-two degrees. He witnessed several of his fellow pilots disappear from his radarscope ahead of him. The American fighters were heading straight for the MiG-23s.

"IRST up. Arm your weapons." Qasmi ordered the three other MiG-29 pilots to bring up their passive infrared search and track sensors. "Break formation . . . NOW."

The Libyan fighters fanned out, leaving Qasmi as their point man.

"Confirm, Cadillac package. I'm showing four new bogeys, Fulcrums, at flight level 16,000 heading your way." Oliveri's sensors had picked up the surging of the MiG-29s' J-band radar.

"Roger, Queen Bee, I see them." Bowes already had contact, showing the new bogeys seventy-three miles to the north. His RHAW system had identified the radar as a class one threat.

Murphy heard the call but presently had other things on his mind, mainly the two MiG-23 targets out in front of him.

"Range to target," the colonel demanded.

"Ten miles and below us. Negative on enemy radar transmissions. You should see them any time." Bowes's RHAW equipment was quiet except for the distant throbbing tone of the MiG-29s' search radar.

Murphy concentrated on the HUD but couldn't shake the nagging feeling that the MiG-23s should be using their weapons radar. *Why aren't they using their radar?* he thought, trying to find them. He swept the sky looking for any signs that would give away the position of the planes. He continued his pursuit, every mile drawing him closer to the apparent enemy.

"Eight miles." Bowes didn't look up from his radar screen. "Seven miles, Colonel . . . six miles . . . two bogeys straight ahead. They just activated their radars. Lock up! They've got lockup on us!"

Still looking at the screen, Bowes watched the two smaller radar returns speeding toward them. Both of the MiG-23 Floggers had just launched on them. "Break hard right. I show a—"

Murphy smashed the stick to the right, putting the fighter in a 7.2 G turn, breaking off his WSO's sentence. The force of the turn pushed each man deep into his ejection seat as the F-15E cut through the sky, coming across the front of the two missiles.

"Where . . . are . . . they?" Murphy grunted, struggling to speak under the force of the Gs. It was a strange language only fighter pilots spoke and understood.

"To the north, to the north. Two missiles," Bowes grunted back.

Murphy used all his strength to turn his head and look to the left. As he did so, he brought the fighter out of the turn, letting the Gs drop off. The sudden turn had stripped the fighter of energy; his airspeed was below 400 knots. He caught sight of two telltale smoke trails in the distance. Only one was coming at him.

Murphy was annoyed he hadn't seen the Libyans first. Putting the F-15E into full military power, he turned into the first missile, popping two decoy flares behind his fighter, and then released a bundle of chaff. He banked slightly and dropped the nose, giving him a wide picture of the anterior. With the downward movement his airspeed began increasing rapidly.

The nine-foot missiles, radar-homing AA-2-2 Atolls, were not advanced enough to get a solid frontal lock on the narrow radar profile of the F-15E. They were designed to pick up and track the large radar cross section of a B-52 bomber. Both AA-2-2s tracked toward the stronger radar cross section of the chaff cloud, missing the American fighter by a quarter mile.

Murphy traced the ashen smoke paths of the missiles back to their source.

"There you are, you bastards!" he shouted, nosing his fighter up. Two dark spots were banking toward him at high speed.

With the missile threats gone for the moment, Murphy put his aircraft into afterburner, closing the distance between the targets. At four miles, he heard the dull chirping of his Sidewinders trying to lock up.

Oliveri's tactical display was animated with turning aircraft and supersonic missiles flying in every direction. It resembled a high-tech video game, only you couldn't control any of the action.

He had counted three more MiGs slain, casualties of the lethal F-15E and Sidewinder combination. That meant that the Strike Eagles had destroyed half of the first wave in less than ten minutes. Three neon-blue, computer-generated blips appeared, moving across the lower part of his display screen. The F-16 Wild Weasels had arrived. If any of the MiGs leaked through now, the Falcons would be there to greet them.

Oliveri diverted his attention to the MiG-29s, which were just minutes away from entering the air defense zone. Fulcrums carried an impressive

weapons mix, including the long-range AA-10 radar-guided and medium-range IR homing air-to-air missiles.

"Cadillac package, be advised. Fulcrum threat, north, in two minutes.
Repeat, Fulcrum threat, north, in two minutes."

The third MiG-23 cut across Murphy's nose a half mile away, nosed up,
and struggled to climb.

His reactions were quick and precise. He popped the speed brake, cut
right and left, bleeding off energy, and slid in behind the MiG. The
launch tone in his head was sharply clear.

"You watch number two . . . number two," the colonel instructed
his WSO. Murphy put more pressure on the stick. Even though he had a
solid, even launch tone, he couldn't fire the Sidewinder, knowing it
might not separate cleanly from the weapons pylon. He had to let the Gs
fall below 3 and then let loose with the missile.

"He's breaking left. Number two's trying to come around behind
us." Bowes was twisted halfway around in his seat watching the other
MiG-23.

Murphy now had his hands full. The first MiG suddenly dove over and
banked to the right in a 5 G turn, releasing a string of hot flares.

The F-15 easily followed, turning with the older aircraft, slicing
through the flares. As he turned with the MiG, his G meter was fluctuating between 3.5 and 4.5.

"Hurry up and kill him, Murph. This other guy's coming around,"
Bowes warned.

The pilot of the MiG-23 was fairly good, not what he was expecting.
Murphy reminded himself to concentrate and just be patient. He waited,
throttling back a little.

The MiG was slowing, losing energy rapidly, as it banked back to the
left, trying to evade the American. In an effort not to lose his maneuverability, the pilot swept the wings forward and forced the nose down
again to pick up some needed airspeed. The MiG, going too slow,
abruptly stalled at 500 feet in front of Murphy.

"Bull's-eye!" Murphy had him. He put his thumb on the weapons
release button, leveled the fighter, and checked the G meter. It went
from 3.8 to 1.5 in a split second.

"Thirty seconds, Murph. He's going to have us in thirty seconds." The
second MiG was lined up directly behind them.

In the heat of the battle, the pilot flying the number one MiG panicked, putting his fighter into afterburner, and tried to break high to the
left. It was an incredibly stupid thing to do.

The Sidewinder flew right up the MiG's tail pipe, blowing off the left
wing and horizontal stabilizer. As the aircraft emerged from the fireball,

Murphy banked up out of its path. He watched the canopy blow off, the pilot eject and separate from his seat.

"Break left!" Bowes shouted.

Murphy looked over his shoulder as he rolled his fighter into a hard left turn. He caught sight of the second MiG above at a forty-five-degree angle coming straight for him.

Experience told him he had only one choice. He drove the throttles forward and the stick back at the same time, putting the fighter into a steep nose incline and releasing decoy flares. He watched his airspeed increase and the altitude climb as the sheer power of the engines propelled him upward. The HUD clicked the rising altitude, 12,000 . . . 13,000 . . . 14,000. He was ascending at 500 feet a second. It was impossible for the single-engine MiG to keep up.

At 15,000 feet, Murphy drove the stick back, barreled over, and thrust the nose down. Just as he had anticipated, the MiG-23 was lingering below, straining to maintain his pursuit.

"Fulcrum threat . . . twenty-five seconds," Oliveri called out.

Murphy's lap restraint dug into his groin as his big fighter headed for the ground. He opened the speed brake, waiting for the distance to close. At 430 knots and 2,000 feet from the MiG, he hurriedly launched a Sidewinder. It shot out toward the brown-and-green MiG.

Qasmi's IRST system was picking up the first soft heat signatures of multiple aircraft in the foreground. He flipped the radar to the standby track mode. The radar was off but was now bound electronically to the IRST system. It would automatically reactivate if the heat source in the IRST system was somehow lost.

Qasmi switched his two AA-10s, code-named Alamo-Bs, from standby to autolock. The liquid nitrogen–filled supercooled seeker heads weren't powerful enough to detect any of the far-off targets from this point. The targeting data on the HUD told him the distance to lock was thirty-four kilometers.

Because of the sharp angle of attack, the Sidewinder only had a lock for a short time. The MiG-23 broke north as the missile sped past, failing to explode.

"Ahhh," Murphy protested, not believing his eyes. He kept the F-15 pointed straight down, picking up airspeed. The MiG-23 Flogger flashed by his canopy several hundred yards to the east. He could see the writing on its side and tail section.

"I'm blowing past, you stay with him." The colonel needed his WSO's eyes to execute his plan of diving, going into max G, pulling up and then firing from below.

"I got him. Just fly this thing and get him before those twenty-nines get here."

Murphy let the airspeed build to 700 knots before beginning his latest strategy.

"Here we go," he groaned, pulling back on the stick.

The stinging Gs increased relentlessly as the F-15 shuddered to climb, 4.5 . . . 6 . . . 7.5 . . . 8 . . . 8.5. At 9 Gs the Strike Eagle bottomed out at 10,780 feet.

Each man breathed in the cool oxygen to keep from losing consciousness. Bowes was wrenched back with the force of the Gs, feeling the vertebrae in his neck crack and pop. Squinting, he preserved eye contact with the Libyan fighter.

Oliveri punched the audio button, cocked his head, and listened, trying to confirm what his computer was indicating. One of the MiGs had just shut down its radar. He could see its radar return on the scope. It just wasn't broadcasting anymore.

"Cadillac package, Fulcrum threat now . . . Fulcrum threat now!"

The two IR signatures on Qasmi's scope were a brighter orange. Range to targets was twenty-seven kilometers. A quick scan of the instruments confirmed that everything was operating properly.

Four thousand feet above him, silhouetted against the deep blue sky, Murphy saw his prey. The black spot of the MiG-23 frolicked in the center of his HUD as he again easily closed the distance between the target.

"Lock, baby. Come on, lock up," Bowes urged, not relishing the prospect of still playing with this guy when the big guns showed up.

Murphy listened to the throbbing launch tone. As the MiG broke left and started to push over into a dive, its hot engine inadvertently came into perfect view.

"Now!" To ensure a kill, the colonel sent both of his last AIM-9Ms darting toward the MiG. Each missile had a solid lock and tracked straight for the enemy aircraft. The MiG weaved, trying to elude them.

With the cool morning air as a background, the heat-seeking heads of the two remaining Sidewinders indulged him and struck their target dead on.

* * *

"Damned Americans," Qasmi muttered, as another target fleeted from his scope. There was only one left. The IR target on his scope was now a bright red. He was in weapons' range.

35

"Queen Bee, this is Cadillac Lead. Splash one more MiG. We're winchester at bingo fuel. Headin' for home plate," Murphy called. Winchester signaled he was out of missiles.

"Roger, Lead. Watch your back. I show a Fulcrum twenty-three miles north of your position."

Murphy leveled the Strike Eagle at 13,000 feet, banking to the southeast on a heading of 153. He put his fighter into afterburner and felt the exhilaration of several swift Gs push him back into his seat. The KC-10 tankers were 112 miles away.

"Cadillac Lead! THREAT . . . THREAT!" Oliveri warned, as calmly as he could. *"Missile launch at your six. No radar . . . no radar."*

Murphy, automatically going defensive, shifted his fighter out of afterburner into a steep climb.

"Get me a visual, Hank," he ordered.

Captain Delattre, piloting Cadillac four, was three minutes to the south at 18,000. He had heard the threat call and was now racing toward the two aircraft shown on his radar screen. The IFF transponder indicated that his flight leader was between him and the Fulcrum.

"Lead, this is Four. I'm three minutes out. Hold tight."

"Roger, Four. Quit screwing around. I'm as naked as a bear's ass up here."

As the missile disappeared and fell to the desert, Qasmi advanced the throttles, taking his fighter closer to the target area. The bluff had worked. Firing one of his four AA-10 Alamo-B IR homing missiles was futile, but he had hoped he could force the American to react just as he did. In an effort to evade the missile, the F-15 stayed in range and the pilot was not going to escape.

The soaring MiG-29 broke through the sound barrier with ease. The target grew closer on the IR tracking screen. The American fighter had slowed and was unknowingly turning across his beam.

"I don't see anything," Bowes called out in frustration. "There's nothing out there."

Murphy keyed his mike. "Queen Bee . . . Cadillac Lead. Where's the threat now?"

"Negative on missile threat," Oliveri answered, as the missile fell from his screen. *"I show one Fulcrum eighteen miles and closing fast. North bearing one seven three. Get the hell out of there, Murph."*

"Cadillac four, that Fulcrum is yours. I'm gone." The colonel banked back to the southeast and added power.

The Libyan swung his fighter to a new heading of 173 degrees, following the red IR signal centered on his screen. Just a few more seconds. Two of his AA-10s were locked up. His forward airspeed was 1,300 knots. Twenty-three kilometers . . . the distance closed, 22 . . . 21.

When his HUD flashed 20 KM TO TARGET, Qasmi responded by opening the speed brakes, dropping his flaps, and throttling back. The MiG shuddered in protest, slowing as briskly as it had accelerated. Qasmi's shoulder straps strained against his weight pushing forward. His helmet forced his head downward as he strained to watch the dropping airspeed—1,000 . . . 900 . . . 850 . . . 780. The instant he dropped below Mach 1, Qasmi fired. Two AA-10s, one from under each wing, rocketed away. Qasmi cleaned up his fighter, putting it back into afterburner, chasing after his missiles and heading straight for the American.

Murphy heard the new threat warning from Queen Bee as the first missile came into view behind his fighter.

"This fucker is pissing me off!" the colonel exclaimed, as both men searched the skies over their shoulders. "There it is." He spotted the tiny white speck quickly gaining on them.

Returning his attention to the HUD, Murphy gripped the throttles tightly. It would be useless to try and outrun the heat seeker. About all he could do was attempt to outturn it.

"Evasive action . . . ready?" Murphy checked his WSO.

"Ready," Bowes answered, keeping track of the missile.

It was a planned sequence of events they had practiced many times over the training range.

The missile made a high, arcing turn toward the F-15E three quarters of a mile away. It swerved east and west as if trying to reacquire its target, then banked directly for the fighter.

Bowes waited, estimating the range out loud. "Twelve hundred yards . . . a thousand . . . eight hundred. Break hard *left!*" he shouted, hitting the flare dispenser button.

Murphy reacted instantly, throwing the F-15E into a biting 7 G turn away from the Alamo. The Strike Eagle, sharply cutting to the east with the force of the turn, slammed both men deep into their seats.

Bowes grunted, "Break . . . break," waiting for the heat seeker to lose its lock on their fighter.

The Alamo's nose-mounted thermal head commanded the top and bottom frontal control fins to swivel left, forcing the missile into a twisting corrective turn. The AA-10 strained under the energy of 12 Gs as it continued to track the target.

Bowes realized he had called the break too soon. *I hope this works,* he thought, trying to remedy his error by sending a flood of flares streaming out behind the aircraft.

The plane quaked in the burst of the explosion, hurling both men forward. Bowes's helmet hit the top of his instrument panel, shattering the sun visor, cutting his face. He lifted the remaining section up and wiped away the loose pieces. Immediately, he began hunting the surrounding sky. *Where's that second heat seeker,* Bowes thought, knowing that an unseen threat kills.

Murphy leveled the fighter and watched the fire warning light blink on for the left engine. To his surprise, the aircraft was still responding to his commands.

"Number two inbound! Hold—" Bowes yelled, as the second AA-10 hit the left rear section of the Strike Eagle, blowing off the tail section.

The F-15E clattered to a stall, hanging suspended, before rolling over to the right. The cockpit filled with the sweet smell of smoke from an electrical fire, as the aircraft began to spin toward the ground.

"Eject . . . eject . . . eject!" Murphy shrieked as he blasted out.

Delattre, approaching, saw the twin bright flashes of the ejection rockets from the descending aircraft. Two parachutes popped open, drifting toward the surface.

"Cadillac one is down. Cadillac one is down," he radioed. Taking his thumb off the button, he cursed himself for not getting there sooner.

*   *   *

Qasmi let his MiG continue to climb, not taking time to celebrate his victory. With the first target rapidly spiraling down, he brought his attention back to the screen, spotting an aircraft entering the area eighteen kilometers to the south. His IFF readout told him it wasn't Libyan.

He checked his weapons. He had one AA-10 remaining, along with two smaller AA-2 short-range heat seekers. His MiG was slightly higher in altitude above the American as they headed straight for each other, closing at over 1,200 knots.

"All right, come and take your shots," Qasmi said softly.

"Bearing one eight niner. AMRAAM up, going for radar lock," Baxley shouted.

"I have him," Delattre calmly answered back, seeing the radar blip. His HUD indicated the two fighters were six miles apart.

"Radar lock . . . AMRAAMs ready," Baxley said. He was quiet, expecting the missiles to fly any second. "Radar lock, sir. Fire when ready."

Delattre didn't respond, and instead continued his trek toward the MiG 29.

"Repeat, radar lock. Let's smoke this guy and get the hell out of here," Baxley implored, wondering what his pilot was waiting for.

"I want to see him when I shoot him down." Delattre's voice was menacing as he switched from AIM-120s to AIM-9M Sidewinders. He adjusted his sun visor, trying to get a visual on the enemy aircraft.

"Two miles." Baxley didn't question the man's decision.

A light gray spot suddenly appeared on the horizon.

"Tally ho! Right, one o'clock," Delattre called, as he banked 180 degrees. The two fighters blasted past parallel to each other less than a thousand feet away.

"Holy shit!" Baxley exclaimed, as the unexpected pass took him by surprise.

"Don't lose him." Delattre brought his stick back and the F-15E climbed straight up, gaining several thousand feet of altitude.

"He's behind us . . . to the right," the WSO grunted.

"That's your first mistake, asshole!" Delattre shouted, coming wings level at 19,000 feet, curling the Strike Eagle over. He snapped his head around to see the gray and blue fighter arcing up after him.

"Gotcha, sucker." Delattre added power and scissored left, then right, putting his nose on the MiG. Two of his Sidewinders locked up.

*   *   *

Qasmi hadn't taken his eyes off the F-15E. He watched the larger aircraft climb straight up, push over, and attempt to bring its weapons to bear in a series of wrenching turns.

In response, Qasmi pushed the throttles to neutral, hauled back on the stick, and waited for the nose to push up and over. The G meter went to 6 a split second before he felt the pressure jar his body. He kept the stick back, forcing the agile MiG to complete the pushover.

As its airspeed slowed, the MiG started to quiver, striving to stay airborne. On the edge of a stall, Qasmi jammed the throttles forward, somersaulting the MiG over on its back. The stall warning light flashed on and off.

Qasmi hung suspended, his body held in place by the nylon restraints. Then the Fulcrum squeezed out enough forward airspeed to complete the maneuver. For an instant he lost sight of the American below him.

Delattre, miscalculating his opponent's ability, immediately went into afterburner and climbed past the MiG to the east only 500 hundred feet away. He grinned, remembering a saying an instructor had warned him never to forget: A pilot's arrogance that there is no one better than he will be his own downfall. As the Fulcrum nosed over and headed for the ground, Delattre continued his climb, breaking through 22,000.

"He's pushing over . . . heading for the deck." Baxley's reliable eyes were still locked onto the enemy warplane.

Qasmi waited for his airspeed to hit 240 knots before he started to maneuver again. Descending through 17,000 feet, he lit the burners and pulled the stick toward him. The MiG's nose turned up, slowly at first, and then more quickly as the afterburners kicked the aircraft into action.

The American was above and climbing away from him. It was a classic fighter strategy: Gain the advantage by rising above your opponent, then turn on him for the kill. Qasmi snickered to himself, wondering if the pilot was so stupid as to think his MiG-29 couldn't climb and turn with the F-15.

With his left hand still on the throttles, he used his thumb to switch from his last AA-10 to the shorter range AA-2 heat seekers. Doing so, he automatically engaged the helmet sight system used to aim the AA-2s. Two sensors below his HUD picked up the movement of Qasmi's head. Wherever the pilot looked, the weapons' computer would follow, signaling the missiles in which direction the heat-seeking pixels should move to lock up.

Qasmi saw an opening and, with the American still above him, he slid in behind the F-15, putting the HUD's targeting cursor on the fighter.

"He's behind us. Break now!" Baxley cried out.

Delattre pulled out of the vertical climb upside down, allowing his WSO to maintain eye contact with the MiG. He was 3,000 feet above the Fulcrum, heading to the southeast. He rotated his head, catching sight of the fighter beneath him.

The MiG was in perfect firing position. The launch tone grew even, signaling that the AA-2s had locked on a heat source. Qasmi hesitated, continuing to force the stick back, gaining a few more degrees of angle on his adversary. With the F-15 on the edge of his HUD, but still well within the missiles' targeting cone, he pushed the button twice, sending both missiles toward the American fighter.

"Missile launch . . . two launches!" Baxley shouted.

Delattre banked slightly to the south and pushed the nose over toward the ground. He rotated the stick, putting his nose right on the MiG. He could see the silvery smoke trails of the missiles racing toward him. Instinctively, he slid his fighter farther to the south. The sudden glare in his rearview mirrors assured him the sun was directly behind him.

The first missile obligingly veered to the right, confused by the heat of the rising morning sun. The second AA-2 continued to track for a few more seconds, then it, too, swerved toward the larger target of warmth radiating from the sun.

Qasmi swore as the graceful F-15 vanished in the glowing yellow rays. He averted his gaze before being blinded and engaged his GSh-301 thirty-millimeter cannon. He tilted the MiG back in the direction of the target. The orange circle of the gun sight and laser range finder materialized in the center of his HUD. Qasmi worked the stick and throttles, attempting to put his gun sight on the dark gray speck coming straight for him. The HUD flashed, DISTANCE TO TARGET—778 METERS.

"Second mistake, jerk. One more and you're out," Delattre said, cutting through the smoke trail of the second AA-2. The MiG was 1,500 feet below him. The two aircraft were closing on each other too fast for him to try and lock up his AIM-9Ms. Delattre switched to guns and pressed the firing button for the twenty-millimeter cannon. He extended the speed brake and jinked the fighter right and left.

The circular gun sight flashed red, telling Qasmi the targeting laser had found the range. He squeezed the trigger just as the F-15E turned.

"Death to you," he whispered, not letting off the firing button.

The first few tracer rounds darted past Delattre's canopy, missing his fighter by only twenty feet. He pulled back on the stick.

As the nose of the F-15E reached up, the Fulcrum appeared centered in the HUD's gun sight and in that split second Delattre depressed the trigger. A stream of armor-piercing bullets burst out the left side of his fighter, heading directly for the MiG.

"That's your third mistake. You're out, asshole!"

The sprinting rounds gashed into the front of the MiG-29, shattering Qasmi's cockpit window and instrumentation. Fragments of shattering bullets, Plexiglas, and metal sliced into his body and face. He was blinded by the debris and his own blood.

Qasmi's hand slipped off the stick as his mind told him to return fire. A swell of pain shooting through his upper body prevented him from locating the stick. Another cannon round smashed into the tail section of the MiG, causing it to vibrate wildly.

Qasmi attempted to clear the blood from his eyes, searching for the ejection handle. The Fulcrum fell from the air, tail first, spinning as it picked up speed. Black smoke poured out of the engine intakes and nozzles as a few flames of fire erupted behind the cockpit. A long stream of white fuel gushed from the MiG's main tanks.

Delattre pitched the nose down, falling in behind the battered fighter. Just as he keyed his mike, the MiG exploded, showering the sky with segments of the fiery Fulcrum. He hesitated, studying the area for a while, not seeing a parachute.

"Splash one MiG-29," he radioed in. "Have you gotten Cadillac Lead out of the area?"

"One of the sixteens was vectored to patrol the area where they went down. S and R Pave Low reports they're in the area to pick them up now," Oliveri answered.

36

Six red blips, representing a mixture of MiG-29s and MiG-23s, were breaking out of the west, trying to slip through the battle area.

Oliveri and Madison watched the electronic images of two missiles, one from an F-15 and the other from an F-16, streak across the computer screen, blowing two more of the escaping MiGs into multiple pieces. Colonel Madison was more than relieved that the unexpected invasion had turned out to be a minor setback. The entire engagement had lasted only fourteen minutes.

"All right, so much for the Libyan air force. Cancel Scarlet condition and get those A-10s in there. Inform Ghere and his men I want them on the ground in twenty minutes." Madison glanced at his watch. "This whole thing will be over within an hour."

"Redhawk Lead . . . Queen Bee. The skies are clean. Do your stuff, hotshots, and sweep things up," Oliveri instructed the six A-10 Thunderbolt IIs orbiting east of Madadhi Air Base.

"Roger, Queen Bee. This is Redhawk Lead. We copy and we're rolling thunder."

A-10 Redhawk Package

The flight leader of the A-10 Redhawk package changed radio frequencies so he could talk with the other five aircraft under his command. "All right, it's our turn. Follow me in and let's mop up the resistance."

Redhawk lead was flown by Captain Gaines W. Bristol, Jr. The brawny, redheaded Clemson fan had grown up in a tiny town near Spartanburg, South Carolina. Born into a poor family, his father had taught him and his five brothers how to shoot squirrels and possums for

373

food. Bristol soon became a deadeye with a .22 rifle. That had been thirty years ago and he still hunted with sharp accuracy. Only today, the targets fired back and his rifle was one of the most powerful weapons ever to be strapped to an airplane, a thirty-millimeter Gatling gun.

Unlike most pilots in the USAF, Bristol had spent all of his flying career behind the stick of the A-10, first as an instructor, and now as the leader of what he regarded as the best damned bunch of Warthog drivers in the world.

The A-10 was an unusual-looking aircraft, with straight wings and the engines mounted above its fuselage and twin tail. The Warthog had been built for a highly specific mission, killing tanks. But the aircraft's versatility made it invaluable to missions such as the one they were about to undertake. It was slow and heavily armored, able to endure the pressures of a battlefield for several hours, providing air cover for ground troops. Its single-barrel Gatling not only could destroy a tank, it had the capability to take out difficult targets such as machine-gun nests and one-man bunkers.

Coming out of the holding pattern, Bristol dropped his A-10 down to 300 feet and started to follow the contour of the desert, flying west. The other five A-10s were strung out behind him, spaced fifty yards apart. They moved with such exact rhythm, they seemed to be hooked together like cars rolling over the winding tracks of a coaster.

Captain Bristol referenced the moving tactical display map below his HUD. The display was linked to a GPS transponder, which showed Redhawk company's preprogrammed flight path into Madadhi, plotted to skirt the known air defenses. Occasionally, Bristol, as a matter of routine, would compare one of the desert landmarks to the satellite-enhanced paper map, verifying that they were on course. The slightest course change could prove fatal.

"Attack pattern Delta on my order," Bristol radioed in his twangy voice. They were seven minutes from entering the target area.

PATHFINDER TEAM ALPHA: ICEBOX

Vasquez, lying stomach down on the ground, froze as a camel spider, or wind scorpion, as the Arabs called it, sauntered across his hand. It scurried up his forearm, stopping at the crease in his fatigues at his elbow. Its big yellow eyes came in contact with Vasquez's, daring him to move.

The sergeant watched it, not shifting his gaze. Firsthand experience told him the brown-and-gold-striped meat eater had an antisocial nature and a nasty bite. Its fangs had inserted a venomous local anesthetic to the point Vasquez hadn't felt it munching on his leg while he slept during a training mission in Egypt. It had left a deep, ugly scar and a definite animosity for the little buggers.

But being positioned the way he was, there wasn't a lot he could do but remain stationary. If he jumped, an alert terrorist could possibly spot his movement.

"Vasquie . . . F-15s inbound. They're going for the power supply," Rath whispered, turning to see the standoff between his sniper and the hideous creature. He quietly tugged a dead twig from a nearby bush and slowly brought it under the spider. As it bit the wood, Rath shoved it under a nearby rock.

"Thanks, man. I hate those things." Vasquez's face was contorted as a shiver raced down his spine.

"I know," Rath replied. He was the one who had found it having breakfast on Vasquez's leg that early morning in Egypt. "Maybe you should change perfumes." He turned back to his spotting scope to gaze at the far eastern side of the bunker complex.

The F-15Es were going to bomb the section of the complex believed to house the camp's electrical generators. If they were wrong, they'd be digging through a pile of smoking rubble looking for the bodies of dead American astronauts.

The suddenness and power of a Strike Eagle hitting a ground target was an enthralling sight to witness, as long as you were on the right side of the bomb. A lone GBU-15, a guided 2,000-pound slick bomb, struck the hillside 2,500 yards away. The ground rumbled a fraction of a second as the bomb easily sank through several meters of earth. It exploded five yards below the surface, causing a cloud of swelling dust and a booming roar of destruction. Rath and Vasquez watched as the ground operations got under way. They both knew the last half of the game would determine the victor.

MADADHI AIR BASE

Ajami briefly lost his balance as he felt the ground shake furiously, and an earsplitting crashing rumbled through the bunker complex like an earthquake. The explosion came from the eastern part of the complex, where the diesel and jet fuel were stored.

He looked up at the ceiling, expecting another bomb to be on its way. Ajami did not stop to think that the Americans might value the lives of three people more than ensuring the warheads did not leave the camp. The overhead lights swung back and forth, flickering on and off, then went out. The bunker complex was darkened, the generators demolished in the blast.

"Don't move!" Ajami shouted, waiting for the emergency batteries to kick in. "Stay where you are!" Seconds later, several of the lights glimmered back on. He turned to see his men lying face down on the ground inside the fortress built around the shuttle.

"Get up, you fools! The Americans have no way of knowing which bunker the shuttle is in. Your orders remain, don't let anyone near it."

Ajami rushed into the main tunnel. It was filling with smoke, dust, and debris. "Americans . . . *infidels.*" He turned and ran toward the command room.

Jibril was picking himself up off the floor. "Get one of those choppers in here at once, Sergeant. This operation is over. We're getting out of here."

"You are going nowhere, coward," Ajami announced, entering the room.

"You are a fool, Ajami. You cannot believe Nittal would let you have those warheads—" Jibril went for his pistol.

Ajami pulled his nine-millimeter first, shooting the captain squarely in the face. The Libyan's body was thrown backward by the drive of the slug ripping through his head. He was dead before hitting the ground, his body twitching from the massive head wound.

The terrorist swung the gun around in a half circle at Lieutenant Mizrahi and the two other men left in the room. One of the technicians didn't move. The other, in front of the radio, abruptly swiveled around. Ajami fired again, the bullet from his weapon hitting the man in the throat. He then shot the last technician in the chest. Ajami pointed the gun directly at Lieutenant Mizrahi.

"Get on that radio and call in those choppers . . . now!" The stunned lieutenant did as he was told, stepping over Jibril's limp body to the communications console.

The sound of gunfire reverberated through the tunnels. *The moment has come,* Majeed told himself. He couldn't wait any longer. He walked into the holding cell and stood for an instant looking at Duke and Andrea. They were both standing, staring at him. The Americans looked tired and afraid. He was sure they expected him to kill them.

"Majeed!" Kamal shouted, spotting the man by the entrance. "Let me out of here. You need me now. I can help kill the Americans. Let me fight alongside you and redeem myself."

Majeed walked into the center of the holding area, probing Kamal's features as he moved closer. Over the last three years he had watched and listened to this man plot the murder of Jews around the world, listening to him brag about the Israeli soldiers he slaughtered in Lebanon and the heinous schemes that killed or injured Jewish women and children. A strong emotion surged in the depths of the security officer's soul. Majeed turned away from Kamal and pulled a key out of his pocket. He unlocked the Americans' cell door, then walked inside. Duke stood in front of Andrea as the soldier motioned for them to walk in front of him, firmly saying, "Come with me quickly and do not make a sound."

"Majeed, don't be a fool. You know I would never betray Ajami. I would not be in here if Jibril had not filled his mind with lies," Kamal pleaded further.

Majeed swung around, staring into his eyes.

"Where are you going?" Kamal asked suspiciously.

"You will never leave this place alive, Kamal." Majeed's voice seethed with hatred. His expression stern and unwavering, he spoke harshly. "I will see to that. Every man here will die for the crimes you have committed against my people."

"Against *your* people . . . what are you saying? Are you crazy?" Majeed closed his eyes, sighing heavily. "You are a pig, Kamal." He swung the cell door completely open and followed the two Americans out, swiftly shutting the door behind him.

Duke took Andrea's arm and moved her ahead of him, turning to look at the Palestinian and then at Majeed. He had a feeling there was something odd going on and he wondered if he should try and wrestle the soldier's gun away, sensing there was no one else in the area.

Majeed, seeing the mistrust and doubt in Duke's eyes, spoke softly. "I am not who you think. Be very quiet . . . and you must do as I say if you wish to live."

"You are the traitor, Majeed! It was you all along," Kamal hissed loudly in Arabic.

"Do not go with him, American! He is going to use you as a shield to escape like a coward," he urged, his mind working deceitfully well.

Majeed pointed with his gun to the doorway, repeating, "Hurry, we must leave now." Duke stood his ground, not sure what he should do. Trusting either man seemed stupid.

"Take his gun, American!" Kamal shouted, heightening the tension. Majeed stepped back away from Duke. He slowly pulled the sling of his Uzi off his shoulder, saying, "I will not harm you." He placed his gun on the floor. Keeping his eyes locked with Duke's, he walked up to the American and cautiously untied his hands. Duke felt the ropes fall away from his wrists. He rubbed his wrists, trying to get the blood flowing again. Duke then removed the restraints from Andrea as she looked over, relieved at the soldier retrieving his weapon.

Kamal backed slowly away from the bars, quietly stooping over his filthy mattress.

"You are not one of them?" Andrea's blue eyes softened as she saw the man in a different light.

"Come, I do not have time to explain. We must hide—"

"Majeed." Kamal's eyes, full of fire, shone out of the shadows of his cell.

Duke and Majeed lifted their gazes back to the prisoner at the same time. Kamal raised his right arm, firing a bullet from the rusty .45. Majeed's arms flew open as it struck him in the upper chest. He fell against Duke, knocking him off balance, then fell to the floor.

"Now you die, American pig." Kamal leveled the pistol at Duke's head.

Duke flinched as two bullets sailed by his ear, striking Kamal in the stomach.

The husky Palestinian stumbled a few steps backward. He looked at his stomach, watching his clothing turn dark red from blood.

"Allah help me." Kamal raised the pistol again, trying to fire. The hammer fell on a dead round. His body hunched over toward the ground as two more shots rang out. The bullets passed through him, impacting the far wall.

Duke spun around to find Andrea holding Majeed's rifle, bluish smoke curling out the end of the barrel.

"Help me, Duke. This man is still alive." She dropped the Uzi and leaned over Majeed, smoothing the hair from his forehead.

Duke sighed and shook his head, letting out a slight jittery breath.

"Where to?" he asked, fetching the discarded weapon.

Majeed struggled to his feet with Duke and Andrea on each side of him. "Down the tunnel. I know a place where we can hide. It should be safe there until this is over." Majeed winced as blood bubbled out of his wound with the movement.

"I'll dress that when we get there." Andrea's fervent glance over to Duke let him know she was worried about the man's condition.

SPECIAL TECHNICAL OPERATIONS CENTER, PENTAGON

Harris watched the final KH-14 pictures fade from his screen. The hot IR spot, marking the newly formed bomb crater, was the last image to disappear.

"That's it, sir. We just lost our picture. The Keyhole is out of range now. *Shit.* I was hoping—"

"Captain, you did a good job. Madison and the EC-141 can handle the rest," Clark said firmly, understanding the disappointment he heard in the man's voice.

"The EC doesn't have an IR capability. If those last few mobile SAMs start to move . . ." Harris' voice trailed off. The implications of his last statement were clear.

PATHFINDER TEAM ALPHA: RUSHMORE

Rodriguez slipped on his headset and nodded to Sergeant Lange that he was ready. The communications specialist plugged in the cord and punched in the prearranged radio frequency, hooking them in to the A-10s.

"Redhawk Lead, this is Rushmore. Do you copy?" Rodriguez said.

"Loud and clear, Rushmore," Bristol replied.

"Stand by for Stay Safe signals, Redhawk." Rodriguez glimpsed back at Lange. "Activate the systems, Sergeant."

Lange flipped the switch for the SSN-28A1 ultra-low-frequency "stay safe" transponders, located inside his radio transmitter. His communications antenna began broadcasting a continuous coded radio signal. The signal was encrypted and hopped from frequency to frequency, via a computer program, making it impossible to jam. It tied directly into the A-10s' navigational and weapons targeting computers.

The signal, picked up by the A-10s' radio receivers, plotted a ground team's position on the pilot's computer-generated map. It then communicated with each aircraft weapons system, alerting it not to fire missiles or rockets on their location. The system had been developed out of Desert Storm to cut the number of friendly fire incidents. However, like anything human or mechanical, it wasn't foolproof. A pilot could still fire manually, but it was better than nothing.

"One's up . . . two is up," Lange said. The number two transponder was Rath's and Vasquez's position.

"Redhawk Lead, we're on-line. Do you see us?"

"Roger that, Rushmore. We see two. You confirm?"

"Roger, Lead. There's two. Be advised, the area directly across from number one position is hot. Two ragheads with hand-held SAMs. There are also two mobile triple-A sites on the east end of the runway," Rodriguez reported.

"Appreciate the info, Rushmore. We're three minutes from the party. Redhawk out."

Rodriguez stared out to the east. "I wonder if these camel jockeys have any idea what an A-10 can do."

On the southeast side of the base, out of the OP's surveillance area, a mobile SA-6 SAM started its engine and drove out from under its camouflage covering and several large boulders.

C-17 SKY FIRE

"We're ninety miles northeast . . . fifteen minutes from the objective. Check your weapons," Lieutenant Ghere announced roughly.

Collins made sure the twenty-round magazine was in place in his M-16, but didn't chamber one. He stared ahead as several of the soldiers left their seats and climbed into the various vehicles in the rear section of the cargo bay.

"Mr. Collins, when we land things are going to happen extremely fast. Remember to stay with me," Ghere shouted.

"Yeah," Collins said. "Plan to."

At 24,000 feet the radar image of the mountains north of Madadhi was clearly distinct. Oliveri studied the image patiently. Cadillac four confirmed that six tanks had crossed the bridge at Al Kisawa before destroying it. Oliveri's WAS/MTI had only been able to follow them for a short time. The T-72s moved away from the bridge and onto a road, cutting through several high sierras. If his estimates were right, the Libyans should be breaking out into the open at any time. They would then have to make a run for it, crossing eighteen miles of flat, dry desert before reaching the west side of Madadhi.

"Thunder Bolt bait," Oliveri replied, as the first black-and-white likeness of six T-72s and two ZSU-23-4s appeared on his screen. "Redhawk Lead, Queen Bee here. I am tracking eight ground targets moving southeast. Down-loading now." Oliveri dumped the new data into the Warthogs' navigation equipment.

The skies were filled with only the sounds of the desert as Major Wazir led his squad of T-72 main battle tanks out of their final turn. His map showed he was twenty-four kilometers northwest of Madadhi. The sandswept road ahead of him stretched out across the vast openness. This would be the most vulnerable part of their mission.

As the last ZSU-23 pulled out from around the turn, Wazir opened up a channel to the other tank commanders. "Diamond formation, behind me . . . maximum speed." Wazir closed the hatch securely and settled into his seat as the tank lurched forward with massive power. In under a minute, they were moving across the desert at forty-four kilometers an hour. The two Shilkas lagged in the rear, following the tanks.

*   *   *

Bristol's first reaction was to go after the tanks on his own, but his better judgment ruled that out. Stay on course, he lectured himself. The T-72s were secondary. His finger hit the communications button.

"Redhawk Lead to Redhawk five and six. We have six T-72s accompanying a couple of Shilkas that want to play ball. You two go hit some runs in."

"Five's in."

"Six is in . . . on the way to the ballpark."

Bristol dropped another fifty feet and leveled at 210. He glanced at the instrumentation; his number two engine was running a little hot. He made a mental note to watch it before looking back at the HUD. Coming into view he could see the two large mountain ridges ahead of him. *The runway must be between them,* he thought.

"Two, this is Redhawk Lead."

"I'm listening, Redhawk." Bristol's wingman, Dennis Sanders, was flying in the number two spot.

"I'm going to come in at about 300 feet. Give 'em some time to look me over and see what fire I can draw. I want you, Three, and Four to stay behind me high enough to get a fix on anything that shoots."

"Understood, Redhawk Lead," Sanders replied. *"I'm in."*

"I'm in," called Three.

"I'm in," echoed Four.

Bristol jinked his aircraft hard right and then left, checking the feel of his plane. He increased his airspeed and popped up to 500 feet. The runway was still not in sight.

Rodriguez held the binoculars as steady as he could once he spotted the shadowy dots in the sky.

"A-10s inbound. Let Rath know."

Lange responded immediately, telling Rath to be prepared.

"One minute out, Vasquie . . . get ready," Rath told his sniper while he kept looking to the east. Coming into view was a single aircraft.

Vasquez pushed the safety off his rifle and placed the cross hairs between the two rocks where the elusive terrorists were located. He could see only one of them. The man was sitting with an SA-16 across his lap. It was apparent he had not noticed the jet yet.

Ajami approached the holding area with his pistol cocked and ready. He had anticipated this moment. He would use the astronauts to subdue and escape the American force.

As he walked closer, his heart seemingly stopped. There were no guards outside the entrance.

"Majeed! Why are there no—" Ajami came to an abrupt halt just inside the room. Majeed was no longer there. The Americans' cell was vacant and his heart pounded furiously. He frantically searched the area, his eyes coming to rest on Kamal lying face down on the ground.

"Kamal, where are the Americans? Where is Majeed?"

Kamal didn't answer, lying motionless as his leader shouted through the bars. "I demand you tell me where the Americans are!" Ajami's blazing stare finally focused on the pool of dark blood pooled around the man's face and upper body. Ajami aimed his pistol at Kamal's lifeless body, pumping three rounds into it. The sound of the gunfire rippled through the room.

"Ahhhh!" Ajami bellowed, running out of the room. "Find the Americans! I order everyone to find the Americans!"

Andrea, Duke, and Majeed dropped to the floor as several armed guards stormed past the door of the pilots' briefing room. They heard several men shouting as they crawled toward the rear of the room.

"Here . . . we can hide in here," Majeed gasped, pointing to a door in the back.

Duke peeked up through the wire-reinforced window in the center of the door, making certain it was okay for Andrea to open it. Seeing that it was safe, they hurried into the room and placed Majeed flat on the floor, closing the door behind them. Duke pulled a chain hanging from the ceiling to turn on the light bulb. They appeared to be in a small closet containing brooms, towels, and stacked cardboard boxes. On one wall was a free-standing metal bookcase with four shelves on which were some cleaning and medical supplies.

Andrea went to the shelves, looking for something of use to help the wounded soldier. Duke crouched in a corner out of her way.

Andrea knelt down next to Majeed and carefully unbuttoned his brown khaki shirt, exposing the wound. She took sterile pads she had found and piled several of them together directly on the wound to absorb the bleeding. Taking another pad, she poured alcohol on it and began cleaning the skin around the area. Andrea's hands were steady and firm as Majeed gazed up into her face.

"Who are you?" Duke asked. "Why did you rescue us?"

The man flinched with pain as some of the alcohol seeped into the wound. "My name is Yitzhak . . . Rafi Yitzhak. I am a . . . a Mossad officer."

"Mossad . . . Israeli intelligence," Duke replied, holding the rifle in his hands.

"That's why you didn't—" Andrea began.

"That explains nothing," Duke interrupted her. "Why should we believe you? Why didn't you help us sooner? We don't even know what's happened to Willie, Andi." Duke stood, his anger rising at their mistreatment.

"I am sorry, General, but you must understand I couldn't do anything sooner. My efforts would have been futile out here in the middle of the desert. It would only have put you all in more jeopardy. It was best to wait until your troops arrived."

"How is it you came to be in such a trustworthy position?" Duke wasn't sure if this man had something to gain by deceiving them, but he wasn't just going to follow him blindly.

"I was placed here when they started to build . . . Ahh—" he cried out, taking a deep breath as Andrea wrapped torn pieces of towels around the pads, waiting to secure them in place when he exhaled. "Eight, nine months ago."

"Why would you allow this to happen? If you're Mossad, why haven't you stopped these people?"

"It is much more complicated than that, General. It was only a few days ago I was promoted. I would have gained valuable information for my country to be able to annihilate this camp. Abu Ajami is smart and distrustful. One mistake and my mission would have been finished. Ajami and his men would still be free to continue their horrendous acts on my people and yours." Majeed sat up, resting against the cloth bag filled with laundry Andrea had placed behind him.

"For heaven's sake, back off a little, will you? You know he was hurt getting us out of that cell. And you're the one holding his gun. I believe him," Andrea chided Duke, as she tried to adjust the man's position so he could breathe easier.

"I tell the truth." Yitzhak smiled at Andrea, then looked firmly at Duke. "Because of this assignment, there is no way I could contact my country. I am just as much a prisoner as you."

Duke searched the man's face, remembering the story Andrea had conveyed to him of her interrogation. She had not been harmed or molested by him. And it was Ajami who had ordered Willie taken away.

"Majeed . . . Yitzhak . . . whoever the hell you are. Where is my pilot?" Duke asked, not offering any apologies for his mistrust. He worked the action on the Uzi, making sure it was loaded.

"In an aircraft hangar. He was still alive when I saw him last. It's located in the main bunker along with the shuttle and bombs."

Duke and Andrea exchanged glances.

"How do I get there from here?" Duke scooted over to Yitzhak, waiting for him to give him the details.

"You must not go there!" The man choked and coughed, catching his breath. "Ajami has it wired with claymore mines. Guards are posted around the shuttle, armed with heavy automatic weapons. There is no way you will be able to enter."

"What other defenses does he have?" Duke asked, sorting things through in his mind. He knew what he had to do and no one was going to stop him.

"Ajami is removing one of the warheads . . ." Yitzhak closed his eyes, knowing he must give Duke the help he needed. He proceeded to give directions to the bunker and outlined the ground defenses Ajami had put into place both inside and out of the bunker complex. When he finished, Duke asked one more question.

"Yitzhak, what is Ajami planning to do?"

"He will try and flee with the warhead. Several escape tunnels have been constructed. But they are small; I do not think he will be able to move the warhead through them." His breathing became shallow and his bronzed face was growing pale.

"All right." Duke crawled to the door and opened it a crack, peering out into the briefing room.

He turned and looked at Andrea. "There's going to be a ground team coming soon. When they land, all hell will break loose. I want you and Yitzhak to stay here." Duke reached over and pulled Yitzhak's pistol from his holster, handing it to Andrea. "Use it if you have to. Even if it's to finish him off. That's an order."

"Yes, sir," Andrea answered, taking the gun and thinking Duke was unduly worried about Yitzhak.

Voices erupted as the outer door of the pilots' briefing room opened and two guards entered. Duke reached up, turning out the light, and held his hand up for silence.

"One A-10, three o'clock." Rodriguez could see the forest green aircraft approaching out of the east. Streams of condensation were curling off its wingtips.

"Icebox, confirm." Rodriguez radioed.

"I see him," Rath responded. *"And we're ready."*

The A-10 bounced up then down as it cut through an air pocket rising 500 feet off the desert floor. Bristol hardly noticed with the speed he was traveling. His attention was on the tactical warning display. A hostile radar had just come up.

"Spike. Ten o'clock. Near. Looks like an SA-6," Bristol called out a warning. The display showed the radar beam coming at him. The AN/ALQ-131 identified the radar frequency and began to jam it.

The seasoned pilot knew the air defense pod, located under his left wing, would confuse the Gainful's radar long enough for his waiting team to clear the area.

"Roger that, Lead. We'll clean it up," the number two Warthog replied.

Bristol could see the black runway ahead of him, with the mountains on each side. He inched the throttles forward and leveled at 600 feet. He was now flying a live decoy.

"Rushmore . . . Redhawk lead. Fifteen seconds out. Stand by to mark targets," Bristol radioed to the Pathfinder OP.

"Roger, Redhawk. We have visual of area," Rodriguez responded.

"All right, assholes, give me what you got," he said into his oxygen mask.

As if someone on the ground had heard him, bursts of twenty-three-millimeter cannon fire spouted into the air. The first rounds missed by fifty yards as Bristol watched the tracer rounds floating up ahead of his jet.

He scanned his instruments again. The only hostile radar was coming from the SA-6 site behind him. The antiaircraft guns were operating visually. He dropped the nose and added power, coming in under the second and third barrage of fire.

"There's one," he grunted, under the strain of the Gs. Bristol let his airspeed build, continuing the dive. When his altitude hit 200 feet, he pulled the attack jet straight up into a spiraling climb. The cannon sent several hundred armor-piercing bullets chasing after him.

"They're moving, Lieutenant," Vasquez whispered, still waiting for the right moment. "I can't get a shot." He could see the two guards through the scope. Each was carrying SA-16 shoulder-fired SAMs. Vasquez followed them as they shifted between several huge boulders, trying to get into position to fire on the A-10.

"Come on, a little to the left," Vasquez urged, forcing himself to be patient for the choice shots.

Rath had spotted a ZSU-23-4, draped in camouflage, sending controlled bursts of fire into the air. It was located directly east of their position. He relayed the info to the OP and continued his scanning.

"More enemy fire . . . to the right, sir." On the edge of Vasquez's scope he saw puffs of white smoke.

Rath instantly identified another ZSU-23.

Bristol watched the G meter swing from 1.0 to 6.5 in the time it took him to think about maneuvering right then left. He threw the throttles to the stops and pointed the nose of his A-10 upward for the infinite sky above. Behind his jet, four decoy flares floated to the ground.

He had done his job. The targets were located, at least the ones that wanted to fight. It was now time to get the hell out of the area, regroup, and attack with the other A-10s.

He topped out of the climb at 5,000 feet and turned to the south, checking the condition and handle of his aircraft.

"Rushmore, Redhawk Lead. I show two triple-A threats. Do you confirm?" Bristol asked.

"Roger that, Lead. Two twenty-threes. We have them marked. Also, be advised we're watching two SA-16s above center bunker."

"Redhawk two, three, and four, this is Lead. We have three hot targets. Formation November two-follow-two. Linkup in three minutes."

They were going to come in pairs. Bristol and his wingman would lead, helping take out the SA-6 site first, although they would need some help from one of the Wild Weasels. The other two A-10s would follow, taking out the other threats.

Bristol leveled his Hog and backed off on his airspeed, trying to conserve fuel.

The noise of jet engines combined with the clamor of multibarreled cannon fire filled the air before either of the Shilkas could react. Major Wazir's worst nightmare was about to come true. His squad was caught out in the open without any air cover and no place to run or hide.

He snapped his head around in time to see a lone American A-10, only fifty feet off the deck, silver puffs of smoke exploding out its nose.

"Air attack, air attack," Wazir shouted over the radio.

He gave the order to break formation and turn into the enemy aircraft, just as one of the Shilkas exploded in a shower of sparks. The sound of the American A-10's GAU-8/A seven-barreled cannon was unique, and the pelting of the depleted uranium penetrator rounds pulverizing his antiaircraft artillery turned his stomach.

"Break left . . . break left!" Wazir cried. He heard the rumble of another aircraft coming from the right behind him. The second ZSU erupted into flames, a missile smashing into it dead center.

"Move this thing. I need more speed," Wazir shouted at the driver.

The American jets popped back up from low level, zeroing in on two more targets. They flew by as Wazir watched helplessly as two of his tanks were ripped to shreds. In under thirty seconds, his already diminished ground force had been reduced to half its original strength.

The two A-10s crossed in front of him, speeding up into a vertical climb. They curved up and high overhead, toward the northeast, behind the mangled troop.

"Move out. Ready your antiaircraft guns!" the major roared, knowing the A-10s would return. The four remaining tanks doggedly lurched away, leaving the burning, empty hulls of metal behind them.

37

Duke pressed up against the wall, grasping the rifle tightly to his chest as the door slowly began to open. A dull gray light filtered in as he held his breath. He slid his finger down on the trigger.

Andrea and Yitzhak were huddled in the rear of the cramped closet. A row of dingy, water-stained cardboard boxes, stacked several feet above, blocked the incoming light from illuminating their presence as the door opened further.

Duke eased the barrel of the rifle up. The smell of the man's body odor reached his nostrils.

"Ramilah . . . Ramilah!" a voice from outside the closet hollered at the approaching, shadowy figure. Yitzhak stifled a cough and Andrea glanced nervously at the doorway.

The guard stopped moving, turning his head, and Duke impulsively lifted his rifle.

"Ramilah, we must move on, quickly. There is no one here in this room." The man speaking was standing at the doorway waiting for his comrade to join him.

"I'm coming," the guard acknowledged. He turned his gaze from the well-lit briefing room, quickly looked over the closet, then exited.

Duke let out a prolonged sigh, thankful the man had not heard his heart thumping in his chest.

"Oh God, that was close," Andrea whispered.

"Yeah. How's he doing?" Duke felt drops of sweat roll down his neck. Andrea looked at Yitzhak's chest, seeing that the bandages were soaked through. She touched his arm; it was cold and clammy.

"I think he's going into shock. Help me lay him down and get his feet up." Andrea and Duke worked to get him situated.

"Take off his pants," Duke ordered, unzipping his own sweat-stained flight suit.

"Huh?" Andrea asked, looking up to see Duke stripping down to his underwear.

"I'm not going to be able to get around in my clothes." Duke reached over and picked up Yitzhak's shirt as Andrea awkwardly struggled to pull off his pants. Duke put on the shirt, feeling the moist blood from the man's wound.

EC-141 QUEEN BEE

The radar images were unmistakable. The fast-turning rotors of a helicopter reflected radar waves like a mirror on a summer day.

"Four . . . five . . . six," Oliveri counted from his seat on the EC-141 command and control aircraft. "I have six Mi-24s airborne."

"Headings?" Madison asked.

"Four are heading away to the northwest. The other two are heading toward Madadhi. Shall I delay the C-17?"

"No. The A-10s and F-16s will have to handle them. What's the ground team's ETA?"

"Seven minutes."

Madison paced, thinking and talking at the same time. "What's the fuel status of the fleet?"

A couple taps of the buttons and Oliveri answered. "Average, about an hour and fifteen minutes per aircraft."

Madison slipped on his headset, linking him to the C-17 transport. "Ghere, this is Madison. The area is still hot, but I need your men on the ground. If we wait any longer, it will give the Libyans a chance to regroup. Make sure you move in fast."

"Understood, sir," Ghere responded.

"Alert the tens and sixteens about the threat of those choppers. And move us in closer," Madison said to Oliveri.

Madison can smell blood, Oliveri thought.

The dots were growing larger. Wazir wrapped his hands around the dual grips of his 12.7-millimeter antiaircraft gun, swiveling the independent command turret around to the north. His T-72 was in the lead, racing over the sand at its top speed of fifty kilometers an hour. The rough terrain of the desert made it difficult to keep the heavy gun leveled at the targets.

"On my command," Wazir ordered the other tanks, the wind whistling threw his hair.

"Now!" he shouted, with the targets still over two kilometers away. *The bullets will fall short, but it might keep them away,* Wazir thought. The gun vibrated in his grip as he shot at the lead aircraft, rotating his position.

Wazir observed the first and then the second A-10 bank away from the incoming fire and push up into a steep climb. The two aircraft gained altitude, rapidly eluding all the hits. The two tank killers were now directly above them. Wazir let off on the trigger, waiting for the A-10s' next move as they continued to barrel over the sands.

Both jets scissored back and forth, falling abruptly toward the ground. The lead A-10 opened fire, spraying the tank directly behind Wazir with deadly cannon rounds. The T-72's diesel fuel ignited with a blast. The armor on top of the tank was no match for the penetrating bullets as they cut into its engine compartment. The T-72 veered right, then rolled over. A final explosion erupted, silencing the screams from within the burning tank.

Wazir maintained his fire on the lead A-10 as it pushed nose up and banked sharply, climbing away. The tracer rounds from his gun swirled around the retreating plane, not making any contact.

"Where are the MiGs?" Wazir shrieked into the air, shaking his fist at the sky.

He turned his attention to the second jet, but the American fighter was exiting the area, having already destroyed a fourth tank. Only Wazir's and one other tank were still operational as they sped the last ten kilometers to reach Madadhi.

A-10 REDHAWK ONE AND TWO

"Let's do it. Jammers off. Pop up," Bristol ordered.

"I'm with you, Skipper." Dennis Sanders, the wingman, stayed in tight on the left side, following his flight leader. Each pilot turned their radar-jamming equipment to standby.

Bristol came off the deck at 430 knots and lodged the throttles all the way forward. The Warthog climbed, breaking through 2,000 feet fifteen seconds later. Bristol swung to the right, heading straight for the radar emission being transmitted from the base of the nearest mountain. His tactical warning display showed that the SA-6 was painting his aircraft with a search and track frequency. It hadn't locked up . . . yet.

Bristol adjusted his radio so he could talk with the F-16 Wild Weasel orbiting at 6,000 feet to the east.

"Corona two, three, Redhawk Lead. We're in place and he's looking at us. You copy?"

"Yeah, I copy that, Redhawk. I see the bastard. When he locks up,

break a few thousand yards to the south. I don't want this HARM to zap you."

"Roger, two three." While holding at 2,000 feet, Bristol banked slowly away from the SA-6 site, then straight back toward it. His instruments told him the Libyans were taking a good, hard look at him.

The TWD changed with the radar frequency. The SA-6 site had just locked up on both A-10s. If their strategy worked, the radar operator was thinking they were one target.

"Corona two three . . . magnum." That was their signal. The F-16 had just fired.

"Break," Bristol radioed to Sanders.

The two A-10s split, one rolling left, the other right, each diving for the ground.

Bristol watched his HUD: 1,200 . . . 1,000 . . . 850. At 600 feet, he banked to the south, looking in the rearview mirror, hoping to see the impact of the HARM. A bright flash told him the missile had hit its mark. His eyes went to the TWD. It was quiet.

"Hot damn, one SA-6 has just been terminated." He added power and came round to a new heading of 203. They still had two Shilkas to take care of.

PATHFINDER TEAM ALPHA: RUSHMORE

The A-10 orbiting above the base was going to get his ass shot off if he didn't listen to him. Twice he had dived at the target, missing it each time.

Rodriguez was frustrated, trying to direct the pilot to a location he could not see clearly.

K. C. Franklin, piloting Redhawk three, was pushing his luck. Every time he dove at the target and missed, the enemy gunner was able to adjust his aim point. Franklin was the youngest member of the A-10 team, with only 1,200 hours of experience. But what he lacked in seasoning, he made up for in raw determination, sometimes to the point of putting himself in danger.

"Give me the location again," Franklin demanded.

"To the east . . . east of the largest rock formation. It's covered in brown camo. I can see the top of the damn thing, but that's all."

"Roger, Rushmore. Talk me in."

Rodriguez watched the A-10 twirl over and dive, pointing his nose straight for the ground. He put his binoculars back on the target as a shower of smoke and broken rocks exploded to the north of the ZSU-23.

The pilot was off the mark . . . again.

"Redhawk three, walk it south about thirty yards and you have the son of a bitch," Rodriguez called.

Redhawk three didn't respond; he had his hands full.

Yellow muzzle flashes turned into pink tracer rounds as the four guns of the ZSU came alive, filling the sky with hot flying metal.

"Break—" Rodriguez didn't finish the sentence. He watched several of the cannon rounds smash into the front section of the Thunderbolt, ripping several wide gashes in the nose section. Two more rounds burst into the canopy of the A-10, shattering it.

"Pull up, man, pull up," Rodriguez urged.

The A-10 continued its spiraling dive. A twenty-three-millimeter round had penetrated the pilot's helmet, killing him instantly. The aircraft crashed into the ground a hundred meters away from the ZSU-23 it had been trying to exterminate.

Everything seemed to stop. Rodriguez's gaze lingered on the burning wreckage. "Oh God, I should have—"

"Inbound," Lange called out, interrupting his thoughts.

Rodriguez focused back on the target area. Redhawk four was heading toward the ground, flying through an assault of twenty-three-millimeter flak, several tracer rounds narrowly missing his cockpit. With his guns blazing, Redhawk four pinpointed his mark. The ZSU-23 vaporized in a fiery explosion. The area of dried grass erupted into an inferno. Lange and Rodriguez watched the pilot pull up and away from the target, climbing to the southeast.

"Redhawk four . . . target destroyed," Rodriguez radioed somberly.

The pilot didn't respond.

Cannon rounds pummeled the earth directly in front of the T-72 tank. Major Wazir felt his tank come sliding to a stop. A cloud of dust swirled up around him.

"What are you doing?" he shouted in surprise and anger as the driver and gun operator emerged from under the hatch directly below the 125-millimeter gun.

"I cannot aim with the way you are driving!" Wazir shouted.

"You are mad . . . you will kill us."

"Get back to your post!" Wazir howled. "I *said* back to your—"

The shock of the cannon fire threw Wazir forward, rocking the mighty tank. He grasped the antiair gun and used all his strength to turn it toward the approaching A-10. Two torrents of fire struck the side of the T-72 below the main turret. The armor-piercing bullets slashed into the hard steel of the tank, blowing one of the treads off and spewing chunks of molten metal in every direction.

Wazir's legs stung with pain as the bullets continued their path, severing them both at the knee. He dropped to the platform of the turret and could see the A-10 flying in closer. Wazir closed his eyes, not wanting to see or feel the next burst that would end his life.

The black smoke twisting up from the wreckage had a sobering effect. Bristol had witnessed Franklin's destruction. He came level at 4,500 feet flying over the southeast portion of the base. *It could have happened to any one of us,* he thought.

"Shut up," Bristol said to himself under his breath. It didn't happen to any one of them. Lieutenant K. C. Franklin had been a good man. He had been the youngest in his squadron and had a wife with two small children. Franklin had always worked hard and never gave up. This fight had cost him his life, and Bristol decided those pricks on the ground were going to pay.

"Rushmore, Redhawk one. I want a laser designator on my next target area. If it's not out in the open, I'll blast the son o'bitch into the open."

"Roger, Lead," Rodriguez answered with the same conviction.

He picked up the AN/PAQ-1 laser target designator, placing it on his shoulder. The riflelike device weighed fifteen pounds and would illuminate a ground target with an invisible homing laser up to 4,000 yards away. He put the cross hairs of the designator on the ZSU-24 and depressed the trigger. A digital readout told him the target was in range, 1,059 yards away. He confirmed the distance a second time and keyed his radio.

"Redhawk Lead, target is marked."

Bristol clicked the communication switch twice, confirming the transmission. Rolling to the east and losing altitude quickly, he checked his systems. He was still carrying a full load of six AGM-65A laser-guided Maverick air-to-ground missiles. Designed for tanks and heavily armored vehicles, the Maverick was Bristol's first choice of weapon.

"Two, I'm going in fast. Stay with me or stay out of the way," Bristol curtly informed his wingman.

"I figure you'll need someone to cover your backside. I'm in," Sanders answered, turning with his flight leader as they skimmed across the desert floor at 400 knots, banking toward the center of the complex.

* * *

Ajami pushed the Libyan ahead of him. "Move it, Mizrahi."

Shmuel Mizrahi kept his hands in the air. "This is not going to work, Ajami. Who is going to fly your helicopters?"

"You and your men."

"It is too late. The Americans are here; we will be shot down. Your plan has failed."

"I *will* escape with it. Do you hear me? I will." Ajami's fear that Mizrahi's words were true overwhelmed him. Mentally, he was on precarious ground.

"We should give ourselves up and be thankful to be alive." Mizrahi felt he would be safer with the Americans taking him hostage than with the frenzied man behind him.

Ajami stopped in his tracks, irate at the man's cowardice. *This is Allah's will. He has done this to test me, to make sure I am worthy.* A feeling of false confidence came over him. His emotions suddenly seemed focused and his thoughts clear. Allah had given Ajami this. It didn't make sense that Allah would now take it away. He felt that Allah would never let him die.

"You are of no use to me now," Ajami said calmly, relieved to feel a new understanding of his situation. He pumped two hollow-point bullets from his nine-millimeter automatic pistol into the back of Mizrahi's head.

"Take a heading of two one seven," Sanders radioed. *"I'm coming in from the south."* Redhawk two broke formation, crossing behind his flight leader and going to maximum power. Attacking a ground target at two opposite compass points prevented the enemy from assaulting both aircraft.

"Roger, Two. I'm holding back." Bristol throttled back, letting his wingman fly around him. His head had cleared a little. Sanders was correct; they needed to do this right or another A-10 would be burning on the ground.

Booting the right rudder, Bristol steadied his aircraft at 300 feet. He estimated he was three miles from the target. He turned the Pave Penny laser seeker on and started his climb. When he hit 1,500 feet the symbology on his HUD changed, signaling that the Pave Penny had acquired the laser designator target.

Bristol didn't waste a second. He locked on two AGM-65A Mavericks, then glanced at the MFD to confirm the seeker head was looking at the same target he was.

"Rifle, rifle," the pilot sang out, as his two missiles left the rail on the port side.

Boosted by Thiokol TX-481 solid-fuel rocket motors, the two Mavericks began climbing up and away. At 2,000 feet, each missile leveled, now having a clear picture of the laser mark below.

Bristol broke hard left, putting his Warthog into a gut-wrenching turn toward the deck. He let the front windscreen fill with the desert before pulling up and away.

Rodriguez heard the hiss of the missiles, keeping the laser locked onto the target. The ZSU-23 was cradled inside several large boulders. He didn't dare move the cross hairs from what he believed to be the upper section of the ZSU.

Just a few more seconds, he thought. *Just a few more.* The Shilka opened up, expelling a myriad of gunfire. Rodriguez's heart jumped as he picked out the camouflage netting trembling around the big weapon. He was aiming too far to the right. He jerked the AN/PAQ-1 target designator left and steadied it, hoping he wasn't too late.

The Warthog came out of the banking turn, wings level at 500 feet. He was looking down at the MFD in his cockpit when suddenly the picture blurred as if the missile had been pulled off course.

"What the hell!" he shouted over his radio.

The control surfaces on the rear of the missile made turbulent adjustments as the seeker head fought to stay locked onto the laser beam.

The screen cleared in time for him to see the first missile slamming into the Shilka. The 137-pound hollow-charged warhead instantly channeled a stream of vaporized metal and plasma into the interior, fatally choking the ZSU-23's crew. The four guns of the Shilka stood motionless and erect as the magnesium chassis began to burn.

Sanders rolled west of the target at 1,200 feet, surveying the burning ZSU.

"*Good kill, Captain . . . good kill,*" he radioed proudly. He now had a perfect view of the aircraft bunkers below.

"What the hell is he doing?" Rath questioned. He watched as the second A-10 cut back across in front of the two SA-16s. "Holy shit! Get out of there!" he screamed into his mike uncontrollably.

Kneeling behind a group of rocks, one of the terrorists heard their tracking tone murmur unevenly. The American fighter was coming across his line of sight, not turning away. He watched it continue its course, then bank to the east, exposing its hot tail pipes.

It was a perfect opportunity. The man centered the aiming dot on the aircraft's back and flipped open the trigger guard. He depressed the firing mechanism halfway, unmasking the liquid nitrogen IR seeker head. Without delay the tone became a uniform pitch. He tightened his grip and squeezed the trigger.

"Break . . . break!" Bristol warned, seeing the yellow streak headed for his wingman.

He watched as Sanders tossed the A-10 on its side, nosing over, putting the jet into a hard right turn. The lieutenant succeeded in breaking the lock of the approaching missile, but only for a moment. The SA-16 corrected itself and overtook the aircraft in a matter of seconds.

The heat seeker detonated alongside the port engine, sending bits of shrapnel into the engine cowling, ripping the low pressure turbine, and cutting the TF34-100 to pieces. The rear section of the fuselage was sprayed with chunks of the warhead and the exploding missile body.

Sanders felt the unmistakable bump of a missile hit. His eyes went to his instruments as he leveled the aircraft and backed off on the power. The port engine was rapidly losing RPMs and oil pressure.

"I've taken a hit," Sanders called.

"You okay, Two?" Bristol queried excitedly.

"Yeah," Sanders answered, as a fire warning light flickered on. He hit a lever activating the fire extinguisher. The flames died instantly. He nosed over, watching his airspeed climb. When the HUD read 260 knots he added power and pulled back on the stick. The Hog responded sluggishly.

"I'm under control," he announced.

"Good. Because now I'm going after those shits." Bristol curled over ninety degrees, pointing his right wing to the ground. There was still a trace of smoke loitering in the air, denoting the missile's path. The bastards were on foot, making them hard, diminutive targets to find and hit. It was their only defense.

Using his thumb, Bristol shot half a dozen decoy flares out the back of his A-10 and popped the air brakes. He switched the rate of fire from 4,200 rounds per minute to 2,100. They were down there, hiding in the rocks.

Using his spotting scope, Rath observed one of the terrorists crawling along the base of a rocky ledge. He watched the man for a few seconds, then whispered to his sniper.

"Vasquie, can you hit him?"

"Negative. Not cleanly. Do you see the other one?"

"No. He's staying low."

"Redhawk Lead, Icebox here. Aim your first burst thirty yards to the left of missile trail. Target at base of ledge," Rath instructed the pilot, taking the kill away from his sniper.

Six hundred feet above the ground, Bristol pointed the nose of his A-10 where Icebox had directed him to. If someone was down there, he was camouflaged well, because the pilot couldn't see him. He pushed over and the blurred ground filled his HUD. Bristol squeezed the trigger once and then a second time.

The smoke pouring out of the A-10's cannon signaled Rath to continue scoping the area around the terrorist. He searched for any movement, waiting for the cloud kicked up by the A-10's rounds to dissipate, to verify that the target had been nixed. If the man was still alive, Rath would be surprised.

"Vasquie, keep your eye out for that other guy."

"Yeah, this sucker's mine. I'm not going to let those A-10s have all the fun," Vasquez said, disgusted Rath had to let the Hog take the moving target.

Bristol pulled up at 150 feet and swung around the front of the center bunker, being careful to keep his tail pipes away from the terrorist's position. Dozens of muzzle flashes sprang up as the various men in covered positions began to fire with their machine guns and light rifles.

The bullets slammed into the side of the A-10. The thick titanium bath, built around his ejection seat, would protect him from any of the deadly projectiles that happened to find their way through.

Bristol smiled to himself. The soldiers had given away their locations. He took note of a few, then banked sharply to the south, climbing straight up. He had to finish what he had started out to do first. Bristol leveled off at 1,500 feet, all the while looking over his shoulder for another SAM. He moved his stick left, swinging the straight-wing attack aircraft back around 180 degrees.

Rath spotted the second terrorist as he tried to move into position to fire on Redhawk Lead. The man was more slippery than the first, running from rock to rock. He settled on hiding behind a clump of dead bushes. Though he was staying low, Rath could see the black tube of his SA-16 pointing upward.

"Redhawk Lead, I see number two. Ready when you are."

"Roger that, Icebox. Coming in for the kill."

"From your last aim point, forty yards to the east. When you see a clump of dried bushes, shoot 'em."

Using his rudders, Bristol centered the round aim point on the HUD. Lowering the nose and increasing his airspeed, the distance shortened in no time. At 600 yards from the target, Bristol placed his finger on the cannon trigger. He waited, moving in closer.

Abruptly the target area swelled with smoke and flames. Bristol impulsively closed his eyes, lowering his head before the blaze blew past his windscreen. The anxious terrorist had fired an SA-16 without it being locked onto a heat source. The missile had missed by only thirty feet, flying off to the south, locked onto the sun.

"Eat this, fucker!" Bristol shouted, looking up at his HUD, realizing he was safe. He centered on a ten-foot circumference from where the missile had departed. His finger hit the trigger and the thirty-millimeter cannons pulverized the zone. He pumped the trigger three more times. "And that's from my mother."

The HUD read 260 feet when Bristol pulled off, banking back to the east. He searched the sky for signs of his wingman. A hint of smoke indicated that Redhawk two was heading southeast a couple of miles away. He was low and slow.

"Two, state your condition," Bristol demanded.

"Number one engine is shut down. Aircraft is stable, a little squirrelly from time to time."

"Can you make it back to base alone?"

"Well, I sure as hell don't need you to hold my hand."

"Roger, Two, you better be there when I land. Queen Bee, this is Redhawk one. Twenty minutes to bingo. Staying on station." Bristol would remain, using up his fuel before heading for the tanker.

"Roger that, Redhawk. Keep this channel clear. No Fear Ghere and his boys will be there in three minutes," Oliveri reported from the EC-141.

Bristol looked out to the east. Sure enough, he could see the large T-tailed C-17 coming in fast on final approach.

EC-141 Queen Bee

Lieutenant Victor Garnsey, the electronics threat officer, scrutinized his warning panel, hoping the emissions weren't what he thought.

"Missile threat, Colonel. It just came on-line," he finally warned, sure of the threat.

"Jam it!" Madison ordered.

Garnsey beat on the keyboard, instructing the EC-141's jamming pods to lock onto the powerful radar painting the aircraft. It was an SA-6 sweeping from the west. The RHAW equipment plotted the SAM site as being only ten miles away. At their altitude of 32,000 feet, the SAM might as well have been right under them.

"We've got trouble—" Garnsey stopped midsentence. The threat panel blared a solid red. Two SA-6s lifted off, heading for the EC.

"Shut everything down. Get us on the deck *NOW!*" Madison shouted.

SPECIAL TECHNICAL OPERATIONS CENTER, PENTAGON

Secretary of Defense John Turner had been in the STOC for the last thirty minutes. He folded his arms and stepped out of the way as Clark rushed over to the main computer screen.

"What's going on, Harris?" Clark asked.

"Unknown, sir. I believe there may have been a SAM threat, but I'm not sure. The EC has gone defensive, shutting down all electronic emissions." Harris looked at Clark. They had just lost the eyes and ears of the operation. With Madison off the air, Cobra was on its own.

"What are your options, General?" Secretary Turner asked.

"I have only one choice—wait and hope to God Madison comes back on the air."

Turner closed his eyes, drawing in a long breath. He wished he didn't have to say it. "I can't wait, and I don't have a choice. Put me in contact with the B-1Bs."

B-1B LANCER, HOLE CARD FLIGHT

The tactical air navigation display showed the two-ship formation crossing over the Egyptian border into northern Sudan 210 miles northeast of Madadhi. The dark green and gray bombers were heading south on a parallel course with the Libyan border, their wings swept back as they screamed over the desert at Mach 0.98. Only 200 feet off the deck, their vortices caused a cloud of dust to boil up behind their massive airframes.

"Over fence number one, sir," the communications officer informed the pilot. His video display plotted their preprogrammed flight path.

"Roger," the pilot, Lieutenant Colonel Milton Jackson, answered from the left seat. The B-1B's terrain-following radar automatically pitched the aircraft up slightly, modifying its altitude several hundred feet in order to clear the next hill a half mile away.

Jackson's disciplined routine brought his eyes across the instruments every few seconds, monitoring the array of dials and electronic read-outs. His bomber, affectionately named Toxic Avenger, was operating flawlessly.

"I have a radio transmission coming in from Crystal Palace, sir." Crystal Palace was the code name for the STOC.

"Patch me in." Jackson let his thumb off the internal mike button.

"Colonel, do you read me?" Secretary Turner's voice was easily distinguishable over the coded UHF radio channel.

"Loud and clear."

"We lost all contact with the EC-141 about a minute ago." The channel hissed as Turner paused. *"I order you to initiate plan X-Ray."*

Jackson's eyes met his copilot's. "Understood, sir."

"Keep this channel open."

"Roger. Hole Card out." Jackson looked right. He could see his wingman 500 yards away.

The colonel radioed his wingman. "We're going in." Jackson wrapped his hand around the stick, disengaging the B-1B's TFR. "Give me a weapons check and bring the ECM on-line."

MADADHI AIR BASE

Duke inched the door open without making a sound. He brought his head close to the crack, peering out into the room, and searched for the location of the voices. He spotted a row of chairs and a podium near the front. Standing outside the entrance were two guards. Duke studied them, watching for a moment. They seemed relaxed, unaware that the camp outside was being attacked. One man leaned against the wall smoking a cigarette as the other talked intently about something.

"Listen, do you hear that?" Andrea pressed in close to Duke, speaking in a hushed tone.

"What?" Duke asked, irritated, then turned his gaze back to the two men.

"Jet engines. I hear jet engines," Andrea whispered urgently.

"Shhhh. I don't hear anything," Duke answered back.

Andrea cocked her head. "I hear jets."

"Quiet. There are two men out there."

"General, I know what I heard."

"Okay. Now shut up." Duke didn't argue. The twenty-some years he had spent on the flight line had dulled his sense of hearing. He closed the door and crawled over next to Yitzhak. The man appeared restless and his breathing had become very shallow. Andrea joined Duke and wiped the sweat from Yitzhak's forehead.

"Rafi, can you hear me? I need to know where the controls for the claymore mines are hidden." Duke hoped the mines the Israeli had warned him of were all wired to a central area.

Yitzhak's eyes fluttered open. "Ajami . . . controls . . . the mines."

Duke nodded. "I know that, but where? Where are the control boxes?"

"Ajami . . . he controls."

Duke placed his large hands firmly on the side of the man's head, trying to get him to focus. "Where are the controls? Is there a remote control?"

"Remote control . . . Ajami . . . remote . . ." Yitzhak's eyes suddenly rolled back and his body slumped.

"No, Yitzhak, no," Andrea protested, pulling his head onto her lap. "Don't give up."

Duke sat back, sighing. The Israeli was still breathing, but just barely.

"He's hurt too badly. You're going to kill him if you don't let up," Andrea hissed angrily.

"I know," Duke spoke lowly, returning to the door. "But if I do let up, Willie could be a dead man."

Rath and Vasquez each carefully continued their sweeping of the area through their scopes. Vasquez stiffened as some figures came into view.

"Three new targets, left fifty yards."

Rath picked them up in his scope at once. "Confirmed."

"What do you make of them?"

Rath's 24-power spotting scope could get a wider, clearer picture. "They're carrying rifles." To the west a rumble caught his attention. *"Oh, fuck,"* he muttered to himself, then keyed the radio. "Rushmore, we have company coming from the west."

"Holy shit. I see 'em," Rodriguez responded. Two Mi-24 helicopters jumped up into the sky out of nowhere. They dropped over the hill and began flying low, kicking up quite a dust storm in their wake. "Queen Bee, this is Rushmore. Do you guys see this? I show two enemy choppers entering the area and they look pissed."

Rodriguez waited for a response, the sight capturing his attention. Then he realized there wasn't one and stared at his mike as if there was the malfunction.

"Queen Bee, this is Rushmore; do you copy?" Again there was no response. "Queen Bee, this is Rushmore. Damn it, will somebody answer me!" He switched radio channels. "Redhawk one, Rushmore. I'm looking at two, repeat, two, Mi-24s coming out of the west. Do you copy?"

"Ah, roger that, Rushmore. I see the gremlins heading this way." Bristol checked his fuel, then swung his A-10 toward the foreboding sight.

EC-141 Queen Bee

"Heading, heading!" Madison called out. They were now seventy-three miles southeast of Madadhi.

"Two four seven . . . altitude 1,500 feet." Oliveri's voice shook as the big command center bounced up and down, speeding over the desert floor.

"Get us back to altitude," Madison ordered. He braced himself against a chair as the EC-141 nosed up into a maximum seventeen-degree climb. If the missile was going to make contact, it would have by now. The large aircraft trembled as the pilots pushed the engines and airframe to the maximum.

"Three thousand, thirty-five hundred," Oliveri called out. His scope was void of any information other than altitude, airspeed, and heading.

Madison checked his watch. A nervous knot was growing in his belly. "When we hit eight thousand, activate the air-to-air radar and get us back on-line," Madison said intensely, thinking things through.

Oliveri's hand floated above the keyboard. It seemed to be taking too long . . . 7,000 . . . 7,500 . . . 8,000. Finally. He hit the buttons as fast as he could. The screen blinked and then cleared as it filled with data. The IFF transponder showed five F-15Es and three F-16s in the area around the EC-141.

"All aircraft, this is Queen Bee. We are back on the air," Oliveri announced.

"Welcome back, Queen Bee. The area is clean. I repeat, the area is clean." It was Captain Delattre.

"Roger. Climbing back to altitude," Oliveri answered back. Out of the corner of his eye he saw the flashing code numbers of two new IFF transponders in the upper right portion of the screen. He scrutinized the IFF signal for a few seconds, making sure he understood what was happening. The flashing numbers told him the fast-approaching aircraft weren't part of Cobra team; however, they were friendly. The EC had been off the air for sixteen minutes; that was plenty of time for an aircraft to enter the area undetected.

"Colonel Madison, look at this, sir," Oliveri said, pointing to the triangles representing the new aircraft.

"Explain," Madison commanded, bending over Oliveri's shoulder.

"They're big and fast and if I didn't know better I'd say they were heavy bombers. I show them at 300 feet at Mach 0.98. Heading is," he looked at Madison, "Madadhi, sir."

Madison picked up the phone tying to the STOC. "Clark, Madison here. We're still in one piece. The skies have been cleaned. I repeat, the skies have been cleaned. We are minutes away from ground operations."

Ajami walked into the bunker, shoving his pistol back into its holster. He stood tall, his rage boiling inside him as his eyes swept the area looking for Majeed.

"Have the other Americans been located?" he questioned the men standing guard nearest the shuttle. They all exchanged glances, not sure what he was asking. As far as they knew, the others were still in their holding cell.

"No, Ajami," one of the men finally answered bravely.

"What of Majeed? Has anyone seen him?" Again they stared at each other, then looked back at him. Their expressions gave away their uncertainty.

"No, Ajami," the same soldier replied hesitantly.

"Listen to me. The Americans must not take away our power. Allah is on our side and he will protect us. Stay at your positions. Prepare for battle," Ajami said, then marched up to Willie, who was still hanging from the crane.

"I will not lose this battle," he vowed to the unconscious man.

B-1B LANCER, HOLE CARD FLIGHT

"Abort . . . abort." Colonel Jackson heard the call in his headset.

"Gladly," he grunted, keying his mike. "Break off, Two. We're outa here."

"Roger, Lead. I'm right behind you."

Jackson used both hands to pull back on the stick and felt the massive bomber climb toward the dark blue desert sky. A half mile away the second B-1B arced skyward, slipping in behind the first.

Rodriguez was back on the frequency linking him to the EC-141. He smiled outwardly, hearing the chatter come back over the radio. Cobra's eyes and ears were back.

"Queen Bee, this is Rushmore," Rodriguez spoke urgently, breaking in to the reestablishments.

"Go ahead, Rushmore."

"I'm looking at two Mi-24 choppers entering the defensive zone around the bunker complex. Visual on one A-10. C-17 is touching down. We need additional air power at once."

"All aircraft are converging on the airfield, Rushmore. I repeat, all aircraft are converging on the airfield."

38

C-17 SKY FIRE

"Radio check, radio check . . . one minute," No Fear Ghere informed the members of the ground team via his PCR-77C radio. He adjusted the headset, securing it under his lightweight Kevlar helmet.

Mark Collins sat stiffly, his body tensing with the news they were getting ready to unload. The interior of the Bradley was dark and cramped. The ten men crowded inside the small infantry support vehicle were jostled about with every bump of the flight. Collins's mouth was dry and his anxiety prevented him from speaking. Each man was quiet, keeping to himself. He wondered if their outwardly cool appearance was just a big macho act.

Collins nervously went over the assault team's attack plans that Ghere had outlined earlier. Sky Fire's first objective would be to take the high ground above the bunker. Using their firepower and the mobility of the motorcycles, they would sweep the area of gun positions and snipers. While this was happening, Ghere would move his team into position next to the westernmost aircraft bunker doors. Using C4 explosives, the door would be blown away, allowing his team to enter the underground complex. Room by room, they would then move through the bunker, taking out any resistance. The Pathfinder team had provided intelligence that the center bunker contained *Atlantis*. It was there that Ghere expected the most resistance. Collins couldn't disagree.

The lieutenant had been candid and open with the members of his team. The intelligence they had on the base was sketchy at best. Essential data for a rescue mission such as this was nonexistent. Sky Fire was going in without any knowledge of how many men they would be fighting, what kind of defenses to expect, or the setup of the interior layout of the bunker complex. Ghere warned them to be alert. It was possible the astronauts were still alive, and he didn't want them to be killed by men under his command.

The whine of the hydraulic motors was barely audible from inside the Bradley as the C-17's rear cargo bay door opened. As with most air-drops, the rehearsed procedure appeared to be much simpler than it really was. The plan called for the C-17 to come in fast with its rear cargo ramp open. The big jet would hit the runway a few seconds after the pilot put all four engines in reverse. As the aircraft slowed to thirty-five knots, the restraints holding the equipment in place would be released, allowing the team to exit the C-17 while it was still moving down the runway.

The C-17 was now traveling at 147 knots, wings level. The copilot, a thirteen-year veteran, counted down, "Over the runway . . . forty feet . . . thirty . . . twenty . . . ten. Get ready, Lieutenant . . . five."

The pilot braked and reversed the engines, slowing the jet to 100 knots of ground speed.

The C-17 hit the runway with a hard thump, and the vehicles in the back jumped up into the air. The men braced themselves against each other, sliding to the front of the Bradley with the force of the aircraft's slowing.

"Sixty knots . . . coming down fast." It was the copilot again. "It's a go."

"It's a go," Ghere responded.

The copilot, watching their ground speed continue to drop, then flipped a lever up at thirty-five knots, releasing the reinforced nylon restraints holding the vehicles in place.

The Bradley lurched forward, soaring off the ramp of the C-17 along with the other Hummers, fast attack vehicles, and Enduro motorcycles.

Ghere changed his radio frequency, tying into Rushmore. "This is Sky Fire. Do you copy?"

"Roger, Sky Fire . . . Rushmore. We see you."

"Advise of situation."

"Area is hot. Two Mi-24s coming in from the west. Several active machine-gun nests and the enemy is moving."

"Roger that."

Ghere let off on the radio mike switch. *That's just great,* he thought, wishing the air team could have arranged a better welcoming party. Helicopters, particularly Mi-24s, flying into the area meant trouble in several different ways, none of them good for a ground team.

A-10 Redhawk One

"Bingo fuel . . . bingo fuel," Bitchin' Betty sounded the warning. Bristol switched the voice admonition off, glancing at the fuel gauge. He could stay in the air approximately seven, maybe eight, more minutes if he flew straight and level. By now the other four A-10s should have refueled and were on their way back. He was the only close air support directly above in the area. The fifteens were flying MiGCAP and the sixteens maintained their vigils in an attempt to support both areas.

"Redhawk one, Sky Fire has landed. I repeat, Sky Fire has landed and is heading toward complex. Hinds closing." The call was radioed in from Rodriguez in the OP.

That was all the warning Bristol needed. Ground troops and enemy helicopters don't mix.

The Hind was the only foreign chopper in the world that could go head to head with an A-10 and have a damned good chance of winning. Bristol banked to the north and climbed away. He didn't take his eyes off the two camouflaged gunships as they twisted their way down the valley floor.

"Redhawk one rolling to engage." Bristol flipped his fighter over and headed for the lead chopper.

Pathfinder Team Alpha: Icebox

"Rushmore, Icebox here. Moving in to cover ground team," Rath reported to the OP.

"Go slow and low, Icebox," Rodriguez advised.

Rath and Vasquez crawled out of their position and headed down the hill. To their right, the C-17 leaped off the runway, climbing away. Rath kept his eyes on the Hinds as he and Vasquez slithered to their new location.

The two choppers were a mile and a half away, crossing in front of him. They carried a full mix of air-to-ground and air-to-air ordnance. The enemy pilots hugged the edge of the rocky mountain. Their camouflage blended well with the sand and shale. If it wasn't for the billowing dust they were tossing into the air, it would have been difficult for Bristol to see them.

He pushed himself back into his ejection seat as he lined up on the lead Mi-24. His rate of descent was 3,000 feet a minute as he used a combination of stick and rudder to center the target on his HUD.

"Come on, stay on course," Bristol urged, needing a few more seconds before he could pulverize the approaching aircraft. His finger went for the trigger just as the lead chopper maneuvered to the left and climbed up out of his target sight. The pilot had seen him.

"Come back here, you . . ." Bristol shouted, as he hauled back on the stick and, jerking right, tried to compensate. He struggled to bring the nose of his jet up and over in an effort to follow his prey. The A-10 clamored as the Gs built and for a second the helicopter filled his HUD. He hit the trigger, filling the air with bullets.

The front windscreen of the Hind was designed to withstand a direct hit from a twenty-three-millimeter antiaircraft round. The Libyan pilot flinched as the armor-piercing bullets ricocheted off his front window after shattering it. He put both hands on the stick, beginning evasive action as the next round of bullets punched through the upper canopy.

The gunner, sitting in the front seat, swiveled around to see the top half of his pilot's body explode in a shower of red blood and bone. The Hind nosed over, dropping the short distance to the ground, erupting in a ball of flames and smoke.

"Airspeed . . . airspeed," Bristol commanded, as he put his plane into an abrupt climb. The A-10 strove upward and he knew he had screwed up by reacting too quickly. Bristol had lost his maneuverability. The Hog slowed on the edge of a stall before the nose went down and his airspeed began to creep up. But it wasn't happening fast enough. The second stubby-nosed Mi-24 came out of a hard banking turn, bringing its weapons to bear.

"Ah, *shit*!" Bristol played with the loose stick but didn't get any response. There wasn't enough air flying over his control surfaces. He was falling right down to the chopper, less than a thousand feet away. He jammed the throttle to the stops, vying to gain airspeed. The Hind was approaching too fast, looming out directly at him.

There was an unexpected white flash then, BOOM! His HUD suddenly filled with a churning sphere of fire and the flying debris of the chopper. Bristol felt the air quake around his aircraft as he banked to the right to avoid the wreckage of the Libyan Hind.

MADHAHI AIR BASE

Ajami circled Willie, wondering what inner strength kept him alive. The ropes had cut deeply into his wrists, and long lines of fresh and dried blood ran the length of his arms. His face was now swollen beyond recognition. Willie opened the slits that were once his eyes and looked straight at Ajami as if he were aware of his presence.

"Your friends are dead. I just killed them. They died begging for their lives."

"Liar . . ."

Ajami smiled. "I alone know the truth." He reached out and touched the American's face. "Your comrades have arrived. They think they can rescue you and this space plane, but it is not Allah's will.

"Azhar! Come here," he called, keeping his eyes on Willie.

Al-Azhar walked over from the fortified machine-gun site he and two other men were manning. Azhar was a short, fat, foul-looking man with deep scars running across his face. A patch covered his left eye. He had lost it and part of his ear in a knife fight with an Iraqi.

"Azhar, are the men ready?"

"Yes, commander."

"Good. You must kill anyone who enters this bunker."

"But what of Majeed?" Al-Azhar asked.

"Majeed is a coward. He has abandoned me. I want you to kill him first. Now, give me one of the claymores and the detonator," Ajami ordered, an eerie calmness in his voice. The soldier turned to retrieve the items.

"My people have suffered long enough and I alone, Abu Ajami, will be their savior," Ajami spoke, lost in his own thoughts.

Azhar returned, handing him the M122 firing device along with the mine. The convex-shaped M18A1 claymore, weighing over two pounds, contained 700 steel pellets backed by a thick layer of C4 plastic explosives. The detonator was a six-by-eight-inch black plastic box with a three-foot antenna protruding from its side. The radio remote control operated the mines around the interior of the bunker.

"Get into position," Ajami ordered.

He then hurriedly climbed up the wooden stairs and into the cargo bay of the shuttle. He stepped onto the top of the satellite and dropped down next to the base of the exposed warhead. Next to it were the bloodstains from Ziad's crushed body. Ajami placed several tools in his pocket, along with a flashlight. He stroked the cool gray outer skin of the bomb for a moment. He would have to finish what Ziad had started.

On the lower side of the warhead casing was a thick fiberglass panel

that provided access to the weapon's internal guidance system and arming structure. The panel was held in place by six screws. Removing them
would allow Ajami to see inside the bomb. Once inside, he would have
to remember what Ziad had said needed to be done.

A gray and blue F-16, its afterburner roaring, rocked its wings, coming
within several hundred feet of Bristol's canopy. It pulled up to escort the
A-10 momentarily. Bristol realized that the white flash he had seen was a
Sidewinder streaking toward its mark. And not a moment too soon.

"Splash one chopper," the F-16 pilot radioed, and then turned, giving
Bristol a thumbs up as if it were routine.

Bristol waved his hand in the air at the unknown pilot. Then he used
the back of his hand to wipe the sweat off his forehead. The two planes
split as Bristol banked to the left, recomposing himself. He swung his
aircraft toward the main part of the base. In the distance he could see
the ground team fanning out as they raced for the bunker complex.

Duke walked silently across the concrete floor. He worked his way
toward the front of the room, stopping at the entryway. He listened
intently for voices, or any noise for that matter. The two guards had left
just minutes ago, but he was uncertain which way they had gone as he
surveyed the tunnel.

Taking a deep breath, he stepped out into the open, turning to his left.
Although he had been blindfolded when taken from the shuttle, his
military training had prepared him to pay careful attention to the details
of their walk to the holding cell. That, coupled with the information he
got from Yitzhak, should allow him to manage fairly well in finding his
way to the bunker.

Duke conscientiously pointed the muzzle of the rifle down while
keeping his finger on the trigger. The safety was off. He had walked
only ten feet when two men abruptly appeared out of the darkness
ahead of him. Duke's first reaction was to raise the rifle and fire, but he
stopped. *No. Stay calm. I am one of them,* he thought.

The dim emergency lights strung through the tunnel cast scarcely
enough light for Duke to see their faces. They were standing next to one
another, talking in low voices.

This was a bad idea, he thought, not breaking his stride. The men
stopped talking as Duke approached them. One of them moved closer
to Duke as the other walked away into the shadows. Duke stared
straight ahead, avoiding the man's eyes.

"Where have you been?" the man asked in Arabic, stepping in Duke's
path. Duke faltered, breaking his stride.

"You . . ." The man walked up closer, repeating himself. "I said, where have you been?"

"Ahhh," came Duke's grunting reply, hoping the bluff would work. It didn't.

"I don't know you." The terrorist's eyes shifted down to the stain on Duke's shirt. His face changed expressions as his hand began to go for his weapon. "Who are—"

The stock of the Uzi hit the man with the force of a sledgehammer, shattering his nose. Before the terrorist could react, Duke swung the rifle again, this time hitting him along the side of his head, knocking him out. His body went limp and he fell to the ground.

"Good job, James. One down, only a few more to go," Duke mumbled, grabbing the man under his arms and pulling him into the darkened room.

A former Fatah Special Operations officer, the Syrian named Ahmed Sulta had been waiting for this. He and his men had trained for it a hundred times. He turned his head methodically, making sure each man was neatly hidden away in their chest-deep foxholes, obscured by the natural surroundings, brush, dried grass, and rocks. Their positions had been carefully selected, spaced in such a way that each terrorist could fire in a full circle covering 360 degrees. In addition to light and heavy machine guns, they were armed with rocket-propelled grenades. Theoretically, they could defend the camp from any ground attack.

Sulta watched the Americans approaching. He counted seven fast-moving vehicles and six motorcycles speeding toward the center of the complex. The Syrian had to admire his enemy. It was a gallant move, hitting them from the front. But they would pay for their courage.

Sulta steadied his weapon; he wouldn't have to say a word. The men under his command would only fire after him. It was all part of their practiced plan.

"Forward elements are reporting no resistance." The first report cracked over No Fear Ghere's radio equipment. Although Ghere was seated in the center of the Bradley, he saw the situation happening in his mind. The motorcycles were speeding several hundred meters out to each side of the Bradley, their drivers hunched low behind the handlebars. The KLR-250 Enduros were maneuverable targets. The Bradley by now was traveling at fifty miles an hour and was being followed by the FAVs and HUMMERs. If the A-10s had done their job, the lieutenant and his squad should only encounter light arms fire. Yet Ghere knew better. In battle the way things should be was rarely the case.

The team's first objective was to make it to the fifteen-foot-high earthen hill directly in front of the aircraft bunkers' doors. Whoever had designed the base had planned on using the man-made hill to stop a direct attack on the bunkers by air-to-surface weapons. It was obvious they never expected an attacking enemy to use the mound as cover for an attack. Once his men were positioned behind the hill, Ghere would use the firepower of the Bradley's twenty-five-millimeter gun to saturate the surrounding mountainside, putting down any resistance. This would allow members of Sky Fire to take the high ground directly above the bunker complex. When that was done they could regroup and the SRT would assault the bunkers.

"Five hundred yards," the Bradley commander called.

Ghere looked at Collins. "We're almost there."

"I can't see them," Rodriguez grunted in futility. He had lost sight of the terrorists he was watching. "Where did the bastards go?"

He moved his binoculars along the base of the mountain. Below him Rath and Vasquez were coming into view as they approached the edge of the runway.

Rodriguez opened the radio channel. "Hold up, Rath. I don't want you to move until that ground team is on station. They might think you're one of the bad guys."

Rath didn't acknowledge the transmission verbally. He and Vasquez fell to their bellies, crawling in behind a clump of rocks.

Rodriguez put his high-power spotting glasses back on the mountainside. The enemy was up there, hiding in the rocks.

Duke opened the heavy metal door and looked inside the room before entering. It was dark, but empty. He dragged the man's body inside and shut the door behind him. The square chamber looked to be some sort of command center. There was radio equipment and several computer stations. The screens were on, casting a blue glow against the far wall.

He walked around to the front of the radio consoles. It was there he noticed three men lying on the floor in a pool of blood, each with a bullet wound. They were wearing Libyan military uniforms and they were all dead. He unsnapped one of the men's holsters and removed his nine millimeter, stuffing it in his belt.

Duke then turned to the radio equipment. The digital numbers were lit up, telling him the equipment was still operating. His eyes swept the controls as he tried to figure out what frequency the Libyans were using. It didn't matter. Duke didn't know what frequency the Americans would be transmitting on and he didn't have all day to figure it out.

He walked back to the doorway and listened. He heard footsteps a moment before three terrorists ran past, heading down the hall in the opposite direction. Duke ducked back in the room.

The M242 twenty-five-millimeter gun, mounted on the Bradley's rotating turret, roared to life. The loud, ripping sound vibrated throughout the interior of the M2 as the big gun pumped 200 armor-piercing and incendiary rounds into the mountainside. The Bradley's commander hit the smoke discharger, firing a pattern of four smoke grenades in front of the M2, masking its approach to the hill.

Without warning, the vehicle slowed and the powerful hydraulic hinges thrust open the back ramp, filling the interior compartment with sunlight.

"Go . . . go . . . *go,"* Ghere shouted.

Collins remembered to unbuckle his lap belt and followed Ghere outside the Bradley. His eyes hurt as his pupils adjusted to the sunlight.

Ghere swung around to the back of the fighting vehicle, keeping it between himself and the mountainside. "You men stay with me."

As Ghere moved away from the Bradley, the M2 continued to fire into the side of the mountain. Collins glanced up and through the dispersing smoke saw rocks and dirt flying off the mountain in front of him.

"They're firing at us," he shouted.

"No shit. Keep your head down."

Ghere ran at full speed to the base of the hill in front of the bunkers. He dove into the dirt so hard it nearly knocked the wind out of him. He rolled over on his back, keying his radio.

"Rushmore . . . Rushmore. Son of a bitch, I thought you said little to no resistance. Where the hell is all that fire coming from?"

Collins listened as he tried to push his head further into his helmet.

Rodriguez was already on top of the situation. *"Sit tight, Sky Fire. Situation is under control."*

"Under control, my ass. You're not the one down here."

Collins looked up in time to see and hear a single A-10 bank out of the southeast and line up, heading for several enemy machine-gun positions to the right. Other members of Sky Fire were already answering back with bursts of .223 and .308 fire.

Ghere crawled up the hill, stopping a few inches from the top. Orange tracers from the terrorists' guns zipped over his head, barely missing. The Americans were using green and white tracers. It was as if they had planned it.

*   *   *

Ajami removed the last screw and jammed the screwdriver into the side of the square panel, forcing it away.

Flipping on his flashlight, he peered inside the lower half of the warhead assembly. The access hole was large enough for him to get his upper body into it. Scanning the interior of the warhead, he looked for what might be the guidance system.

"Think . . . think." He closed his eyes and tried to remember what Ziad had told him.

Immediately below the opening was a compact black box secured with shock-absorbing springs that were attached to each of its corners. On the side was a shiny gold metal plate with Russian writing. Ajami focused the flashlight's beam on the protruding circuit cables running out the top center of the box. He guessed it was the guidance system's main computer. He was looking for what Ziad had described as the inertial platform. It would be a sphere about the size of a basketball, with six tubes protruding out of its sides.

Ajami followed the cables until they reached the midsection of the warhead. Refocusing the flashlight, he saw the circular black guidance unit. The sphere contained the weapons systems accelerometers and gyros. And directly above the sphere, he would find the glass arming fuse.

"RPG, RPG!" Sulta shouted for a rocket-propelled grenade over the sound of his machine gun and enemy bullets hitting the dirt around him.

He turned, firing at the Bradley, spraying the area around the light tank with a volley of fire. Out of the corner of his eye he could see several of the motorcycles swinging around to the left, trying to get up the hill and behind him. He was more concerned about the fighting vehicle.

"RPG on the Bradley—" The area to his right exploded in a bombardment of erupting bullet fragments and fire from the American incendiary rounds.

Al-Gargi heard the desperate shout for an RPG from his squad leader. He rolled out of his protective position, hauling the launcher with him. The long-haired man was only twenty-two years old, one of the camp's newest freedom fighters. Yet he was skilled in the use of the rocket-propelled grenade, able to hit a target the size of a car at 300 meters.

He crawled several meters. Lying on his belly, with bullets flying over him, Al-Gargi screwed the OG-7 HE-Frag round warhead and the sustainer rocket motor together. He rolled over on his side, slinging the launcher between his shoulder and neck to steady his aim. Then, turning the rocket launcher sideways, he looked through the eyesight, placing his finger on the trigger. Next he positioned the cross hairs of the optical sight on the side of the M2 Bradley. The range lines, marked in 100-meter intervals from 200 to 500, told him the American light tank was just over 200 meters away. It would be an easy shot.

Al-Gargi moved the bore sight cross hairs until they were below the M2's turret. He waited for the turret to swing to the left so he could clearly see it. With the cross hairs rock solid, he squeezed the trigger, sending the grenade to its target.

Ghere saw it first and shouted, "RPG . . . RPG!" The warning was too late.

The long, thin warhead accelerated as its rocket motor burst away from the launch area toward the target. Ghere would remember where it was fired from.

The piezoelectric fuse armed the grenade within five meters of leaving the launch tube. Four rear stabilizing fins opened, putting the rocket-propelled grenade into a stabilizing right-hand spiral. In a heartbeat, the warhead was traveling at 300 meters a second.

The antitank projectile, a mixture of ninety-four percent RDX high explosives and six percent wax, hit the side of the Bradley in a fiery splash. The M2 rocked and for a moment its main gun quit firing. The explosive gases and hot liquid metal fragments penetrated the Chobham-type compound armor of the Bradley only a fraction of an inch before the force of the impact dissipated over a wide area, lessening the effect of the blast.

Ghere didn't move, his eyes fixed on the M2. As the fire quickly burned away, he watched the main gun start up again. A surge of relief came over him. His men inside were thankfully still alive.

Ghere crawled to the top of the hill and fired several three-round bursts in the direction of where the RPG had been fired. He was too late. Several other members of his team were already saturating the area with gunfire.

Al-Gargi was flat on his back. He had hit the target but not where he had wanted. His grenade had impacted several feet below the turret. He had to redeem himself. He had to reload and fire again.

Swinging the launcher around, he held it a couple inches above his chest. He reached behind him and grasped another grenade out of his knapsack. Then the dirt started to fly in front of his face as bullets crashed into the ground all around him. The Americans were saturating his area with an amazing amount of firepower. He was not ready for this. He had not trained to fight under these kinds of conditions.

"RPG, RPG." Al-Gargi heard the order again.

With his insides churning, he started to screw on the launcher rocket motor. A volley of fire started to roar above him. A .223 bullet ripped into his hand, blowing off three of his fingers. He howled in pain, dropping the RPG. He was afraid to move again.

"S . . . R . . . T." Ghere shouted for the special reaction team and signaled with his hand, telling them it was time to move. He jumped to his feet and ran down the back of the hill at full speed. One of the camouflaged HUMMERS sped up next to him, and the squad of eight men climbed in.

Collins was breathing heavily and was angry at himself for not being in better shape.

The four wheels of the HUMMER tore across the sand, kicking up dust as it sped away. Collins hung on as the small truck accelerated across the open desert at fifty miles an hour.

"Take your helmet off and put this on." Ghere handed Collins a black watchman's cap. "When we get inside, things are going to happen fast. Don't ask any questions, just follow my lead. Understood?"

Collins nodded yes as he slipped on the cap. From the lieutenant's expression and tone of voice it was evident he really wasn't welcome.

The HUMMER began to slow as it neared the left side of the bunker complex. The reinforced concrete door was the only way they could gain quick entrance into the complex. The members of the team piled out of the vehicle, followed by Collins.

When he reached the side of the bunker, one of the team members was already placing large bundles of gray plastic explosives around the edge of the door. Before Collins knew it, the detonator plugs were inserted into the soft puttylike clay and the M122 firing device was armed.

"Goggles on," Ghere instructed, as he slipped the NVGs over his eyes. "Weapons check . . . radios on. Okay."

Each man turned his head away from the coming explosion.

"One . . . two . . . three."

The deafening sound of three separate plastic explosive charges going off in quick succession had a numbing effect on Ghere. The two-foot-thick steel-fortified door crumbled into several pieces. There was now a four-foot hole the team could crawl through.

Ghere was the first through the jagged-edged hole, thrusting his way into the dark tunnel. He flipped on his NVGs and brought his H&K silenced assault rifle down, sweeping it right to left and back again.

Operations Sergeant Hayward Chappel, an E8, followed him. He crouched low, anticipating a volley of fire.

They were in the bunker.

Duke spun around to the sound of the blast. His insides jumped. It had to be the rescue team.

He ran down the tunnel, ducking into the next doorway, and squatted down. Duke estimated he had walked a hundred yards and passed a number of empty rooms. He reassured himself he would have to run into the aircraft bunker containing *Atlantis* shortly.

He rested his head against the wall and tried to gather his thoughts. His hands were swollen and sore from being tightly bound.

The muted sound of footsteps and voices forced him to gather his strength once again. Duke leaned forward and counted three men running past him carrying weapons. The terrorists were moving quickly toward the explosion.

He took a deep breath. He was close to the main bunker and to Willie.

Ajami had found it. The gyroscope and accelerometer assembly looked like a series of steel shafts joined together in the center by a circular frame. The frame was mounted to the side of the warhead with pivoting hinges that allowed the system to move independently as the bomb pitched and yawed on its way to the target area.

Ajami reached up and grabbed the assembly near one of the hinges. Firmly anchoring his feet on the wall of the satellite, he used all his strength to tear the mounting bracket away. He yanked once and then twice before the first hinge pulled free. He grabbed the next bracket, breaking it off at the hinge.

With half the assembly pulled away, Ajami caught a glimpse of what he was looking for: a dull, heavy-gauge titanium pipe. It was the shield Ziad had said would be around the arming fuse.

A line of sweat rolled down his forehead. Beneath the shield was a glass tube containing the pressure-sensitive fuse. He would have to remove the protective armor encompassing the fuse. When the glass tube was broken, the pressure-sensitive switch would perceive the change in atmospheric pressure, arming the warhead. Thirty seconds later, the twenty-five-megaton nuclear device would start its detonation sequence.

Rodriguez and Rath were now halfway across the runway, moving toward the hill as fast as they could. Most of the enemy fire had died down; only a few scattered rifle shots could be heard. The terrorists had not been much of a match for the Bradley and the A-10s.

Rath looked up at two more A-10s weaving their way across the valley floor as if saying, we are here when you need us.

"Looks like we missed all the excitement," Vasquez said, running alongside Rath.

"Don't bet on it, man. I haven't seen the shuttle yet."

"Clear . . . move," Ghere whispered in the mouthpiece of the PRC-77 radio, as he moved deeper into the hallway. He swept his head right, the uncanny green glow of the NVGs allowing him to see every detail of the interior. The wall of the tunnel was a light green and the floor a darker shade of the same color. Ahead he could see a doorway and where the tunnel turned to the right.

"Two doors." The lieutenant pointed to a room on the right side of the tunnel.

"Chappel right." The square-shouldered sergeant darted past Ghere.

Two members of the SRT hit the door, knocking it off its hinges. The room flashed white as two stun grenades exploded. The team members waited a few seconds before entering the room.

Ghere lunged past the room to the other doorway. He stopped, listened, looked, then moved again very rapidly.

Collins was doing his best to keep up with Ghere. He knew enough about special operations not to follow him footstep for footstep. The enemy would be looking for a pattern. But he also knew enough that when he did move he had to do it quickly.

"Collins, here," Ghere radioed.

Collins bolted to the entryway where Ghere had disappeared. The lieutenant was standing next to a cell door. "Do you know who this is?" Ghere asked.

Collins studied the man's body and then removed his NVGs, looking at him in the low light. "I've never seen him."

"Let's move." An instant later they were back in the tunnel again.

Duke inched his way down the tunnel with his back against the wall. He was listening and looking for any movement. He came to a corner and stopped. This was the place. He could sense and smell it. The odor of humans mixing with burned metal was extremely unique.

He knelt down, placing one knee on the ground. Making sure his rifle was out in front of him, he moved closer, looking around the corner. He saw it, the entrance to the bunker. But something wasn't right. There weren't any guards around . . . nothing.

"This is too easy." It was as if they wanted him to enter.

Duke sprinted to the opposite side of the tunnel and started to move toward the entrance.

39

The SRT was now operating in three separate groups, spaced evenly apart, as they maneuvered through the maze of tunnels. Ghere and Chappel were leading the clearing team. Their job was to command the unit and make sure each room or section was safe before moving ahead. Behind them was the covering, or cutoff, group. These two men were responsible for backup fire in case the lead group ran into heavy enemy resistance. The final group of two well-armed men were for reserve cover. If any of the enemy were clever enough to hide and wait for the forward elements of the team to pass, thinking they could attack from behind, they would run into a nasty surprise.

"Team down," Chappel ordered.

Immediately each man stopped moving and found cover.

"What's up, Chappel?" Ghere asked.

"I saw something up ahead. We have company."

"Shit. How far?" Ghere's first thought was that of an RPG screaming down the tunnel at them.

"Thirty, thirty-five meters," Chappel answered.

Ghere wasn't going to wait around and find out who was out there. "Move on my signal," he grunted, unsnapping a rubber-coated grenade from his flak jacket. He pulled the pin. *One . . . two . . . three,* he counted. Ghere tossed the grenade down the hall. The quarter inch of rubber surrounding the grenade deadened its sound as it hit the concrete and rolled toward the enemy.

"Live one," he warned.

The upper section of the warhead was narrow, making it difficult to get at the arming fuse. Ajami used all his strength attempting to pry the protective covering away from the glass tube. He wrenched the screwdriver into the heavy metal welding around the top of it. It didn't work. The tube was fixed firmly in place. The Russians had known what they were doing when they used titanium. The metal was extremely strong.

It is no use, he thought. A simple screwdriver wasn't going to work. He would have to get the cutting torch and he didn't have time.

Ajami started to back out when it occurred to him. He could use the claymore, the one he had planned to defend himself with inside the shuttle.

The force and sound of the explosion rocked the tunnel at the same time. Pieces of shrapnel dug into the wall above Collins's head. He stumbled to his feet as Chappel jumped in front of him.

The enemy had only one place to hide and that was in the doorway ahead of them. If the grenade hadn't killed them, that was where they would be. Ghere and Chappel were already on the move. The men dashed down the main section of the smoke-filled tunnel. They had to hit the terrorists before they had a chance to recover.

Chappel put his rifle to his shoulder as he watched his commanding officer move away. They were walking several feet apart with Ghere in the lead.

"Right—" Chappel shouted, not completing his sentence.

Ghere had seen the figure a split second before his number two man. He used his left hand to squeeze the laser designator button on the side of his rifle, sending out a solid red targeting beam. He didn't need to aim the rifle, just put the red laser where he wanted the bullet to hit.

The dot, no bigger than a pinhead, cut through the dusty air and came to rest on the forehead of the terrorist. Ghere tapped the trigger once. His silenced MP5 jumped, sending one hollow-point nine-millimeter round into his head. The terrorist, still half dazed, never knew what hit him.

Ghere swung his rifle around in the other direction, catching sight of another terrorist bringing up his AK in preparation to fire. The lieutenant didn't have to think. His training had made it a reflex. Dropping to one knee, he centered the laser on the man's face and fired twice, killing him instantly.

"Dust one . . . dust two," Ghere muttered into the radio as he moved his head from left to right looking for more bad guys.

Chappel came even with him, rifle at ready. Neither man had seen a third terrorist emerge from the first doorway, which was now behind them.

Collins was thirty feet behind, walking as close as he could to the wall. Through his NVGs, he saw the glimmer of the man's gun barrel swing toward Ghere. He didn't have time to aim. Holding the M-16 at his waist, Collins fired.

The claymore was now resting next to the warhead's arming fuse. The explosive charge of the mine would easily cut through the metal surrounding the glass fuse.

Ajami was becoming overwrought. There were gunshots and explosions ringing out inside his complex. The enemy was growing closer each second; his base of safety and operations was no longer. Abu Ajami, the future leader of the Palestinian world, was going to die.

"There is a reason for this. Allah has a reason," he reassured himself. *Allah will protect me. I will live,* he finally rationalized.

Ajami primed the antipersonnel mine by inserting the electric blasting cap into the top. He turned it, making sure it was locked into place. Connected to the blasting cap was a two-meter wire attached to a radio-controlled M122 firing device. He was careful to make sure the wire didn't tangle as he backed out of the bomb's cavity. He uncoiled the wire inch by inch until the firing box was dangling outside the warhead.

"Son of a bitch, that was close." Ghere glanced at Collins. "We don't have time to celebrate. Let's move."

The team was halfway to its objective.

Vasquez and Rath reached the base of the hill and climbed into position next to several other members of the Sky Fire team.

"Icebox is here," Rath announced to the senior intelligence sergeant.

"Welcome to the battle, Lieutenant." The sergeant looked at the two men in amazement. They both had three-day-old beards, were a ball of dirt from head to toe, and smelled as bad as they looked.

"Glad you could join us. I think we've taken out all the enemy, but you need to keep your heads down just in case," the sergeant cautioned.

Rath turned and watched as the cleanup operations continued. A dozen team members were still combing the hills above them.

"What's the game plan?" Vasquez asked.

"Wait until we hear from Ghere," the sergeant said, looking at the bunker.

The gunshots had seemed incredibly close, echoing down the tunnel. But now everything was quiet again.

The entryway leading to *Atlantis* was open and unguarded as Duke took several more steps toward it. He stopped and looked at the opening. The aircraft bunker appeared dark and empty, and standing only five yards away, he couldn't hear a thing.

This is strange, he told himself. *It could only mean one thing, a trap.*

Duke felt the cold steel of a gun barrel against his neck. He instantly froze. Whoever it was had come out of nowhere and he was angry at himself for not having heard him. His first thought was to try and swing around, killing whoever was behind him. On second thought, he doubted the plan would work.

Then someone whispered something in English. Or at least he thought it was English. He started to turn around but stopped; he would take a chance.

"I am General Duke James, U.S. Air Force," he said in a low voice.

"Say again?" came an answer. Duke could sense the man's apprehension.

"General Duke James. I'm the shuttle commander. If you're who I think you are, then you're here to rescue me," Duke answered back. His voice was measured with confidence.

"How do I know you're James?"

"Apple pie, mom, hotdogs. Look, damn it, we don't have time for this." Duke's relief was starting to turn into anger.

"Turn around."

Duke deliberately turned to find a half dozen American commandos, all wearing NVGs, with their guns pointed at him.

"General James," a voice murmured in the back. It was Collins.

"That's right." Duke looked at the men dressed in their brown camo fatigues. "Who the hell are you guys?"

Ghere stripped off the black tape covering the American flag on his shoulder. He then grasped the general by the back of the collar and pulled him toward the main part of the tunnel. The rest of the men took up positions around the entrance leading to the shuttle. Having a conversation thirty feet from their main objective wasn't a very good idea.

Ghere slipped off his goggles and looked at Duke's face. He recognized him from the NASA photo.

"Andrea Tilken is hiding in the pilot's briefing room and my pilot is in there, with the rest of the terrorists," Duke said.

"Okay. We'll find Tilken in a minute. How many men are in there?" Ghere pointed to the bunker.

"A dozen, maybe two. I don't know," Duke guessed.

"What about their defenses?"

"Hey, slow down. Do you even know who you're fighting? These are terrorists and they have nuclear bombs," Duke protested.

"We know that. What about their defenses?"

"They're set up with machine guns and the bunker is mined with claymores. That's all I know."

Ghere thought for a moment. "Do you know who's in control here?"

Duke nodded. "He calls himself Ajami."

"So it is Ajami," Collins said.

"Yeah, and the man is insane," Duke popped off. "He's probably killed Willie, my pilot." Duke looked at both Ghere and Collins. "Well, are we going to sit here or what?"

Ghere removed his radio. Using his thumb, he boosted the power level to maximum.

"Sky Fire, this is Blazer. Move to plan Jungle House . . . move to plan Jungle House," Ghere repeated.

"Roger, Blazer . . . Jungle House in three minutes."

Ajami cut Willie down from the aircraft engine crane. Willie fell to the ground and didn't move.

Ajami grabbed his roped hands. "American, you must stand." He forced Willie to his feet. He then clutched his bruised face. "Open your eyes and look at me."

"Where are you taking me?" Willie struggled to see the man in front of him.

"You will come with me."

Ajami led him to the side of the shuttle. They climbed the stairs and stepped into the cargo bay. They were both standing on the satellite next to the warhead. Ajami picked up the M122 wireless firing device that controlled each of the nine claymore mines.

"When your comrades come for you, they will die." Ajami smiled.

"Aim to please," the A-10 pilot flying Redhawk five responded to the radio call. "Tell your men to head for cover."

Banking to the north, the pilot, Captain Scotty Marshall, throttled back, reducing his airspeed by twenty knots. He didn't have to fly fast, he just had to be accurate.

He adjusted his oxygen mask and the position of his feet on the rudder pedals.

"Laser designator on. Target is illuminated," came the call from the ground.

"Roger, Ground. Here we go."

Marshall leveled the Warthog three quarters of a mile from the target. He systematically worked the rudder pedals, placing the nose dead center on the hill ahead of him.

Unlike making a strafing run on a column of tanks, hitting the base of a bunker door, knowing Americans were inside, was something different. He would have only a small window in which to drop his bomb and turn away. If he dropped the GBU-12, a 500-pound laser-guided bomb, too soon, it would crash through the bunker door, possibly destroying everything inside. If Marshall dropped it too late, he wouldn't be able to turn away in time and would hit the side of the mountain. To sum it up, he didn't like the odds on either end of the equation.

The main bunker door would be hidden for most of his target run. He'd have to be right over the bunker before the symbology on the HUD changed, signaling that the Pave Penny laser spot seeker had acquired its target. Only then could he drop the bomb.

"Keep designating," Marshall ordered, not taking his eyes off the HUD. He could now see the top of the bunker door. He kept his hand firmly on the stick. The A-10 was rock solid and he was only seconds away from bomb release.

Marshall unconsciously stopped breathing, his full attention on the mission. Half of the bunker was now visible. The round targeting symbol began to flash orange. The target seeker was starting to pick up the first reflected traces of the invisible laser beam.

Marshall thrust the throttles forward and fingered the weapons release button. He required more airspeed going into his turn and the engines would need a few seconds to spool up.

The HUD's target designator flashed to a solid orange. He had a lockup.

"Now," he grunted.

As he hit the trigger, one GBU-12 separated cleanly from the wing-mounted weapons pylon. The bomb's seeker head pushed the nose down as it started the short drop to its target point.

Marshall didn't waste any time. He forced the stick right again using both hands. The G meter climbed, 4 . . . 5 . . . 6 . . . 7, topping out at 7.5 Gs. He watched the ground through the windscreen. The pain of the Gs bit into his chest and upper legs. He didn't let up, forcing the unwilling aircraft to stay in the sharp turn. The brown blur suddenly turned to blue sky. He had made it.

The 500-pound smart bomb hit the base of the bunker, exploding on impact. The force of the blast blew a twenty-foot section out of the door in a torrent of fire, smoke, and debris.

The unexpected explosion knocked both Ajami and Willie off their feet and back into the shuttle's cargo bay. Ajami hit the top of the exposed warhead, the shock knocking the M122 firing device out of his hand. He now had no way of controlling the claymore mines.

He rolled over, dazed but unhurt. The exploding bomb had thrown a massive amount of rock and steel reinforcements into the air. Ajami's body was covered with small pockmarks, and his clothes were ripped in several places. He looked down, searching for the M122. His entire plan was about to come undone. He saw it. The black box rested on its side about halfway down the side of the rocket. It was lodged between the burned outer skin of the satellite and the warhead assembly. He would have to climb down into the cargo bay to retrieve it. He grabbed Willie and forced him down the ladder into the shuttle bay with him.

Ghere and the SRT were ready. The instant the bomb hit they moved through the door into the bunker. Ghere knew his men would have to put down any enemy fire in the first ten to fifteen seconds after the bomb exploded. And if the terrorists were well trained, they would have only seven or eight seconds to kill them.

Collins followed but wasn't expecting what he saw as he propelled himself into the bunker complex. The room was a fog of dust and smoke. Sunlight streamed through the large hole in the massive door, making his NVGs useless. He ripped off the goggles, throwing them to the floor. As his eyes swept the bunker from right to left he saw at least a dozen fires burning on and around *Atlantis*. More Americans were entering the complex through the opening, and men were shouting all around him.

Collins flinched. The sound of gunshots rang out next to him. The machine-gun nest next to the shuttle's nose gear disappeared in a burst of gunfire. The three terrorists manning it never fired a shot as a hail of bullets ended their lives.

"Follow me," someone said to Collins. He looked to his right. It was Duke James and he was headed for the shuttle.

Ajami had crawled down inside the satellite as he tried to reach the M122. The black remote control box was just inches away from his fingers. He tried to wedge his body further into the satellite. His fingertips were on the box.

"There," Ajami muttered. He clutched the box tightly in his right hand. "Now they will pay."

Duke ran up the makeshift ladder, followed by Collins. When he reached the top, he stopped. Standing in the cargo bay, between the burned remains of the satellite and the wall of the flight deck, was Ajami. And he was holding Willie in front of him with a forearm across his throat.

"Don't move, American, or you will all die." Ajami held up the M122.

Duke didn't move. He knew the box controlled the claymore mines Yitzhak had told him about.

"Put down your weapons," Ajami demanded. He thrust the black box toward the two men.

Duke and Collins did as they were told, setting their rifles down so the terrorist could see them. Ajami had the advantage. He was fairly well hidden from the rest of the ground troops, so it would be impossible for a sniper to take him out. They could use a grenade, but that would also kill Willie. Duke had run out of options.

"Abu Ajami. Son of a drug dealer and an American woman. How can a man call himself a true Palestinian when his mother is an American?" Collins asked. "What was she, Ajami, some prostitute your father dragged home?"

Ajami looked at the man, his face rigid and eyes ablaze. How did he know who his parents were? "Who are you?"

"I know all about you, Ajami. We have been watching you for a long time. All the men in your own camp have betrayed you at one time or another."

"Liar . . ."

"We have known your every move for the last five years. Adib Hamen's MiG was not shot down. We made that story up. He landed in Israel. He now drinks wine and has many western girls looking after him." Collins didn't waver. "And you call yourself a Palestinian. The entire Arab world thinks of you as a fool."

Ajami felt every muscle in his body begin to tighten. Was the American telling the truth? Were his people not loyal to him? Was this why Allah was punishing him? Ajami's rage was about to erupt into a violent tantrum. Allah had promised to protect him and now the Americans were right in front of him.

"Ajami, where are your loyal men? Where are they?" Collins shouted. "Why are they not by your side? Look around. You are alone. All the men are gone. They have run away."

"*Ahhhh!*" Ajami shouted, dropping Willie. His mind was a blur of fear, anger, and betrayal.

Now was his chance. Duke jumped on top of the terrorist, knocking him to the floor. He took his fist and hit the man several times in the face with all his strength.

Ajami brought his forearm up, striking Duke across the face, breaking his nose and driving him back and away. In the confusion, he released the M122 and it skidded across the floor of the cargo bay, coming to rest against the wall.

Duke swung at the terrorist again, this time hitting him in the stomach. The man cringed with pain and doubled over.

"You *bastard*," Duke said, hitting him in the face with an uppercut.

Ajami flew back, losing his balance, but only for a second. He righted himself, and in a twisting roundhouse kick, hit the general in the side of the face.

The thrust of the kick sent Duke flying. He fell back, hitting his head on the shuttle's fuselage. Ajami jumped on top of him, going for his throat.

Ghere reached the top of the stairs. "What the hell!" he shouted, leveling his rifle at the terrorist.

"Stop, lieutenant. This is personal," Collins stated.

Duke grasped Ajami's hands and rolled over, breaking the viselike grip. The two men tumbled across the bottom of the cargo bay until they both hit the wall. Ajami was on top of Duke when he raised his fist to strike the American.

BAM . . . BAM.

Ajami didn't move. He looked at Duke, his clutched fist still raised. His eyes seemed to soften for a second and then went dull. He slumped over. Two red patches of blood were spreading in the center of the chest.

Duke climbed to his feet. In his right hand was the Libyan nine millimeter he had taken off of Jibril. He stuffed it back into his belt.

Duke looked up at Ghere and Collins. "Get a medic down here. My pilot needs attention."

"It's confirmed, sir. The base is secure." Oliveri smiled. "No Fear Ghere reports that all three astronauts are alive. All ten warheads have been accounted for."

Madison folded his arms, not showing any emotion. "Signal job well done and get us on the ground. I want to see things firsthand. And contact the STOC. Inform General Clark Cobra has struck. We have everything under control."

"Yes, sir."

SPECIAL TECHNICAL OPERATIONS CENTER, PENTAGON

General Clark sat down and took a sip of coffee from his nearby cup. He didn't notice that it was cold. "Harris, get on the phone; let the White House know all is well, astronauts alive, warheads recovered. And tell them we don't have a read on casualties; I know they're going to ask." He turned and looked at Staffer and Turner. "Well, gentlemen, we did it." A tired grin came across his face.

"No. You did it, General. Thank you." Turner stood and shook Clark's hand. "I'm going back to my office and get some rest. I have to brief the press in a few hours, and they're going to have a hundred questions."

"If anything else develops, I'll let you know, sir," Clark said, as Turner left the STOC.

Staffer slipped on his jacket. "Warren, I'm going home. You know where to reach me." He smiled at Clark. "I've had just about as much excitement as I can stand in a day."

"Well, I'll be here a couple more hours. NASA's got some questions and I want to make sure reinforcements arrive on time to relieve Cobra."

"All right. I'll probably see you midmorning." Staffer turned and exited the room.

"Sir, I have General Dawson on the phone. He says well done."

"Tell Dawson the men he needs to thank are still out there in the desert." Clark grabbed the phone from Harris. "No, I'll tell him."

"It was wired to blow, all right," Ghere said, holding the claymore. "It was a good thing you acted when you did, General. This place could have been one giant mushroom cloud."

Duke was quiet as he watched the medics load Willie and Yitzhak onto the stretchers. Willie would live, but they weren't sure about the Israeli. He had lost a lot of blood. Andrea was next to the Mossad officer, doing her best to keep him comfortable.

Duke James looked up at his shuttle. She was a bit worse for wear. A section of the left wing had been ripped away when the GBU-12 had hit the bunker, and of course the fire from the satellite had caused a great deal of damage. But it was nothing so bad that it couldn't be repaired. In the next few days NASA's rapid-response team would be making over seventy trips into the base, flying C-5s and C-141s to bring workers and equipment to ready the shuttle for her trip back to the States. *Yeah, back to the States.* The thought of a hot shower and the arms of his wife came to mind.

"How did you know he would react that way?" Duke asked Collins.

"I didn't. Well, not for sure, anyway. It was just a hunch," Collins said, smirking.

"A hunch . . . Right. I believe that," Duke replied. The CIA analyst's modesty didn't work. He knew better.

The two men walked outside the bunker into the warm air. Duke didn't move for a moment, letting the sun warm his tired body. The heat felt good for a change as he looked up into the deep blue sky. The air was light and fresh. In the distance he saw several fighters as they turned on their final approach to land. In a few more minutes the base would be crawling with Americans.

"All you went on was a hunch." Duke James turned to Collins and smiled. "I like the thought of that."

WITHDRAWN